The Children
Left Behind

BOOKS BY LIZZIE PAGE

Lizzie Page

The Children
Left Behind

bookouture

Published by Bookouture in 2023

An imprint of Storyfire Ltd.
Carmelite House
50 Victoria Embankment
London EC4Y 0DZ

www.bookouture.com

ISBN: 978-1-80314-959-2
eBook ISBN: 978-1-80314-958-5

To all our Ukrainian friends but especially Dina

How pleasant it is, at the end of the day,
    No follies to have to repent,
    But reflect on the past, and be able to say,
    That my time has been properly spent

Jane Taylor

DEAR SIR,

I WISH TO MAKE ENQUIRIES ABOUT A CHILD, PHYLLIS BURNHAM, WHO I BELIEVE YOU HAVE IN YOUR CARE.

I AM HER RIGHTFUL FATHER.

PHYLLIS WAS PUT IN YOUR CARE BY HER MOTHER IN APRIL 1944. REGRETTABLY I WAS NOT IN A POSITION TO TAKE ON PHYLLIS AT THE TIME, BUT I HAVE SINCE MADE SUBSTANTIAL CHANGES TO MY DOMESTIC SITUATION AND WOULD LIKE TO MAKE A HOME FOR PHYLLIS WITH ME.

SHE WOULD HAVE ALL THE CARE AND ATTENTION SHE COULD WANT FROM ME, AND FROM HER DOTING GRANDPARENTS.

MR K. BURNHAM

Dear Mr K. Burnham,

Thank you for your letter. There is no child of that name in any Suffolk Home.

Mr P.P. Sommersby – Head of Children's Services

1

JULY 1951

Suffolk, England

Clara Newton, the housemother of the Shilling Grange Children's Home in Lavenham, pulled her suitcase from the top of the wardrobe where it had been gathering dust, wiped it, then clapped her hands together in disgust. It was even grubbier than she had expected.

Setting the suitcase on the floor, she went about filling it, as quietly as she could because she didn't want the children to wake up yet. She felt guilty enough about this as it was. Stella the cat came in and sat in the lid, which Clara didn't mind too much; it was nice to have company. Stella sometimes made her sneeze but the dust was making her nose twitch anyway.

As she took a first dress from the hanger in the wardrobe, Clara was smiling to herself. Ivor had made this outfit for her and she was very much looking forward to wearing it for dinner tonight. It was knee-length, figure-skimming, and she knew she looked nice in it. She added a checked sundress, a blouse and trousers, although she wasn't convinced by the trousers yet. However lovely the girls in the fashion magazines looked in them, the pockets and her hips were not the best combination, but she wanted a choice.

Finally, still smiling – Stella must have thought she was crazy – she went to the bottom drawer, from where she took out a long white silk nightgown with spaghetti straps. It was quite possibly not only the most expensive item of clothing in there but the most expensive item Clara had ever had. It was also a hand-me-down (Anita really was a dear friend), but you wouldn't know it: it was in perfect condition and beautiful.

Later today, Clara and her beau, Ivor Delaney, would go to Hunstanton, Norfolk, and check in to the Ocean Breeze as Mr and Mrs Jones. They could perhaps choose a less obvious surname, but what was the point of that? They were all adults. Everyone knew what was what. Plus, the Ocean Breeze was a bit obvious too, wasn't it?

Since Clara and Ivor had got together two months ago on the day of the orphans' performance at the Royal Festival Hall, they had only been alone with each other a handful of times. They were still together, but despite their proximity (he lived opposite on Shilling Street), they were not actually together an awful lot. They made plans for dates, but anything could scupper them: if Clara's cover, Sister Grace, had a parish obligation, if Peg, one of the orphans, had a head cold, or if Gladys, another of the orphans, fell down the stairs and thought she had broken her wrist. (She had not broken her wrist.)

When they did have time together, it was often only snippets. If Clara had a free moment, she sometimes went over to his workshop, where she watched him working. Despite having lost an arm at Dunkirk (in a military operation that gained him several medals for valour), Ivor was a craftsman. Clara loved listening to the hum of the sewing machines and admiring the concentration in his dark brown eyes. He brought stale armchairs back to life and covered dreary sofas and dining chairs with patterns. And he seemed to conjure up colourful curtains, thick tablecloths and cosy cushions out of nothing.

Friends sometimes offered to come and 'sit' the orphans so that Clara and Ivor could spend time alone together, but Clara didn't want to burden anyone – not for her love life, that would be wrong. And she couldn't leave the children alone in the evenings. Peg (who was probably ten, no one knew for sure) and nine-year-old Gladys were as well-behaved as any children you could imagine, but both were too young and vulnerable to be left for long. Other families might, but housemothers had to obey a different set of rules. New girl, thirteen-year-old Florrie, was settling in nicely but, although mature, she had no inclination to watch the younger ones – she'd made that clear.

So, other than the odd snatched moment together in his workshop, Clara and Ivor were back to the old yearnings across the street, waving from windows, a quick chat while putting out the milk bottles, a snatched kiss outside the library, or a squeeze at Anita's house. Only it was much better than before – it was the kind of yearning that put a smile on your lips, not agony in your heart, for this was a yearning that was reciprocated.

'I'll get you alone one day,' Ivor liked to whisper.

'One night...' Clara would think.

Clara was smitten now. No doubt about it. It wasn't like first love. She had been there and done that with American serviceman, Captain Michael Adams, during the war, before Lavenham was even a twinkle in her eye. The love she had for Ivor was more measured and yet wilder; she was more confident yet more timorous, more careful yet more feckless. She wanted to wrap their relationship up and spirit it away in special tissue paper – yet at the same time she wanted to shout about it from the rooftops. Ivor made her heart sing. She just needed more time alone with him.

And today – for the first time since the happy evening they got together in May – she would have it. Clara shooed Stella away and closed the suitcase. Today, even the rusty clasp worked like a dream. From two o'clock that afternoon – fingers crossed, touch wood – Ivor would be all hers.

Since she would be away from the children for the weekend, Clara was more attentive over their breakfast than usual. She did feel terrible about leaving them. She cut Peg's toast into quarters and gave Gladys a choice of honey or lard. She measured the milk into the glasses carefully – inequality could trigger a row – and she told them a story she had read in the newspaper about baby owls who had been looked after and were now going back to their burrows. Peg was a foundling, left on a Lincolnshire church doorstep, while Gladys had been in care for years since her mother and father died.

Florrie came down later than the younger girls and was in too much of a hurry to eat. She also had been in care for many years, although she'd only been at the home for three weeks. With a breezy goodbye, she dashed away to high school, a whirl-wind. She was taller than Clara – what was it with this genera-tion? – they were like giants – but she was thin and bony too, with knees that knocked together as she walked and her feet in old shoes pointing inwards, the opposite of a duck. There was something endearing about it.

Once Peg had found her ruler and Gladys had put on her summer dress, this time the right way round – *honestly!* – Clara walked them to their junior school. The sun was shining, and the sky was a promising blanket of blue. Summer had come early to Lavenham and showed no signs of letting up. Clara had already taken the girls strawberry picking once in Farmer Buck-le's fields and planned to go again.

As they approached the junior school gates, Gladys seemed her usual exuberant self. She threw her arms round Clara and squeezed.

'Have a wonderful trip!' Then she ran off, satchel bouncing at her side, without looking back. Gladys had only joined the home in April, but had settled in beautifully, both with Clara and at school. It was nice to have her blessing.

Peg, though, was different this morning: subdued and uneasy. She never spoke apart from an incident a couple of years back when she had yelled out 'cows' (which probably saved Clara's life). Now Clara gave Peg a kiss on the forehead and a pat on the back. She was aware that some mothers watched her at the gates and that rumours about her swirled through the school community – *Miss Newton is too affection-ate/she is not affectionate enough. She's too lenient/she's too strict.*

Other people's opinions didn't bother Clara too much, but she didn't want them to filter down to the children.

'Off you go, Peg. Work hard at school. I'll see you on Sunday.'

Peg's face fell, and she puffed out her pink cheeks. It was as though Clara was about to board the doomed *Titanic*. Clara just had to keep her fingers crossed that she did not get a telephone call from the school – 'Miss Newton, could you pick up Peg, she has vomited on the desk'. If Peg *did* want to vomit, Clara had told her, only half-jokingly, she must keep it in until after two o'clock.

But still Peg dawdled and, just as Clara was about to go, Peg shyly handed her a handwritten note.

'Are you coming back?'

This was why Clara felt guilty. 'You don't think I will?'

Peg nodded slowly, her big eyes downcast.

'Of course I'll come back. What on earth makes you think I wouldn't?'

But Peg shrugged and refused to write anything else down.

'Oh, Peg, I promise!' The little girl snaked her hot arms round Clara's neck as Clara carried her to the gate.

. . .

After Clara returned to the home, she washed the sheets – unusually, Peg had wet the bed twice – and finished clearing up the breakfast things, although they'd already done most of that together. Now that there were only three quite amenable residents and one small *fairly* amenable cat, life was easier than it ever had been at the home, but Clara knew it was just a lull, a temporary pause on proceedings.

The postman had been, and Clara scooped up the letters delightedly. She loved hearing all the exciting things her ex-residents were getting up to with their adopted families. On the top of the pile, there was a postcard with a scenic painting of a field at sunset on one side. Her first guess was that it was from ex-resident Terry – who couldn't resist anything outdoorsy. The next possibility was intellectual Alex, who loved both history and art.

She was wrong on both counts. As she turned it over and began to read, Clara grew cold all over and for a moment it was hard to catch a breath.

Dear Clara,

I am staying in Constable country and understand that it is not far from you. It has been some time since we saw each other, and I wondered if I might pay you a visit. I enclose my telephone number for future communication.

Yours sincerely,

Augustus Newton

The absolute bloody cheek of him! Clara was infused with astonishment and then rage. Yes, *Augustus Newton*, she thought, it had been 'some time', but whose fault was that? There was barely room for the scribbled signature, but no doubt he couldn't bring himself to call himself 'Father' or 'Papa'. With trembling fingers, Clara stuffed the card in the bottom of the box that she kept in the kitchen of 'things to deal with later'. She would not let her father upset her, not today.

Sweeping the bedroom floor extra-vigorously helped her calm down. She gave her suitcase a final check and then left the house for her appointment at her hairdresser's, Beryl's Brushes. She wanted to look extra special for Ivor. And if her father's message was thrum-thrumming in her ribcage – what *further communication* did he expect? – she would ignore it. He was the one who had cut her off, left her adrift, there was no way she would jump to his commands like she used to. She would concentrate on the people who were important to her.

Hairdresser Beryl disapproved of Clara's lack of vanity and always reproached her for not coming often enough, which wasn't a great sales technique and made Clara feel even less inclined to come. Nevertheless, Beryl did a nice 'do' and Clara had grown fond of her visits (although she point-blank refused to hold the glass ashtray on her lap for Beryl's pungent cigarettes).

Today, Beryl was preoccupied with the antics of her elderly tenant, old Mr Hargreaves, who was an ex-tax inspector and, worse, a Taurean. Clara didn't know what Beryl had against Taureans in general, but this one in particular had a penchant for wandering around at night in just his underpants. Beryl, who underneath her gruff superstitious exterior – a typical Virgoan apparently – was kind, had found herself looking after him rather more than she'd bargained for.

Beryl – still talking about the woes of being a landlady – enclosed Clara under the hairdryer. Each customer was a captive audience. She would have grabbed one of the magazines stacked in the corner, but Beryl preferred her to listen to her.

Nevertheless, Clara drifted away, dreaming about dinner – she would take care not to have anything heavy. She hoped the restaurant might offer a prawn starter. She'd had that just once before, when she was courting Julian White (of local law firm Robinson, Browne and White), and it was hard to imagine anything more exotic.

Beryl always took longer than she said she would, and soon Clara started panicking she'd be late. She could not allow her plans with Ivor to be scuppered yet again, but Beryl always had to dab, fluff and hairspray, 'no more spray, Beryl, BERYL, it's hard to breathe.' Finally, she produced a hand mirror for Clara to admire the back of her own head.

'Fine, thank you.'

But 'fine' was not enough for Beryl. Beryl demanded superlatives.

'I love it!' corrected Clara quickly. Who cared about the back of her head? The trouble was, Beryl was determined to give Clara every inch of her money's worth.

'Good enough for your dirty weekend?' Beryl cackled, to Clara's mortification. 'I must say, I didn't think you had it in you.'

Back at the home, Clara ran upstairs for last-minute checks. Florrie's part of the room was tidy, but a drumstick had rolled under Peg's bed next to a singular white sock with a grubby heel. Under Gladys' pillow was a note: 'Miss Nuton is the buest'.

Who knew what went through their minds?

Clara made sure the lights were off in the bathroom and then it was 1.55 – suitcase dragged downstairs, freshly lipsticked; blessedly the hairspray had lost its potency. She did not dare go back to the 'things to deal with later' box to reread her father's postcard since it was nearly – almost – completely out of her head already (*how dare he?*). Anyhow, it was time to go over to Ivor's to present herself: 'Ta Da!'. She might even stick an arm or a leg in the air for fun! May as well start the weekend as she meant to go on. All this effort – it had to be worthwhile.

She was just casting one final look around the kitchen, oven off, cupboards shut, nothing in the sink, *where was the cat?* Stella was the unsentimental sort who didn't seem to need a goodbye cuddle – but Clara did – when there was a knock on the front door. The postman? Again? Unlikely. No, on the doorstep stood a young woman with one hand shading her eyes and a folder in the other. Clara's heart sank.

The woman was wearing a navy skirt suit, a white blouse with a pussy-cat bow and clumpy heels. Her hair pulled back in a bun made her look like she wanted to seem older than she was, but her smooth, unlined skin gave her away. She had a jolly, well-spoken voice. 'I'm from Suffolk County Council,' she said, letting out a high-pitched laugh – Clara wasn't sure why. 'The childcare department. I'm Miss Webb, the replacement for Miss Cooper.'

'Miss Cooper's going?' Clara couldn't help herself.

'Miss Cooper's gone!'

That the last childcare officer had disappeared was not *altogether* out of character. She was what Clara's father might have called 'flighty'. Miss Cooper did not have much of a grip on administrative tasks, showed little interest in children and was more into the machinations of the Labour Party than the minutiae of council life. She had also suspiciously spent the last few weeks off 'sick'. But still, the sudden change made Clara uneasy.

'It's good to meet you, Miss Webb. I'm Clara Newton, the housemother, but I'm afraid I was just going out,' Clara said. She picked up her suitcase, displaying the evidence. She wouldn't let the young woman in, she told herself, she'd never get away if she did.

'It's the only time I could come.' Miss Webb laughed that irritating laugh again. 'I'm glad I caught you.'

She placed a clumpy shoe an inch over the threshold and, defeated, Clara let go of the suitcase handle with a sigh.

In the kitchen, Miss Webb peeled off her gloves – she had pretty, plump hands like a Regency lady – and looked around appraisingly. 'It's nice here,' she said. 'Just as I heard.'

Clara did not want to get in Miss Webb's bad books already (no doubt that would come), but did she have to offer her a drink? Yes, she probably did. Boiling the kettle, Clara blinked resentfully into the steam. The clock struck a jolly note of two as though it was enjoying seeing her life ticking away. She should have known something or someone would spoil her weekend. That's the way her life was.

'I don't have long,' Clara reminded her as she poured hot water into the best china teapot.

A beaming Miss Webb said it shouldn't take too long. 'An hour maybe?'

A whole hour? This was a nightmare! Miss Webb came across as young and a little too keen. If she were in a better mood Clara might have said she was like a child in a sweet-shop, but right now she found her like a pig snuffling for truffles.

'I've brought you the transition notes.'

On the handwritten ones, the black strokes leaned slightly backward – only a pedant (like Clara) would notice – but they were uniformly clear and impressively even.

The typed pages were also beautifully presented; this was someone who not only knew their way around the margins but also the footnotes' function. Clara recognised a fellow paper-work enthusiast – or, as Ivor would tease, 'a pen-pusher'. She would have commented, but it was already a quarter past two. She and Ivor were supposed to be on the half past the hour train!

Miss Webb asked if, after their tea, Clara would show her the rest of the house.

'I can show you now,' Clara offered, but Miss Webb wanted to sit and contemplate first. She had the mannerisms and expressions of a woman three times her age. Clara half expected to have to help her out of her chair.

'It's so important to get a *feel* for a place,' she said.

Clara had liked her first childcare officer Mrs Horton, and they were still great friends. She had not liked (nor trusted one inch) the second – Mrs Harrington. The third, Miss Cooper, she hadn't minded... Miss Webb would be her fourth. This was normal, apparently. Childcare officer was one of those professions where young women came and went, went and came. Occasionally, they went to other jobs. Mostly they sailed blithely along the conveyor belt from council worker to wife and then mother to their own children. Clara did have things she would have liked to discuss with her childcare officer about the children, but not now, not today. This was her long-awaited holiday.

Miss Webb had a cup and a half before she was ready – but Clara didn't show her the house. Instead she followed Miss Webb around as the childcare officer strutted through the rooms, touching the beams and the walls and nodding like it was confirming what she already knew. It was going to take longer than an hour at this rate.

In the parlour, the games were haphazardly piled up on the sideboard and the library books next to them. Once, this room had been adults only – a showroom – but now it was where the children relaxed, argued, or did whatever else children do. Miss Webb sat in Peg's favourite armchair.

'So, I have some questions...'

Why had she left them until now?

'As I said,' Clara interjected, imagining a tight-lipped Ivor, locking up the workshop and shaking his wristwatch. 'This is my weekend off. I booked it a while ago and I get hardly any time to myself, so...'

Miss Webb managed to look both startled and disapproving at once. 'Oh,' she responded, 'and what will you be doing?'

'A... trip to the seaside,' Clara said blushing, thinking of Beryl's embarrassing summary. Despite Miss Webb's youth, Clara had a feeling that she was not the type to call herself Mrs Jones to check into the Ocean Breeze. A small hotel advertised in the *Suffolk Gazette* under the subheading, '*Escape the city, embrace the sea air*'.

'Embrace' was another word that was kind of obvious too.

Miss Webb looked at her and snipped, 'I see,' and, just like that, Clara's boldness disappeared. *Was* she doing something wrong? Something immoral? Maybe she was. Her father probably would have said she was.

But then her father wasn't in London during the Blitz and Miss Webb probably wasn't either. Miss Webb probably hadn't dug in rubble for a kitten who had hobbled off. Miss Webb probably hadn't had her arms round four children crying for their mother. Miss Webb hadn't held an old man weeping after his house had collapsed like a deck of cards. It gave you a different set of values. Maybe it focused your mind on what was important and what wasn't. And getting away for a weekend with Ivor WAS important. They didn't get the chance often – no, they never got the chance.

'May I have the full names of each of the children who live here now?'

Surely she already knew this? It was like she was prevaricating on purpose. 'Peg Church, Gladys Gluck and Florrie Macdonald.'

Miss Webb peered at her notes while Clara drummed her fingers on the table. 'I've got a Maureen Keaton?'

'She left four weeks ago.'

Maureen had been one of the residents in the home when

Clara first arrived (and had caused her plenty of anguish too!) Now she was studying full-time at a secretarial college in Liverpool Street, London – 'Not Liverpool, Peg, it's not that far.' She hadn't let Clara come with her on the train, or even walk up to the station with her, but she had made a Victoria sponge on her last day, and she had given Clara the lightest of hugs.

'Did you let the council know – in writing?'

'Of course.' Some housemothers might not be good at paperwork – there were rumours one in Norfolk was illiterate – but not Clara. It was her forte.

'You really are down to just three!' Miss Webb looked surprised. 'Three children rattling around like peas in a can in this big old place. There is room for more.'

She said it like Clara would disagree!

Clara remembered how when she first arrived, she'd kept repeating to herself: *eight children*. She had felt like the old woman who lived in a shoe – she had so many children she didn't know what to do.

'I'm glad the children who were here have found permanent homes,' Clara said. 'I am also looking forward to the house filling up again.' And she was. This is what it was for. This is what *she* was for. 'And I don't know if you are aware, but the house is no longer called Shilling Grange – it is the Michael Adams Children's Home,' she added proudly (although no one called it that but her and Michael's mother, Marilyn). 'Although it is under the auspices of the council, it doesn't belong to the council. They rent it from an American benefactor. It should all be in the notes.'

It was done legally. Sometimes Clara wondered if she should have pushed for more independence, but, much as Suffolk Council irritated her sometimes – like now – they were a safety net, a safeguard and sounding board – and much more besides. (Although Clara wondered, as she grew more experienced, whether the advantages outweighed the disadvantages).

Stella strutted in.

'You have a cat?'

Clara winced. And then sneezed. That was another thing against the council – although it was perfectly above board, their officials tended not to approve of Stella.

'This is Stella, Stella, this is Miss Webb,' she said.

'I didn't know pets were allowed,' Miss Webb said, as Clara expected her to. But then her expression softened. 'I do love cats,' and, obligingly, Stella – fickle beast – rubbed the backs of her ankles.

Clara and Ivor had missed the fast trains. Was this weekend going to be yet another washout? Clara felt... what was the word? *Thwarted*. Miss Webb was thwarting her. And at the same time she felt ashamed for feeling that, and for everything really. Should she be going away at all? She thought of Peg's downcast face, Gladys' fixed smile and Florrie's scowl as she'd scurried away. Was she allowed a life? Sometimes the answer seemed to be no. Was this a sign that she should cancel?

'There *is* something else,' Miss Webb said. 'The council seemed to have neglected something important in their requirements of you to date.'

This didn't sound good. Clara narrowed her eyes. 'Oh?'

Miss Webb rummaged in her briefcase and, once again, it was like she was being deliberately slow. Clara stood with her hands on her hips. Finally, she found what she was after and took out a clipboard, a pencil and a sheet of paper, from which she read before frowning. 'I understand that the children formed a singing troupe and sang on the wireless, the television and in the Festival of Britain?'

'Oh yes, they had a wonderful—'

'Which is all very good,' Miss Webb interrupted while her expression said she thought it was not good at all. 'Yet it is apparent you are pursuing a godless agenda.'

Clara knew she must not react negatively, she must not.

And yet she felt another spark of fury. It was like her father all over again. 'I wouldn't call it that...'

'Then what would you call it?' For such a young woman, Miss Webb had a powerful beady eye.

'I'm not pursuing *any* agenda,' Clara muttered mutinously. 'Except to provide a safe happy home for the children while they are here with me.'

'Do you take them to church?'

'Uh, no...'

'Bible studies?'

'No, but—'

'Say grace at mealtimes?'

Here, Clara sprang in: 'Yes, sometimes. And also, the girls have assembly, Religious Education at school and...' She racked her brains before adding spuriously, 'no shortage of churchgoing friends.'

It was only when she saw Miss Webb's smug expression that she realised she had walked right into her trap.

'In which case it will be no problem for you to take them to the local Sunday School, where they will receive a fitting spiritual and moral education, yes?'

Clara sighed. She could get into a long discussion with Miss Webb about it now and waste a further precious hour, or she could sort it out later.

'Fine.'

By the time Clara hurried over to Ivor's workshop, it had already past three o'clock. Seventy minutes of their long-awaited together time had been wasted.

'I'm so sorry!'

'It's all right,' he mumbled. Contrary to Clara's fevered imaginings, Ivor was not ripping his shirt in despair: he was kneeling on the floor with a pair of scissors in his hand, his other elbow was keeping the material stretched taut and his mouth was full of pins. He was cutting an outline for a sofa cover. It looked like the outline of a large rectangular man.

'Aren't you ready?'

'Let me just finish this.' The scissors sliced through the material like air. Ivor had strong feelings about scissors and paid an eye-watering amount for them at an exclusive haberdasher's store in Mayfair.

'We're late!'

'Are we? I lost track of time,' he said mildly. 'Anyway, Patricia is still napping upstairs.'

Ivor was a devoted parent to two-year-old Patricia, yet he was not her birth father. Ruby, Patricia's birth mother, and Ivor had been sweethearts for years, a relationship that had begun when they were teenagers at the home. Ruby didn't want to look after Patricia, and Ivor had taken her on last year (a decision that Clara still secretly, and perhaps not so secretly, struggled to come to terms with).

'I'll get her then,' Clara snapped, feeling disappointed at Ivor's apparent lack of urgency while she was desperate to get away. 'You *are* ready, aren't you?'

'Of course.'

Patricia was not napping, she was standing up in her cot, clutching her favourite toy – a small wooden mallet from an old croquet set that a customer had given Ivor. It was an odd favourite, but then Patricia was an odd child and while Ivor could be an anxious parent, he was surprisingly relaxed about eccentricities.

Recently, Patricia was losing her chubby-baby looks and was becoming a little girl – the creases in her neck that used to catch falling crumbs were gone. She had blonde wispy hair, curls on her forehead and a tiny, pointed chin that she stuck up frequently when she was annoyed. Like now.

'Polly is naughty,' she said, pointing her mallet at the straggly brown ted she shared her cot with.

'Are you ready to see baby Howard?'

Patricia shook her blonde curls. 'Want Daddy. Only Daddy.'

'Let's go downstairs.'

She folded her arms and stuck out her lower lip.

'Want Da-deeee,' she wailed.

'It's all right,' said Clara, desperately now she could hear Ivor's feet on the stairs – once again, Patricia seemed determined to show up Clara as incompetent. She threw poor Polly on the floor.

'Shuush,' said Clara, but Patricia did not shush, she never shushed, and Ivor was stood at the door, an unreadable expression on his face.

'Don't worry, Clara, I'll take her.'

Clara chewed her lip. She dropped down to pick up woebegone Polly but Patricia shook her head; she didn't want her ted any more.

Sometimes Clara had strange half-waking dreams where Patricia was a tiny high court judge wearing one of those funny white wigs, scowling as she thumped down a gavel.

Guilty, guilty, guilty.

Patricia wouldn't let Ivor put her in the pram. She clung to him like a limpet all the way to Anita Cardew's house. Mallet dangling in hand, she burrowed her face into Ivor's shoulder. Occasionally she looked over as though Clara had done something unspeakably terrible, and, when Clara caught her eye, Patricia turned up her little nose and looked away. She was so like her mother.

Clara pushed the pram over the cobblestones. There was

something unnerving about pushing an empty pram that made her feel more agitated than she already was.

If it wasn't for Miss Webb, they'd be miles away by now. It was nearly time for school to be let out and the last thing Clara wanted was to bump into one of the children. It would be confusing for them – and her. Peg's eyes might fill with tears and then what would she do? Gladys would be more effusive, but who knew what she was hiding behind all those over-the-top declarations of love? Florrie would probably just cross her arms and say something fantastically condescending.

Perhaps they shouldn't go?

Anita Cardew's house, which was also the doctor's surgery, was on a quiet street just off the high road. They knocked on the door round the side, which was for visitors, rather than the front one, which was for patients, and the nanny answered. The nanny was 'trained at Norwood', a prestigious childcare college. Anita, who had arrived in England shortly after the war, was a remarkably enthusiastic learner when it came to English status symbols. The nanny was an earnest young woman who had a knack with babies (although not adults).

The Cardews' house was both grand and 'continental'. Clara could imagine it being lifted straight out of Vienna or Warsaw. It was full of musical instruments, leather-bound books and indoor plants. It always smelled medicinal too – which Anita complained about, but which Clara found reassuring.

Baby Howard was wearing a hand-knitted yellow cardigan and a matching hat. He rolled over and kicked his legs in the air in excitement at their arrival. He had only recently started walking, which Anita had informed Clara about with some relief: 'Howard might be a late developer, but he gets there in the end.'

Patricia loved the Norwood Nanny and she loved Howard; she squealed and raised her mallet in salute at him. So it wasn't like she was going to have a bad weekend – but you would have thought she was about to be tortured from the way she struggled in Ivor's arm.

Clara had brought along a going-away present for her – six shiny glass marbles full of promise. Ex-resident Clifford used to spend hours knocking them into one another, when he wasn't doing the more dangerous things that had him put in a reform school for boys.

'Marbles?' Ivor said when she passed them over to him. 'She's way too young for those!'

'Is she?' Ivor had definitely told her Patricia had stopped putting things in her mouth, otherwise Clara wouldn't have brought them. She wasn't *totally* stupid. 'Oh, that's fine,' she said nonetheless, red-faced. 'I'll save them for when she's bigger then.'

But, of course, Patricia had caught wind that she was being denied something and was furious. 'Give me!' she squealed, grabbing air. 'Want, want!'

'It's my fault,' Clara said guiltily.

'Maybe I'm being overprotective,' Ivor said.

'Better safe than sorry,' the Norwood Nanny said. She always used phrases like that. 'Better out than in' and 'Better late than never' – they must have been a specialist subject at Nanny School.

'We'd better go,' Clara said softly. If Ivor changed his mind now, then she would go home, put the kettle on, read a magazine and have a good cry.

Ivor gave Patricia a kiss goodbye. There was something private and tender about it that Clara wished she hadn't seen. The Norwood Nanny was breezy again.

'Oh, a sweet for my sweet, who's a lucky girl?'

Ivor whispered something to Patricia that Clara couldn't catch – and Patricia nodded solemnly, judge-like. And then, Clara and Ivor left, the door shut behind them and finally,

finally! they were free. Not quite two whole days, but – here was the important bit – *two whole nights*. Two whole nights without children, babies or other obligations. Bliss!

The bright Suffolk houses looked lovely in the July sunshine as they walked up to the station. It was such a pretty town that Clara supposed it strange to be in such a rush to get away from it. The high road was a mismatch of medieval timber buildings, of cute shops with their rounded window-fronts, the butcher's, the baker's, the post office, the library. Their walls of yellow and pink and pale blue were like those in a children's illustrated book. The birds were chirruping as though they were unanimously pleased with their conditions too. The town of Lavenham was not particularly popular with tourists – thank goodness – but it did, on a day like today, have something of a holiday mood about it. A scent of lavender ran through it, although Clara wondered sometimes if it was actually there or if, like a placebo, she just smelled it nowadays.

Ivor insisted on carrying Clara's suitcase while also making fun of her. 'What did you pack? The kitchen sink?'

'Ha.'

The first day they'd met – nearly two years earlier – Ivor had carried her bag to the station and asked if she had a dead body in her luggage. Her feelings towards him back then were mostly animosity or irritation. But then, her feelings about a lot of things had changed. Back then, she hardly spoke to children, they intimidated her and she felt like they were a different species. Now barely an hour went by without a weird conversation with a child, and she was more at home with them than most adults.

She smiled at Ivor. Now that all the children were where they ought to be, she felt less frantic and more certain. It had taken them a long time to get to this point. But as they say, sometimes the most circuitous journey has the best views.

'It was lucky that you were there that day.'

On that day of their first meeting, Clara had crept out of the children's home to run away, but there had been no trains. Funny to think that her fate had depended on there not being a late passage back to London.

'Hmm, not just luck.' He grinned. 'I had been looking out for you. The innocent new housemother...'

Clara blushed and pretended to be interested in her shoes. Innocent was a compliment, right? Ivor, who was good at so many things that she privately thought he was quite the Renaissance Man, was not so skilful at flattery.

As they approached the station, Clara resolved to put her resentment at the delays behind her. After all, against the odds, they had got away. All she had to do was forget her worries about the children, accept Patricia's attitude towards her, put her father's desperate cry for attention behind her and focus on the now – she breathed in, yes, it was definitely lavender – life was sweet.

2

On the train, after the last bowler-hatted passenger got off, Ivor snoozed with his head on Clara's shoulder, which made reaching into her bag for a copy of *Good Housekeeping* impossible. She had an unfinished letter to ex-resident Rita (now reunited with her long-lost mama in Switzerland) in her handbag too – and a card ready to post for ex-resident twins Billy and Barry, who lived with their aunt and uncle in Highgate. Clara liked to write a letter every day: it was a good thing to do to relax in the long light evenings once all the chores were done. She'd tried knitting and she'd tried gardening; she was never good at domestic things, but letters – and her precious files on the children and the workings of the house, of course – were different.

Staring out of the grimy window at the telegraph poles whooshing past, she tried not to dwell on that postcard – no, she would *not* reply to her father. And yet, in the midst of her anger, there was a nub of curiosity. Why had he got in touch, why now?

Her thoughts turned, as they often did, to Patricia. She'd had to repeat the word 'daughter' to herself many times before it made any sense: 'Ivor's daughter', 'his adopted daughter'. Whenever Clara saw Bandit, Julian's dog and Clara's favourite pet in Lavenham (Stella included), his tail would whip upright, and he would shake with excitement. Sadly, Patricia was the opposite. If she'd had a tail it would have drooped at Clara. Her lower lip trembled when she saw her, sometimes her eyes even filled with tears. She had bright blue eyes, unlike Ivor's, which was a relief. Clara wondered if she would have been able to bear it if her eyes were the same colour as his.

Occasionally she did get a watery smile out of the little girl. But not often. Mostly Patricia just cried in her company. Anita said she also cried when she was with her and had once pondered, 'Maybe it's older women she doesn't like.'

'Speak for yourself, Anita!'

Anita had laughed. But it wasn't funny, Patricia simply hadn't taken to Clara.

And this was painful because nowadays, Clara seemed to win over most children like a spell (certainly Peg and Gladys wouldn't want to be without her). And because if there was ever a child she needed to win over then it was Patricia Delaney.

With two connection changes, the train journey was going to take four and a half hours, although if they had been on the earlier train as planned it would only have taken three. Clara fretted that they would miss dinner at the Ocean Breeze. She also realised that in the kerfuffle with the new childcare officer, she had forgotten the brand-new hat she had bought at the market expressly for this weekend. She wanted to look respectable at the front desk. Although she was doing what she knew many – most? – couples of her generation did, it was going against convention. It still felt brazen.

At the idea of respectability, Clara's thoughts returned once again to her father and his position of respectability above all else. 'What will people say?' was one of his catchphrases. What the neighbours might think had always been more important to him than what his daughter was feeling. Nowadays, there were jokes about people like him on the wireless – but that's what many families were like. The rules were made by the men like her father, but the women, like her poor mother, enforced them.

She and Ivor weren't like that; they wouldn't be nullified by convention. Clara plucked a sherbet lemon from Ivor's pocket without him noticing. They had been planning to save them, but if she was going to hell, she might as well have some sweets on the way.

And then they were nearly at Hunstanton station and, good timing, Ivor woke up, smiling, his hair charmingly askew. The seafront ahead of them was vast. Since when was there so much sky? It was as though the sky was all here – not in London or Lavenham. It was such a wide-open space, it reminded Clara how closed-in she had felt recently. Sometimes it felt like she was living in a glass box, a sweet and comfortable box, but captivity, nevertheless. Ivor laughed at her as she breathed in deeply, as though she was trying to inhale the whole vista. *And relax.*

'It's good to get away,' she said, twice. She had felt divided but now she couldn't encapsulate this sense of freedom she had. The feeling of her spirit returning to herself. The sense that she was not an overstretched housemother, not a disappointing daughter, not Miss Newton, not Mama, not an employee 'pursuing a godless agenda', for heaven's sake. She was just Clara. Clara, restored.

It certainly was breezy at the Ocean Breeze. Clara was almost pushed up the crazy-paving path towards the front door, past a rock garden on the left. She wasn't keen on them but the magazines said they were fashionable.

At the front desk, Clara regretted forgetting her respectable hat more than ever; she could have pulled down the netting and her blushing would have been less visible. *What would my father say about this?* She felt transgressive, although she wasn't worried enough to put her ring on her wedding finger and go the full hog. *Let them think what they like*, she thought, *it's the 1950s now.*

The woman the other side of the desk had curly tendrils by her ears and a heavy smoker's voice not dissimilar to Beryl's. She didn't seem to think much of this Mr and Mrs Jones.

'Room 4. Dinner is served at seven,' she rasped.

'Oh,' exclaimed Clara, 'but that's...'

'Twenty minutes ago, yes.'

'We have paid in advance and we're awfully hungry.'

Ivor was polite yet firm and Clara was glad to see it. The manager huffed and then said she would see what she could do. She slouched off, then returned slightly less annoyed: 'Chef says no starters, mind, and hurry.'

Room 4 had twin beds and a bedside table in between. Eiderdowns, nothing fancy. The rug had a nasty stain, but other than that it was fine. Better than fine: the window was wide and, behind the lace curtains, there was a view of the expanse of sea.

'I like it,' Clara said, thinking it *was* worth all the effort.

'I'm glad, Mrs Jones.' He winked.

'Don't!'

She ran her finger along the bedside table – it was cleaner than her suitcase. Ivor kissed her, but only in a friendly way, and then he asked, 'Which would you prefer, window side or...'

Clara said she didn't mind, and he flung his bag on the bed nearer the door. The velvety eiderdown rippled. It had patches that looked damp, but they weren't – it was just the material.

'I'll go this side then.'

There wasn't enough time to change into her special dress,

although she didn't have the will to either. Get all dressed up for a half a dinner? Instead, she freshened up in the bathroom down the hall and then in a fake bright voice called out, 'Ready!' This time, she noticed the stairway carpet was swirly and orange, which made her think of the time ex-resident Denny had vomited, dear thing. The dining room was two rooms knocked together and had dark velvety curtains. (Velvet was clearly a thing here.)

Ivor wrinkled up his nose at the menu. She knew he would probably rather take her somewhere more salubrious but, actually, she would be happy anywhere with him and that was the truth.

The waiter had an accent and dark glistening eyebrows. He might have been Mediterranean, she thought, but supposed it rude to enquire. A prisoner of war who stayed, maybe – she knew there was a camp and they had built the new housing on the edges of Norfolk – or an economic migrant? Or something completely different? Either way, would he want her pointing out his foreignness over dinner? He might not know she meant it in a friendly, inquisitive way, not in a 'you shouldn't be here' kind of way. Perhaps both felt the same to him.

Ivor, who was not bothered by such pedantries, asked the waiter for a recommendation of wine.

'In Italy, we have this one!' the waiter said proudly, producing a bottle of red, and Clara smiled. She felt grown-up as she had a sip and reported, 'It's lovely, thank you!' Julian White had taught her the first try was about the corkage and not the taste but she could never quite believe it.

Gulping the red back, she hoped this would help them relax. She was feeling a bit uptight – shy or nervous maybe. Maybe Ivor was too, because he also swallowed his down and then swiftly poured them both another.

She told Ivor more about the new children's officer, Miss Webb. 'She's a bit of a pen-pusher.'

He laughed (which was why she had said it). 'Takes one to know one.'

'Oy, someone needs to do the paperwork!'

'We'll all go to hell in a handcart if it's not written down,' he beamed back.

She could have stared for ever at his face, across the table, his lovely face. He had gone for chicken pie, while she went for the cottage. Although they had had buffets and picnics and snatched lunches at the home, she had never eaten in a formal setting with Ivor before, and just before the dishes arrived she had a twinge about it. Would he manage with only one hand? If she offered to cut his food, he would surely shrivel up and die. She wondered if he had chosen the soft pie deliberately, rather than the harder-to-cut steak: yes, of course he had.

The pie wasn't as good as the ones ex-resident Maureen used to make, but it was probably way better than hers. Clara always lost interest at the glazing-of-the-onion stage.

There were about eight other people in the room, all older couples. Ivor winked at her and whispered, 'I feel young,' but there *was* one other couple who were about their age. Another Mr and Mrs Jones, perhaps, although possibly they were the real thing. Clara could see the man staring at Ivor's missing arm and hoped Ivor wouldn't notice. The man said something to his wife and then she stared over too.

Don't start, thought Clara, not today. Could they not have a romantic night away together without people interfering?

She left a tiny spoonful of pie – she didn't want Ivor to think she was greedy – but then couldn't resist it. Ivor wasn't like that, anyway. She wanted to go straight up to their room, but he suggested sharing an ice cream. He requested two spoons, which made her feel like they were in an American movie, but the waiter didn't seem to think it was out of the ordinary.

Did she want a coffee? Clara looked at Ivor before respond-

ing, no, no, she didn't. Was he delaying the inevitable on
purpose? Wasn't it time – wasn't it long overdue? – to go up to
their room?

As the couple opposite got up, she realised that the man
who had been staring was missing a leg. It stopped above the
knee and – she should have noticed it before – there was his
crutch leaned against the pillar. People underestimate how hard
it is to walk with a crutch, thought Clara, thinking of ex-resident
Joyce's struggles. The woman with him looked over and, where
she had originally thought it was curiosity, she now understood
that it was more sympathy or understanding. Clara smiled back.
She could afford to be generous now. She and Ivor were nearly
on their own, properly on their own, and she was feeling heady.
Nervous but in a welcome way.

As they reached room 4, Clara was still giggling *at long last*,
but once they were inside, Ivor confessed he didn't feel well.
Was it the wine or the chicken pie? Should have had the
cottage. He disappeared to the bathroom along the hall and she
waited – he surely wouldn't be long – but after five minutes or
so he still hadn't come back. Never mind. She changed into the
beautiful nightdress and sat on the bed. The velvet rippled and
the pillows were comfortable enough.

As time went by, her hopefulness began to wane. How long
had he been? She felt like Penelope waiting for Odysseus (obviously Ivor wasn't going to be away at sea for twenty years nor
was he going to be ravaged by a minotaur), but then how long
should she wait?

The room whirled. It didn't make her feel sick, but she had
to put her foot on the floor to stop the carousel. It was the wine.
It was probably lust too. It was awful this desire for him, it made
her feel part-animal.

He still hadn't come back so she got under the covers and
read *Good Housekeeping*, a five-minute-fiction called 'The

sailor who returned from the dead' that was about just that. But of course, she couldn't concentrate.

She didn't know whether to just turn out the light and fall asleep – that seemed rude – or if she should wait up. But that seemed ruder. Eventually, she did turn off the light, yet wasn't able to sleep.

He didn't return until about an hour later.

'Are you awake?'

'No,' she said, to make him laugh.

He didn't laugh. He said, 'I'm sorry.'

The three feet between the beds might as well have been the Persian Gulf. She wished she were in an ordinary flannel nightdress instead of this elaborate one. It was the same feeling she had got pushing the empty pram that afternoon – it was like she was pretending to be something she was not.

'I wanted tonight to be special,' he said. 'I don't know what's wrong with me...'

She would have reached out her arm to hold his, to comfort him, but she was on the wrong side. She should have thought. She felt like crying but he groaned and added, 'I feel terrible,' and she knew it wasn't about her.

'It's fine,' she said. 'Don't worry about it. Honestly.'

She remembered once Anita saying when baby Howard was poorly, 'This is my punishment,' and the thought floated there. Everything had been going well – which meant there *had* to be some minor disaster. She should have known. That was the way her life worked.

After a while, Ivor hurried from the room again, and this time he didn't come back for over an hour. When he did return, she pretended to be asleep.

Tomorrow will be a better day, she thought to herself as she finally drifted away.

In the middle of the night, Clara woke, momentarily confused about where she was and who was there. She had dreamed about her father, or rather a strange version of her father. He was a very old man, bent double, and they were standing in a church, but not in any church she knew. He was gripping her wrist. She wanted to see to the children, who were behind a door, but he kept holding her back and telling her they were not there – when she knew they were.

Ivor was fast asleep, breathing deeply, in the single bed next to her. She remembered that he had told her once that he too sometimes had bad dreams. His were flashbacks to the war, nightmares that made him thrash around, waking up in a cold sweat. He was quiet as a mouse now. She had asked him only once about the war, and he had said he didn't want to talk about it. This was perfectly reasonable – more than reasonable – but all positions, even reasonable ones, have consequences. On one level, she understood that he didn't want to talk about it – but on another, she wondered if he didn't trust her enough to offload onto her. It also made it difficult for her to confide in him about her war. And she would have liked to talk about her experiences sometimes.

She would also have liked to have curled up with him in his bed, but she didn't feel able to do so. They didn't know each other in that way yet, and she didn't know how he'd react. She knew that undisturbed sleep was a thing he craved, probably more than he craved her.

She couldn't fall back asleep, so she got up, went to the window, and pushed back the net curtains that smelled of cigarettes. The sea was somewhere out there, a moving black mass, like a living thing. The rest of the moon was there, although you couldn't see it. When she thought of how many people might have stared at the sea or the moon when feeling lost, it bucked her up. After all, nothing was seriously wrong; the children were safe, and Ivor was snoring gently.

She crept to the bathroom down the hall. Although she

came back quietly, silent as Peg, and managing not to knock into anything, he called out. 'Patricia?'

'It's me, Clara.'

'Oh, Cla-ra,' he mumbled softly. Then he fell asleep again, just like that.

Ivor was already dressed in a cotton shirt, braces and grey, slightly baggy trousers when she next woke up. He was a sight for sleepy eyes. She did adore him, *especially* without a jacket. Can you say that someone has a wonderful outline to them? Whether you could or not, Ivor did.

'Breakfast is until eight, and it's ten to,' he said. 'I only just woke up myself.'

Clara would have skipped breakfast for an 'embrace' to make up for the night before – but Ivor seemed determined to go. He said he felt much better, he was hungry actually, and he apologised again for the night before without looking at her. 'It wasn't what I had imagined.'

'Forget it.' It came out more harshly than she intended, so she added, 'We've got the rest of the weekend,' which was not quite what she wanted to get across either.

'I'll go ahead, Mrs Jones,' he said, 'so you can get ready.'

She was sad as she slipped out of the nightdress. And as she put it under her pillow, she felt embarrassed. *What was she doing with such fine things?*

Downstairs, she found Ivor had taken what had become their 'usual table', and he gave her a nervy smile when she came in. The waiter wasn't there, it was the manager serving, but she seemed more enthused than she had been the previous evening and she visibly perked up when they both ordered eggs.

'My girls are the best layers in town,' she boasted. 'Even during the war, they were at it like nobody's business.'

Clara couldn't decide if she liked her or not.

Ivor finished first and went up to their room while Clara drank a cup of tea. As she was going, the woman they'd noticed with the man with the crutch last night put her hand out and said, 'I see your one lost his arm.'

Clara was taken aback, and not just by the 'your one'. The woman must have known that it wasn't the done thing to speak openly about things like this.

'It's hard, isn't it? Not just the physical challenge but...' The oversharing woman tapped her head. 'Up here. They're never the same again, are they?'

Clara didn't know what to say. While the woman confiding in her was generous, it was also unwarranted. Clara hadn't known Ivor before the war. Presumably he wasn't the same – but the Ivor she knew now was the one she loved.

Ivor asked the manager which beach she recommended and, enthusiastically, she grabbed some guidebooks and maps from the shelf behind her. Clara gave her a smile, but she was thinking, we're going to be stuck talking here for ever.

'It depends what you're after.' The manager peered into Ivor's eyes. He had definitely won her over. Clara repeated to herself: *My girls are the best layers in town*, and it made her want to chuckle.

'We'd probably prefer a quiet one,' Ivor responded. The way he said 'we'd prefer' was sweet, like they were of one mind, but her mind was not on the beach.

They went back to their room to fetch their bags and Clara sat on the velvet eiderdown, stroking it. She said, 'Or... we could just stay here.' She was trying to be coquettish but it didn't come naturally. She was no Miss Cooper, effortlessly desirable, and she was no Mrs Harrington the bulldozer. She was pen-pushing, file-keeping Clara, the housemother. It was hard to switch hats, even if you'd left your respectable hat at home.

Ivor blushed – he knew what she meant. And he said, 'I've got plans for us this morning.'

For every two steps Ivor took, Clara had to take three. It seemed to sum it up. She'd made a pass at him and he'd rebuffed her. Apologetically, yes, but it still stung.

The sun was beating down and the air was heavy. Clara sometimes got a headache when the weather was humid like this – when it was so overcast that it felt like the sky was pressing in – but today she was all right. What a place. Even feeling as humiliated as she did, she had to admire the white sands. It was not just patches of it either, great long beaches stretched as far as she could see.

As they stopped to gaze at a lighthouse on a cliff, Ivor held her hand – and then after a moment, he kissed her salty lips – *so he did still like her in that way* – her snoring or her way of eating pie hadn't repulsed him. When she said, 'What's that for?' he said it was because she had been sweet about last night and how sorry he was – and he'd make it up to her. She felt better after that.

After a while though, she realised they weren't going to the quiet beach.

'We'll go there tomorrow,' he said, 'if that's all right.'

Of course it was all right. Everything was all right. (She didn't want him to think her highly strung.)

'Where *are* we going then?'

'You'll see.'

It was a long walk and he kept asking, 'How are you managing?' and 'I had no idea it was this far.' And she had to chew back her questions. She wished she'd dressed for comfort rather than the checked sundress (which was decidedly tighter on the hips after the hard-boiled eggs), and Anita's dainty sandals, which were not built for treks to surprise destinations. Clara already had two angry red lines near her toes on her right foot. She had always suspected her feet were different sizes – here was the proof. And again, she lamented forgetting her new hat; she could have done with some shade. But she didn't want Ivor to think her a complainer either.

After about one hour's walking, just as Clara was thinking of saying that they should perhaps admit defeat, Ivor led them inland towards an imposing building on the cliff, grey brick with small square windows. At first Clara thought the bars on the windows were a trick of the light, but then realised they were real. She stared at Ivor and then back at the building again. She didn't have a clue where they were or why until they were closer and she saw the sign over the door: 'Hunstanton Reform School for Boys. No trespassers'.

She turned to Ivor, and his expression was apologetic yet keen.

'You said a while back you wanted to see Clifford...'

'Can we really *see* him?'

'They said we might, on the phone.'

Clifford had been removed from the home in the spring. The council had sent him to an institution that would be better able to deal with his needs and Clara hadn't seen him since. How typical it was of Ivor to think of this – and how generous of him too. The children were in her bloodstream now, even the ones who'd left, like Clifford. Perhaps *especially* the ones who'd left. And Ivor understood that. He didn't try to divert her from the children like a lesser man, a jealous man might. He understood that the children came first – he understood her *purpose* – and that made her adore him even more.

They were told to wait in a panelled hall, where there was a picture of a canal and some boats at a lock. Clara sat down and then stood up to stare at it, and then at the marble bust of another stern-faced man. At the bottom, the motto: 'Spare the rod, spoil the child' was written. Is that how they dealt with Clifford's needs?

Clara was feeling nervous now. She wanted Ivor to take her hand but he was staring at his shoes – maybe he had stomach ache again.

Eventually, Clifford emerged, ruddy-faced and terse behind an unsmiling woman in a suit. He was in a creased shirt, his shorts were too tight and his skin was tanned, but other than that, he looked much like the sullen boy she had shared a cigarette and confidences in the kitchen with. It was only four months or so but it felt longer.

The woman made a fuss about unlocking the doors and giving instructions to Clifford. She barely looked at Ivor or Clara except to say, 'We don't normally allow visitors.'

Clifford rubbed his elbows, embarrassed.

They took him straight down to the beach, where was a hut with a grizzled old man selling tea and coffee. In this heat! Clifford said he didn't want one, but Ivor bought him one anyway, in case he changed his mind and because the old man needed some trade.

You haven't set fire to anything, have you? she thought. She would not ask that. Since he'd left, she had done some reading about why children and young people might turn to destructive behaviour. 'A cry for help,' that was the phrase. Food stealing, arson: signs of a disturbed mind.

'Have you any friends?' she asked instead.

'A few,' he said, showing no inclination to elaborate. And why would he? thought Clara. Imagine if someone asked her that!

'Still singing?'

Much to Clara's surprise, Anita had discovered that Clifford had a talent for performing. Clara hoped his success in singing on the wireless and television was standing him in good stead here.

'Not really.' He chewed. The lemon sherbets, at least, were going down well. 'There's no one to sing with, so...'

She didn't want to interrogate him. The things you want to say to teenagers, you have to halve and halve again. 'Do you like it here?' she asked, after a while.

He screwed up his nose. 'It is what it is.'

The colours were beautiful. Back in Lavenham, it was greens and purples, sometimes brown. Here it was all yellow, blue, grey. The sea was flat as a millpond, as though it also was too hot to rouse itself.

Gradually, Clifford started to relax. He asked after Anita. He was still talking about her when the plane flew over. It was so low – it must have only just taken off – and it made such a roar they all had to stop talking. Goosepimples came up on her arms. She squinted up and the belly of the beast was right over-head, glittering in the light.

'There's an American airbase not far from here,' shouted Ivor, and he put his hand on Clara's shoulder.

'Yeah,' returned Clifford. 'Same time every day.' And then, once the sound had dissipated, 'Are you feeling all right, Miss Newton?'

'Of course,' Clara said brightly. 'It just took me by surprise, that's all.'

Her late fiancé, Michael, used to say that in peacetime, the most dangerous time in flying was in those first few seconds when a plane takes off, and in the final seconds when it comes in to land.

'And in wartime?'

'It's all dangerous.'

The other thing he used to say was: 'I'm not afraid of flying, I'm afraid of crashing.'

. . .

Soon after the plane, about thirty boys marched past – they must have been from the school – in red jumpers and shorts. Their leader shouted something, and Clifford flushed.

'She's my old housemother,' he shouted back, a rictus grin on his face, 'she came to visit me.' Someone wolf-whistled and another called out, 'She can visit me any time,' and was hastily told off by the leader.

Clara asked Clifford what the other children were like, and he fidgeted and then with his head held higher, he said, 'I told them that I sang on the television, but no one believed me. I don't know why they think I would make it up.'

Clifford went back to his school, and it was just her and Ivor again: it was weirdly nerve-wracking. It shouldn't have been – they knew each other well – but perhaps they didn't know each other so well in this incarnation. Patricia and the children were a moat and bailey to intimacy, and it was hard to know how to behave without them.

'Shall we... I mean, is there anything you want to do now... in particular, I mean?'

He raised his eyebrows at her. 'We could go back for... for a rest?'

'Oh, are you feeling poorly again?'

He shook his head, then smiled without looking at her. She felt shy now and when she was shy, she tended to babble: 'I heard that in hot countries they have a nap in the afternoon, and they call it a siesta or something like that. I've always thought it sounds like a good idea...'

Goodness, she did talk *nonsense* sometimes!

When Clara woke up, the room was dark. She was in Ivor's bed, his body radiating heat, and everything was different. They had walked back quickly, invigorated, holding hands – mostly she was nervous he'd change his mind and she'd feel mortified again.

And as they crept into the hall, she was thinking, *please don't let the manager be at her desk*; yet for once, fortune had favoured them and no one was there.

Ivor had drawn the curtains and given her a come-hither look and she had come-hithered. And it was marvellous, even if she didn't have time to put on the silky nightdress.

Wrapped in a sheet, she went over to the desk and finished the letter to Rita and began one to Terry. It was lovely to do that, and occasionally to look over her shoulder to watch Ivor there, sleeping so peacefully.

That evening, finally, she put on the dress he had made for her. It was fitted – unlike her usual attire – and once she had put on her heels, he nodded approvingly.

'But do you really like it – on me?' She surprised herself with how needy she could be with him sometimes. She would hate anyone else to know this.

He looked like a deer in headlights and then whispered, 'I do, but I like you not in it too,' which made her laugh, but it was fun scolding him.

'Ivor, that is not the point.'

There were plenty of empty tables in the dining room, but the Italian waiter led them to the table next to an old couple. They were a lovely pair but they looked over at them a lot, and Clara wished she'd worn a ring on her wedding finger after all.

Clara wasn't sure how they got on to it, but they talked about his missing arm. How it affected his work, not the quality, thank goodness, but the speed. He used to be able to do things twice as fast with two hands and that was frustrating.

'It was worth it anyway,' he said quietly as he forked his

mash. 'To do my bit. To free our country of tyranny. I try to have no regrets.' He smiled up at her.

She tried to be charming. (If only she could raise a single eyebrow like film stars did!) 'I think you manage without it.'

He laughed.

After they'd eaten, the old man on the next table leaned over, dabbing his mouth with his serviette. 'We've been married forty years,' he said. 'How about you?'

Ivor coughed. 'It *feels* like for ever, Mrs Jones.' He winked at Clara, who blushed. She was blushing a lot this weekend.

'You look beautiful in that dress,' the woman said. She had something – could be mustard? on her chin. 'Doesn't she, Gil?'

'She does. If only I were fifty years younger,' the old man said, chuckling to himself as he tucked into his chicken pie. Clara wondered if she should warn him. Goodness, she had no evidence that it was the pie that had affected Ivor. It might have been nerves! Nevertheless, she willed the old man to put down his knife and fork.

'Take care of each other,' the man said as they left, and the woman leaned over to say, 'It's nice to see young love.'

When they were out of earshot, Ivor whispered, 'How long have we been together?'

'Since May,' Clara tutted – the date was engraved on her heart. 'Less than two months...'

'Oh, it was long before then,' he said. His eyes were crinkled at the edges. 'I feel like we've been together from the moment we met.'

It was definitely love, thought Clara, but it wasn't young – she felt like they'd been through a thousand years together.

Ivor seemed twitchy the next morning, and Clara wondered if they'd been away for too long. 'Are you worried about Patricia? We can call Anita if you like?'

She thought about calling Sister Grace too. Forty hours –
yes, she was counting – was a lot without hearing from the children. However, she resisted. Bad news travels fast, she told
herself. Ivor too said he wouldn't call, he was fine and dandy,
but on the way to the dining room he doubled back, saying he'd
forgotten something, and then at the table he knocked his boiled
egg out of its cup and it rolled onto the floor. She had been
looking forward to the breakfast, but this time the toast was
underdone and there wasn't enough butter. Perhaps it was the
heat? Men hid behind newspapers as their wives stared into
space with forced smiles. The wireless crackled and Clara
could just make out presenters pontificating about faraway
places and King George's health. She thought about telling Ivor
about her father's postcard, but she didn't want to lower the
mood (although probably it would only be her mood that was
lowered).

They agreed they'd spend the day on the quiet beach that
the manager recommended, then they'd go up to the train
station about three.

There were so many questions Clara wanted to ask him.
Was she the first woman he'd been with since Ruby? How did it
feel? (He had seemed happy enough.) She kept having flashbacks that made her cheeks flame so much that she put her
hands on them to cool them down. Did he like her? She knew
he *liked* her. Did he like her as much as she liked him? Was that
even possible?

The beach wasn't that quiet after all. There were families
spread out over picnic blankets, and children darting in and out
of the water, shrieking about the cold. They had been there
about five minutes, making their own nest a few yards from the
shore, when some six or seven horses galloped across the sand,
and a little dog darted over to yelp at them.

Ivor laughed. 'I don't think he'd stand a chance, do you?'

'That's the thing about little dogs,' she said, laughing too. 'He probably imagines he's the same size as them.'

They took their shoes off – what a relief to unbuckle the sandals – and Ivor promised he'd paddle, but not yet. They kissed, but only once because of all the people around – no one wants to see that – and then he sat back on the deckchair with his pork pie hat over his face and his socks pointing to the sky. He refused to take them off. He kept his jacket and shirt on, of course, but he undid his tie.

After a couple of minutes, Clara sat down too. A small stone was digging into her back, but it was not worth scrabbling about for. The sky was bright blue, and wholesome somehow. It was odd to relax in public and she was not sure if she could. She closed her eyes, feeling the sun beat down on her face, and wondered if she had brought the last basket of washing in. Miss Webb had thrown her off her stride on Friday. Was it just Friday? It felt like ages ago.

Clara thought about her ill-advised promise to take the children to church, and she thought about the ex-residents she was fond of. Alex was going to a summer school for 'the advanced child' with Bernard. Bernard's father, Victor – one of Clara's old beaus – was marrying his librarian friend. Joyce had sent some photographs of a trip to Butlin's.

She hadn't heard from Terry for a while – but that was good. It meant she had moved on. She had had a card from Denny's adoptive parents which hinted at some dark moments – Denny had only recently lost his parents in a car accident – but it appeared Denny was getting on with things too. The twins Barry and Billy didn't write; they were busy playing football every day. Occasionally she had phone calls with them, their voices so loud she had to hold the receiver away from her ear.

And then she thought about what the current residents of

the home would be doing. She still fretted about them even when they were apart. In her care meant under her skin. When she was with them, she dreamed of not being with them, yet even when she was not with them she couldn't get them out of her mind. Peg and Gladys might be reading or playing or cooking with Sister Grace. Florrie however would probably be up in her room alone. Some children played in the street with hula hoops, prams with dolls or football – but that was too young for Florrie and she was too young for the things she was most interested in: cigarettes and boys.

Clara had hoped learning a musical instrument would help – or at least get the girl out of the house for an hour or two. Anita was always looking for new protégés, but Florrie said she hated music.

'Penny for them?' Ivor was smiling.

'Just thinking about...'

'The children?' he finished.

'Always.'

'I thought so,' he said affectionately.

'I'd love to bring them here one day.'

Nearby, a man was lying flat on his back and his children, in fits of laughter, were covering every part of him, from the neck down to his boots; his suit was being covered with a thick layer of sand. They patted and flattened the sand with spades as he exhorted them to go gently. He was entirely trapped with his arms crossed over his chest. His children were delighted.

'I got a postcard from my father yesterday,' she said presently.

'Oh?' Ivor's feet shifted in the sand. 'What did it say then?'

Everything about it had disturbed her but something about that banal phrase 'Constable country' made her inexplicably furious. She hated that her father had this power over her emotions. The postcard had made her realise she was a long way from being indifferent to him. Would she never be out of his control?

'Nothing much,' she said. Already she regretted bringing it up and couldn't understand why she had. It only made her miserable. 'Just... I'll ignore it, I think.'

'Right-o,' he said and then he too went silent, which was unusual, because Ivor was usually insightful about her family issues.

The father next to them was completely covered up to his neck and his children were thrilled at their handiwork. It was kind of him to indulge them, Clara thought. She liked to make the children at the home happy too, but she wouldn't have let them bury her. As for her own father... he never would have.

'Daddy, you're a mummy!' one yelled and they all laughed again.

The sun was on Clara's arms. Her face would be tomato-red tomorrow, but she didn't care. 'I'm glad we came.'

'I didn't know there'd be so many people about,' Ivor was saying. 'But here goes nothing.'

Clara turned away from the family, smiling to herself. 'That poor man is going to have sand *everywhere*...'

'Clara,' Ivor's voice was suddenly serious, 'I want to ask you something.'

Clara's head was not there. She was still impressed by the patience of the father in the sand. Nevertheless, she smiled up at Ivor. 'What is it?'

He'd sprung forward suddenly and was fumbling in his jacket pocket.

Clara guessed he'd have an emergency sewing kit in there, a handkerchief, and his wallet. What was he looking for now? If it was lemon sherbets he was after, he'd be out of luck because she'd been snaffling them all weekend *and* the packets were small these days, not at all like she remembered them as a girl.

But no, it wasn't any of that. Ivor was kneeling in front of her, and he had produced a box. It was small, dark green velvet, ring-sized. She knew what it was as soon as she saw it.

'Ivor?'

Before she could stop him, the box had opened up with a click.

3

The instant Ivor asked, almost the same time as he asked, she said, 'I don't know...'. Shock was running through her as though cold water had been tipped on her head. She wasn't expecting this. *Should* she have expected it? *Goodness, Ivor. Where did that come from?* It was a beautiful ring – an amber on a silver band.

He said, 'You always liked art deco style,' and she could hear that behind the nerves, he was proud, proud that he knew her preferred style better than anyone. 'And it's a bit different.'

She couldn't bring herself to speak, and he continued.

'But it doesn't have to be this one. We can get another if you like. Change the stone – or if you're worried about the size...' His voice trailed off. 'They said to come back any time...'

'The ring is lovely,' she said, and then he understood. The ring wasn't the problem.

Ivor leaned back into the sand on his elbow, putting space between them, like the two single beds, a disappointed, embarrassed look on his face. He grabbed his collar as though it were suddenly too tight and then said in his low, measured voice, 'That's me told.'

Next to them, the man who had been buried rose up suddenly like a sand monster. He shook the grains off his clothes, then chased after the squealing children, roaring, 'I'll get you!'

'If I was going to marry anyone, it would be you,' she said quickly. 'It's just... I'm not ready to be married yet.' God, she loved him but if she married, she would have to give up her work looking after the orphans. She would have to give up little Peg, who was just coming along, and sweet-tempered Gladys and Florrie, who always expected the worst. And all the desperate children she had yet to meet. The children who gave her this feeling of peace in her stomach that, although she was doing the tiniest thing in the world, like throwing stones into the sea, she was making a big difference for them.

She would have to give up her life at the home, she would have to give up everything. Ivor wouldn't. He would keep his name, his job, his bank account, his identity. She'd only just found hers – and she could envisage it slipping away. She'd only just made herself comfortable as Miss Newton the House-mother – to then turn herself into Mrs Delaney? Mrs Delaney the what?

And she didn't want to live in a suburban house like Mrs Horton even if it had modern gas fires, soft toilet roll and hold-back ropes for the pleated curtains. She certainly didn't want to be restricted and beaten to smithereens, like her best friend, Judy. She didn't want to flirt and hopelessly flutter at the attention of other men, like Mrs Harrington. She didn't want to tut every time her husband spoke, like the florist, Mrs Garrard. She didn't want to follow a husband everywhere, like her mother, like a shadow, even if she did get to see Africa. All different women – all the same situation: marriage. The institution. She didn't want that.

Ivor wouldn't be like those husbands; surely, Ivor was different? She loved him so much. But this had come as a shock. She was not ready.

Somehow, her father slammed back into her thoughts again, as he had much of the weekend. Respectability. Duty. She remembered her mother's fearful 'Don't tell your father.' She remembered the long drives up to school: her father admonishing her mother for being emotional – 'for God's sake, it's only six months,' and her mother withering under his glare. It was like Clara was in a tug-of-war sometimes – until her mother stopped tugging.

Ivor wasn't wealthy – he had to paddle like a dog to keep his head above water – and she certainly had nothing to bring to the table on that score. And much as she loved Ivor's damn workshop, she couldn't imagine the two of them – no, *the three of them*, living there.

And then there was that issue too, perhaps the biggest issue of them all... *the three of them.*

Patricia: the high court judge baby who didn't like her – perhaps that was normal, but Clara didn't feel she had the expertise with babies to overcome it. Mrs Horton advised her, 'She won't be a baby for ever,' but Clara found that thought frightening rather than comforting. Patricia wasn't just going to grow out of the antipathy she had towards Clara. She would be a child, and then she would be a teen – and that would be worse.

Patricia's recalcitrance seemed as much a part of her as her curly hair and long eyelashes. And what about her history? She had another mother and a father out there – what of them? Patricia came with big question marks hanging over her. At least with the children in the home, Clara was performing a service and everything was transparent and compartmentalised. She had background files, information on the lot of them. It was because of this clarity, this order somehow, that she felt free to care. Free to be devoted. Meanwhile, Patricia's status was murky, nothing was formalised; it all seemed to perch on a vague expectation of goodwill that meant Ruby, her birth mother, could take Patricia back at any moment. Clara didn't work that way.

Ivor needed an explanation. He hadn't asked for one, he was just biting his lip, staring out to sea as though he wished he were under the waves, but he was owed one.

'I don't want to be a housewife,' she began.

'Who says you'd be a housewife?'

Everyone. From *Good Housekeeping* to Donald Button's TV show to newspapers to the council. And even if they didn't, it wasn't like there were a billion alternative paths to choose from either. What would people think?

She said, 'It's complicated, isn't it?' *For women*, she thought. And *you have a baby. What about her?*

'It doesn't have to be.'

'Can't we just carry on as we are? For now, I mean. I have my work, and I don't want to stop...'

'I'm asking you to marry me – not abdicate. You're not the King.'

She couldn't tell if he was joking. There was a jagged edge behind it. She heard *what makes you so special?* She sensed he was saying what her father always used to say: that she was prickly, that she was 'above herself'. Or *who does she think she is?*

Right now, she felt like a small, deluded dog, unaware of its own limitations, barking at horses.

Ivor fumbled by his side, then threw something which jumped twice in the water, then disappeared into the sea. Clara covered her mouth with her hands. 'No! Ivor, wait.' She thought it was the ring.

'No, it's here,' he said, patting his pocket. He understood. And she felt mortified and relieved.

'Save it for another time,' she said, her heart still racing.

'I won't ask again.'

Her heart sank. No, it plummeted. Immediately. It was a childish response. She thought, *ask every day, ask every week, please*. 'I just need to think it through – the implications with... work, with the children.' She didn't say 'with Patricia,' but he must understand how complicated that was – he must. 'You just took me by surprise...'

'But your first reaction was no,' he stated.

'My first reaction was *I don't know*. I do want to— in the future, yes, definitely...'

'But for now...'

'For now, I just...'

'Don't know,' he finished for her.

An aeroplane went overhead. It must have been that time again. She could feel herself shiver at the roar; it was something she seemed to have no control over. Even though her mind said there was no threat, it was fine, the hairs on her arm stood up and her skin turned like goose skin. But Ivor didn't put his hand on her this time. And then there was a cacophony of squawking from the birds; they must have scattered then regrouped.

She wanted to say more, but she didn't know what. Something had opened and something had shut. She remembered Alex telling her about Pandora's box. Something had shifted. The light, the sea, everything was the same as it had been five minutes ago, but maybe the shadows had drawn nearer, these grains under her feet were packed more compactly than the others.

Finally, he took her hand, and she loved him more than ever. 'I understand.' Ivor; the most rational, clear-thinking man she knew.

'I meant not now, but yes, some day, yes.'

'When?'

'Uh, ten years?'

He sighed. She had got it wrong again. 'Maybe five?'

They had walked back to The Ocean Breeze, hand in clammy hand, and, if you had seen them, you might have thought she had said yes.

When Clara arrived back at the home, Sister Grace opened the door. Her lovely smiley face with its big flat plate-like cheeks and gentle grey eyes was more welcome than ever, and Clara could smell Sister Grace's favourite dish of mince.

On the train, Ivor had fallen asleep again, but this time with his head against the window. She had read articles in her magazines about fit-and-flare skirts being all the rage and why you should keep bees – *it's not just for the honey!* – while rolling the marbles between her fingers: there was something soothing about their cool roundness. Clifford had told her to keep them.

It was a relief to be back.

'They've been good as gold. Peg is playing in the shed, and Gladys is practising the flute. Florrie is in her room. She didn't eat much though. Even Stella has been no problem,' Sister Grace said, and then, studying Clara's expression, asked: 'What happened?'

'Everything's grand,' Clara lied. 'Couldn't be better.' She hoped Sister Grace wouldn't pursue it. She would cry if she asked any more. Gosh, it was awful. She couldn't bear thinking of it, and yet she couldn't think of anything else.

Peg was twirling at the bottom of the stairs. She handed Clara a notebook. Page one said 'I MIST YOU'. Page two said 'don't GO way again'. Clara gathered her close and kissed her.

'But you had a good time?'

Peg nodded eagerly, then tried to lick Clara's cheek.

Florrie hadn't come down when she was called so, once Sister Grace had left, Clara had gone up to the girl's bedroom. (Florrie hated having to share with 'babies'.)

'You're back,' noted again Florrie flatly.

'I am,' said Clara. If Clifford made her nervous, Florrie made her feel frustrated. 'Everything all right?'

Florrie shrugged her shoulders. 'I suppose.'

Gladys burst in, a ball of energy. 'Can we play Newmarket tonight?' Everyone loved Newmarket. That is, the children did; Clara didn't. Actually, Florrie didn't either.

'Another day, maybe,' she told the sunny girl, smoothing down her hair.

At bedtime that evening, Gladys brought up her brothers again. She had been separated from them some time ago, and she was desperate to be reunited. When she had first told Clara about them, Clara had assumed that finding them would be impossible, and that she should help Gladys to be resilient without them. But this evening she remembered that moment at the Royal Festival Hall when, despite the terrible odds, Rita's long-lost mama had returned. Everything had turned out well for Rita, hadn't it? It was perhaps time for Clara to lose her cynicism. If Rita, and now Gladys, believed that dreams come true, then she should try to make them. What is an orphan without hope?

It might help take her mind off Ivor's proposal too.

So this time, Clara asked Gladys to tell her more (which Gladys was delighted to do), and soon Clara felt as though she knew the brothers. Trevor was the oldest – Gladys thought he must be eleven – born on New Year's Day. And Frank was the middle one. He would be nine – born on Valentine's Day.

'Easy to remember,' Gladys said.

Clara said her mummy must have been clever to organise all that, and Gladys gurgled with pleasure and then said seriously that she couldn't remember much about Mummy, but she could remember everything about Frank and Trevor, even the way they smelled—

'How do they smell?'

'With their noses!' Gladys screeched gleefully.

Trevor was the clever one while Frank was funny. Trevor loved games, and he always won at thumb wars. At Clara's quizzical look, Gladys explained. 'You have to crush the other person's thumb'.

'Oh, of course.'

Frank was loud and loved planes.

'A lot of children do,' Clara said, remembering Alex's fascination with the Wright brothers.

'He really does,' Gladys said. 'All day long he is like this...' She stretched out her arms and made a vrooming noise.

'I will try to find out where they are,' Clara promised and was rewarded with a huge smile and another squeeze.

Gladys had always been affectionate – sometimes overly so. And Clara constantly wondered if it was too much, but pushing her away would have been worse. In any case, after the weekend she'd just had – which had been marvellous and yet mortifying – the physical comfort was welcome.

4

_____

After the proposal, Clara didn't go to Ivor's workshop for a few days and he didn't call on her: it was best they cooled off. Plus, there was always something to do in the home. Even with only three residents, Clara couldn't sit around twiddling her thumbs. Lovely as the home was, it was ramshackle, and its problems were so large she could only tweak around the seams. There was an invasion of flies (Stella and a hidden dead mouse), a leak at the sinks in the basement bathroom, and always something to do in the garden. She painted the door a brilliant blue, which delighted Peg and Gladys, but still Ivor did not come over.

Finally, on the Wednesday morning, Clara went to his workshop with some clothes that needed darning – she could resist no longer – and Ivor greeted her warmly, made her tea, and at first nothing seemed amiss. She talked about the children, he talked about Patricia, and she showed him a letter she'd had from Alex (mostly concerned about the Princes in the Tower in 1483).

He asked if there was more news from her father. She told him that there hadn't been, thank goodness, she hoped the postcard was a one-off.

'Good,' he said uncertainly, 'I mean, if that's what you want.'

'I do.' Clara nodded her head fervently. 'He's the last thing I need.'

But then Ivor said he had a busy few days ahead, which Clara thought was suspicious. Was he making a point? Was he saying, *I am no longer at your beck and call?* Which is how she probably would have felt if it were the other way round – only it wouldn't have been the other way round, would it?

A lot of Ivor's work was in London, and this time Patricia was going with him. He had a house to price up – he'd never had to dress an entire house before – and then if he got this commission, who knew? Lots of new clients. He wasn't snubbing her, he was still sweet and attentive with her, still keen to make plans with her for when he got back – for her next day off, Sunday week – but that was days away.

Before they had got together back in May, Ivor had said that he was nervous that they would ruin what they had. They had had something precious, and now Clara had smashed it. Should she have just said yes?

No.

But why hadn't she said yes?

Ivor did call her from London, on Thursday morning, to check that his upstairs light was off; and then he told her that Patricia had lost her ted, Polly, on a double-decker bus. On Thursday evening, he called again. Patricia was learning words and she may have said, 'Clara', he said, and then he laughed. 'Or it might have been "car".'

Clara leaned against the wall, loving Ivor's voice. He still liked her, she thought, despite everything.

The Friday was the last day before the schools broke up for the summer holidays, and the children went off in great spirits. It was a fine day for washing too, and Clara was hanging out her second load when she heard a firm knock at the front door. She hoped it wasn't Miss Webb from the childcare department. She had a moment's terror that it would be her father, but that wasn't a realistic concern – surprise visits weren't likely his thing.

It was a serviceman: a serviceman in American military uniform. Oh, she knew it well. He was smoking a cigarette. She would have known that American tobacco smell anywhere. He was tall – Clara only came up to his throat – and broad; he seemed to take up the whole of the doorway and was tanned golden like a crispy roast potato skin. His buttons were so shiny, she could see herself reflected in them.

At the sight of him, Clara couldn't breathe. Her heart was thumping. *Michael.*

Of course, it wasn't Michael. Michael died on Christmas Eve, 1944. She'd been to Michael's funeral. She'd cried on Michael's friends' shoulders. She'd cried on this one's shoulder, in fact – Davey Selby. He was one of Michael's best friends. Yes, he looked like him in his uniform, but when you looked closer it was obvious it wasn't him. Michael was just as tall, just as broad, but not tanned, and Michael was different – it was just wishful thinking, that's all.

'Looks like I found you,' he said. 'May I?' He crossed the threshold, picked her up and twirled her around. Clara went limp in his arms. 'Good golly, Miss Newton, I would have known you anywhere.'

Sgt Davey Selby of the Eighth Air Force, 838 Bombardment Squadron sat in the kitchen with his long legs stretched out in front of him. Clara couldn't stop staring at him. He seemed out of place here; he was gigantic and, like Michael and Marilyn, he was so American. He was familiar yet exotic. He was her past, yet he was here now.

Michael, Dave Selby and their other friend, Jacob she-can't-remember-his surname. She'd preferred Jacob but Davey was a good man too, 'the most loyal man I know,' Michael used to say, 'like a brother to me.'

She boiled the kettle and hurriedly arranged left-over biscuits. She couldn't believe it. The postcard from her father, now Davey – it was like the past kept intruding. She didn't mind Davey being here though, but she wished he'd given her some warning.

He stared around him. 'It's quaint,' he said. 'I hadn't expected this.' When she asked what he had expected, he chuckled to himself. 'Something more like a prison, I guess. An institution...' He loved the biscuits. 'You always were a great cook.'

Was he mistaking her for someone else?

'You've done well for yourself, Clara,' he said, nodding his head both up and down and from side to side.

'You realise this is not *my* home – it's my job?'

'Of course,' he said, but she wasn't sure he did.

She remembered nights in Central London. Basement bars and secret drinks. She had made it her mission to find him a girl-friend, and she tried to fix him up with Judy once. That was a mistake; they had nothing in common and, worse, both seemed insulted by it.

'She's not my usual type of gal,' Davey had said. He was more diplomatic than Judy; at work the next morning she had refused to speak to Clara, before wailing, 'Oh, Clara, don't you know me at all?' in the canteen.

Not long after that, Davey had found someone without Clara's help (which was aggravating), an English girl called Nellie Coleman. Didn't they meet on the London Under-ground when he was on leave? Yes, that was it, and their romance had been fast and passionate. Even faster than Clara and Michael's relationship, and they were no slouches in that department! And Davey and Nellie were 'public' in their affection too. Clara could remember complaining to Michael about their kissing in the street: 'Maybe he doesn't know English customs, but she does, and it's too much.'

Nellie was younger than Clara and more outspoken. She knew her own mind, Clara thought (she was intimidated by people who did).

Michael used to say, 'The thing is, Clara, friendships aren't like when you are at school or something and you pick friends who are like you. In war, your friends are the ones you trust. It's deeper than in peacetime.'

'Is that what we're like?'

'We're both. You *are* like me – and you are the one who I trust with my life.'

She blinked back the tears. Davey was Michael's best friend. Of course she would make him welcome. 'Make yourself at home,' she said. And he promised he would.

When after about an hour he was making no signs of moving on, she asked him if he wanted to stay for lunch. She gave him the last slice of kidney pie with some lettuce from the garden and got him a beer from Christmas. When he saw the spread, he shook his head incredulously.

'I can't take all this. You English had it bad the past few years.'

'We manage,' Clara said proudly.

'Clara, you knockout,' he said as he tucked in. 'Don't you want any?'

'I had some earlier,' she lied. 'Tell me, how is Nellie?'

Michael had gone to their wedding, but she hadn't. She couldn't remember why – probably work. 'Overtime will be written on my grave,' she remembered moaning to Judy, 'I'm missing out on all the excitement.' Judy used to retort: 'We get plenty enough excitement here.' Judy meant bombs, sirens and explosions – an altogether different kind of excitement.

Clara had been aggrieved at the time; Davey and Nellie had

met each other *after* she and Michael had met, and yet they'd beaten them down the aisle. How were they so fast? Clara remembered Nellie saying: 'Can't wait to get out this dump,' and 'America is the future,' at least once every time they met. She suspected that had been one of Nellie's motivations for marrying Davey.

Now Davey stabbed the pie and then, putting it into his mouth, said: 'You cook better than my old ma – don't tell her I said that.' He winked at her.

'Where is she then, Nellie?'

Davey had a habit of batting questions away. What was he doing here? How long was he staying? There was never a straight answer. He talked a lot, but not much information was conveyed. She had to ask twice more before he finally spelled it out.

'She's visiting folks in London town, so I thought I'd revisit my old haunts in Suffolk. I heard you were here – looked you up and hey presto.' He spoke as he chewed. 'I can't believe you're single when you cook like this.'

And then Clara realised it was almost three o'clock and she had forgotten Peg and Gladys. Sometimes they walked home without her, but she had promised to be at the school gates since it was the special last day, and they'd have lots to carry. She'd never been late before. Nobody likes to be kept waiting, but for her girls being kept waiting was huge. They lived in the shadow of abandonment and a false step from Clara could bring that back with a vengeance.

She leapt up. 'I'm meant to be up the road.' She flapped around, not sure what to do first. 'The school. Wait there, I'll only be twenty minutes.'

But Davey had scraped back his chair and got up too. 'I'll give you a lift.'

'Are you sure? Okay, thank you.'

But outside, gleaming in the afternoon sunshine, wasn't a

car, as Clara had expected, but a motorbike. It was all chunky wheels, shiny handlebars and fenders.

Clara's heart fell. This was not her.

'She's a beauty, isn't she?' He climbed on. 'Ready?'

'Oh, I couldn't possibly.' It was far too reckless, far too... intimate. Clara backed away. She'd run instead. But on second thoughts, she knew she didn't have much choice. She would be late otherwise, and the image of Peg and Gladys fretting for her was appalling. And Davey was looking at her like the solution was straightforward.

So Clara clambered on and held on to him. She wished she didn't have to press herself close, and she certainly wished she didn't have to clutch him when they picked up speed. It felt unfaithful, even though it wasn't. She hoped Nellie wouldn't mind, but she could imagine Nellie would mind very much. Her skirt flapped and she didn't know whether to take her hands off Davey to hold it down, or if that was too risky and she should just let it be. A glimpse of suspender was hardly the end of the world (although in Lavenham maybe it was).

They rode up the high road with the wind in her face and she felt like a devil-may-care girl, only she did care.

She didn't want Davey to deposit her too near the school, but he couldn't hear her shouting, 'Here is fine', so he drove right up to the gate in the middle of everything.

Everyone was looking at her as she dismounted, mums with prams and toddlers on reins, while she felt like Calamity Jane. She was already the odd one out – 'Miss Newton the housemother' – and this wouldn't help. One of the teachers, Miss Fisher, was waiting with the stragglers, a quizzical look on her face. Clara was sweating and her legs felt like jelly. They hadn't been shaking when she had squeezed them around Davey but now she was back on dry land, they did. She told him nicely to go and, thankfully, he didn't put up a fight, but he did say, 'See you back at the house,' and her stomach clenched.

'That's not Ivor Delaney, is it?' said a woman, picking up a scrap of a girl who Clara recognised as a child who often put things up her nose.

'He's an old friend from America,' Clara said, smiling quickly. God, people loved to talk. She'd be hung, drawn and quartered and splattered over mid-Suffolk in no time.

'Is he now?' said the mother of last year's May Queen, Hazel Richards. She was a gossip.

'He served at Cockerham during the war,' Clara said, and it was satisfying to see her expression change. 'A brave pilot.'

That kept them quiet. Everyone respected *those* boys, the Americans who helped save us.

Clara's legs were still trembling as she walked home with the girls, trying to fend off Gladys' constant questions: Who was that? Why were you on his bike? Do you love him?

'An old friend.' 'So I could get here in time.' 'No, don't be daft.'

Davey was waiting for them in the street outside the home. Clara assumed it was time to draw their reunion to an end, but he said he didn't have anything else to do, so she invited him in. What else could she do?

The girls ran off, full of glee at weeks of freedom ahead of them, and Davey helped her get the stripey deckchairs out of the shed: he was as strong as he looked. They sat on them in the shade under the trees at the back of the garden. She couldn't cope with him AND the bright sunlight. Her undergarments were on the line too, which was embarrassing. It was a headache waiting to happen. The grass had grown back; there was only one scrubby patch where Peg liked to skip.

The bees were loud and busy in the lavender. Clara grew restless but Davey seemed happy just to sit, his hat on his chest, his face in direct communication with the sun.

'Nice roses,' he said. 'And I like the vegetable patch.'

Then Florrie came home, indifferent to the prospect of the summer holiday, and Clara gave the children their tea while Davey was still soaking up the last of the rays outside (and she pretended there was nothing unusual about this at all). Florrie didn't even ask who he was – that was how little she cared.

Ivor knocked on the door later, holding a sleepy Patricia. He'd just got back from London, and she could see the tension in his features that he often had after long days in the city.

'I can't stop,' he said, rubbing his shoulder. He rarely complained, but he often had pain there. 'Just thought we'd come by to say hello.'

'That's fine,' she said quickly. 'Hello, Patricia.'

Patricia stared straight through her.

'Whose is the motorbike?' Ivor said. And she realised that was why he had come over so soon. It wasn't *just* to say hello.

'It's a... he's an old friend of Michael's.' Ivor was looking so quizzically at her that she felt the need to fill the gaps. 'He looks like him too – gave me a fright.'

'Oh?' He leaned against the doorframe, his face shadowed, and Patricia stuck her tongue out at Clara.

'He's in England with his wife, Nellie. I used to know them both. In the war.'

He still looked stern.

'Don't be silly, Ivor, I'll introduce you.'

'I don't think...'

But Davey had come in from the garden, and stuck out his big military hand ready for a big military handshake. Ivor was perfectly pleasant, but Clara could guess what he was thinking. And Davey was so... large, not just in height but breadth too, he made even burly Ivor seem pint-sized.

At the sight of him, Patricia swung her mallet wildly.

'Hey, what you got?' Davey said in a sweet for-children voice.

'It's a mallet,' Clara explained. 'From croquet.'

'I bet that's good for knocking out baddies!'

Patricia giggled, showing her tooth stumps. She was clearly a sucker for a handsome man.

'Cute kid,' Davey said to Ivor.

'Thank you,' replied Ivor, stony-faced.

Davey retreated and Ivor stared after him. One part, one small silly part of her, liked to think that he might be jealous. The bigger part of her told herself not to be daft.

'He's staying over?'

'No, he'll head off...' She didn't know when. 'Soon. Ivor, there's no need to be funny. He's just a friend.'

'I'm not being funny,' Ivor said, and then he paused like he was waiting for her to say something else. 'All right,' he said finally. 'We're staying in Norwich for a few days working on another commission.'

'You're going away again?'

'It's easier than going backwards and forwards.'

He let her kiss his cheek, and she watched him go back to his responsibilities. She kept her eyes on him until he was inside: the shape of his trousers and the back of his head – the haircut that wasn't that short, but just enough to expose where the sun caught the nape of his neck.

Davey had taken off his boots and put his feet up on a chair in the parlour. '2–1,' he said and she thought it was a remark about Ivor, but he was scanning the sports pages. Then he asked if she had ever seen a baseball match. She said not, and he said, 'You'd enjoy it.'

She just wanted him to leave now. It felt wrong and she imagined Ivor would be watching and waiting for him to go too.

Picking up on her mood perhaps, Davey said he'd only meant to come for a quick drink – hadn't meant to take up her afternoon. He added, defensively, 'But you did say to make yourself at home.'

After they'd had more tea, she asked when he was going to head off and he scratched his cheek and shuffled his feet. 'I thought you had plenty of room. All those little beds...'

Clara gulped. 'Oh no, we're short of space,' she said nonsensically.

'I'm not sure where I'm going to stay then.'

Clara felt panicky. She hadn't realised he hadn't arranged anything, and she felt she had to suggest a solution and quickly. 'You could go to Ivor's – the... man you just met with the baby...' But she could just imagine Ivor's face if Davey appeared on his doorstep. Fortunately, Davey didn't seem to think that was appropriate either.

He chuckled. 'What would his wife say if I turned up out of the blue?'

Clara swallowed, weighing up whether to tell him about that or not, but he was continuing obliviously, 'Just give me the name of a hotel.'

She told him to try the Shilling Grange Hotel or the Lavenham Arms, and he scrunched up his face. 'On second thoughts, I'll head back to town.'

This was a relief. 'Nellie would prefer that, I imagine,' Clara said in a happier tone.

He rubbed his chin, chuckled. 'Yeah, you know Nellie!'

He held Clara's hands for just a little too long, like he didn't want to go. She pulled away her fingers. 'Give my love to Nellie. Why not bring her here some time?'

She wished Nellie had come. She'd have more in common with her than she did with Davey. In fact, she thought, she'd love to hear Nellie talk about her life.

'Will do.'

And then he was gone – and, washing her hands, Clara breathed deeply. Although that chapter of her life had been an exciting one, she wasn't sure she wanted to go over it again, not now. And it was bad timing because after their weekend together, Ivor was disappointed with her. Davey's appearance wasn't going to help with that.

That evening, she took the photographs of Michael out of the drawer where she had put them a long time ago. The one of him as a baby, the one of him with his plane, and one of him with her. After someone dies, their photographs take on a different quality. Now, as the years between them grew, Michael was locked into that time, locked into that smile. It seemed more profound, more poignant than ever.

Maybe it was only by the past coming into full focus that you could see just how far you'd come. Davey's visit was a reminder, thought Clara, that she ought to concentrate on the here and now. Still, she was surprised to find tears prickling her eyes as she put the pictures away once again.

5

When Clara was told to attend a meeting with Miss Webb in her office at the council, she felt unenthusiastic. She hadn't warmed to the officious young woman and she didn't like the chaotic childcare officer's office or the gloomy council building either. On the other hand, Clara supposed it would be a chance to make some progress on the issue of Gladys' brothers – she was determined now, and she might get a word in with Mr Sommersby, the head of the council. Also, she did enjoy a trip into town. Lavenham had everything, but sometimes it could feel narrow. You couldn't be anonymous in Lavenham; everyone knew your name and your business.

Clara's spirits couldn't help but rise at the sight of Miss Webb's orderly workspace. Miss Webb kept a tidy ship; gone were Miss Cooper's Labour Party posters, photographs of Clement Attlee, overflowing ashtrays and spare shoes. Instead, there was one calendar of churches and a painting of Jesus in a pretty bronze frame. And Miss Webb was sitting at a new model typewriter and – unlike one-fingered typist Miss Cooper – she appeared to be a whizz at it. It was shallow, but Clara was impressed.

Miss Webb handed over some balance sheets and started to explain their contents. Clara saw that her files were in excellent order and beautifully presented. Miss Cooper had not been a file person. The only time she would pen-push would be to shove one off a cliff.

When Miss Webb finally drew a breath, Clara jumped in and outlined the story of Gladys' missing brothers but Miss Webb was immediately defensive. She said she didn't know where they would look for them and, what's more, she didn't think looking for them was a good idea.

'Let sleeping dogs lie,' she suggested with her high-pitched laugh, until Clara pointed out they were neither asleep nor dogs – 'they are boys.' She reiterated, 'Much-loved boys.'

'There is nothing about them here,' said Miss Webb peevishly, staring at her files. 'Could Gladys be mistaken?'

Mistaken? You didn't just lose brothers!

'Or lying?'

Clara struggled to keep her temper. Sometimes, she thought it was a shame Mrs Horton had been her first childcare officer – she hadn't appreciated what a diamond she was. Miss Cooper and now Miss Webb both seemed to be on another planet. Miss Cooper had been distracted by men and politics, while Miss Webb... well, Miss Webb seemed to be suffering from the tunnel vision that Clara used to have – yes, paperwork was important, but no, paperwork was not *everything*.

'Or attention-seeking? Don't tell me that's never happened before?'

Clara blushed. She couldn't say that had never happened before. But not Gladys, surely? Gladys was a good girl.

'All I'm saying is that we need to investigate,' Clara insisted. 'Where are the boys living now, and whose idea was it to split them up?'

The more Clara thought about it, the more it mystified and

enraged her. Arbitrarily putting siblings in separates homes: why?

Miss Webb frowned. 'Even if we did find them, they will be more difficult to place as a group. One is easier than two...'

'And three is impossible.' Clara finished for her. 'I know, but it's important for Gladys.' Miss Webb's eyebrows were knitted together. Clara went on, 'It's only information I am searching for at this stage.'

'If Gladys makes contact with her brothers, you could be condemning her to care for her whole childhood.'

'Everything is a risk,' Clara said helplessly, 'but Gladys needs this, and if I can help in any way...'

Miss Webb leaned forward with her elbows on her desk, the New Testament on her right. 'We have limited time and resources. And Miss Newton, I need to talk about something far more important.'

Once again, Miss Webb was concerned about getting the children to Sunday School – 'You agreed,' she said.

'I did,' admitted Clara, 'and I will try, but Sunday morning is difficult.' Sunday morning was catching up on chores. The thought of more commitments made her feel weary.

'Difficult' didn't go down well with Miss Webb.

Mr Sommersby's considerably larger room was just opposite Miss Webb's, and on her way out, Clara peeped through the window in the door. Perhaps the head of children's services might have some answers. He had several cups on his desk, and letters in front of him and a franking machine. He was head down in some papers and as he rubbed his red eyes, she thought for a moment that he was crying. He might not have been, but the once-jovial man certainly seemed to have been afflicted by a malaise.

So Clara changed her mind. Instead, she caught the tram to

see Mrs Horton in her new suburban house in a cul-de-sac, where she lived with her new husband and her mother-in-law. The last time she had visited, Mrs Horton senior had called out from the back room, and for a few seconds Mrs Horton ignored her. It made Clara feel uncomfortable, and Mrs Horton noticed and said, 'She does it all day long, you'll see.'

And she did.

Clara hadn't seen her old friend since she got back from Geneva, where she and Mr Horton had taken ex-resident Rita to reunite her with her mother. Today Mrs Horton's stories revolved around cheese.

'The hot cheese fondle?' repeated Clara.

'Fondoo,' corrected Mrs Horton.

Then there was the cheese with the holes in it.

Since they'd got back, Mrs Horton senior had deteriorated, and Mrs Horton said now, 'It's like she's punishing us.' When Clara said, 'How do you mean?' she grew flustered and said, 'It doesn't matter, forget it.'

Mrs Horton wheeled her mother-in-law in for tea and they talked about the weather and how good the raspberries were. Clara realised Mrs Horton was deliberately trying to keep things light. Mrs Horton senior repeated herself, but Mrs Horton answered each question or observation patiently. Mrs Horton senior was adamant that she had never met Clara and Clara couldn't help but feel disappointed that she'd made that little impression on her. She knew it was silly – the poor lady was ill – but for some reason it prickled.

Clara asked about emergency care – had Mrs Horton looked after any babies recently? Now she was no longer a council childcare officer, Mrs Horton instead provided emergency foster care for children. A few months back, she had cared for a baby for three days while the mother got back on her feet. The time before that, she had looked after twins while an aunt was located.

But now Mrs Horton coloured, gesturing to her mother-in-law. 'I had to give up that as well – too much on my plate.'

This wasn't a surprise but still, Clara felt saddened. Her friend and ally was giving up work entirely?

'How is Ivor?' Mrs Horton added as though she was trying to draw Clara's attention away from her. And it worked. Clara always liked hearing Ivor's name. She liked saying his name too. Her lips made a shape almost like a kiss.

'Ivor is well.' She permitted herself a small smile. 'Working hard as usual.'

'Who is Ivor?' asked the old lady as she put her fingers over all the cakes.

'Her...' Mrs Horton looked up helplessly. 'Gentleman friend?'

'Oh, I remember him,' Mrs Horton senior said to Clara's surprise and slight chagrin. Why did she remember him and not her? 'Handsome fella, upholsterer, lost a leg in the war.'

'Arm,' corrected Clara.

'An arm *and* a leg?' She shook her head. 'War is cruel.' Tears pooled in her eyes and Clara felt suddenly sympathetic towards her.

Mrs Horton leaned forward. 'You never did tell me – how was your trip to Norfolk?'

Clara couldn't tell Mrs Horton about the proposal, not while Mrs Horton senior was wagging her ears – but she probably wouldn't have told her anyway. Increasingly, she wanted to forget it ever happened. It was a mortification, an elephant in the room. If she could have packaged it up and left it in number four at the Ocean Breeze, she would have. Clara tried not to think of the jewellery box on the beach. The sunlight glistening. The smell of the sea, Ivor's crumpled expression. The sting of his dismay.

He had forgiven her though, hadn't he? He *said* he had, and he didn't mention it, but it made her feel ashamed.

'Who is she?' Mrs Horton senior said before Clara could reply. She pointed at Clara and then squinted at Mrs Horton. 'Do we know her?'

Clara decided to ask Mrs Horton for help with Gladys' brothers. She didn't expect busy Mrs Horton to be able to do much but Miss Webb had been about as helpful as a chocolate teapot, and Clara was running out of ideas. A trip to the library had proved fruitless too.

'I do like a mystery,' Mrs Horton said, and Clara remembered her substantial Agatha Christie collection. 'I'll do some digging for you.'

'Who died now?' said Mrs Horton senior and Mrs Horton shook her head, patiently. 'No one's died.'

There were other things Clara would have liked to confide in Mrs Horton had it been just the two of them: the unsettling blast from the past that was both Davey's visit and her father's unsolicited approach; but now Clara couldn't wait to get out of there. The experience was disorientating – it made Clara feel that time was running out. Mrs Horton was happily married, as far as Clara was aware, but she had inadvertently become a carer too. She used to be a proud independent career woman, and she didn't seem to be any more.

6

_____

The summer holidays were long! The children said they weren't long enough, but Clara wondered if they really thought so, since there wasn't much for them to do: Florrie skulked around the house while Peg and Gladys grew nut-brown and wild-haired as they played out in the garden, helped with the chores, occasionally played their instruments or painted. The younger girls continued their music lessons, but other than that there was little structure to their days. Peg still said nothing, but Gladys talked enough for two. She constantly wondered what amazing things Trevor and Frank would be doing. Clara called Mrs Horton every so often for updates but Mrs Horton had no news (yet!).

The children-in-care summer holiday to the seaside was cancelled – or rather, it turned out that Miss Cooper had failed to put the application in. Clara was annoyed at this, but she doubted Gladys or Peg would have wanted to go. They were homebodies.

Ivor and Clara were together still, but Clara knew she had hurt him. The postcard from her father also prickled at her. The thought of him coming back and interfering in her life made her nerves jangle.

Ex-resident Maureen was now living in a Victorian lodging house not ten minutes from her college. She was doing shorthand, typing, 'all of it', as she explained vaguely.

Maureen was fortunate that Sir Alfred Munnings – an elderly wealthy artist and Lavenham resident who had taken a shine to her – was paying her rent. She had also made friends with two women in her accommodation, both named Joan. Big Joan was deaf in one ear from being a baby in the war, but apparently you wouldn't know it. Little Joan's point of interest was she liked the fellas.

'She's wild for them, Miss Newton,' Maureen said cheerfully. 'It's embarrassing.'

On Sundays, Big Joan visited her mum in a two-up two-down in Islington, while Little Joan's parents came and took her out for spam sandwiches. Maureen telephoned Clara and asked if she could visit.

'There's never anything to do here on Sundays,' Maureen said cheerfully. 'So I may as well come to you.'

Clara was used to Maureen's double-edged compliments, and so she laughed. Of course Maureen could come. She could be good with the younger ones and now Clara hoped she would be a friend to Florrie. Clara had hoped Florrie would make friends with Anita's daughter and ex-resident Evelyn. They had gone for a picnic together, but Florrie had spent most of the time flapping and squealing about wasps and Evelyn, who was almost painfully sensible, had not been impressed.

Clara had gone up to meet Maureen at the station and although she'd have loved a reunion hug, like the family next to her who were embracing like baboons, Maureen was anti-most physical contact, so a stroke of her hair had to be enough.

Maureen's hair was almost as stiff as she was too since she had bleached it blonde. It was hard to get used to, but once she did, Clara liked it: Maureen was growing up.

'I'm like Snow White now!' she said, and Clara didn't have the heart to tell her that it was Snow White's skin, not her hair, that was white.

Maureen was big on sweeping statements, light on the specifics, thought Clara as they prepared lunch and chatted back at the home.

'Do the Joans not mind being called Big and Little?'

'They love it,' said Maureen unconvincingly.

Big Joan already had a job lined up in her father's book-keeping firm when she'd finished the course. Little Joan was hoping to meet and marry someone before the dreaded end-of-year exams. Maureen said that they had fake interview practice, but – she smirked – they hadn't done fake dating practice. Clara said it sounded like Little Joan didn't need any, which, gratifyingly, made Maureen laugh.

When Florrie finally agreed to come downstairs and say hello, the first thing Maureen said was, 'Oh, there's already a Florrie in my class, she's tiny, I'll have to call you Big Florrie.' And it went downhill from there. Maureen suggested baking a cake, Florrie screwed up her nose. Maureen suggested listening to the wireless, Florrie said she'd rather go up to her room. Maureen shrugged. 'Your loss.'

Clara and Maureen put apples in the oven with syrup and raisins and, as they waited for them to bake, Maureen said she was hoping to see Ivor and Patricia. Clara explained that they were in London again, and they weren't back until the following evening.

'Are you two still in love?'

Clara checked on the apples. They were softening up

nicely. 'I think so.' Next Sunday, she and Ivor had another date planned, just an afternoon – if nothing scuppered it. They might be able to talk some more then.

'What do you mean, *think so?*' Maureen screwed up her face.

'I hope so,' Clara said. If only she could be as certain about things as Maureen.

There was still no breakthrough about Gladys' brothers, so the next day Clara returned to the council office and knocked on Mr Sommersby's door. She wasn't going to let this go. As she entered, he was unpeeling brown wrapping paper from a sandwich with one hand and was immersed in some letters. The office smelled of egg.

'Miss Newton?' His voice was tired. She apologised for bothering him, but he said he was needing a break anyway. He put down his lunch, lit a cigarette and proceeded to smoke miserably. The ashtray was full of half-smoked cigarettes. Now she was here she wasn't sure how to proceed. Her impression hadn't been wrong when she spied him last – he was not the sprightly jovial fellow he used to be.

'New children coming along?'

'Uh, not too bad...'

'And you're getting along with our new childcare officer, Miss Tebb?' He gestured to the room opposite.

'Miss Webb? On the whole, yes.'

'I was very sad when Miss Cooper left.'

'Yes.' While she expected he was, she was surprised he mentioned it.

Mr Sommersby took several deep breaths, looked at her like he was trying to figure something out and then stubbed out his cigarette. 'How can I help?'

'We have a girl at the home, Gladys, who has been separated from her older brothers. It appears they are missing, and I don't understand where or why.'

'Missing children are not our responsibility.'

'Oh,' Clara said. 'Then whose...'

'You have to prioritise. You have to make judgements every single day, that's the reality.'

'I know but they're missing.'

'No one is missing,' he barked. Then he curled up the paper over the sandwich as though she had made him lose his appetite. The yellow and white squelched at her.

'Gladys believes they are... I just don't understand – what could have happened?'

Mr Sommersby slapped his hand on the desk so hard that the feathers on his pen quivered. 'If children have been separated – and I don't believe they have been – it will have been for their own good!'

Clara stared at him uneasily. He wasn't reacting at all as she'd expected; he seemed to think she was accusing him of something.

'For their own good,' he repeated, this time quietly. 'Do you understand me?'

'I do,' she said, 'but why would it be for their own good? Orphans especially need those close relationships.'

He seemed horrified that she would be so persistent.

'Don't bring it up again! There's just no point. Leave it. This is not your job!'

'It's all our jobs!' she insisted. 'We are in the service of the children – at least we should be.'

'Miss Newton, you're only a housemother – this is not your place.'

Know thy place, Clara thought furiously. This was another of her father's phrases. *Who did that serve?*

'You can't change the world,' he hissed. 'Stop this charade.'

It was like an admission of something, but she couldn't

think what. Guilt? Shame? Was she grasping at those emotions because they were often her own? Perhaps it was complacency or laziness or just callousness. She considered the papers he had been reading, lying across his desk. There was a letter of some kind – all capital letters – it looked like someone was trying their best to be neat.

Clara left the offices more resolved than ever. She would find the brothers, whether Mr Sommersby wanted her to or not.

7

Early the next morning, while the children were still eating breakfast, a motorbike revved its engine outside the home and made Peg jump and Gladys squeal in terror. Clara took them to the kitchen window but all they could see was birds flying away. It was a good thing Ivor was in London, for he would not like the return of Davey one bit. What had he come for this time? It was only a few weeks since he'd last been here. But then she thought, *perhaps he's brought Nellie,* and she hurried to the front door.

Davey was alone.

'Did you miss me?' he asked and she laughed. He wasn't being serious, was he? She let him hug and twirl her again and it was less clumsy than last time. And this time, he led her into the kitchen. He was like Michael in many ways: he filled a room.

Davey sat while Clara whipped around the breakfast things. Florrie left her buttered toast and Davey picked it up, winking at Clara.

'Don't mind if I do,' he said, crunching it with his big healthy teeth.

Peg wrote, 'What does he want?'

'That's rude, Peg.' The girl looked tearful and Clara regretted her sharpness instantly. She scribbled in her notepad so Davey wouldn't know. 'I'm not sure!' Then she winked at her.

'How's Nellie?' she asked him.

'Tell you in a bit,' he said, gesturing to the children.

Oh goodness, thought Clara, so there *is* something to tell?

Soon Florrie went upstairs and the younger girls outside to play. Clara waited for Davey to say something but he didn't, so, self-consciously, she asked.

'What were you going to say, Davey?'

'Ab-out?'

'About Nellie?'

'She wants to see you.'

Why didn't she come here then? 'Oh, okay. You've never heard of a telephone?' she said.

'I don't have your number,' he said, and Clara felt she had been as rude as Peg. She wrote down the telephone number on a piece of paper and said, 'If you need me in future.'

He said, 'I'll keep this for ever.'

She wasn't sure what was going on.

'Is next Friday night any good? Or Saturday night?'

'I can't do evenings.'

He laughed. 'They must give you some time off.'

'This isn't like most jobs...' Why didn't anyone understand this? This was a life choice. 'I have to be available to the children virtually all of the time.'

'Okay, let's make it lunch in London. Surely you can do that?'

'Maybe.'

He looked at her slyly. 'Michael used to say he'd do anything for you...'

His bringing up Michael made her uncomfortable. She knew what Michael would have said. Michael was a people person, he never said no to anyone. 'All right. I'd like to see Nellie.'

'I'll take you on the motorbike. You enjoyed it, didn't you?'

'Nooo. I mean, I did but I'll get the train, thanks.' If she went to London, she would make sure to see ex-resident Peter too. A lovely boy with a great talent for illustration, he now worked for a comic company and Clara always enjoyed visiting him. She had to mention Ivor though, it was pulsing at her. 'You will tell her I've got a boyfriend, won't you?' she said awkwardly.

Davey shifted in his chair. He kept his eyes lowered, a small smirk on his lips. 'Who is he then?'

'It's Ivor, you remember? The man who lives across the road.'

Davey looked puzzled at first, and then as though it had come back to him. 'But he has a baby, doesn't he? – that's a lot to take on.'

'I'm not "taking on" anything.' Clara bristled. That phrase was another something her father might have said. Reminders of him were everywhere.

'H-okay,' Davey said, his palms upright. 'You wanna bring him along too? Nellie would be pleased.'

Clara couldn't imagine a double date with Ivor, Davey and Nellie. It just wouldn't be his thing. 'No, I was just saying, so there's no confusion.' So now it looked like she thought she was irresistible! Good grief.

He seemed to expect to be invited for lunch, but this time Clara held strong and he left just before midday.

Clara had been calling Mrs Horton every day to no avail, but that afternoon, Mrs Horton strutted into the home holding aloft a piece of paper. Eureka! She had managed to dig out an address. Gladys' brothers might be living with a Johnson family in Ipswich, in a road not far from the theatre, the library and the waterside there. This was fantastic news and a great antidote to Clara's mood after that morning's encounter.

With great excitement, they got a map of the area out and leaned over it, like they were planning a military operation.

'Looks like a nice spot,' Mrs Horton said when they'd found it.

'It's all right for some,' responded Clara.

Gladys would be able to visit her brothers there. She deserved some fun; she was the most agreeable child Clara had ever known. In fact, if she had any criticism about the girl it was that she was *too* agreeable. She adored everyone and was enthusiastic about everything. How weird that Gladys' brothers had turned out to be close by in the end. Only twenty miles as the crow flies. They might have walked past each other in the street.

'We'll go there next Sunday,' Mrs Horton said.

'Can't we go today? Now?'

Clara still felt bruised from her encounter with Mr Sommersby. Why had he been so negative? she wondered. And it didn't seem like a specific negative, it was more a general weariness. He didn't want her to upturn the apple cart. Well, she would, if she had to, for the children. He must know that about her by now. 'No, Sunday is best.'

Next Sunday was Clara's long-awaited day off. Sister Grace was booked in, and she had been hoping for some 'alone' time with Ivor. Nevertheless, it was what it was. Ivor would just have to understand.

8

The next Sunday, Ivor took Patricia to the local market. Although he said he was disappointed not to be going on their planned date, Clara thought he was annoyingly perky as he waved her and Mrs Horton off.

Mrs Horton always drove like they were being chased, but for once Clara didn't much mind. She was keen to meet the boys and their foster family. And she was even keener to get back to tell Gladys the good news. She hadn't told Gladys anything yet, just in case something went wrong.

When they arrived at the waterfront, Clara's first impression was that it was nothing like Hunstanton; it was like someone had let all the air out of the place. And as they approached the house, Clara couldn't help feeling deflated too. This wasn't... it didn't feel *auspicious*.

Perhaps the fox poo on the path to Gladys' brothers' home couldn't be helped, but everything else was awful too. Flies buzzing fervently, an upright bedframe in the straggly yard, a filthy-looking mattress, and empty boxes scattered around. *Don't judge a book by its cover*, Clara reminded herself, but she knew Mrs Horton's tight expression probably mirrored her own.

They knocked at the door but, although no one came, and although it was quiet, there was clearly something going on in the house. You could just feel a fuzzy movement through the windows, the thin walls. There were people inside.

Finally, wearing long shorts, sandals and black socks, a man appeared at the door. His legs were brown, but his arms were pale and thin. He looked like his body was made up of several ill-fitting parts. On his head he had a knotted handkerchief that made him seem like one of Peter's cartoons of someone going to the seaside, only he wasn't cheery. He scowled at them; he looked like an angry potato.

Mrs Horton took the lead. 'Mr Johnson? Sorry to disturb you.'

'I was in the back,' he explained gruffly. 'What do you want?'

'We understand that you have two young brothers in your care here.'

'Might do. Who wants to know?'

'It's just a social call,' Clara trilled. 'A relative of theirs in Lavenham would like to meet up.'

He eyed her up and down. 'I'll pass it on.'

'We're from the council,' Mrs Horton added.

He folded his arms over his chest. 'You are supposed to give us warning.'

'How much warning do you need?' Clara responded brightly. It was taking all her effort not to storm into the house.

A boy, the spit of the man but with even more of a potato look about him, came out. He was a good foot taller than Clara, heavily set and sweating. He took up the entire doorway. 'Who is it, Dad?' he asked the man. Clara recognised the way he looked at him, searching for approval.

'Nothing, son, get back inside.'

But the big boy hovered. 'What do you want?' he addressed Clara. Then, 'What does she want, Dad?'

'I just explained to your father, we're here about two boys. Why don't we have a nice sit-down together?' Mrs Horton was saying. She had a voice for pacification. She rummaged into her handbag. 'I've brought fly biscuits.'

A child appeared at the top of the stairs behind him, and wobbled there.

'Back to bed,' the man snarled and the child retreated out of sight.

'Bed?' questioned Clara, a flush rising across her chest. 'It's two o'clock in the afternoon.'

'They're home-made, my favourite!' Mrs Horton was trying to keep things civil but Clara had had enough. She couldn't restrain herself any longer. Mrs Horton and her softly-softly approach just weren't enough. Clara raced past the pair of them and ran up the stairs two at a time. At the top were three shut doors. She opened one, and three, no four faces stared up at her. They weren't what she had expected. Their clothes and their skin were filthy – they had the look of the long-term unclean. They stared at her unblinkingly, disturbingly. The place was a state, a hovel.

She asked them, 'Are you all right?' and they ignored her. Before she could open the second door, the potato boy was behind her. Her hair was sticking to her head in the heat, and her anger was building. 'These conditions aren't appropriate,' she said, her arms outstretched in despair.

'It's fine...'

'What *is* going on?'

The father looked at the son from the bottom of the stairs, and the son looked down at him undecided, waiting for an answer. Clara thought she saw the father nod. The potato boy rushed at her.

It all happened so quickly. There was the fear of his proximity, the sweaty smell of him, and the way everything else receded, overwhelmed by his shirt, his size, him. Then, he punched her in the face. The shock was dazzling. She felt a sharp pain in her left cheek, but somehow kept her balance, she did not go down. His expression was almost as surprised as hers.

Mrs Horton ran out into the street and then to a neighbour's house, and soon the police came, two cars and three bicycles. But it was the father who dragged the boy away. 'What have you done?' he kept saying and Clara wasn't sure if he meant to her or the boy. 'You've spoiled *everything*.'

'I thought you wanted me to, Dad!'

There were children everywhere. No one looked like they welcomed her intervention. They looked like today was just another day in this place. 'What's your name?' she asked one child, but he just walked away.

She had been about to hug the littlest one when Mrs Horton put her hand on her shoulder. 'I wouldn't.' In a low voice, she explained, 'They'll need to be de-loused and de-nitted first.'

Gulping, Clara stepped back. 'Of course.'

The last time the children at the home had got nits, Clara had unwittingly taken them on her own head to Beryl's. Her hairdresser was not impressed at having to fumigate her brushes and combs: 'It's not decent.' Clara knew she wouldn't live it down if it happened a second time.

The police drove off with all but two boys, who were put in the back of Mrs Horton's car. Clara kept looking round at them. Their faces were petrified. The smaller one in a hat, clutching a small metal plane, was Frank. The older one with freckles and sticky-out ears was Trevor. Clara noticed for the first time that they weren't wearing shoes.

That man was a tyrant. No other word for it.

She thought of Ivor fighting against the Nazis. 'It was worth it anyway,' he had said, his voice reverberating with sincerity. 'To free our country of tyranny.' Michael had lost his life in that struggle. But the shame of it was that there were other tyrants – tyrants *within* the country, within their community. It was just efficacious to ignore them sometimes or to plaster over them, because in some way they were our own.

Those poor children.

'I had it under control,' said Mrs Horton in that way she had when she was telling Clara off. 'There was no need for you to rush upstairs like a... like a banshee.'

Do banshees rush upstairs?

'How was I to know?' said Clara. 'As far as I was aware, your only plan was to dish out some fly biscuits!' She imitated Mrs Horton's voice. 'Home-made...'

'It wasn't only that. And you shouldn't have told them anything about Gladys.'

'Oh well. It worked out in the end.'

'Except your face is purple, orange and red.'

And I have a banging headache, Clara thought regretfully.

Clara was going to keep Gladys' brothers, and the other three children would go to emergency carers. Two new children in the home at once was enough.

Miss Webb was waiting on the doorstep of the home, and for once Clara was grateful to see her. Mrs Horton went off with Sister Grace in the passenger seat, nearly driving into a horse and cart coming the other way. Clara imagined she could hear Sister Grace's Hallelujahs.

'I came as soon as I heard,' Miss Webb said self-importantly. 'You'll need to open files, get to the council, shop for clothes, get rid of the old clothes and—' she peered at Clara. 'Whatever happened to your face?'

'Nothing,' said Clara through gritted teeth, her gratitude at Miss Webb's presence quickly disappearing.

Gladys was still at Anita's for her lesson, so they had approximately half an hour to get the boys presentable before they met their sister. Clara filled up the bath but Frank shook his head and folded his arms across his chest. 'I won't get in,' he said. He wouldn't talk directly to Clara. 'She can't make me.'

'I will,' suggested Trevor, clearly the more amenable child. 'We can get in together.' He got in. 'He used to hold our heads down,' he explained apologetically. Clara couldn't meet Miss Webb's eyes. It made her shiver to picture it. *What kind of person did that?* And to children? And how had he got away with it for so long?

When Trevor got out, beaming, he tried again with his brother: 'Honestly, it's okay, Frank.'

'Take off your hat first,' Miss Webb ordered.

But Frank wouldn't and in the end, Miss Webb yanked it off. Frank cried and Clara couldn't bear to see it. Miss Webb folded her arms while Clara cropped Frank's hair short, trying to gently comfort him as she did so. He had tears running down his face. After that, he popped in and out of the bath and then the brothers put on Peter and Alex's old pyjamas and she showed them to their room.

'For us?' Frank bounced on a bed, pulling a face at Trevor, who pulled a face back.

'That's yours.' Clara pointed to each bed in turn. 'And that's yours.'

'One each?' Trevor's voice was shrill with shock.

'Yes,' she said gently. 'Although, if you prefer you are welcome to share at first.'

'He's not sharing with me,' Trevor said sternly. Now he lay on the bed like a starfish. 'My own bed, well, well, well,' he said, laughing. 'And will we get our own shoes here too?'

This time, even impassive Miss Webb had 'something in her eye'.

If Florrie had been unimpressed at sharing a home with two small girls, she looked even more put out now. 'More young-sters?' she said to Clara as though she herself were middle-aged.

'They won't interfere with you,' Clara claimed opti-mistically.

Florrie raised her thin eyebrows and shrugged. 'They had better not.'

'Rat-atat-atat-atat,' shrieked Frank, coming in flying his plane, and Florrie shook her head in despair, but then she peered at Clara, her face suddenly appalled.

'What *is* that?'

'Oh, it's nothing, just... bruising.' She had almost forgotten her injury.

'Have you got steak?'

'Florrie! I'm not hungry,' Clara snapped. *Good grief, dinner was the last thing she was thinking about.*

'It's for that,' said Florrie pointing to Clara's cheek. 'My dad always said.'

Miss Webb and Clara looked at each other.

'Actually, that's not a bad idea,' Miss Webb said.

When Gladys finally walked in, it made everything worthwhile. Peg hopped up and down (she could never contain herself) and Miss Webb leapt up while Gladys looked around her, mystified.

'Is something going on?'

Then the boys jumped up from behind the table like jack-in-the-boxes. Gladys squealed, covered her face with her hands, then ran to hug them both.

They squeezed each other and then Frank hid under the

table and Gladys and Trevor cried, but they were happy tears, Gladys explained, wiping her eyes.

'Is it really safe here?' Frank whispered.

'It's brilliant,' Gladys responded, her arms outstretched. 'You'll love it. Miss Newton is the kindest lady in the whole world.'

Pulling the meat off her cheek, Clara blushed. They didn't have steak, so she had been stuck with pork mince. 'It's lucky we've got the room,' she said.

Gladys was even more emotional than usual. 'It's what I always hoped for, Miss Newton,' she said, *happy* tears pouring down her cheeks.

'Everything happens for a reason,' said Miss Webb brightly, a phrase that never failed to make Clara scowl, but especially now given Miss Webb had been obstructive about it all.

There was more hugging and shrieking. Frank still wouldn't talk directly to Clara, but he chatted ten to the dozen with Gladys. Trevor said he'd never been anywhere so cosy in his entire life and he couldn't believe it was all for them. Now Clara wanted to weep too. She hoped the children could put their tortured pasts behind them.

They were too excited to sleep, and Clara said that since it was a special occasion, they could stay up until nine. She suggested they make a den in the parlour – something Peg and Gladys loved to do. The boys stared at her uncomprehendingly.

'It's fine,' yelled Gladys, 'Miss Newton lets us do whatever we want.'

'Not quite,' said Clara, more for Miss Webb's benefit than anyone else's, but Miss Webb just gave her loud laugh.

While the children were occupied, gathering blankets and then stretching them haphazardly over the furniture, Miss Webb and Clara had a cocoa together in the kitchen, and Miss Webb awkwardly patted Clara's arm. 'You did a good thing today.'

'Thank you,' Clara said, warming to her at last. She was glad her determination had paid off, yet she was still feeling peculiar. She wondered if it was the knock to her head. They had rescued Gladys' brothers and it was amazing – but why had it had to come to that? Why had Mr Sommersby or even Miss Webb not helped? It was as though the children's department was averse to any kind of change or any kind of real effort on behalf of the children at all. Which was crazy.

Perhaps not *any* kind of effort...

'I still think they could benefit from Sunday School.' Miss Webb gazed at Clara over her cup.

'I know you do,' retorted Clara, and for once Miss Webb didn't say anything else.

9

At breakfast the next morning, Gladys was on cloud nine and Peg was giggling at Trevor and Frank pulling funny faces. The atmosphere was pleasant – until Florrie huffed off upstairs.

'Not hungry,' she said. 'I'll eat at school.'

Trevor had slept well in a bed by himself, 'Thank you, Miss Newton.' But Frank was still not speaking to Clara. She tried to engage him on his favourite subject of planes, but he was proving stubborn. He did chat to the other children though. Plenty of children didn't like talking with grown-ups, she knew that. She hadn't been that keen on it either when she was young.

Clara had a long list of things to do, and the first was to take the children to Dr Cardew. He winced when he saw her bruised cheek.

Clara held up a hand. 'I'm not here for me.' She shoved the boys in front of him. 'This is Trevor and this is Frank, new residents at the home.'

'Welcome to Lavenham, boys,' Dr Cardew said warmly. He had a fabulous bedside manner, especially with children. He pointed his pencil at Clara. 'I will see to that later.'

Dr Cardew spent a long time examining the boys before he told them to go and spy on the fish in the waiting room. At that, their faces lit up: everyone likes to spy on a fish. His expression gave nothing away, so when he told Clara that he had a number of concerns she was taken by surprise.

'Anaemia, low iron – it might be due to the nits. Bruises. Trevor's had a break and it hasn't set right. All the signs of neglect are there. Frank's twitch – again, it might clear up by itself, hard to say. I can only imagine what they've been through.'

She walked out to where the boys were sitting cross-legged on the carpet, studying the tank. Trevor looked petrified.

'It's dead,' said Frank, the first words he ever said to her. He looked devastated.

'What?'

'The fish,' Trevor added, rising nervously. 'Is not right.'

'Ah dear,' said Clara. 'Shall we go?' She tried to steer Frank away or to cover his eyes; she wasn't sure what he might do. But now standing on tiptoe, Trevor tugged her sleeve.

'Look, it's floating.'

'It's just a silly fish,' Clara said, concerned that Frank wouldn't be able to deal with this. 'Nothing to worry about.'

Dr Cardew emerged from his surgery, letting the door swing behind him. He went pale as he strained to see into the tank.

'Good grief.' He delivered his verdict. 'A. I think you're right, boys. B. It's kicked the bucket. Well spotted.'

Frank looked up at him, his eyes shiny and devout.

That night, Clara lit a fire in the garden and – with the boys' permission – threw their stinky lice-ridden clothes on to it. The flames crackled and hissed. Clara threw the postcard from her father in the fire too. It had been bothering her, sitting in the box in the kitchen casting a dark shadow, and it was satisfying to get rid of it. Enough looking backwards. The boys were starting new lives afresh– it was an example to her too.

The children ran around shrieking, throwing dry leaves. Peg had her hand in hers, mesmerised, and even miserable Florrie looked fascinated by the flames.

'I like the way the colours change all the time,' she said, momentarily forgetting herself. Clara went to put her arm round her shoulder, but Florrie shrugged it off and went the other side of the fire.

Ivor brought Patricia over to watch the bonfire and sticks to toast some crumpets. He was good with the new boys, Clara thought proudly, before correcting herself – Ivor was good with everyone.

He had been given some pinstriped suits last year and said he could quickly whip up some shorts and blazers from them for the boys. And because he didn't want the girls to feel left out, he would make some bathing suits for them (after the wool ones the council had supplied last year had proved disastrous) if they liked.

Later, he stood close to Clara and she flushed, and not just from the fire. She wanted to kiss him and pull him to her, but they had agreed they didn't kiss in front of the children, nor even hold hands. He met her eyes though and, one time, he touched her jawline and said, 'Ow, Clara, that looks nasty.'

Clara wondered what she'd do without him. She thought, if he asks to marry me now, right now, I might say yes. Screw the consequences! But then Patricia started crying about something or other, and Ivor said he was off again the next day.

'Do you ever go to the same places... the places as when you were with Ruby?'

'Some of the same places,' he said shortly. 'It's strictly work, Clara. I go where the demand is.'

She told him Sister Grace was coming again in a couple of

weeks' time and she would finally have a free Sunday, so perhaps they could have some alone time? She raised her eyebrow to underline what she was getting at, and he nodded, and said solemnly, his dark eyes on hers, he'd see what he could do.

Miss Webb seemed to think that she needed to keep a close eye on Clara, but after three years of being a housemother, dealing with or fending off all sorts, Clara did not need or want to be micromanaged, especially by someone fresh out of training college, thank you very much. It was a good thing Miss Webb didn't drive; she visited far too often as it was.

Two days after the boys' arrival though, Miss Webb came back to the home clutching handbag and clipboard but this time also carrying a cardboard box. She didn't mention it, so Clara didn't either – not until the children came home from school.

'I bet you're wondering what's in the box?'

'No,' lied Clara. She didn't want to give Miss Webb the pleasure.

The children hadn't noticed it, but when they did they grew excited, even Florrie.

'Is it new shoes?' Florrie's were worn to the bone, and she had slender feet, so none of the second-hand shoes fit.

'Is it A. an aeroplane or B. an aircraft carrier?' wondered Frank.

'Things for school?' suggested Trevor, more reasonably.

'A television?' Florrie said. She was grumpy that they didn't have one.

'A gramophone?' shouted Gladys.

'A gas fire?' Florrie was enjoying listing the inadequacies of the home.

In a scribbled note, Peg wrote: 'Is it a puppy? For us!'

'It's better than a puppy,' Miss Webb said proudly.

Arms crossed; Clara tried to look enthused, but she was not feeling it. Whatever it was, it was unlikely to be better than a puppy. What was better than a puppy? A kitten? A trip to the seaside? All seemed unlikely.

They tried to open the box with their fingers but couldn't get through the tape. Trevor got a knife and slit it and pulled up the box's sides. Peg dove in and pulled out the contents...

'Bibles?' Florrie couldn't have sounded less pleased.

'Oh no,' said Gladys.

Peg looked like she'd been punched. She dropped the book onto the table and slumped back in her chair, arms crossed. The Bibles were leather-bound with embossed fronts. They looked expensive. (How many new pairs of shoes could they have got for this?)

'I suppose we can try,' Trevor said doubtfully.

Good grief, Clara thought. Miss Webb did go about things the wrong way.

'There's one for each of you. To keep. For ever.'

'Do we have to read them all the way through?' asked Gladys.

'Of course not,' said Clara.

'You don't have to,' Miss Webb said, 'but I expect you will want to.'

Clara blinked at her.

'Mr Sommersby has never —'

'Mr Sommersby agrees with me,' Miss Webb said, her back arched. 'Church or there'll be words.'

That evening, the books stayed in a tower on the kitchen table. Clara didn't know what to do with them. It annoyed her that even though she had rid herself of the postcard and was trying to look forward, her father still managed to wheedle his way into her thoughts, her life. He would have loved this, and that was part of the problem.

. . .

After the Festival of Britain, Anita had decided she wanted to do more conducting and performing, thus she had formed a choir, which rehearsed three times a week. And she was busy with that and her own children so it was especially kind of her to invite the boys to see about learning a musical instrument. Frank and Trevor sat uncharacteristically still in her beautiful living room with its expensive furniture. Even when Clara told them they were allowed to move, they didn't dare.

It was decided: Frank would learn the recorder. Clara groaned (this was not kind of Anita). But Frank said he would rather play the drums like Peg because 'A. We could practise together. And B. I have arms like Popeye.'

He rolled up his sleeves, revealing tangerine-size bumps.

Anita shrugged serenely. 'If that's what you think...'

And Trevor, who in Clara's mind was secretly 'the intelligent one', could learn piano. Anita suspected he would have a talent – 'He might be the new Rita,' she said, admiring Trevor's fingers.

But a few days later, Trevor asked if he could drop the piano lessons.

'I'd like you to learn something,' Clara explained. 'It's good for you.'

'Florrie doesn't,' Trevor pointed out reasonably.

'Yes, well, that's Florrie,' said Clara. *Oh dear.*

Still, it wasn't all bad news. It had been a responsibility to look after a musical prodigy and Clara was quietly relieved that she did not have another one. But Trevor said there *was* something he was interested in learning. At Anita's, on one of the low tables next to the sumptuous chaise longue, he had noticed a game with figures of knights, a king and queen and other pieces: 'Would I be allowed to play?'

Before long, Trevor was playing chess with Dr Cardew, who was enjoying having a new protégé. Sometimes Evelyn joined the games too, and they spent many a happy afternoon ruminating over opening strategies and checkmates.

The two boys were a lovely addition to the household, and Gladys – who was effusive enough at the best of times – said she would never forget how Miss Newton got her brothers out of their terrible situation and back with her at home. 'You're like an angel,' she said.

One time, Clara overheard Evelyn ask Trevor what he thought about the home so far and she felt quite emotional when she heard him say, 'No one is trying to hurt you here. Makes a change.'

DEAR MR SOMMERSBY

MANY THANKS FOR YOUR RESPONSE. I HAVE TO SAY THAT I WAS STARTLED AND NOT SURE HOW TO REPLY – BUT REPLY I MUST.

WHEN PHYLLIS'S MOTHER LEFT HER, IT WAS ONLY FOR A MATTER OF MONTHS. IT SEEMS INCONCEIVABLE THAT SHE HAS DISAPPEARED OFF THE FACE OF THIS EARTH. IT IS JUST NOT POSSIBLE. YOU MUST HAVE SOME IDEA WHERE PHYLLIS IS NOW. I BEG OF YOU.

MR BURNHAM

10

At the beginning of September, the children went back to school. Trevor joined Florrie at the high school, Frank went with the younger girls to the juniors and Clara began to get used to being home alone in the day again after the long holidays. Without children under her feet, she could get much more washing, cleaning and paperwork done. She could also get a few hours to herself.

Clara loved an excuse to go to London. She didn't miss her home city but she did find a dose of it every few months medicinal. The lights were brighter, the pigeons were fatter, the buildings went up faster there. In Suffolk, she couldn't walk for five yards without bumping into anyone she knew. In London, she could spend weeks buried in blessed anonymity. And it wasn't like you had to do anything in particular – it was enough to say to oneself, 'We're in London, we're here,' and it was like you had done something remarkable.

But she didn't feel excited about this trip because she knew Ivor wouldn't be pleased. (Which was also why she left it to the last minute to tell him.)

She was leaning casually against his work counter, yet she

was not feeling casual. He was snipping off a piece of material, and he looked up at her and grinned.

'Give Peter my love.'

'Will do.'

He looked up at her, still smiling. 'It's good you still see him.'

'I'm not only going to see Peter this time.' She paused, smoothing down a piece of fabric that was close to hand. 'I'm going to meet Davey and his wife, Nellie.'

She said the 'and his wife Nellie' clearly so he wouldn't be in any doubt.

Ivor looked puzzled but carried on scissoring. 'How many times have you met him now?'

Met seemed like the wrong word.

'Uh, once. Since the first time.'

'This will be three times?'

'I suppose.'

'Why are you going to London to see him?'

'To meet them. His wife, Nellie, we used to be...'

Well, they didn't used to be friends exactly.

'We used to know each other. And I was going to London anyway – I'll be back before teatime.'

His expression was stormy. She'd seen him like this only a couple of times before, once when she told him that Peter's uncle was hurting him and that other more recent time when she'd said 'I don't know' at Hunstanton.

'I don't get why you're seeing him so much.'

'Because he was a friend of Michael's.' She laughed nervously. 'For a moment, when he turned up, I thought it *was* Michael.'

Ivor blinked at her. And then he ripped his material apart as though he couldn't be bothered to cut it any more, the nub of his arm holding it so it was trapped under his body weight.

'So, you're meeting his wife this time?' He grabbed his scissors.

'I already said that.'

Her cheeks were flaming.

Snip. Snip. Snip.

'Have a good day then.'

'Oh, I will.'

She went into the house and everything she was cooking was burning. The mash stuck to the bottom of the pan and there was smoke coming from the oven.

It's a good thing we're not married, she thought. How dare he think he could tell her what to do? She turned everything off, then swept the floor self-righteously. She would see who she liked, thank you. Ivor would not make her feel like she had done something wrong. Who did he think he was?

Upon her arrival in London, Clara met Peter outside his place of work. He bounded out of the building like a proper young-man-about-town, his face bright and freckly, his short hair that adorable orange. Carrot-top, he called it; Clara called it the more flattering 'copper'.

He kissed her cheek and said, 'Is that one of Anita's dresses?' and she laughed because it was, and he knew her well.

He lit a cigarette and offered her one. Cigarettes were to Peter what Patricia's mallet was to Patricia or shells were to Peg.

He was wearing clothes she'd never seen before. 'Oh, this old stuff,' he said self-consciously. 'I got it at Camden Market.'

They walked to a public square, one of those curious green patches in the city, with a stuttering water fountain in the middle and benches with messages on them:

To Alan, who loved this place.

To Marion who, despite her severe hay fever, liked sitting here in spring.

Peter said he was starting work on his own cartoon.

'Another orphan?' she teased him, because Peter always said that the best cartoons were about orphans, foundlings or foster children.

'Of course.' He laughed. 'The good guys always are.'

Peter enthused about his work. He told her sales figures that made her eyes pop, but when it came to his sweetheart Mabel and his forthcoming National Service he clammed up. Clara didn't push him to open up. He'd tell her what was going on in his own sweet time – or maybe he'd never tell her; that was up to him. He asked her about her bruised cheek – she was surprised it still showed. There was no point upsetting him, so she told him it was from playing ball with the children.

'That's why I stick to smoking,' he said with a laugh. 'Far less dangerous.'

'Where are you off to now?' he asked as they got up from Marion's bench.

'Shopping,' she said. She didn't want to tell him about Davey and Nellie, she just wanted to get it over with. And when he asked about Ivor she said that he was excellent – which he probably was – what else could she say? *'We had another row?'*

Peter gave her a selection of comics to take back for the children, which was lovely, and then he kissed her on the cheek, which was even lovelier.

'Thanks for coming, Mum,' he said.

It made everything, every single thing, worthwhile.

Clara could still feel where Peter's kiss had landed when she went to meet Davey at Piccadilly Circus in a better mood. Leaning against Eros, Davey raised one eyebrow at her, then enveloped her in a big bear hug. He complained he had been waiting ages, but he did so with a broad grin on his face, and then said it was 'worth it, wow.'

She didn't know what she was supposed to say to that; she wasn't late.

She was already hoping no one from Lavenham had seen them. She could just imagine Ivor – *you were hugging him next to the God of Love and you don't think that's strange?*

Even in London, Davey stood out. He was better-looking than anyone else; hard to say how exactly, he just was. Was it his posture? He looked stronger, broader, his teeth were straighter. He had a kind of well-nourished glow about him.

They wandered around, taking in the huge adverts for Coca-Cola and Rolls-Royce, but after a while Davey took her elbow and steered her to a Lyons tea room.

'What time are we meeting Nellie?' she asked, annoyed that she wasn't here yet.

'Soon,' he said.

Then he said he had been to Cambridge to visit Michael's grave, and Clara was so shocked, she nearly dropped the menu.

'I'll take you there if you like,' he went on.

'I've already been,' she told him.

She had visited with Julian two years ago. She didn't like being at the grave – Michael was in her heart, not the earth. She knew visiting was a comfort to some, but it wasn't to her.

Clara tried to steer the conversation away from Michael. It wasn't only painful, it made her feel obligated to Davey somehow.

'What time is Nellie coming?'

Why was Nellie running so late? Clara was now looking forward to seeing her – it surprised her how much. Nellie had been in America for over six years. Clara had missed out on all that – on what might have been. She wanted to find out about Nellie's life, her routine, her everything. It could have been Clara's life. And, silly as it was, with Ivor's proposal still hanging over her like the sword of Damocles, she wondered what Nellie would advise. (Clara had no real grounds, no evidence, but she imagined Nellie would tell her to accept.)

'She'll be here soon.'

When she hadn't arrived after half an hour, he insisted they ordered. 'Typical Nellie,' he said, and she thought, *uh-oh.*

She chose an egg sandwich because the place wasn't cheap and she didn't want him to pay, but it reminded her of Mr Sommersby. It was strange to be out with Davey. All around them were courting couples: women fanning themselves, men staring back with red, shiny faces. She was glad of the third chair at their table, like a silent chaperone. She could just imagine what her father would say if he knew she was still *fraternising* – that was one of his sneery words – with the Yanks.

An hour passed, and he was still talking about the great friendship he had with Michael. He told her one convoluted story she already knew involving midnight alarms and swapped uniforms, and another she didn't know, and she said, 'You were a great team,' and he said, 'You can say that again.'

She tried to discreetly keep her eye on the clock behind the bar but one time, he caught her watching it and said, 'Am I boring you?' And she had to say, 'No, just wondering where Nellie is!'

That's when he said, 'I need to be honest with you, Cla.'

No one called her Cla.

'Go on...'

'Nellie came back to England – six weeks ago.'

Clara nodded. 'I know, you said.'

'I mean for good, she's come back to live here.'

Nellie had left America? It had been Nellie's dream to go there in the first place. America is the future, she used to say. Sometimes Clara used to wonder if Nellie loved the idea of America more than the reality of Davey.

'Wow. I mean... why? What happened?'

'The weather,' he said. He opened his cigarette box and rolled a cigarette. 'It was too much for her.'

Clara paused. *The weather was too much?* It sounded like a joke in search of a punchline.

'I followed her over,' he said quietly. 'I need to convince her to come back.'

11

Clara saw Ivor the next morning, carrying Patricia on his shoulders. She had wrapped her arms around his head, her feet were tapping a beat on his chest, 'Da-de, Da-de...'

As Ivor kissed Clara's cheek, Patricia swung her mallet around, missing Clara's ear by inches. Clara winced. Sometimes, she thought, Patricia did it deliberately.

'How did it go then? Your meeting with Davey and his wife?' Ivor asked. Although he had clearly forgotten Nellie's name, Clara wouldn't hold it against him. He smelled gorgeous as usual.

She cleared her throat. 'Actually, Nellie didn't turn up. They're having difficulties.'

If you can call one of them running away 'difficulties'.

Ivor looked at her. His expression said, 'You must be joking.'

Davey had nearly broken down in the tea room. His shoulders were shaking nineteen to the dozen; there was something startling about a uniformed man crying in public. He blew his nose on the cloth serviette. People were staring, and a worried-looking waitress scurried over with a scone and jam, said it was 'on the house'. Clara's heart broke for him. 'I'm here,' she promised, patting his big knee. 'Michael would have been here for you, and I am too.'

'Davey is having a terrible time of it,' she said now.

'I can imagine,' said Ivor lightly.

'I'm going to see if there's anything he can do. I need to help him... for Michael.'

Ivor's face!

'So he got you up in London under false pretences and now you're inviting him back?'

Clara laughed. 'It's not like that, Ivor. Your marriage doesn't break down every day, does it?'

That didn't mollify him. 'How are you planning to help him?'

'We reunited Gladys and her brothers, didn't we? Despite the odds! I bet Mrs Horton will be able to think of something. She should have been a detective.' Clara put on her Mrs Horton voice: 'That's elementary, my dear.'

Ivor didn't laugh. He pulled Patricia off his shoulders and placed her feet on the ground. Remarkable that he could do that with just the one arm.

'Run ahead,' he told Patricia in a firm voice. 'The door is open.'

And Patricia skipped away, her white socks gleaming and black shoes shining.

For some reason, Clara imagined Ivor was about to lean in and kiss her. But she was wrong. Once Patricia was in the workshop, Ivor turned and glowered at her.

'You're unbelievable,' he said.

'What...?'

'How do you think it feels?'

'I don't...'

'From my perspective?'

'It's not like that. He's a friend in need.'

'Friend?' he said. 'Wake up, Clara.'

Why did he have to be so possessive?

'I'm wide awake, thank you. I know what I'm doing. He and Michael were—'

'I can't believe your cheek.'

Clara stared at him. She had suspected he wouldn't be pleased but she couldn't believe he was losing his temper over it.

'You refuse to marry me—'

'Not *refuse*.'

'Refuse – then you go off galivanting around with a man who – in your words – looks the spit of the love of your life.'

'He... they were best friends, Ivor. Like brothers.'

The closest friendship she had ever had was with Judy. And it made her ache to think how that had ended. She'd let Judy down. And Michael and Davey had been the best of friends, and now Davey had no one, poor soul. What would Michael have done? She *knew* what Michael would have done. He'd have got involved, because that's what he always did. And she owed this to him.

'How do you think I feel? Everyone knows you turned me down.'

'You didn't have to tell anyone,' she retorted awkwardly.

He ignored that. 'And now everyone is saying you're swanning around with an American on a motorbike with your garters on show.'

This wasn't the time to tell him they were suspenders. 'Who on earth is saying that?'

Miss Webb was charging down the street towards them, with her handbag, files and officious expression.

'I have to go,' Clara said. 'We'll talk about this later, Ivor.'

'Nothing to talk about,' he snapped, shaking his head and then stalking back to his workshop, his feet kicking up dust.

Miss Webb had reached her. 'Am I interrupting?' she asked in her deliberately jolly tone.

'Not at all,' Clara responded smoothly, leading her into the home. She felt in turmoil. Ivor had never been demanding of her before. It was almost exactly what she'd feared: that once they got close, he'd try to tell her what to do. He'd order her about and she'd lose her autonomy. Well, she wouldn't submit, she wouldn't. As she put on the kettle, she kept picturing it: Ivor had been positively trembling with rage.

'Big news,' said Miss Webb. 'His name is Jonathon Pell.'

Clara told herself to concentrate. She had to keep work and her personal life separate. Even though it felt impossible.

'Whose name?'

'Your new boy. He's a PELL. PE double L.' Miss Webb said his name as though that should mean something to Clara. It didn't.

'Excellent,' said Clara. 'Double L. I see.'

As they drank tea, Clara tried to listen to Miss Webb's instructions, but it was hard to stop thinking about Ivor and that awful row. She felt misunderstood and she felt judged. By no means were these new emotions, but from Ivor? Yes, they were new from him. He was supposed to be the hearth where she could relax, the cushion into which she could sink. He had promised to be by her side. He told her once that instead of counting sheep to help himself sleep, he had taken to going over moments they shared together. So, he did feel the same – and yet now, he'd let her down.

She forced herself to take some interest in the files – Jonathon Pell. Double L. Once again, she had to admire Miss Webb's impeccable note-keeping. They were what she had always hoped for from the council. And as usual, the nervous excitement at the prospect of a new resident grew. Would the boy feel at home? Would he get on with the others? Would he get on with her? The revolving door of orphans sometimes made her head spin, but she always tried to keep in mind that she was providing a safe refuge for forgotten children. This was what she was here for, after all.

Miss Webb also seemed to have other things on her mind and finally, as she stood at the door to leave, they spilled out.

'I understand you still haven't been to the Sunday School yet.'

Clara felt as though all the fight had gone out of her.

'I will go this Sunday,' she promised, and Miss Webb was so overjoyed, she squeezed Clara's hands and couldn't thank her enough. So now Clara was committed to that too.

She wished she could go over to Ivor's and pretend nothing had happened. To watch him sewing for a while or to have him reassure her that all would work out with new boy Jonathon Pell, Sunday School, whatever it was. To hear him say that she could handle it. She decided she would wait though, wait until after she'd helped Davey once and for all. Ivor never was furious at her for long anyway. Whatever was eating him, he'd get over it. She picked up the file and then went to see what clothes and furniture she had in the boys' room.

Clara didn't have long to wait until she had to deal with Davey. The next morning, the children had gone to school and she had just made dinner (an uninspiring meatloaf) and swept the floor (and picked up one Tiger Moth, two seashells and a note), when she heard the motorbike roaring in the street and hurried to the door. *Please let Ivor not hear it.* Although how could he not hear it? Everything in a ten-mile radius must have heard it.

'Are you home alone?' Davey asked as he came in.

'I am,' she laughed. 'And it's not often I can say that...'

Davey sat across from her at the kitchen table, and there were no more tears. In fact, he seemed quite enlivened.

That's often the case, Clara told herself. These things were better out than in. Didn't she sometimes feel invigorated after a good cry?

'I guess I need to tell you the full story.' Davey said, picking at the grains in the wood like Frank did (although Frank got told off for it).

'Good idea...' Clara said, although she was also thinking what needed to be done: wash sheets, darn socks, check accounts. It was a perfect day for drying.

Davey explained that he wasn't a good husband.

Oh, and return library books.

'I drank a lot. My best friend had died.'

He meant Michael.

'I miss him,' she said and she forgot her chores. And as they smiled at each other, it was a moment of connection. They had been through the war and Michael's death together. And Ivor never wanted to talk about the past. He hated raking things up. But it was good to talk; you can't bury these things for ever. They have a way of contaminating the present.

'And my best friend died as well,' she added suddenly. 'After the war. You met her once... Judy, do you remember? I do understand how it feels.'

He nodded. 'I couldn't get a grip on it. Nellie begged me to sort myself out. And I tried and tried. Maybe I didn't try hard enough. I kept remembering that night, that night of the raid when Michael died, planes falling out of the sky to the side of me... Everything was pointless after that. Even her. Even our marriage. And then she left.'

'I'm sorry, Davey,' Clara said. They held each other's hands and then she let go to wipe her face.

Was this what would have become of her and Michael?

What if Michael – like Davey – had changed? What if the war came after them too? It was a wily monster; you'd think it had receded, faded into the background, but there it was, sinking its claws in. Drink. Women. Violence. The triumvirate of the traumatised ex-serviceman. Would Michael have been immune to such issues? The time they had together had been like the hottest part of summer – who knew how they would have coped with the winter storms?

She'd never know. The thought that she would ever have left him seemed surreal or impossible to her – but it could have happened. Stranger things happen. She thought they'd have lived happily ever after. Was it possible they might not have done?

Until recently she had had no such doubts about Ivor either. Whatever life threw at them, they'd manage. But she kept thinking about that place, that hellhole Frank and Trevor had been plucked from, and the worst thing was that it *wasn't* atypical, it was fairly normal. The thought of Peg, Gladys, even Florrie ending up in a home like that because she'd abandoned them, because she'd given up on them, didn't bear thinking about. She couldn't do right by everyone, but she could do right for some. Children's needs came first. Marriage would have to wait. Just a few years. It wasn't too much to ask.

She looked up to see Davey leaning right back in his chair. He was smiling at her but with tightly closed lips.

'Thank you for inviting me again.'

'My pleasure,' said Clara and it was, but she was also thinking, *I didn't invite you, you invited yourself.*

'You understand. You were as close as anyone could be. I feel I can be honest with you.'

'You can, absolutely.'

'You suffered.'

'We all did.'

He paused and then reached his hand out again.

'You sure look pretty today, Cla.'

She had that feeling again. She sat still, as if he were a wasp, and hoped he'd soon get fed up and buzz off. But he didn't get fed up; he must have been determined. And people said about wasps that 'they are more scared of you than you are of them', but she knew it wasn't true about wasps, and it wasn't true about Davey either.

Suddenly, she found herself hoping that Ivor *had* heard the motorbike.

'I saw a sign for a dance in town tonight. I'd like to take you.'

'Oh no...'

'Call it a thank you.'

'Honestly, I can't.'

What did he think she would do with the children? Just abandon them?

'What was that stuff you English gals used to put on your legs?'

He pursed his lips and did a whistle.

'Uh, gravy powder?'

'We couldn't wait to catch a glimpse of those pins.'

Clara swallowed. Everything seemed to have changed at a dizzying speed. One minute Davey was broken-hearted, now he was leering at her across the teapot. Now the light-hearted 'Are you home alone?' seemed to have a far more sinister connotation. Ivor, she begged silently, please rescue me.

'You used to love dancing...'

'I don't any more,' she lied.

'All work and no play make Clara a dull girl.'

'I don't...'

'I remember how your skirt used to whip up – you did it on purpose, didn't you, an eyeful for the boys?'

She got up.

'Everyone was crazy about you. Michael was one lucky guy.'

Clara screwed up her face. She did not want the conversation to go here.

He went for her hand but she pulled it away.

'He wouldn't want you living like a nun, Cla.'

'It's Clara and I'm not.' She had to close this down. It had gone on for much too long.

'Oh, but you are – why so uptight? There's nothing to be afraid of.'

She squirmed. 'I'm not, I'm happy.'

'If you were happy, you'd be engaged, no?'

She winced. That cut. *Is this what people thought? Isn't this what Ivor thought?*

Davey had his arm round her waist and his fingers were digging in. 'Michael wouldn't mind.'

'*I* mind. I don't feel like that.'

'Course you do...' He leaned across the table, caught her face in his big hands and kissed her, hard.

It was like she'd been stung. She pulled away. 'Nooo.'

He flopped back in his chair. He looked not mortified, shifty more than anything – she could discern in his expression the person he might have been if everything hadn't happened. She remembered that Michael had loved him. She remembered Nellie saying, 'he kisses like a kitchen sink'. She knew what she had to do.

'It's time for you to go,' she said. 'Don't ever contact me again.'

12

She had blown it. Fancy putting that... that awful man before Ivor. She had indulged Davey for weeks. Why? Was it because she was – as Ivor suspected – interested in him? Did she want a relationship with him? No. Clara searched deep in her conscience, and it was clear of anything like that. And yet it was murky with other things.

Did she just fall for his down-on-his-luck story? No, not quite. She knew about boundaries. No, it was more – it had something to do with Michael.

Old friends. She owed him.

But Ivor was the one she owed. Or did she? No, she didn't *owe* Ivor. She *wanted* to be with him, didn't she? So now she should behave as if she did.

Once Davey had left, she ran upstairs, nearly falling over Stella the damn cat, and she changed her blouse, brushed her hair and did her face. But it was too late. Ivor's workshop was closed and padlocked. He'd gone away again, but this time he hadn't said goodbye. She wrote a note, choosing her words carefully and posted it under the door.

Dearest Ivor,

You were right and I was wrong.

Please forgive me, my love.

Clara

That afternoon, Clara saw ex-childcare officer Miss Cooper in town and it was too late – they were too close for Clara to pretend she hadn't seen her (which is what she would have liked to have done). She had just popped out for some baking powder and was not looking how you'd want to look when you bang into someone you haven't seen for a whole six months.

Miss Cooper was smoking a cigarette and each time after she inhaled, she held the cigarette up high in the air. It was something Clara had never seen before, and it seemed a strange habit, for the ash was more inclined to fall on her. Miss Cooper spotted Clara and looked rather satisfied (although that was her normal expression).

'Darling, how are things at the home?'

Miss Cooper didn't used to say 'Darling'. Like the cigarette angle, it was a new affectation. This one suited her, though.

'Fine.' Clara sounded strained in comparison to Miss Cooper. She tried to perk herself up. 'Good, actually. The children seem to be thriving.'

She knew from past experience never to say the children ARE thriving because although she didn't count herself as superstitious, that seemed too much like an invitation to the gods to throw a spanner in the works.

'You do wonders for those lost souls, don't you? You always give them your all.'

Much as she liked a compliment, Clara didn't like the patronising phrase 'lost souls'. She felt offended on behalf of the children.

'What are you doing now, Miss Cooper?'

'That is the question...'

'It was *my* question,' Clara snipped.

'I'm working in Parliament. Westminster,' Miss Cooper explained. 'The seat of power.'

'Wow.'

'You'll agree it's more me,' Miss Cooper trilled. 'I've always been passionate about the way the world is run. You know, day to day isn't my style. I'm more interested in the bigger picture. But aren't we lucky to be doing what we're meant to be doing?' She pawed Clara's arm. 'Some people spend their whole lives searching for that.'

Clara supposed it was true but when she thought of Ivor's lovely face and his expression after she turned down his proposal and over their recent dispute, it made her feel torn.

As though reading her mind, Miss Cooper said, 'And how is your handsome neighbour?'

'All right.' Clara blushed. He couldn't have seen her note yet.

'I've got my eye on someone now,' Miss Cooper said suddenly. Clara tried not to look surprised. Miss Cooper had never confided in her much in the past. 'At work. Nothing has happened yet, but he is a dreamboat. Puts a spring in your step, doesn't it?'

'That's nice.' Clara couldn't think what else to say.

Only when Clara asked Miss Cooper if she had seen Mr Sommersby recently did Miss Cooper's demeanour betray the tiniest darkness. She said that he had not been pleased at her leaving but then she shrugged coquettishly: 'You've got to keep on moving or you go stale.'

When she said that, Clara thought suddenly of poor Florrie – the home was her sixth place in three years; the poor girl had never had the time to 'go stale' – and the boys, who had lost count of the number of foster carers they'd been shunted to.

'Did he imagine I'd stay at the council for ever?' she said, then abruptly kissed Clara's cheek goodbye.

When she got home, Clara realised that the flowers in the back garden – her roses – were flattened. This didn't help improve her filthy temper one bit. First Ivor, then Davey and now this. She was fond of those roses – her mother's favourite flower – and to see the children treat them with such disregard made her furious. It looked like they'd been trampled on.

She was muttering to herself – a real sign that she was cross. *Did no one care about anything? What was the matter with everyone?*

When the children came back from school, she marched them out to show them. Their faces fell at the sight too. They went silent, even Frank. Peg rubbed her eyes as if she couldn't believe it.

'Oh dear,' said Gladys first, in a babyish voice.

'Oh dear indeed,' snapped Clara self-righteously. 'Who did it then?'

None of the children played football in the garden like Billy and Barry used to, but one of them must have run through the patch repeatedly to cause such devastation. Fleetingly, the damage Clifford used to inflict on the home crossed her mind. Please don't let this be the start of a campaign like that, she thought, although she couldn't imagine it of any of the children.

They were all shaking their heads.

'Come on,' she said impatiently, 'I'm not angry.' (She *was* angry.) It felt like something was burning in her chest. Was she the only one keeping things together here? (Yes, probably.) 'I just want to know.'

Still they shrugged, and then Florrie just turned and walked off.

'Come back here,' Clara bellowed – she only rarely shouted at the children, so they all looked startled. Florrie shuffled back, her eyes downcast.

'I haven't finished yet,' Clara continued furiously. Yet she didn't like the rage running through her veins. It was straight out of her father's handbook – and she didn't like the way they were reacting to her. She had scared them. She wasn't like him, she wasn't. Clara switched her tone, and, although it sounded cloyingly sweet to her, it was an improvement. Hadn't she just ten minutes ago told Miss Cooper the children were thriving? Hadn't she hated the idea that they were poor souls?

'Florrie, are you saying you had nothing to do with this?'

Florrie nodded.

'Then you may go to your room,' Clara said, her voice still shaking a little. If she had Ivor by her side, she might have handled this better. (She would have him by her side again soon, wouldn't she?)

Frank and Trevor were still looking petrified. Trevor had his hand on Frank's shoulder and was murmuring, 'It's all right. She won't hurt us...'

Clara took in their frightened faces and was horrified at herself. She apologised. 'I was angry,' she said, 'but it's all right. I believe it wasn't any of you.'

Gladys piped up, 'The roses weren't my favourites anyway.'

'Okay, Gladys.'

'I love you.'

'Good. I love you too.'

Trevor offered to help tidy up and while they were doing it, he asked her if she believed it wasn't any of them, then who did she think had done it? Unprepared for the question, Clara said it was probably just an accident. Or an animal maybe.

Trevor seemed happier after that, but as Clara surveyed the roses and their stems lay in a mulched heap of mud, maybe it was her black mood but she couldn't help thinking it was most likely that someone had done it on purpose. And if it wasn't the children...

CHILDREN'S REPORT 14
Frank Gluck

Date of Birth:

14 February 1941

Family Background:

The middle sibling. He argues with his older brother (see Trevor Gluck) a lot, but when push comes to shove (which it does often), they get on. He is fond of his younger sister, Gladys.

Health/Appearance:

Very poor teeth. Watch for anaemia. Rickets. Pale and scruffy. Even when he puts on clean ironed clothes, he manages to be rumpled in minutes.

Food:

Frank enjoys his food and eats everything put in front of him with gusto. His table manners need some (a lot of) work. He can't use a knife and fork yet (lack of practice).

Hobbies/Interests:

Loves planes. Real planes, toy planes and pretending to be a pilot. Learning drums with Anita Cardew.

Other:

Frank is sensitive to shouting or trouble involving adults – although he likes shouting and causing trouble too! He is attached to his hat. And Dr Cardew.

13

There was nothing Clara could do about Ivor. It was a waiting game. She felt their fall-out would blow over – but what havoc had it wreaked, had *she* wreaked? She knew she had done wrong, but she had apologised. What more did he want?

Clara visited the schools to find out how the new children were getting on and to distract herself. At junior school she found out that Frank was obsessed not only with planes but also with dying fish: his teacher couldn't work out why.

'Perhaps he could write science fiction novels in future?' the teacher suggested hopefully. 'He has a great imagination.'

At the high school, the teacher talked about Trevor in glowing terms.

'Highly commended,' he said, 'and I don't say that lightly. He should be at the grammar school.' The teacher was an older, grey man with a moustache that he kept scratching. Trevor had told Clara his teacher kept rats as pets – it looked like he was keeping one on his upper lip. Clara was slightly wary of him, but his positivity towards Trevor won her over.

'While I'm here, I wonder if I might find out how Florrie is doing?'

'Florrie who?'

Clara was disappointed but not surprised. Sometimes, it was like Florrie was invisible, as though she *wanted* to be invisible. The teacher rubbed his moustache. If it was *that* itchy, why he didn't shave it off?

'Ah yes, Fliss Macdonald?'

'Fliss?'

Scratch, scratch.

'I thought that was her name?'

'No, it's definitely Florrie.'

It seemed Florrie had asked to be called Fliss at school and, surprisingly, the school had obliged. Clara remembered that Clifford had once insisted on being Cliff. It seemed to her that the children in the home sometimes liked to reinvent themselves: she couldn't blame them for that, she wished she could reinvent her and Ivor sometimes.

A few days later, a van pulled up outside the home and a smart young fella in a grey uniform and a cap jumped out. Clara watched as he walked up to the door holding a sheet of paper, and then answered before he knocked.

'Delivery for C.A. Newton.' He had a delightful Irish accent.

'I'm not expecting anything.'

Clara wasn't as friendly as usual. She'd had a couple of sleepless nights, not only worrying about darling Ivor and dreadful Davey but over the trampled flowers too. She kept playing events over in her mind. The children were innocent – she was almost certain. Which was good, but it meant someone from outside the home must have done it. And Davey had left in a temper, but really, was flower-trampling a Davey thing to do?

The boy thrust an invoice at her, full of columns and rows.

'Do you accept?'

'Do I... what?'

Oh God. Had Davey sent her something? she thought. As an apology perhaps? If he had, she knew that whatever it was, Ivor wouldn't like it. Unless, she pondered, Ivor had sent it as a gift to show that they were still together. Yes, perhaps... Her eyes scanned the paper until she found two words she did understand: 'Marilyn Adams'.

'Oh, of course.'

Marilyn Adams was Michael's mother and Clara's friend and landlady, and she could never resist a surprise present. It was typical of her to send something out of the blue. She was currently touring Canada – like Miss Cooper, she was a woman who could never stay still – but she telephoned fortnightly and demanded stories about all the children. 'Has Frank taken off his hat yet? Has Peg said anything? Is Maureen sticking with her studies?'

So sending presents wasn't out of character – but what had she sent this time?

Oh goodness. The boy pulled down a bicycle from the back of the truck while Clara hovered ineffectually. 'Oh... Yes, put it there.'

But there was more than one: there were three, four, five in total.

'But we can't ride,' Clara mumbled. 'And we have nowhere to put them.'

'Sure you can,' the boy said, smiling. 'It's easy.'

He asked where to leave them and Clara wanted to say, take them back, but the children were running out of the house now and were shrieking, 'For us?'

They each got a bike, and the delivery boy helped them up. Trevor toppled over straight away and nearly took the others down with him. Florrie hung back, but when the boy brought one over to her, saying brightly, 'They're great for staying in shape,' she hopped on.

'Hold up, there's one more,' he went on.

'Six?' This last one was sleek and shiny; the wheels were gleaming white, and the handlebars and the frame were racing green. It must have been the latest model.

'It's a mistake,' said Clara. 'There are too many. Or maybe that one's for you, Florrie.'

'But I've already got this one.' Florrie was holding on to a similar one, but maybe the wheels were smaller. For once, she was grinning fit to burst.

'Or Maureen, maybe?' continued Clara.

The boy looked at his paper. 'It's definitely for a Miss Clara Newton.' He grinned.

'You can take it back,' insisted Clara, feeling sick.

'Can't do that,' he said cheerily.

The children picked up cycling in minutes. Apart from Frank, whose wobbling was just painful to watch.

'If you took off your hat, you might see more,' Clara told him.

But Frank refused. 'A. I can see perfectly. B. My hat does not want to come off.'

He rode off – smack! Straight into the tree.

Cleaning his knees in the kitchen, Clara was glad to have got away from the growing circus outside. Frank insisted on going back on his bike again though. 'A. I want to be better than Trevor—'

'Fine, go,' Clara said, not waiting for B.

Marilyn was modest on the telephone that evening: 'The children deserve something nice.'

She was too generous. She was less good at the fundamentals – the damp – but said, 'It's those extras that make life worth living, isn't it?'

Clara was agreeing with her when she heard a series of thuds from the kitchen.

'Hold on, Marilyn,' she said, leaving the receiver dangling and running towards the noise. She couldn't see anything at first, but then she saw three or four fat tomatoes sliding wetly down the pane. She looked out the window and then out the front door to see who the culprits were, but she couldn't see anyone there.

'Children?' she shouted, and the boys answered from upstairs while the girls responded from the parlour.

She went back to the telephone.

'Everything all right?' Marilyn asked cheerfully. She was off to a theatrical production of *The Mousetrap*.

'Absolutely,' said Clara through gritted teeth. Someone had just thrown tomatoes at the window! She remembered how good she'd felt when Trevor said, *no one is trying to hurt you here*. She realised she needed to do something – but what?

'Give my love to the wonderful Ivor,' Marilyn said.

'I will.' Clara couldn't bring herself to tell Marilyn what had happened between them – she wasn't sure she could put it into words yet.

Outside, Clara picked up the busted tomatoes off the ground – a waste of good food – and set about scrubbing the windows. To be fair, they could have done with a good clean. She couldn't understand it. She grew more bewildered as the glass grew clearer. She missed Ivor with a dull constant ache – but today the pain was becoming quite acute. He would have marvelled with her about the bicycles, despaired with her about this. She didn't want to think that they weren't together but she had to be realistic: it was looking more and more that way.

Peg came out to have a look and then went straight back inside, which was good because Clara didn't want her to see how annoyed she was. She wished Ivor would come over, but the workshop doors remained shut. He didn't want to talk to her.

On the telephone to Marilyn, she had managed to pretend everything was fine. But now the mystery struck her again with force. *What on earth was going on?*

The idea that someone had done this to frighten her or the children was just too horrible.

The next Sunday morning, Clara did as she had for so long been promising and took the children to Sunday School. It was clear that trouble could be brought on her head if she didn't comply. Forthrightness is not just a question of personality but of position and even if forthrightness had been a personality trait of hers, she was not in a position to do anything. And she was tired of arguing; it was exhausting. Was it Churchill who said you had to pick your battles wisely? If it wasn't him, it was the *kind* of thing he said. And she had no date with Ivor this Sunday. Or any Sunday soon, it seemed.

Ivor's workshop was shut and lifeless and, every time she looked at it (often), it seemed to be saying, *I told you so.*

Clara had met the vicar once before and he had asked if the children might want to come along to the church, but at the time they couldn't have been less interested in worship. Alex was almost aggressively agnostic, Peter was distracted, Maureen was indifferent and Billy and Barry's religion was football. Now, the children were aggrieved about getting up early on 'the day of rest', but soon Florrie, Frank, Trevor, Gladys and Peg were all following her out of the house and down the road to the Church of St Peter and St Paul.

'You'll like the vicar,' she told them.

But they didn't find the vicar. Instead, the person who greeted them in the churchyard was a plump and small-footed woman whom Clara recognised from the Jane Taylor Society meetings in the library. Mrs Dorne often had a bag of vegetables from her allotment with her. Before she spoke, Clara remembered she had a whispery voice and you had to lean in as though everything she said was of great importance.

'Can the children attend the Sunday School today?' Clara asked.

'Certainly!' Mrs Dorne may have said (Clara couldn't quite catch it).

Well, that was simpler than Clara had expected. She kissed the younger ones and said to the older ones, 'You can walk yourselves back, yes?'

But the woman looked under her lashes at Clara. 'Sunday School is for the children of church attendees only.'

'Ah, no, I'm not...'

'No attendee, no childrenee.' Mrs Dorne had a peculiar sense of humour. She continued gaily, 'Either you take a pew or you take the children home, the decision is entirely yours.'

The decision was not entirely hers, thought Clara ruefully. And never had been.

The children were all ready for it now. They had their Bibles, notebooks and pencils. They all looked at each other.

'In you go then,' Mrs Dorne said softly, and in they went.

This could be a chance to make friends – the children from the home didn't make friends easily, Clara reflected as she made her way down the church aisle, and then she thought: *some* of the children from the home didn't make friends easily – others did brilliantly: ex-resident Alex had his best friend Bernard. Peg was well-liked among her peers and Gladys was friends with everyone. Still, she hoped Florrie, Trevor and Frank would perhaps make some new connections today, especially Florrie who, apart from her pleasure at owning a bicycle, grew more miserable by the day.

Clara took a pew at the back of the church, where she hoped she might be able to slip out easily. The last time she had been here was for Mrs Horton's wedding and she had enjoyed that, but attending Sunday service was a different beast and it brought back lots of feelings that she wanted buried.

She gave a timid wave to Miss Fisher. There was Trevor's teacher with the moustache, the postmistress, the fishmonger, Mr Dowsett and his wife. This mightn't be too bad, she told herself, but as soon as the priest started intoning at the lectern, her heart beat faster. Oh, she did not want to be here.

She could hear her father's authoritarian voice. You didn't question things said in that voice. She could hear the vicar's voice from when she was a child. She was back trembling next to her mother, and her anxiety was off the scale.

'Don't stand out.' 'Don't make a fool of yourself.'

And her hands were shaking even now. Around her, along the bench, people opened their Bibles, and the musty smell catapulted her backward.

She tried to focus on the perfect colours of the stained-glass windows and the beautiful images captured there. Not Ivor, who she missed so much. Not her father, who she didn't. Not tomatoes and trampled flowers. She would just let the words wash over her. How hard could it be? She didn't have to listen. She didn't have to remember. Two hours, one and a half – she could do this. Just today. There was no way the children would want to come back and at least she would have tried.

The children tumbled out of the side room and jumped down the steps. Clara was still sweaty and it would take a while before her heart stopped racing, but she had survived.

'Did you enjoy it?' she asked brightly.

Say no – give me back my Sundays.

Peg jumped up and down.

'It was wonderful,' Gladys said. If Gladys had a fault, decided Clara, it was not being discerning enough. 'I loved it,' she continued. She explained they'd done singing. Her favourite was: 'He's Got the Whole World in His Hands'. And 'Kum Ba Ya My Lord, Kum By Ya'.

Peg had a pageful of notes. She scribbled quickly. 'FUN! I want to go next week!'

What on earth had the softly spoken woman done with them in there? Hypnosis?

Surely, Clara thought, she could rely on Florrie to resist. Florrie, the girl whose glass was never more than a quarter full. Just as she turned to ask, a tall handsome boy with a fine moustache swaggered down the steps of the hall. He did an exaggerated jump to avoid the snail that was living dangerously on the bottom step.

'See you next week, Florrie,' he called out.

Florrie shrugged at Clara. 'I didn't mind it actually,' she said, a small smile playing on her lips – little traitor.

14

Dear Ivor,

It would be good to talk, find out where we stand.

Clara

Ivor would forgive her eventually, wouldn't he? worried Clara. They had fallen out before and recovered. She would have knocked at the workshop to speak to him in person, but he was never there. Note number two was a vastly less emotional one, yet there still was nothing in return. He was home late at night, but he was out early in the mornings. Anita said Patricia was often there with the Norwood Nanny and she didn't mention Ivor was out of sorts or anything, so Clara didn't mention their recent falling-out.

Clara had just read a *Good Housekeeping* guide on 'Keeping Your Husband Happy'. Tips included:

Sew his buttons on. Ivor would be aghast if she did his sewing.

Take the rubbish out. Ditto.

Give him a kiss. This she could do.

Talk less. This she could not do.

Pink underwear with frills. *For goodness' sake.*

It was too late for all that now. And anyway, Ivor wasn't her husband – which was partly – maybe mostly? – what this mess was all about.

While she was concerned with Ivor, Clara was also disconcerted to realise that someone might have been removing her newspapers from the letter box. It was only occasional, and it seemed such a measly complaint – hardly worth thinking about – yet, like trampled roses and the tomatoes, it gnawed at her. She kept returning to the idea that it was Davey. Hadn't he mentioned the roses? Hadn't he talked about her vegetable patch? And hadn't he left the home in a filthy temper with her? On the bonus side, if it was Davey, it would stop soon, because Davey wasn't going to stay in England for ever. That was another thing she would just have to wait out. Patience, as her father would have annoyingly said, is a virtue. But then would Davey have come all the way to Lavenham to do something so trivial? – (and surely she would have heard his motorbike if he did?). Which meant if not him, it had to be someone in the area. If she discounted the children in the home, then who did that leave?

The thought that Ivor would do this briefly – shamefully – crossed her mind and she hated herself for it. Ivor would never, ever be so petty, so sneaky, so vindictive – what kind of monster was she for thinking such a thing?

But she was *that* bewildered, and she was that hurt.

If Gladys was happy before her brothers came, now she was walking on sunshine. Not a day went by when Clara wasn't delighted she had reunited them. That's not to say it was plain sailing. When Gladys tried to kiss Trevor, he would yelp, 'Gerroff me,' and push her away, and when Gladys went to put her arms round Frank, he said, 'A. I'm busy and B. It's annoying.' But on the whole, the three had a special relationship.

Frank and Trevor no longer wept at loud noises, and, when Clara shouted, they didn't flee but stood their ground. They no longer had nits or looked anaemic. Frank still hated a bath, but Trevor would soak for hours, flapping about like a seal. Clara said he was a merman. Frank said that was impossible 'because A. There are only mermaids and B. Trevor is my brother.'

The children could do wheelies and some could cycle with no hands. (It took a while longer for Clara to stop screeching at them about it.) Frank became proficient at mending the bicycles. Necessity was the mother of invention – he'd had three punctures already.

Clara's bicycle leant against the shed like an albatross round her neck. It looked pretty, especially after she put a lucky spider plant in the basket, but everyone expected her to ride it and she wouldn't. She couldn't even give it away. Maureen said it would muck up her skirts. Mrs Horton was far too attached to racing her car. Anita laughed and said that if God had meant her to cycle, she'd have wheels instead of heels, and Clara couldn't bring herself to ask Miss Webb. And Ivor? Who knew what was on his mind.

The next Sunday, the children trotted off merrily to Sunday School once again and Clara had to sit through *another* church service. This sermon was about forgiveness, and she would have done anything not to be there – anything to have been with Ivor – could he not show some forgiveness? – or even to tackle the mountain of washing or get lunch ready instead.

She was determined to lift her mood on Monday, but in the morning, Anita cancelled their planned visit – she had to organise something with the choir – so Clara just got on with her chores and watched for the light to come on in the workshop opposite.

It didn't.

She planned a card game for after school, but when the children came home they told her they were hoping to cycle up to the playground.

'That's fine,' she said, thinking to herself, even better! But they had only been gone a moment when they came tearing back in. Three of the bicycles had gone. Only three were left: Clara's, Peg's and Gladys'.

Frank was howling. 'My bike!'

Clara hadn't seen him rage like this before and he let her put her arms round him for the first time. 'Now, calm down,' she said into his hat. 'Are you sure you didn't take them out, or maybe you forgot where you put them?'

This didn't seem likely. Frank collapsed on the floor, thumping the ground with his fist. Stella stood over him.

'Are they definitely not there?' Clara persisted as she followed them outside. 'I mean, one missing bike I could understand, but three?'

The children were terrible at not looking for things properly, but Clara did a thorough search and had to admit the three bicycles weren't there. They had vanished into thin air.

Clara gave the children two hours to go out looking for the bikes, and they checked the schools, the library, the churchyard and the playground. There was nothing, no sign of anything. When they got back, exhausted, Peg drew angry pictures of monsters and lightning streaks, Gladys went off to play the flute and the boys sat idly in the parlour, arguing in hissed voices. Florrie didn't really care – shrugging, she said she could always borrow one.

Clara wondered how she would be able to explain it to their benefactor, Marilyn. She resolved she'd call her tomorrow *after* she'd had a good look everywhere, and if they didn't turn up, she'd call the police. That evening though, after their misery was compounded with spam sandwiches, Farmer Buckle appeared at the door. Clara answered before he could knock. He was the palest man, yet now his cheeks were high pink. He had found the children's bicycles—

'Fantastic!' Clara cried out, but Farmer Bucket did not find it fantastic at all.

'How dare you use my land as a dumping ground?!'

They'd been left in his field. When he started shouting Frank fled, and wet himself halfway up the stairs, while Trevor visibly bristled, squared up, fists clenched ready for a fight.

Farmer Buckle noticed that, and a flicker of sympathy crossed his face. He was still fuming but he managed to tone it down.

'It's unacceptable, Miss Newton,' he hissed, trying to regain his composure. 'I'm sorry for the orphans but I will not have you trespass on my fields again.'

Last year, Clifford had set the farmer's shepherd's hut alight. And there had been some mischief before Clara arrived too so this wasn't a *complete* overreaction.

'I can assure you it wasn't us who put them there,' Clara said, as she put her arms round Frank. 'It's all right.'

'Who did, then?' He too was cooling down. 'Who would have done that?'

Surely not Davey?

'That's a good question. Won't you have some tea, Farmer Buckle, and one of Mrs Horton's excellent Bath buns?'

Farmer Buckle took off his hat and rubbed his face.

'Don't mind if I do, Miss Newton. It's been a long day and that was the last straw.'

Clara and the children walked back with him later. Clara tried not to feel guilty – it wasn't her fault – but she did. The bicycles had been thrown together into a metallic clump, a hill of scrap twined together. It was a dismaying picture. The children began to pull at them right away.

Frank's was twisted. Trevor's was undamaged, Florrie's had flat tyres, but the frames were mostly okay.

'Who could have done such a thing?' Gladys repeated over and over.

'I don't know,' Clara said, wondering the same, her heart sinking. The tomatoes. The flowers. Maybe her newspapers. And now this... this was even worse, directly targeting the children.

'Ivor will fix them for you,' said Farmer Buckle. He was in a much better mood now.

'I can do it myself.' Clara forced herself to smile. 'You know how busy Ivor is these days.'

'Oh, Ivor would give you the moon if he could,' Farmer Buckle said fondly. Clara doubted that were true anymore.

To take three bikes and then just dump them in a middle of a field? It didn't make sense. It had to be organised. It had to be deliberate. She wished she could talk it over with Ivor, but she doubted if he'd ever want to discuss things with her again, and the implications of that were really hitting home now. She felt lonely, yet there was no time for self-indulgence. She had to think who was doing this – and stop them.

Clara recalled the squalor of the house where Frank and Trevor had lived – and the aggression of the potato-faced boy. The children had lived under a regime of terror. Could it have been the Johnsons? It seemed unlikely – the young man was brutish and violent, but not organised or wily enough. She asked Mrs Horton about them on the telephone the following morning.

'How did they ever foster so many children anyway?'

'When the mother was living there, it was acceptable. But then she left, and they didn't tell anyone. They were scared the children would be taken away – they had five in total and they were making a tidy amount. It all went downhill from there. It was one of those regrettable things. They fell through the holes in the system.'

'Mm,' said Clara. Regrettable was forgetting your hat on holiday, not leaving children in the care of an ogre. But then, it wasn't Mrs Horton who was to blame. They were all playing in the same system. A system built around saving money and minimising effort.

Within a few days, Mrs Horton had investigated whether or not the father and son could have taken the bikes. (She did belong in an Agatha Christie novel.) She stood on the doorstep and wouldn't come in since she was on her way to Bury to get some cheese, they did a nice Wensleydale – *did her life revolve around cheese?* wondered Clara. *Is this what happened when you stopped working?*

'Who does Ivor think did it?' Mrs Horton asked.

'I have no idea,' Clara muttered. Just as she couldn't explain their latest dispute to Marilyn, she couldn't bear to explain it to Mrs Horton. Mrs Horton was such an Ivor-champion, there was no way she'd see Clara's side – to be fair, Clara didn't know what her side was exactly.

'Why's that?'

'Oh, he's in London,' Clara said – she couldn't resist a pointed *again* though.

'Anyway, the father and son moved!' Mrs Horton explained triumphantly. 'There are some farmworkers living in the house now.'

'Where've they gone?'

'Nowhere near here, according to a neighbour.'

'So it couldn't be them?'

Mrs Horton threw up her hands. 'Never say never but they

have *definitely* left the area. It would seem a strange idea to travel all that way into Lavenham – a five-hour round trip – just to move some bikes or to throw tomatoes at the window.'

Clara thought it was a strange idea to travel all the way to Bury for some cheese, but she didn't say that. She also didn't mention the trampled flowers – that might have been the work of a dog or a fox. And the missing newspapers might have been the result of a poorly paper-boy. The incidents might not even be connected at all, she told herself. In fact, they probably weren't, and she didn't want to seem overdramatic.

But the niggling feeling she had wouldn't go away.

15

It was a warm, sticky day in mid-September, almost a week since the bicycle incident, and Clara still had no resolution. Nor was she any closer to a reconciliation with Ivor. From up the high road, she could see the doors of his workshop were wide open, the way they were when there were visitors or if he was expecting someone. She started to walk faster, her shopping bags clacking against her calves. He had to listen to her, he had to. Davey meant nothing to her – how on earth could he think otherwise?

But as she grew nearer, she noticed a sleek black car parked outside the home, which made her pause. It wasn't Ruby, Patricia's mother, was it? The thought of Ruby's return always gave Clara a horrible feeling in the pit of her stomach. It was what she feared in the middle of the night.

No one was in the car, and no one was on her doorstep either. Her fears multiplied. It wasn't Ruby – but it was just as bad.

It was her father.

For all his disavowal of material things, her father was a sucker for a nice car. Like Frank and Trevor, planes, trains and automobiles fascinated him. Even when he was in Africa, he had paid 'an exorbitant' amount of money to get his Rover shipped over there.

This was the moment Clara had been dreading ever since that postcard had arrived. She had hoped she could ignore it, but deep down she had known her father wouldn't be able to resist picking at the scab.

Tremulously, she entered the workshop. Her father was sitting at the small round table at the back under the window. In the chair where she usually sat. Their special place. Next to the telescope, their gateway to the stars.

Clara didn't even know if she and Ivor were talking to each other now.

Ivor stood up first, his expression pained. He knew exactly how she felt – or didn't feel – about her father.

'Clara, I...'

Her father rose. He was wearing a dark jumper over a shirt and tie – in this heat! He looked like a politician or an over-grown schoolboy; the similarities between the two occurred to her for the first time.

'No one was home...' he began.

Ivor continued. 'So, I saw someone waiting—'

'And he suggested I wait here,' finished her father.

'Out of the sun.'

It wasn't just old married couples who finished each other's sentences, then. Sometimes, it could be strangers.

The kettle whistled on the stove. Patricia was sleeping in her pram, her mallet next to her. Ivor must have taken her out for her midday walk, then seen Clara's father as he returned. A homely scene. A fraud.

Clara was light-headed. To see these two men together, both important in her life for different reasons, was strange.

'Thank you,' she said to Ivor, and he made a strangled 'You're welcome' in reply.

'I was shopping,' she told her father. 'I'd better get back, the children will be home from school soon.'

Unbidden, her father picked up his hat and coat and followed her out. He thanked Ivor before he left. Out of the corner of her eye, she could see Ivor hesitate before he held out his hand.

'Funny chap,' her father said as they crossed the road to the home. Clara felt like she was walking towards disaster. She resented him so much. He had to come here, to this place she'd made her own. He had to spoil everything.

'I suppose he lost that arm in the war.'

'Yes.' Now he was spoiling Ivor just by talking about him.

'Must be hard – hard for the wife too.'

'Ivor isn't married,' she said shortly.

Her father made another face. 'How sad... That poor baby.'

Now her father assumed Patricia was motherless and Ivor was a widower. It was natural, she supposed. And Ivor hadn't tried to set him straight.

So, Ivor hadn't told her father they were together. Did this mean Ivor didn't think they *were* together any more?

She led him into the kitchen, and Stella the cat almost tripped him over as she shot past. He didn't look like the father in her dream; in fact, he looked the same as he always had.

'It didn't occur to you to telephone first?'

'I did,' he said. 'No one answered, and I once left a message with a girl who said she was just off to play piano at the Festival of Britain.'

That would have been Rita. Rita, who never passed on messages.

She wanted to know why he'd come, but he volunteered it before she could ask.

'Heard you on the wireless.'

'You did?'

Clara had feared that estranged family members would be

prompted to get in touch with the children after their performance at the Festival of Britain. This had been an issue in the past. People imagined that all the children at the home were orphans, but some were foundlings and some had been abandoned or even removed from their families. The last thing the council wanted was people who shouldn't be approaching them getting back in touch. Not once had it occurred to her that the estranged family members would be hers.

'Good performance,' said her father.

She was surprised at the compliment.

'You didn't show signs of musical interest when you were young.'

Not true, thought Clara. 'It wasn't me, we had a talented musical director,' she said.

'That explains it. I must say, I thought it was odd.'

'Odd?'

'That you would be doing anything like that.'

Did he mean to be so hateful? she wondered. They hadn't seen each other for three years and the thing he most wanted to do was to remind her that she wasn't good at music.

'What is it you want?'

'Unexpected, I mean. I didn't mean anything by it, dearie me.'

She stared at him.

'I've been living up at Flatford Mill,' he rambled, 'and I remembered you weren't far from here, so I thought I'd drive up – see how you are.'

'Well, now you know.'

He paused. This obviously wasn't the reception he had anticipated, but then what had he expected after all this time?

'Can I have a look around?'

'You've surely seen inside children's homes before.'

'I haven't seen inside *your* children's home before,' he said.

As he took himself off to explore, Clara's turmoil increased.

What should she be doing? And what would she tell the children? Was she supposed to pretend everything was hunky-dory between her and her father?

He was back in the room. 'It's not how I imagined it.'

'Right,' said Clara.

'You keep it nice,' he added.

'Thank you.' Clara tried not to be won over by the compliment – anyone can say sweet things – but nevertheless, she couldn't help feeling pleased. Recognition from her father went straight to the heart of her. 'It's beautiful, isn't it?' she found herself saying. 'I feel lucky. The poet Jane Taylor and her family lived here. Sometimes I imagine I can feel her walking about.'

'The poet?'

'Yes, she wrote "Twinkle, Twinkle, Little Star". The nursery rhyme?'

He looked surprised, said he didn't know that.

She thought about showing him her book of Jane Taylor's poems, but she didn't want to leave him alone again, for some reason. It had suddenly occurred to her that the strange things – the tomatoes, the flowers, the bicycles – had all happened since he'd been in touch, or at least since he'd been in Constable country. It was an outrageous and ridiculous thought – *her father throwing tomatoes!* – but once she had the thought, it was hard to get it out of her head. She knew he had the cruelty it required.

They went out into the garden and the clouds were in pleasing rolls, the air warm and smelling of honeysuckle. She showed him the trees, the hammock that no one swung on now Evelyn had left, the shed with Rita's piano in it. She was suddenly proud of all she had achieved with minimal funding and with even less experience, just her and her Lavenham community. They walked over to the small vegetable patch that Terry had started, that Joe had worked on, that Denny and Cliff had tended and now Gladys, Frank and Trevor sometimes enjoyed.

'We had some roses here. Mum liked them, didn't she?' she went on. He didn't respond but went on an anecdote about a wonderful stately home near where he lived, but when he looked up and saw her face he stopped, took a breath and said, 'I sold the London house.'

This wasn't where she'd expected the conversation to go. 'Yes, I saw.'

She remembered going back to London and watching the people now living in her old house through the window. They seemed like a happy family, and she had been shot through with a powerful longing. Oh, to be like that carefree child, cross-legged on the carpet, immersed in a puzzle. She never was that. Oh, to be given the chance to be that child. Even now, she'd take it.

'It did surprisingly well. The prices in London are exorbitant, and I was able to make a substantial donation to the Church. You know that's important to me.' He looked at her slyly. She knew what he was saying.

'Why are you telling me this?'

'I thought you should know.'

She knew he had no money for her, she had always known that, but she wondered why he wanted to spell out the fact. She knew it then; he would want to fashion it into a spear to poke her with. He was only satisfied when she was hurt. He had come to see her fail and if he did not see her fail, he would damn well make sure she felt like a failure anyway.

'I hope it goes to help poor children – like the ones here,' he said. 'I hope I did the right thing.'

He was waiting for a response. She knew anything she said would be perceived as mercenary. She knew that she had no grounds for anything from him – but it hurt. What had she expected? She thought of what Frank and Terry sometimes said to each other: 'What do you want, a medal?'

(Her father wanted a medal.)

Her father was still there, hanging aimlessly around, when the children poured in after school.

'The new boy is old, ain't he?' Frank observed, his nose curled up.

Clara's father laughed as he held out his hand to be shaken. The boys took it like a mouse Stella had brought in. They weren't good at formalities, although they were getting better.

Peg wrote something: 'I got 10/10 on spellings,' and then there was a drawing of a smiley face. She pursed her lips to Clara for a kiss and Clara kissed her, aware that her father was looking surprised.

He will not define me, Clara told herself. She remembered when the choirmaster at her church had said she had a lovely voice and her father said: 'We want to hear everyone's voices, not just yours.'

The *children* wanted to hear her voice.

But then Gladys clambered onto her father's knee and said, 'Miss Newton says I mustn't say I love you to everyone.'

'Very wise.'

'But you have a sad face like a St Bernard dog.'

Some time ago, Gladys had found one of Alex's old encyclopaedias in the parlour and had grown fond of it. Now, she showed Clara's father her favourite, a picture of a big dog in the Swiss Alps with a casket round its neck. Clara couldn't see the resemblance, but everybody laughed.

Gladys pulled at Clara's father's jowls. Clara couldn't believe it – was it her imagination or did her father have tears in his eyes?

'I like you,' Gladys said. 'Am I allowed to say *that*, Miss Newton?'

Clara muttered that she probably was. Clara's father clearly didn't know what to say to her. He was so awkward that Clara almost felt sorry for him.

'Can you ride a bicycle?' Trevor asked.

'I can,' her father said, clearly relieved to be on safer subject matter. And Clara's head jerked upwards again: *Why would her father take their bicycles and dump them in a field? It would be ludicrous!*

Frank squealed. 'She can't,' he yelped, pointing at Clara. 'She's useless.'

'That's because no one taught me,' Clara said in a low voice.

'That's something I regret,' said her father, looking away. 'I should have.'

She could see he was trying, but it was too little and too late.

Her father said he wouldn't stay for dinner, although at the same time he seemed reluctant to go. Finally, he seemed to understand that his visit was unwelcome. He was realising Clara didn't want him in her life. Or maybe it wasn't that she didn't want him, but more that she didn't know what to do with him. *How* to be with him.

She sent the children away, although she was more nervous with him when they were alone.

'What happened to that solicitor fellow you were involved with?'

'Mr White? I'm not involved with him any more.'

He paused. It was as if he wished to go somewhere with this conversation, but he didn't know where.

'I thought you'd be married by now.'

'Well, I'm not,' she snapped. 'Evidently.'

He nodded. 'They all do seem pleasant children.'

'They ARE pleasant children. People think children in homes aren't nice or have bad blood or something, but they have so much potential, each one of them.' She felt like crying again. 'All children do.'

He wanted to say something, *she* wanted to say something, but nothing came out.

'I'm not good with children,' he said. 'I didn't know how to do it. I always left it to your mother.'

She couldn't think how to reply to that. It was true. He was an Old Testament God of a father, all punishments, retributions and demands in a land of droughts and storms. Maybe that worked with some children, but it hadn't worked for her. And she couldn't forget it. It wasn't just what he did, it was how he made her feel, and not just now and again, it was how she felt most of the time. She always came up short, insufficient, under par.

'I got you something,' he said. 'I didn't know what to get.'

And whose fault is that? she thought crossly. She'd had enough of this day, this week. Had Ivor been by her side, maybe she would have coped with this, but with Ivor barely talking to her every tiny issue became a great big obstacle. (And her father wasn't a tiny issue in any case.)

'It's nothing much, I saw it at the bookshop. I just thought...'

He shoved a book across the table. It was *Baby and Child Care* by Dr Benjamin Spock. On the front cover there was a sleepy baby propped up on its tummy, looking and smiling at the reader, under a sheepskin blanket. It promised answers. It promised to make this look easy.

Something about it made her want to cry. She would have loved this book three years ago. She would have loved presents from her father fifteen years ago. It was all too late.

'It might be just as good as those magazines I know you young women enjoy.' He smiled.

Clara's chin shot up. She wasn't having that. 'Some of those magazines have a lot of good information. Why do people feel the need to mock?'

And he chuckled. 'I'm not saying they don't. I'm just saying this might be equally informative. You don't already have it, do you?'

'I don't have it, no.'

He looked pleased with himself and that sparked a fury within her too.

'I haven't got it because I don't need it. I'm managing on my own – as I have the last fifteen years without your help.'

Finally, she had got through to him. He scratched his chin and put the book back in his bag.

'Silly idea,' he said in a low voice. 'I didn't mean that you weren't managing – I just wanted to get you something that you're interested in.'

He spent ages putting on his blazer, getting up, looking around. She walked him to the front door, opened it for him, and he was still lagging behind. And then he stood with his small brown suitcase and his head lowered as if in prayer, and there was something pathetic about the scene. She imagined it as a painting entitled *Homecoming* or *The Long Goodbye* and it made her insides churn.

She didn't want him to stay, but somehow, in that moment, she didn't want him to go either. Not yet. She didn't know whether to try to stop him or not. She hadn't wanted him to reappear and yet now he was leaving, she felt all mixed up.

'I can see you've got a lot on here,' he said uncertainly. He stroked the paintwork. 'Nice colour.' He was blinking fast. 'Would you like me to come again?' he asked.

'It's up to you.'

'I don't want to impose.' He was looking at her hopefully. She remembered one of the letters her mother had sent from Africa. She had wanted to come home, she had finally admitted it, but she knew she wouldn't make the journey and she didn't want to die in transit. They'd left it too late. *He'd* left it too late. He'd denied Clara time with her mother at the end. And then he blamed her. Yes, he had – he had written that *she* had made her mother unhappy. He preached forgiveness – but who were the chief beneficiaries of that? The people who did the bad things, that was who.

'Then don't.'

'Well,' he said finally, 'May God be with you.'

'And you too.'

She closed the front door, then stood against it. She couldn't believe he'd gone.

And breathe.

Dear Mr Burnham,

I apologise for the brusqueness of my initial response. There is no easy way to say that a child is not with us – and perhaps I should have been more measured – however, the answer remains the same: we have no record of any child by that name.

Since the Children Act 1948, we have more looked-after children than before and we have had to take them from large institutions and put them in smaller homely ones – some have even gone to build new lives in Australia – all this despite considerable budgetary constraints.

I am confident that wherever Phyllis is, she will be flourishing.

Mr P.P. Sommersby – Head of Children's Services.

16

On Sunday, Clara once again dutifully attended church and the children once again came back from Sunday School reciting stories about angels and prophets. Peg was slightly off with Clara when she got home, but she didn't explain why, so Clara tried not to worry. On the way back, she had seen Ivor pushing the pram up the high road, the fallen leaves catching on the wheels. While he greeted the children cheerfully, he avoided meeting her eye. It had been ten days since their row, and four days since her father's visit.

That afternoon, they were all invited up to Anita's.

'How is Ivor?' Anita asked, after the children and Dr Cardew had been sent to collect conkers and it was just the two of them in front of the fire in the parlour. Clara hadn't told Anita about their falling-out *or* the proposal because Anita was just so busy nowadays. Actually, the real reason she hadn't told her was that Clara knew that her friend would despair at her prevaricating. Anita did not understand 'spinsters-by-choice' as she called them, and she certainly wouldn't understand Clara's reluctance to marry just now.

Instead, Clara chatted with Anita about Mrs Horton's Swiss

trip and Anita said there was no cheese with holes in, Mrs Horton must have been mistaken. (Anita could get angsty over the smallest details but Clara didn't want to fight over it.)

Dr Cardew and the children came back with handfuls of conkers, which they emptied onto the carpet. Anita only told them off three times.

Anita talked about her own children. She compared baby Howard to Patricia constantly: 'Patricia speaks over eighty words.'

'Ivor told you that?' It would, Clara thought, be most unlike Ivor to show off, although he *was* dopey about Patricia.

'No, when she was here with Nanny, I counted,' Anita said. 'She even manages to say "triangle" perfectly and that's not an easy word.'

Evelyn, who was quietly listening, rolled her eyes. But Anita noticed and started on her as well.

'The problem with Evelyn is that she underestimates herself,' she announced. She directed it at Clara, but she was saying it for Evelyn's benefit.

Putting the lid on the biscuit tin, Evelyn laughed. 'I don't.'

'Does it matter?' Clara said, meaning *shall we drop this for now?* but Anita was glowering.

'Of course it matters. If Evelyn is going to be a doctor, she needs to know her worth.'

Again, Evelyn rolled her eyes. Then she picked up her violin, placed it under her chin and said in a low voice, 'Or a nurse.'

She started playing a joyful sound, a jig. Clara, Peg and Gladys clapped along and even Florrie looked impressed, although she'd never admit it. The boys were still attempting to make holes in the conkers in the kitchen.

'Or a professional musician?' Clara suggested playfully.

'She's not good enough,' Anita explained. She didn't care that Evelyn could hear. 'She started too late.'

Dr Cardew buried his face in his newspaper.

It was Anita who brought up the bicycles – she said everyone in Lavenham was talking about their appearance in Farmer Buckle's field, and speculated about who could have done such a horrible thing to orphans. Clara asked her to keep her voice down and Anita hissed, 'Don't they know?'

'They do know,' Clara explained. Sometimes talking to her cleverest friend was like talking to a young child. 'But they don't know that it must have been deliberate.'

Anita screwed up her face. 'It wouldn't take Einstein to work it out.'

'Okay,' Clara agreed wearily.

Then Trevor came in, wanting to play Evelyn at chess, and even though Evelyn was a proficient player, she was soon down a queen and both bishops and Trevor's castles were dancing towards her king.

'You should admit defeat,' Trevor said.

'Never,' advised Clara. 'Keep on battling.'

'It's bad form when it's unwinnable,' Trevor said. 'Isn't it, Dr Cardew?'

Clara winced; she hadn't known that.

Dr Cardew grimaced too. 'Not exactly, it's just no point in flogging a dead horse.'

'Exactly.' Trevor could be insufferably competitive nowadays, but Evelyn was tolerant of everyone and she just laughed and conceded on her next go.

Clara wondered if she was flogging a dead horse with Ivor. Was she just keeping on trying and hoping when the relationship was unwinnable?

Then Dr Cardew, Evelyn and Trevor had an argument about which piece was the most powerful.

'It's the queen, of course. She can move *everywhere*,' Evelyn and Trevor insisted, for once on the same side. But Dr Cardew disagreed.

'It's the king, of course. If *he* dies, they all die.'

'He is the most powerful AND the most fragile. Why can't he be both at the same time?' Clara asked.

Dr Cardew laughed. 'Which is your favourite piece, Evelyn?' he asked.

Evelyn considered, and then picked up a pawn. 'This one.'

'Ah,' said Dr Cardew, smiling and patting his girl proudly on her head. 'Because any pawn might turn into a queen one day?'

Evelyn smiled, turning over the piece in her hand. 'No, because, they just get on with it.'

Now Clara laughed. It was such an Evelyn observation. And then she thought of Ivor again, just getting on with it without her, and her heart ached.

17

There had been a hold-up with new boy, Jonathon Pell. A military school were going to offer him full-time sponsorship and then at the last minute changed their mind. Miss Webb said she couldn't say why nevertheless he was a lovely boy.

The children wanted to string up bunting at the front of the house to welcome him. Clara was prepared to go up the ladder, but Trevor offered and said she might be more useful holding it steady for him – Trevor was good at tying and untying knots.

It wasn't only the children who loved a bit of fuss – Clara did too. And it was good to have a distraction from Ivor and the weird incidents at the orphanage. There hadn't been any further incidents for a week or two, but Clara still felt as though she was expecting them. Perhaps that was the worst thing about it – bad things changed your whole outlook, you couldn't help expecting the worst.

'There was *no* bunting up when we came,' pouted Frank.

'I didn't know you were coming, did I?' Clara retorted. 'You were just thrust on me out of the blue.'

She tickled his ribs; Frank was a delightfully squirmy thing and he loved a tickle.

One day, she resolved, she would get him to take his hat off.

'A. Is there going to be cake – for the new boy? B. Can I have some?'

'If you lot get off to school and leave me time to make it, yes and yes!'

Up the high road, she got some flowers from the Garrards' and some red apples from the greengrocer's. No one mentioned Ivor, which was good (but also made her sad because she usually loved talking about him).

She wanted to make the home welcoming. Clara had hopes for this lovely boy, Jonathon. She thought he might be a good influence on Florrie (Florrie needed a good influence), and Frank and Trevor would enjoy having someone to look up to. Role models were important. And by all accounts, Jonathon was an all-rounder, good at academic subjects, excellent at sport.

He'll fit in fine, Clara told herself. *He'll have to.*

And she'd managed without Ivor in the past – she'd manage without him again, if she had to. The idea broke her heart though. She couldn't believe it had come to that.

Jonathon Pell arrived one Thursday while the children were at school. He was a skinny, pleasant-faced lad with thin arms and knees that stuck out like brackets. He was lugging a sack of clothes, and Miss Webb was carrying a small box for him too. At first, Clara thought it was a music box like the one she had given Rita, but when Miss Webb opened it she saw it was chock-full of medals.

Jonathon blushed.

'Tell Miss Newton what you told me,' prompted Miss Webb, her face eager as a schoolgirl.

'I was living with my grandfather until he—'

'No, I mean about your father.'

'He was killed at Normandy. They gave me his medals.'

'One's a Victoria Cross,' said Miss Webb, all raised eyebrows and pointed lips.

The boy's misery was palpable. While waiting for the kettle, Clara picked up the Victoria Cross medal. She had seen plenty of medals in the films, and she had seen plenty in real life, but none this close before. Ivor's were hidden away somewhere, and he had no interest in showing her them – she had asked. This one was exceptional, that was immediately evident. A bronze straight-armed cross with raised edges.

She turned it over in her hand for a moment, lost in its beauty – the lion on the crown, the words *Pro Valore*, and, sitting on the top, that crimson ribbon.

'Tell her what else you told me,' insisted Miss Webb.

Jonathon cleared his throat. 'Uh...'

'Where you went,' Miss Webb prompted. 'In London.'

'Oh, we went to Buckingham Palace...'

'And he met the King!' Miss Webb could contain herself no longer. 'And his wife. And his daughter.'

'Princess Margaret?' asked Clara, who had always had a soft spot for the rebellious younger sister.

'Better than that! Princess Elizabeth.' Miss Webb's face said, this is really something and you should think so too.

'Princess Margaret was also there,' Jonathon added quietly.

'Can you imagine?' Miss Webb continued as if he hadn't spoken. 'There's nothing I'd like more in the world than to meet the princesses.'

Jonathon looked like he was ready to jump into the box and pull the ribbons round his neck.

After school, when Trevor and Frank came in, Miss Webb told them about the medals and they were clearly impressed. Peg and Gladys danced around while Florrie eyed him up and then skulked off.

'He's a special one,' said Miss Webb with great satisfaction, as though she had personally planted and grown him. 'A Victoria Cross in the family? You don't see that every day! Check it's in the notes, Clara.'

Clara leant across to the boy.

'You're welcome here,' she told him as his eyes filled and he looked away.

Sunday rolled around and there was still no word from Ivor. Face it, Clara told herself, her apologies, no, her *excuses* had been too late. Jonathon was quiet as a mouse but everyone seemed to like him. He was unlikely to be a good influence though – it was too easy to forget he was there.

Clara was just telling off Florrie – she was refusing to eat her pie and mash – when suddenly something flew through the window, strewing shards of glass everywhere.

What the hell?

Clara froze. Time seemed to stand still. The children froze at the table too, for two, maybe three seconds, and then they burst into life.

Frank was on the floor. 'It's a stone!'

Trevor was next to him. 'More like a rock.'

Clara swallowed, still in shock. 'Don't touch anything.' Then she found herself taking charge. 'Shoes on,' she insisted, carrying the girls out so they wouldn't get splinters. Florrie leapt away. Fortunately, Trevor was still wearing his boots. He got the dustpan and brush and began sweeping.

She took the rock from Frank in wonderment, as though it might contain a clue. Her heart was pounding. Who hated them this much? *That could have killed someone.*

Jonathon was trembling. Why wouldn't he be? He'd arrived just a few days ago and now this had happened. What a welcome.

Clara swept up as best she could and tried not to let her fear show. Who on earth had done this? There could be no benign explanation for this. The other 'pranks' were bad, but this was the worst yet.

She felt sick, her imagination running away with her. And then she thought about her father sitting here in the kitchen, and Davey too. It couldn't have been either of them, could it? She wondered if the children had acquired any enemies at school without her knowing – or maybe even without realising it themselves.

Only Florrie didn't seem perturbed – it was as though she always expected bad things to happen. 'In my last house,' she said, 'they put firecrackers through the letter box.'

'Really?' asked Clara nervously.

'We kept a bucket of water there, just in case. And we never went near the front door after dark. That was just *asking* for trouble.'

But Peg clutched her knees to her chin and chewed her fingernails. She wrote in a note, 'Can't I go to live with Mrs Fisher?'

'Why, darling?' Clara picked her up and put her on her lap. She was warm as anything.

'Becos scarrey.'

Not for the first time, Clara wondered how she was getting 10/10s for her spellings at school.

Minutes later, there was a knock at the front door. Trevor went to answer and yelled, 'It's the man from over the road.'

Clara had wanted Ivor to come to her, but not now and not like this. Not in the middle of some horrible drama when her face was a sticky mush. Her stockings were as baggy as bloodhounds, and she knew the apron did nothing for her. She whipped it off quickly and loosened her hair.

Ivor had followed Trevor into the kitchen. 'I heard a crash. What the hell happened?'

Gladys threw herself at him and Peg started weeping again.

'Did you see anything?' he asked over their heads.

'Nothing,' Clara said. She too would have liked to throw herself at him or make his shirt wet with tears. 'It was a shock.'

Trevor said, 'Whoever it was, I'll torture them until they confess. I'll skin them alive then throw them to the wolves.'

Frank laughed a demonic laugh in response.

'Make sure everyone is wearing shoes, Clara,' Ivor said.

'Already have,' Clara replied.

He examined the shattered window. 'You can ask Anita to get her man over.'

'I was just about to,' Clara said, and he nodded approvingly.

'I'll put a temporary fix on it for you until then.'

Ivor trotted back to his workshop to get his tools, and when he returned, Clara reminded herself not to swoon. Goodness, she was like a lovesick woman in a *Woman's Own* story sometimes. Ivor had come back! He made her weak, and not only at the knees.

He sawed the wood as she and Trevor watched; the others wandered away. Then Ivor let Trevor have a go with the saw – 'mind your fingers!' – and Trevor was beaming.

Ivor hammered the board over the window. 'That'll keep you safe for now at least.'

He must remember how good they were together... Their weekend in Hunstanton before everything went awry.

'What do you think it was?'

Bewitched by Ivor's loveliness, Clara had momentarily forgotten the dark reason that had brought him here. 'It's a mystery.'

Ivor got up and looked outside again. 'I guess something could have rolled off the shed roof maybe, and bounced into the window.' He smiled at her, and she remembered he didn't know anything about the other incidents. Perhaps not everyone in Lavenham was talking about them.

Peg sat on Ivor's knee as Clara made the tea. It was lovely to see Ivor here in the kitchen, back in the fold, and she could almost ignore the ignoble circumstances – but she knew the battle was far from won. He was being kind to her, but maybe that was all. There was a difference between neighbourly and boyfriendly and she was aware of which one he was being now.

'What's up, Peg?'

Peg had her notebook prepared, which meant it was something serious.

The first page was a drawing: a bonfire – someone on a bonfire. Clara examined it and then tried to meet Ivor's eyes. He didn't look at her and his face betrayed nothing as he said, 'Is that Miss Newton, Peg?'

Fierce nodding.

'This – this is the shed on fire, Peg?'

Peg shook her head vehemently.

'No? I don't know what it is.'

Peg turned the page.

In big letters she had written HELL.

'Hell? You think? Oh, Peg.'

For a moment Clara thought Ivor was going to laugh, but he didn't. Wiping his face, he looked sad. 'Why do you think that, Peg?' His voice was soft.

Peg scribbled furiously. 'Becos she doesn't like church.'

'I go to church actually,' interjected Clara irritably. 'Every week since you've been going to that Sunday School.'

But Peg was still writing: 'She dosnt believe it. She thinks it's lod of codwalop.'

'I never said that,' said Clara, her face as hot as the Clara in the picture. 'Did I?'

'She finks that,' Peg scribbled, underlining 'finks'. 'I know she does.'

Ivor still didn't look at her but gazed tenderly at Peg. 'Oh, Peg, there's no way Miss Newton would be going to hell.'

Fresh tears prickled at Clara's eyes.

'She puts you to bed and feeds you and listens to you and—' his voice cracked, 'loves you, doesn't she?'

Peg nodded slowly at first and then quickly, her mouth still downturned.

'Miss Newton is the best woman I know,' Ivor continued. 'That's a fact.'

Clara got up to go back to the kettle. She couldn't just sit there any more. Ivor continued, 'Isn't that right, Clara? It's not what you believe – it's what you do.'

Now Clara had a lump in her throat. 'That's right.'

Ivor leaned back in his chair. Peg was heavier than she used to be, but he didn't tip her off. She had turned to face him and was fiddling with his collar.

'If anyone is going to hell here, Peg, it would be me.'

Peg's eyes widened in horror. Realising his mistake, Ivor quickly backtracked. 'But I'm not going to hell either, Peg. You mustn't worry, promise?'

Peg nodded earnestly before galloping out gaily, her plaits swinging. A second later, Clara heard the shed door open and the clatter of the drums. (Despite repeated instructions, she never remembered to shut the shed door behind her.)

'Thank you,' she said.

'You'd do the same for me,' he said and shrugged, and she nodded. Was that the only reason he was helping?

'Do you want some tea?'

He checked his watch. She couldn't stop staring at his wrist-bone. The hairs on his arm. The shoulders she had held in bed in Norfolk. He can't have forgotten how lovely it was when they were together.

'Not now, thanks.'

So he *was* still angry?

'Patricia will be returning from the nanny any minute.'

'That's fine,' she said sorrowfully. Everything she touched turned to disaster. It might not be hell she was heading to, but it surely was a big fat mess.

But then he leaned so close to her that their skin nearly touched, and said, 'Can you pop by mine tomorrow morning? About nine?'

Wild horses couldn't keep her away.

18

Clara was not naturally a paranoid person. If the stone through the window had happened in isolation, as Ivor had assumed, she might also have thought it an accident. Or if it were intentional, it was directed at the wrong address. But it wasn't in isolation. The stolen bikes, the thrown tomatoes, the squashed flowers – they all added up to something more ominous.

Someone was targeting the home. Someone was doing their best to disturb them – and she had no idea who or why.

She sent the children to bed early that evening, hoping they wouldn't notice – but of course they did.

'But I'm thirsty,' said Gladys. It was her new delaying tactic.

'Just swallow your spit,' Clara advised. (Good grief, she was turning into her own mother.)

'There's a fly in here,' complained Florrie.

'Just ignore it.'

'It's not always like this here,' Clara said to Jonathon, who whispered, 'I don't mind,' which she thought was sweet, and then, somehow, awfully sad.

'You will tell me if anything is troubling you?' she said to him and he nodded meekly and then in a small voice said that he was fine.

She couldn't sleep. She was agitated about seeing Ivor as well now. Tomorrow couldn't come soon enough. And yet, 'Pop by'?! Pop by wasn't for long, was it? – pop by meant you were barely over the threshold. Or was it just a figure of speech?

There was so much she wanted to share with Ivor. He was like air – when he was there, you didn't notice how much you needed him.

When she finally fell asleep, she dreamed that she was in the car with her father and she knew something terrible was happening to the children and yet they were driving away. She kept shouting at him to turn the car round, turn back, but he wouldn't.

Just as soon as the children were dispatched to school the next morning, Clara trotted over to Ivor's workshop. Her make-up was done, but her hair was beyond salvaging, and she regretted not seeing Beryl more often. She was also wearing trousers, but she knew that Ivor didn't have anything against women wearing trousers. It was difficult not to keep putting her hands in the pockets though.

She tried not to be disappointed that Patricia was still there, sitting up at the table eating porridge. She had hoped it was a Norwood Nanny day. Patricia ignored her; the disappointment was probably mutual.

Ivor said, 'Patricia is helping me work today,' as he made coffee. 'Are you all right?' he asked. 'You looked upset yesterday about the window. More than I expected, I mean.'

She took a deep breath before admitting, 'It wasn't the first time.'

Finally, she told him about the other incidents. Ivor got visibly angry and she felt relieved that he still cared, that he was on her side. He said he felt terrible and he hadn't realised how bad things were.

'You know I'd do anything to protect the children,' he said.

'So would I,' she said, and their eyes locked. In that moment it was like old times, but then he turned away and she realised he hadn't said he would do anything to protect her.

'We also need to talk about us...' he said after a few moments.

Us, she thought. Now that was a better sign. She looked nervously at Patricia and then back to him.

'Yes,' she said gratefully. 'I want to talk... and listen too, of course.'

'The thing is, Clara, I'm not your backup man. I don't want to be your safety net.'

Although he had said they should talk, it all felt a bit sudden and surprising that he had launched in like this with no preamble. Patricia spooned her porridge slowly, her eyes almost as wide as her mouth.

'I don't see you like that,' she started, and then she thought: *Like air.* She *did* see him like that. He wasn't wrong.

'Is this about me not marrying you, because one day, I want to, it just... not now.'

'It's not just that. It's the way you expect me to be here for you for ever,' Ivor said.

'Oh.'

'I wish we could move forward. I feel like we keep getting pulled back into the past.'

Didn't that strike him as absurd when his past was sitting there scraping her bowl, oats round her mouth?

'Your past is with us all the time!' she retorted. And not just Patricia, she meant Ruby too.

'She's not my past – she's my now. Only one of us is *living* in the past.'

'And it's not me,' Clara said defiantly.

'Then why not marry me?'

'I will do, but I need...'

'What? What is it you need?'

'Time. A plan. Ideas. The children. This... what I do... It's a vocation, not a job. I need a way to do it, without giving up entirely.'

Ivor looked like he was thinking. 'I'm here to help you figure it out when you want.'

'You'll wait for me, then?'

This seemed like the opposite of what he had been suggesting.

'I don't want to,' he snapped, but then, shaking his head, he looked at her. 'But I can't seem to help myself when it comes to you.'

'Does that mean you still like me?'

Ivor stood over her. He put his arms round her. Patricia looked up and tapped her spoon against the table. 'All gone,' she said.

Clara inhaled him.

'How could you believe anything else?'

She kissed him and he kissed her back. She would have gone on kissing him for ever, only Patricia threw her spoon on the floor.

Later that afternoon, Ivor said he wanted to teach her how to cycle.

'You'll pick it up quickly once you know how,' he promised. He got on hers to demonstrate, and Clara was left holding Patricia's hand as Ivor circled away. Patricia cried, 'Da-dee,' so Ivor circled back; he was nifty.

'Your turn,' he said, holding out the bicycle to Clara.

'I can't balance.'

He laughed at her. 'If I can and I'm all lopsided, you can.'

Clara could sit nicely on the saddle, and she could put one foot on the pedal, and that was fine. It was when she tried to lift up the second foot that it all went wrong. Again and again, she tried. Again and again, she tipped and had to put her foot down. Ivor even offered to run next to her holding the handlebars upright, but nothing worked. It was upsetting. She wanted to cry but the children had come out to watch, and they were being encouraging (although Florrie was definitely laughing behind her hand). Clara swore under her breath. She thought, *I bet Ruby can ride a bike.*

'I can't. I'm rubbish.'

She hated giving up, especially in front of the children. What did that teach them about life?

Ivor put his arm round her. 'You're good at all the important things,' he whispered, one eyebrow raised suggestively, and she punched him lightly in the arm. They were together again and that was the important thing.

CHILDREN'S REPORT 15
Trevor Gluck

Date of Birth: 1 January 1940

Family Background:

The oldest of three siblings, Trevor has endured several homes where he was subject to terrible treatment and/or neglect. A responsible older brother, he looks after Frank and Gladys.

Health/Appearance:

A sunny personality, resilient and resourceful – he has grown four inches and put on three pounds since he arrived. Previous malnutrition. Growth spurt. Teeth are poor, may need attention.

Food:

Dislikes mince. Perhaps it reminds him of his old home.

Hobbies/Interests:

Has no interest in music although he has a sweet voice. He loves chess to the point of obsession. Cycles proficiently.

Other:

Trevor doesn't like to be reminded of the past. He is a forward-looking, talented boy.

19

As autumn went on, the temperature dropped suddenly. The ground was a golden carpet, and the sky was a fuzzy snowdrop grey. Kicking the leaves on the way to school, poor Frank regularly put his foot in dog's muck. He seemed to have a knack for it.

A. *Why does it always happen to me?*

B. *Have you got a tissue, Miss Newton?*

Clara remained on high alert for more incidents. She pulled the bunting down herself – they, he, whoever it was, hadn't taken advantage of that – and she expected to see some of the pumpkins they were growing kicked around the garden, but they weren't. She quizzed the children about their relationships at school, and listened, ever vigilant, for any enemies they made, probed every recrimination, but there was nothing of any significance. A boy in Florrie's class told her she should 'go back to the workhouse', and Frank was arguing with a child about the speed of aeroplanes, but there was nothing out of the ordinary.

A dead mouse in the kitchen was courtesy of Stella, definitely, and, when sheets went missing on the washing line, that turned out to be Frank and Trevor building dens again. Perhaps it had been Davey after all, Clara thought. Perhaps the stone through the window was the final straw or the last hurrah or something before he went back to America. Either way, it was nice to have this respite from being attacked. But sometimes, she felt they were being watched. It was probably nothing, tricks of the light, autumnal shadows, but shivers would come up on her arm and she couldn't say why.

In other news, Prime Minister Clement Attlee dissolved the government and called a general election. Another election! Clara bet Miss Cooper was having a time of it. She always thrived on a fight.

It was a two-horse race. Attlee versus Churchill. The Conservatives versus Labour. This was a fantastic learning opportunity for the children, a chance to partake in democracy – but unfortunately, they did not seem the most willing students.

Leaflets from the main parties turned up on the doormat almost every day and one afternoon, a car went by with wound-down windows and a man bellowing through a loudspeaker. Clara made a show of studying each of the leaflets, and listening to the bellowing man, but her mind was made up.

On the morning of election day, Clara took Peg and Gladys to the town hall to see the vote. In the street, there were men in oily raincoats jostling each other and handing out leaflets. 'Can we rely on your vote?' She was surrounded by red and blue rosettes and people with clipboards all trying to look more official than the next person. There was just one woman there, an older woman in a headscarf and in glasses with wings: 'Thank you for coming, dear, we appreciate your time.'

She came across Julian White outside, and the children petted Bandit, who was far more patient than Stella. Gladys told Bandit she loved him, and Peg patted his head. Bandit sat nicely, without a leash. He was a dog who could be trusted (unlike his owner).

'I was against women getting the vote.' Julian looked around to see who was listening and a couple of men grinned. 'Or the working classes,' he continued but then he winked at Clara, and she didn't know if he was joking or not. She never did.

They made their way to separate booths, Clara's heels announcing her arrival as they clacked loudly on the floor. 'I hope you do the right thing for the country, Clara,' Julian hissed, which Clara thought was decidedly off. She would always try to do the right thing for everyone, she didn't need Julian to remind her.

The children had been primed to stay quiet inside the booth. The pencil, which was already blunt, was attached to the string: voters couldn't be trusted not to steal. Clara scanned down the list for names or parties she recognised.

She was aware of Julian breathing loudly in the booth next to her. Now he was humming: 'Land of Hope and Glory'. The children giggled; Peg hopped and played pretend drums, and Gladys put her fingers in her mouth and stretched her smile. Clara shook her head. Julian was never serious. It was something she had liked about him – and then disliked. It was a privilege to never have to take anything seriously. She wondered briefly if perhaps Julian was a possible suspect – he had always been against the home being in Lavenham, after all. Children's homes brought down the value of a neighbourhood. But she had to admit anonymous threatening incidents weren't Julian's style. He was more a throw-money-at-a-problem person, not a stone- or tomato-thrower.

Gladys asked if she could tick the box and Clara told her it wasn't allowed, but she let her fold the paper and Peg posted it into the big black box. Both were overawed.

'Is that democracy?' asked Gladys as they left, blinking into the autumn sun.

Julian answered for her. 'It's not perfect but it's the best we've got.'

Clara was surprised he was saying something sensible for once. It was like children's homes, she supposed. The system wasn't perfect, but it was better than the alternative. It was good to do something. But then Julian put his arm round her waist and mumbled, 'I bet you haven't found anyone better than me either,' into her ear.

At dinner that night, Clara served up stew and as usual, Florrie pushed it away.

'I'm on a diet.'

'Just have a few spoonfuls then.'

'And it's burnt.'

Florrie was hardly – as Ivor would say – well-upholstered – she was such a slender thing, a strong wind would blow her down. Whatever Clara served up, charred or not, Florrie ate little. She swirled food around on her plate, and sometimes tried to offload it straight into Stella's bowl when no one was looking. At first Clara wondered if it was her cooking. Not many house-mothers struggled with something as rudimentary as beef stew or toad in the hole. But Florrie said her last home was even worse, so it wasn't that.

'You're not a baby!' Clara admonished when she caught her a third time. This was the sort of thing she'd expect Patricia or Howard to do, not this smart young woman. 'Be a big girl, eat up!'

Florrie was a worry. Her teacher said she behaved, but

Clara knew that behaving at school was something some of the troubled girls were good at.

There was something frustrating in the fact that after all the years of hardship during the war, here was a silly girl depriving herself of nourishment for no good reason. Even when Clara tried the old 'you can't leave the table until you've taken four more bites,' she wouldn't. Even when Clara negotiated it down to two, Florrie was stubborn. Eventually when it was bedtime and Florrie still hadn't capitulated, Clara had to give up. Still, at least she was eating at school, Clara thought, or hoped.

20

Dr Cardew and Anita had wanted to get a television for the Festival of Britain celebrations earlier in the year, but they were in such demand they couldn't get one until now. Florrie said that Evelyn had been showing off about it. That wasn't like Evelyn, who wasn't boastful, but when Clara asked further, it seemed all Evelyn had said was that it came with its own cabinet.

When Clara told the children they were going to watch television at the Cardews', and that Ivor and Patricia would be there too, they squealed with delight, but when they got there and found out it was 'election night special', they begged to go back home.

'Stella needs looking after,' proposed Trevor. He was skilful at working out what adults might want to hear.

'Stella never needs looking after!'

(Most likely Stella was on the prowl, ready to catch unsuspecting birds or hesitant mice.)

'It's almost as boring as your *Archers*,' said Frank. The Cardews were surprisingly big fans of the going-ons at Ambridge in the new drama on the wireless. Clara laughed with them about it but when she had the chance she liked to listen too. Something about hearing about the difficult lives on the farm cheered her up.

'Oh, let them go,' said Anita.

'They can't without me,' said Clara and Anita mumbled something like, 'Other children get left all the time.'

The truth was, even though there hadn't been an incident since the smashed window, Clara was unnerved. Who knew what was going on? It did feel like they were a castle under threat sometimes. And leaving the children there, defenceless, without a moat or a team of trained archers, didn't feel appropriate.

'You know things are complicated,' Clara said through gritted teeth. 'At the home...'

'I thought there hadn't been anything for ages,' Anita said. She could be insensitive sometimes.

'There hasn't,' hissed Clara. 'But still...'

'Anyway, who do we think will win? Shall we bet?' Ivor said loudly, trying to gee everybody up.

'Labour will win the popular vote,' pronounced Dr Cardew, who followed these things. 'But they won't get enough seats.' He proceeded to explain the electoral system in terms that Clara couldn't understand, let alone the children.

'That doesn't seem fair,' said Clara at the same time as Anita said briskly, 'It's seats that are important, not votes.'

Dr Cardew shrugged at Clara as if to say, 'what can you do with my wife?'

Jonathon was biting his fingernails, which he sometimes did until they bled, and Trevor was yawning as part of his campaign to be allowed to go back home, but Frank was following Dr Cardew around, doe-eyed.

'Why does he wear that grubby hat all the time?' Anita asked, which Clara thought was rich coming from her – Anita seemed to think baby Howard would succumb to hypothermia without a knitted bonnet.

And who was helping with the presenting of the election that evening? Clara's heart sank. It was none other than her nemesis – Donald Button. She had gone on a date with him last year. It had not been a success, and every time Clara heard the name Donald Button (star of radio, screen and stage) she felt nauseous.

Gladys squealed, 'I met Donald Button at the Royal Festival Hall,' but fortunately Florrie, Frank and Trevor ignored her. The only Donald they were interested in was Donald Duck.

Ivor had his arm round her.

'Your *friend*, Donald Button.'

'Ho,' she said, avoiding Anita's eye. 'Stop biting your nails, Jonathon.'

The Conservatives *did* win. Dr Cardew regretted not putting money on it at the bookmaker's – if he'd put down a guinea, he would have got £20 back. Winston Churchill and the Conservative Party were back in power.

All that work the Labour Party did, and it wasn't enough? Why had they lost? Some people said it was the boundary changes, which favoured the Conservatives, and that Labour hadn't resisted enough. Others said the Party had simply run out of steam. Was it the Iran problem? The newspapers discussed it, Clara discussed it, everyone discussed it. Was Attlee just too boring? Would he be more popular, as Frank suggested, if he wore a spotted bow tie like one of Frank's teachers?

How would Miss Cooper be feeling? Clara wondered. She liked being on the winning team – didn't everyone?

When Clara saw Anita again, in the street the following day, she tried to make a brave face of it, but she was feeling discouraged. She also knew that Anita was not of the same mind as her.

'I just fear that things for children in care will go backward.'

Anita screwed up her face.

'The Conservatives are not monsters, Clara. They have agreed to keep many of the Labour policies in place.'

'I'm not saying they're monsters, I just don't think they understand what life is like for normal people.'

Anita yawned.

The next day, Clara called in on Ivor, who was hard at work with a stapler. Ivor said Churchill was like a father figure to the nation. People will forgive anything if they feel like someone – anyone – is in charge. Clara liked Churchill: who didn't? Was there ever a better leader to get them through a war? But they weren't at war now, and why look backward when you could look forward?

Ivor was disappointed with the result too, but he had expected it, which was worse. She was glad they were on the same side. Another thing – *oh, there were many things!* – they had in common.

'Labour won the popular vote, just not enough seats – we mustn't lose heart.'

'It feels like 1940 again,' said Clara.

'Except this time, we've got each other,' he said lightly. There was something about the way he said it that gave her pause.

'Of course we have,' she said.

There it was, the elephant in the room again: the marriage proposal. The room was large enough to take an elephant right now, but it wouldn't always be that way – and then what?

'I thought we'd go to the cinema on Sunday.' He raised an

eyebrow at her. 'And then back to mine. The Norwood Nanny is booked.'

'Ah, about this Sunday...' Clara began tentatively. 'I've got church and then Maureen coming, and Peter is calling to talk about his National Service paperwork...'

'Never mind,' he said. 'Another time.'

One day, he would get fed up with her.

When she said that to him, though, he looked puzzled.

'Why?'

She watched him. 'Because...' She suddenly felt tearful. He needed more, she knew that. 'I'm running round looking after everyone – everyone except for you.'

He got up from the square of fabric he was working on and strode over to her.

'Hey, I don't need you running round looking after me. I'm a grown man. You're doing a good thing, Clara.'

'But I want to spend time with you too.'

'I know. And we will,' he said. 'How about the Saturday after then?'

'Um, Miss Webb is bringing some prospective parents. I'm sorry.'

He kissed her again. 'Clara, I'm not going anywhere.'

'Even though I'm useless?'

Patricia was awake: 'Daddeee, Daddeee.'

'We're *both* useless.' He grinned. 'Now get back to work.'

She left the workshop and its rolls of material and coffee smell. She was lucky that Ivor was in her life. Clara knew she had to think about the proposal – she knew 'in the future' wasn't answer enough. It wouldn't keep him interested for ever. The popular vote, or her affection was nothing – it was actual marriage that counted. He had given her another chance. She couldn't let him down again.

21

As autumn gave way to winter, the children were arguing over conker matches and collecting pennies for the guy. They were regular attenders of Sunday School and had got certificates and gold stars. Clara got nothing for her regular attendance at church other than a headache and mountains of washing, but there you go.

Farmer Buckle cancelled the Guy Fawkes Night bonfire because it had rained for days, and Peter telephoned and said the fog was so bad in London that some of the staff had slept in the office rather than brave the streets home. The clothes Clara hung out to dry took ages, and sometimes even came in wetter than when she put them out. Jonathon got an infection in his finger and had to see Dr Cardew every day for a week, and yet still Clara caught him nibbling.

The chances of finding a home for three young siblings were small, nigh-on impossible, so when the impossible happened, Miss Webb was in an excellent mood. She said she had been praying and God always delivered. It certainly felt like a miracle. Clara imagined the prospective parents coming down from a cloud in a flash of light.

'They are regular churchgoers,' Miss Webb had said proudly, rifling through the file. 'Devout people. They want to take the children from February.'

'Why so long?'

'Holidays and then they're getting their house ready. It's a show home.'

Clara didn't like the sound of a show home but she knew she had to reserve judgement. People prepared to take three children? They must be saints.

Miss Webb was so excited to meet the churchgoing Mounts that she insisted she would be there at the introduction. She arrived at the home one hour early and as Clara whipped around trying to make the place look presentable (it was not a show home), Miss Webb talked about how exceptional Jonathon was and how determined she was to find the right family for him too.

'What about Florrie?' Clara asked.

'There'll be someone out there for her,' Miss Webb said, but she didn't sound convinced.

'And Peg?'

Miss Webb said nothing. She seemed selectively deaf when it came to poor Peg's prospects.

Mr and Mrs Mount arrived on the dot of two – so Clara couldn't complain about lack of punctuality. Mrs Mount was angular-shaped and fashionably dressed in a big coat, a hat with a veil and long black gloves that went up to her elbows. She looked like one of the drawings in Ivor's pattern books. Square-jawed Mr Mount was charming, handsome in a good-quality lined mackintosh and suit, but friendly too. Mrs Mount was the effusive one. Clara suspected she was the one driving the adoption perhaps, but he got involved too; he wasn't stand-offish like many of the prospective fathers. Clara hadn't expected to warm to them, but despite herself she was instantly smitten.

After she hung up their coats, Mrs Mount grabbed Clara's hand. Her fingers were long and her nails polished. She was like an aristocratic version of Anita.

'I saw them on *The Great British Songbook*. I cried and wished we could take them all, didn't I, Monty?'

Mr Mount had asked if he might light a cigarette and then said emphatically, 'We did.'

'That boy – what an extraordinary talent.'

'Denny?' Everyone had loved wide-eyed, cherubic Denny.

Mrs Mount shook her head.

'He was wonderful, but I meant the older one – the one who looked like Frank Sinatra.'

'Clifford?' Clara coughed.

'I made enquiries about him, but then I saw that he'd already left – and when we saw there was a family of three, two brothers and a sister available, I said to Monty, why not?'

'In for a penny, in for a pound,' Mr Mount said.

'A ready-made family,' Mrs Mount said with satisfaction.

Shortly after, the children came back from school. A shadow fell over Florrie and Peg's faces when Clara explained who the Mounts were here to see. To watch their friends picked out, plucked away, sometimes to beautiful families, must have been painful. It took an emotional toll; neither Peg nor Florrie got any interest from prospective adopters. Clara noticed the grim set of Peg's jaw and Florrie's faux nonchalance and reminded herself to spend extra time with them both later.

Gladys was sold on the Mounts. She played jacks with Mrs Mount and then when Mrs Mount went into the garden to play ball with Frank, Gladys said, 'Aren't they adorable!'

Clara went outside to watch. They were all laughing a lot. Then Mrs Mount came over to her.

'What's the hat for?' She gestured towards Frank.

'He never takes it off,' Clara explained apologetically. *Let this not be the thing that changes their minds.*

But the Mounts were nothing if not determined.

'I never take my wedding ring off.' Mrs Mount stared lovingly at her husband, who blushed. 'Some things stay on for life.'

'I hope Frank's hat isn't for life. It needs a good wash,' Clara said drily. But for once, she thought Gladys had a point: they *were* adorable.

When Mr Mount heard that Trevor played chess, it was a match made in heaven. The two of them marched into the parlour and commenced a grim game, with both of them determined not to concede defeat.

Eventually they came back into the kitchen. It was fairly even, Trevor admitted. He wasn't used to that, but he had won, just.

'Smart player,' said Mr Mount through gritted teeth.

'We have a garden,' said Mrs Mount. 'And two horses. Chickens, and two large ponds. We keep fish.'

'My hobby,' Mr Mount said apologetically. 'Keeps me busy.'

'I love fish,' said Gladys, and then Frank went on a lengthy explanation about the premature death of Barry 2, which he had witnessed on 'my first day in Lavenham'.

'That must have been upsetting,' Mrs Mount said. She had a soothing, sympathetic tone. Like honey.

'No,' said Frank, wiping his nose on his sleeve. 'A. I never knew him when he was alive, see. And B. As Miss Newton said, he was only a silly fish.'

Clara cleared her throat. 'And what do you do?' she asked Mr Mount, who was smiling at Frank as though he was a cherub and not a ghoulish nine-year-old wearing a smelly old hat.

'Oh, me? I work in government.' He seemed surprised that she was interested.

'Oh?' She wanted to ask what he thought about the results. She wanted to hear that he was upset about the latest general election, but it was best not to mention it just in case he wasn't.

While Gladys played the flute, Mr Mount put his arm round his wife and rested his head on her shoulder. They seemed physically easy together, and Clara realised that she and Ivor were still not. Perhaps these things took time and practice. When Grace finished, bashfully, they clapped, and Mrs Mount knelt at little Gladys' side and said, 'You are wonderful.' Then she looked over at Clara and said, 'We'd make sure she can continue her musical education. There's no question.'

'Thank you,' said Clara. She knew Anita would be happy to hear that too.

'I didn't expect them to be so loveable,' Mrs Mount whispered, her head tilted. 'I only wish we could take them all.'

Mr Mount was now on the floor, telling Frank about aeroplanes. He had flown in a Lancaster bomber.

'He'll be a wonderful father,' Mrs Mount said wistfully. Clara looked at her. The words made her pause. She thought of her own failure of a father and then of Ivor, who had thrown himself into fatherhood with a zeal she would never have anticipated. 'He lost his own when he was sixteen,' Mrs Mount went on. 'It's all he ever wanted.'

Clara offered them more tea but was slightly relieved when the Mounts said they would have to head off. It wasn't them, it was Miss Webb. She could be exhausting company.

At the door, Mrs Mount kept her hand on the frame as though she was reluctant to let go.

'What *will* happen to the other children? The girl who doesn't speak, and the sad-faced older one...'

'Don't worry,' Clara said. 'They'll be fine here.'

'I know that,' Mrs Mount said, biting her lip. 'Despite everything, you make it a happy place – it's just... It's distressing, isn't it?'

Clara was reminded that in her first weeks at the home she used to fill up with tears every night. Sometimes too much empathy could paralyse you. It could freeze you. You had to be pragmatic. You had to try to distance yourself emotionally if you were to achieve something positive.

'I'm exhausted,' Frank said later that evening as Clara tucked him in. No matter what she did, the boys' bedroom smelled of socks and cabbage. 'A. I had a busy day and B. It's hard work being good.'

Clara smiled. 'Did you have to try very hard?'

'A little.'

His hair had grown long over his ears. The school wouldn't like that. She stroked it. 'Once you are relaxed there, you'll be fine.'

'They won't try and drown us – in their pond?'

The words caught in Clara's heart. 'No, darling, they won't.'

'Or take our bikes? Or trample our flowers?'

'No.'

'Or throw stones?'

'You'll be perfectly safe.'

'I didn't like that.'

'No,' she said softly, 'neither did I. But it's over now.'

He held his plane under his arm as though it were a teddy bear.

Three children had never been taken in by the same family before, not from Suffolk County Council anyway, so the

Mounts were a coup. Three siblings! Clara kept repeating it like it was a fairy tale and the Mounts were the treasure chest at the end of the rainbow.

Mr Horton must have told Mrs Horton, for she rang up the next day to congratulate Clara.

'It's hardly down to me.'

'It's good news. And you liked the family?'

'I did.'

'Mr Horton says we'll go ahead in the adoption league against Norfolk County Council.'

Clara laughed. Always with the county rivalries.

The next day, Mrs Mount telephoned to say what a magical afternoon it had been. Clara joked about her having been put off, and she laughed her tinkly laugh: 'Not at all, we are more committed than ever.' She was a good person.

'And also,' she said, 'we're filling in the garden ponds – I noticed Frank's face and Mr Mount and I don't want to leave anything to chance.'

22

It was December and the shopkeepers along the high road had decorated their shopfronts. There was a glorious smell of roasted chestnuts, and small fir trees in the town square, which reminded Clara of the war when the company she'd worked for, Harris & Sons, helped cut them down and put them on roofs for camouflage. The butchers had a wooden nativity scene in their window and the children peered at it, somehow ignoring the hanging pig cadavers in the background. Even though it was cold, they thought nothing of steaming up the glass for as long as Clara would allow.

The children continued to attend Sunday School eagerly throughout the month, while Clara attended church grumpily. She grew used to the service, zoning out at certain points and looking engaged at others. She had to admit, though, that the children were coming on in leaps and bounds. Mrs Dorne certainly had a way about her.

It grew bitterly cold. Ice on the windows, coats on beds, socks on at night. Clara had an argument about that with Florrie. Her lips were blue but she refused to wrap up.

'Feet need to breathe,' she said. 'My dad always said that.'

The council sent over gloves, boots, scarves and hats. Frank and Trevor had never had gloves before and were wild with excitement.

And there had been no more strange happenings at the home. Not for ages now. It must have been Davey, decided Clara, and she was relieved and pleased with how she had handled it. She had not overreacted. She hadn't given the culprit the thrill he was looking for. Despite the odds, she had kept a steady ship. This was the difference between the experienced housemother that she was now – and the Clara of three years ago. And all these lessons she had learned and was learning were all being put to good use. She couldn't give up on the children now. Not yet. Not for a man, even the best man in the world.

Clara told Jonathon Pell he could borrow her bicycle – she had no use for it – but Jonathan never took it out. He preferred running and went out for hours every day. He still seemed unhappy, and Clara was determined to get to the bottom of it. She understood it was probably a many-layered thing. Wasn't it always? Many of the children who came were certain – wrongly – that someone was going to return to them. Was that what it was with Jonathon? she wondered. Did he not accept that his father and grandfather were dead?

One day, as he was getting ready for school, she asked him outright. 'Did you go to your father's funeral?'

He took a deep breath in and then looked at her with narrowed eyes. 'Ye-es.'

Clara paused, *how could she frame this?* – 'It must have been difficult.'

Jonathon squinted at her. He had big ears and now they looked hot to touch.

'You must miss him an awful lot?'

He nodded.

Right, *that* didn't seem to be the issue.

There was another possibility that nagged at her: the great hero, Maurice Pell, perhaps he wasn't the great father after all?

And this, of course, was something Clara understood all too well.

Before long, the junior school gave the children their roles in the nativity play. First Frank was selected as a shepherd, and then he was promoted to innkeeper. Frank didn't mind because A. He could still wear his hat under his tea-towel and B. He could rough up Joseph. (It transpired he didn't like the child playing Joseph.) Clara said she wasn't aware there was any roughing up in the nativity story, but Frank said A. Miss Newton probably didn't listen in class. And B. These were different times.

Peg was playing the drums but she was also a sheep, and she was annoyed about that, but the next day she came back and wrote that she was now a star. Ivor was inveigled to help with her costume.

But Gladys, Gladys was selected to be Mary! The centre-piece of the show. Apparently, it was a reward for her knowing the answer to all the Bible questions – (again, thanks to Sunday School and Mrs Dorne).

'I can't believe she's been chosen,' Clara exclaimed to Miss Webb. 'It's usually the super-popular obnoxious girls.'

'I was Mary,' retorted Miss Webb sternly. 'Three years in a row.'

Frank and Mary had to rehearse their lines, and Gladys didn't have much to say even though she was the main charac-ter, but every evening after tea, they read aloud from their sheets, correcting each other and instructing each other how to do it best.

Trevor was in the school choir, and like Gladys he had a

sweet voice, but he was devoted to his chess and couldn't have cared less. Florrie said no one wanted her for anything and then ran upstairs, her school bag flapping behind her.

Clara was disappointed that talented Jonathon hadn't been selected for anything when he could do with a boost. She asked at the school and the teacher looked offended and said that Jonathon had been asked to participate in lots of things, but always refused.

That Sunday, Maureen came back for another visit and since there wasn't cake, she set about making some – she had always been resourceful like that. Clara dried the dishes from a disappointing lunch and watched as Maureen mixed the flour and baking powder and stirred. It was like she'd never been away.

Maureen loved a gossip, too, and she had lots of stories about Big Jean and Little Jean and the awful man who taught them sometimes, who had a glass eye (that was not why she disliked him, or at least it was not the only reason). Clara had worried that she would struggle to keep up on her course, as Maureen was not an academic girl, but she seemed to be thriving. She talked about the massive room with the typewriters and hard-backed chairs, the posters on the wall left over from the war; and she boasted about her typing speeds and how to end letters – 'There's Yours Sincerely and Yours Faithfully. Or you could say Yours Endearingly.'

It was fantastic: Maureen had never been one of the more forthcoming children, but now she chatted away to Clara as though, well as though they were friends (although she was insistent on still calling her Miss Newton).

Maureen had just put the cake in the oven when she said, oh so casually, that she wasn't sure what she wanted to do after secretarial college.

Clara nearly dropped the dishcloth. 'What? I thought you

wanted to be a secretary!' *Wasn't that what she had gone there for?*

'Maybe,' Maureen said cheerfully, 'but I miss children. And baking. Office life is all about sitting down while creepy old men with bad breath stand over you, watching your every move.'

While this wasn't an entirely accurate description of life at Clara's former employer in London, she had a point, Clara mused. 'There are other things...' she said tentatively.

'Like what?'

Like the satisfaction of an invoice come in and filed. Like a bar chart. Did Maureen not love a bar chart? Or a pie chart?

Maureen sniffed. 'I've not decided yet.'

'It's costing a lot,' Clara said. It was clear Maureen didn't respect the money. And why would she when she hadn't put in the hours for it?

Maureen pouted. 'But if I find out it's NOT something I want to do, then that's worthwhile too, isn't it? Big Joan says it's a *process of elimination.*'

Clara didn't know where she got these ideas from. 'Process of elimination' indeed. The joy of making mistakes was for the wealthy, for people of means, not orphans from children's homes.

Later, Ivor brought Patricia over to play with Maureen, and it was lovely right up until the moment Maureen said in her loud voice, 'So, when are you two getting married then? Patricia will be such a sweet bridesmaid.'

Ivor shrugged his shoulders. 'Clara, perhaps you can explain?'

'Not yet.' Clara swallowed. *God, this was awful.* 'We're... there's so much to do and... one day.'

'Are you still in love with Ruby?' Maureen asked Ivor, her voice clear as a bell.

Ivor laughed. 'Good God, no.'

'Is she still in love with you?' Maureen said, prying in the way only a very bold teenager could.

Ivor laughed.

'There's no love lost between us.'

'Then what's the hold-up?'

Ivor shook his head back at her as though he were saying, *not now*. Clara's cheeks burned and for once she was glad when Patricia starting yelling about hitting her thumb with her mallet or some such and everyone turned their attention to her.

And then one afternoon, Frank fell in the garden. Frank was a clumsy donkey, so Clara ignored it at first. She did clock that his skin was slightly green-tinged. He practised his lines for the play, and then ran off to throw up – but then Frank could be a vomiter too. Frank and Trevor could also be boisterous with each other. They threw each other about a lot, which they called wrestling. But then Frank explained that he had not simply fallen, he had tripped on something in the garden – a tripwire, he called it.

His words shook Clara and she combed the area frantically. It wasn't – was it? She had thought all that was over. Frank must have been mistaken. Then suddenly, when she had been out there for about ten minutes, she found a near-invisible thread – thread like the ones Ivor had all over the workshop – stretched between gate and drainpipe. Only four, five inches from the ground; low enough and discreet enough to go undetected.

Enough to trip up Frank, though.

She looked around her suspiciously. Could she hear laughter? No, well, yes, but it was just the normal noise from the street. She snipped the wire hurriedly with scissors. She didn't know where to turn. She felt sick again. She had thought, hoped, wanted to believe there would be no more incidents. She had been wrong.

Dr Cardew had called round with some cod liver oil and she ambushed him to have a quick look at Frank, which he did.

'It's probably nothing,' Clara said as she hovered.

When Dr Cardew looked up, his face was a picture.

'What is it?'

'We're taking him up to the hospital. Now.'

'Oh, good lord.'

All the way there Clara hoped Dr Cardew was exaggerating, but she knew really that he wasn't. Frank was lying in the back muttering, and Dr Cardew inclined his neck to hear.

'Is he saying he's in pain?'

'No, he's saying he wants his plane.'

In their hurry, they had forgotten his precious Tiger Moth.

Frank soon charmed all the nurses, even the matron with the wine birthmark who usually had a sour word for everyone. The nurses were talking about their Christmas plans. One of them was heading to Blackpool Tower. She said, 'If he doesn't propose there, I'm going to drop him. We've been together six months – what is he waiting for?' Feeling herself growing warm, Clara busied herself at Frank's bedside table.

They put the arm in plaster and one of the porters who wheeled him back gave him a tangerine. Frank didn't know what to do with it and the porter laughed at him, deftly peeling it: 'You want me to feed it to you too?'

'One segment at a time and with your left hand please,' retorted Frank.

'Don't be rude,' Clara said but she smiled. A few months back, Frank would have been frightened by the porter, Clara thought; he was making progress in so many ways.

Once he was settled she told him, shamefaced, that she had to get back to the other children.

But he didn't mind. He was most worried about the nativity: 'Will I still be innkeeper?'

'I can't imagine anyone else delivering the lines like you do,' she said neutrally.

His face relaxed. 'A. I think you're right. B. No one is as good as me.'

At home, she telephoned Miss Webb. The council had to be informed of any hospitalisation of their charges.

'Will you let Mr Sommersby know?' Clara requested.

Miss Webb snorted. 'Mr Sommersby won't give a fig, the man is away with the fairies most of the time.'

So it wasn't just Clara who had noticed.

The next morning, once the children were safely deposited at school, Clara crunched on the frost up to the bus stop. It was a long trip to the hospital by bus and it was one of the older ones with wooden slats for seats. She had chosen to bring three of Frank's tin planes: it was guesswork which he'd like best, but she'd picked the Spitfire, the bomber and the last one because she thought it was pretty. They stuck out from her handbag like puppy-dog noses. On the bus the windows were steamed up and the little girl in front of her was drawing hearts.

She strode down the hospital corridor: a good night's sleep had helped assuage most of the guilt. At least she was here. At least she had brought planes. At least he was in the best place now. But when she arrived at the door of the ward, the matron said, 'He's only allowed one visitor. Rules are rules.'

Clara looked at her in surprise. The matron put her hand on Clara's elbow and squeezed. 'Oh, go on, but only because he's such a doll.'

Clara nodded, because she couldn't think what to say – who else had come to see Frank?

There he was, beaming up at her from the bed, a picture of

health. Wearing a hospital gown, he reminded her of an advert for soap except for the fact he had crumbs around his mouth: it was good he was eating.

Clara pulled up the seat next to him, taking in the pretty snowdrops in the jam jar on the bedside table and the perfect, shiny apple casting a perfect shadow behind it.

Mr and Mrs Mount stepped out from behind a blue gauze curtain like actors for their encore.

'Ta-da!' laughed Mrs Mount.

'We hope you don't mind.'

'We came as soon as we heard...'

Again, Clara was shocked. It was fantastic that the Mounts were this attentive, but still she felt as though she had been caught. Looking after Frank was still her role – although maybe she hadn't done a good job this week.

'Frank thinks someone laid out a trip on purpose!' Mrs Mount said incredulously. 'Who would do such a thing?'

'He does have an active imagination,' Clara said, parroting his teacher's words, but her heart sank. She hadn't wanted the Mounts to know. This was private, this was her issue to resolve, not theirs.

She directed her attention to dear Frank. She could make up for this. Rummaging in her bag, she triumphantly produced his three planes.

'Where do you want them?'

'I've already got some.' He waved something in the air.

'Oh... great.'

He screeched the plane through the air and then said in a nasal presenter's voice: *'Breaking the speed of sound.'*

'Thank you,' she said to the Mounts, who were both sat by his bedside.

'It's the least we could do. So you don't think there's...' Mrs Mount lowered her voice, 'any danger to the children?'

'Not at all,' said Clara and any doubts she had about lying vanished when she saw how relieved Mrs Mount was.

Mr Mount patted Frank's leg. 'And it looks like we're all set for the third of February!'

Mrs Mount looked like she was about to burst into tears. Pushing her hair behind her pretty earlobe, she said, 'We are working so hard to get the bedrooms ready.' She patted Frank's fist, which was clenched around his new plane. 'I asked Frank if he'll prefer to share with Trevor – and he said he will just till he's settled. He wants his own bed though!'

'Wonderful,' said Clara, still feeling overwhelmed. Across the aisle, there was a bed containing a small boy – perhaps around the same age as Frank – with a bandage around his ear. He stared at her with almost exactly the same unimpressed expression as Patricia did.

'You can write on my cast if you like, Miss Newton,' offered Frank. This was the perfect distraction. He'd already covered the thick plaster with Mickey Mouse ears and Donald Duck feet, and there was Dr Cardew's laconic: *'Am I the first?'*

And there was Mr and Mrs Mount's:

To a brave little soldier –
All our love
Mummy and Daddy.

Clara swallowed, told herself not to be jealous. Frank was happy, they were happy, everyone was happy. This was what moving forward looked like. She wasn't going to hold them back. It wasn't a competition, she knew that. She shook the pen until the ink rushed to its head:

Get well soon, Frank.

It wasn't until she was on the bus home that Clara realised there might be another suspect to throw into the mix: Ruby Delaney. Who knew where Ruby was now? Ruby might not have the means but she could have more than one motive: dislike of Ivor, jealousy of Clara, wanting revenge on the home where she was once so unhappy. And although Ivor didn't talk about her much – Ruby very much belonged in a cupboard marked 'keep out' – Clara knew enough to guess that she was unpredictable and reckless.

Her suspicions wouldn't go down too well if she suggested them to Ivor though. In fact, he might think she was the mad one. It was, Clara told herself, something to keep in mind, yet, for now at least, best to keep to herself.

23

To his relief, Frank was allowed out of hospital days before the nativity. The Mounts couldn't come to see it though, as they were going away for their last hurrah of just the two of them. They came to visit the children before they left.

'You don't mind you, do you?' Mrs Mount was nearly weeping as she wished the children good luck. 'If only we could rearrange the dates... We will be there next year, I promise.'

'Break a leg,' said Mr Mount, to everyone's horror.

'As well as my arm?' squealed Frank.

Mr Mount hastily explained that was something actors said. It didn't mean he thought they should... oh, never mind.

Clara knew it was wrong but she was secretly glad the Mounts weren't coming.

Ivor couldn't make it to the nativity either. 'If I'm to have a day off at Christmas, I have to push through,' so Clara went to the junior school on her own. She didn't mind; she was used to it. Mostly, she felt a mixture of pride and apprehension. There was no reason the children should muck it up, but they had a tendency to be unpredictable.

Ivor had done a terrific job as usual with Peg's costume, and she played the drums as everyone trooped in. And Clara thought her cup would overflow when the woman in front of her leaned across to her husband.

'That girl is from the Shilling Grange Orphanage – they're such a talented lot. They were on the television last year.'

Her husband replied, 'Just shows what you can do when someone believes in you.'

And Gladys – Mary – was beaming and waving to the audience. She nudged Peg, who looked at her crossly and then laughed. She petted the boy playing the sheep. She was gracious, and she prompted Joseph when he forgot his line.

'Is there room at the inn? We need to rest our weary heads,' she said finally, and Joseph crossed his arms and hissed, 'That's my line.' And it must have taken her all the willpower in the world not to yell: 'Why didn't you just say it then?'

Frank, with his perennial hat squished under his tea towel, had also clammed up. One of the wise men shoved him and Frank shook his fist at him. Then he squared up to Joseph. 'No room!' he said, which was correct, but then he added, 'Even if we had room, we wouldn't let you in,' which wasn't.

Joseph and the innkeeper started pushing each other's chests – Clara wasn't entirely sure who'd started it, but she was worried about that arm. She couldn't make out exactly what they were saying, or who was saying what, but she could distinctly hear the letters A and B a lot, which pointed to Frank.

Could Joseph be behind the incidents? He was four foot nothing and drooling, unlikely to be a criminal mastermind – but looks could be deceiving, and perhaps he had someone else to do the heavy lifting – the bikes, for example. Perhaps his parents were against the home? It wasn't just Julian who didn't love the orphanage being in the heart of middle-class Lavenham.

In the end, it was Gladys – or Mary – who saved the day. Somehow, she got between the two warring factions and said,

'We're tired, we're hungry, give us somewhere to rest, we don't ask a lot...'

'But—' began Joseph.

'No, sorry. Whatever happened to you in the past is over. I'm having a baby and this baby needs to be safe.'

And everyone went 'Ahh,' and clapped.

The next scene was Gladys with the baby. Gladys had requested a real live baby – a request they hadn't been able to accommodate, and Clara was glad they hadn't because the way she was swinging about the china-faced doll with the slow blink was petrifying.

And then it was the end and she watched children run into the arms of their parents. Joseph came pelting towards her and she tensed up, but then – false alarm –he tumbled into the parents in front. And then *her* children came running out towards her, all three of them, colliding into her like bowling balls hitting the pins.

'You were all brilliant,' she told them, ruffling their hair. And the couple from the row in front – Joseph's parents – turned round and smiled.

24

Mrs Horton couldn't come for Christmas Day this year; she was cooking for Mr Horton, her mother-in-law and her mother-in-law's sisters (it sounded dreadful). But she did come by two days before Christmas with a batch of home-made cheese scones, a branch of Brussels sprouts and a whole lot of gossip too.

'Mr Sommersby just doesn't seem interested in the children's welfare recently,' Clara said as they drank tea and ate the scones together in the kitchen. Mr Sommersby had never been *that* interested before, but it was getting ridiculous now.

'Maybe he misses Miss Cooper?' Mrs Horton looked at her meaningfully. 'It seems they were rather... close.'

'How close?' Clara had long suspected this but to hear it confirmed gave her a jolt.

'Close enough that he was about to leave his wife for her.'

'What?!'

'Apparently Miss Cooper changed her mind and left the council instead. I'm not saying anything,' Mrs Horton said, but she had said plenty already and she knew it. Clara stared at her and then busied herself pulling the sprouts off the stalk.

Ivor was coming for Christmas Day, and Clara asked Miss Webb to join them because she felt obliged to – thank goodness she said no, she would be spending it with her parents. Clara also asked Miss Fisher because Peg begged her to (and because she was brilliant at getting the children to sit nicely). Miss Fisher said yes. So they'd be quite a merry crowd, and Clara was glad. She wanted Christmas 1951 to be an extra-special one. As for the incidents, she was determined to do as she told the children: 'Just ignore them and they'll go away.'

But would they?

On Christmas morning, the children opened their presents in the parlour with great excitement. She could have made them wait until after dinner, but what would be the point? Clara had found a super second-hand chess set at the market for Trevor, which he was thrilled about: 'I'm going to thrash Evelyn and Dr Cardew!' She got Frank a new hat – which he threw on the floor immediately: A. He didn't care if this hat smelled and B. He didn't want a new one – but she had also got him a new tin plane, which he clutched to his heart and declared he loved more than anything in the world.

Gladys got the basket and the bell for her bicycle that she had asked for, while Peg got a music box similar to the one Rita had had. Florrie had gone shy when asked what she wanted and said, 'Don't mind,' so Clara had chosen a perfume for her, and very pleased Florrie was too.

A few days before Christmas, Jonathon had gone out running and come back with sodden, grazed knees, gashes; he'd had a nasty fall and was trying not to cry.

'What would he say if he saw me?'

'Who?'

'My father. What would he say about me?'

'He'd say you are a lovely boy.'

Clara thought of her own father. He had seemed to be trying to say something through the children and yet she'd turned him away. Now, the nativity ringing in her head, for the first time, she wondered if she'd done the right thing. The least she should have done was offer him somewhere to rest his weary head. Would he be alone this Christmas?

'Why *wouldn't* he think that, Jonathon?'

Somehow, she expected him to say, 'Because he wasn't nice,' or 'Because nothing ever pleased him,' or something along those lines. Instead, he had stared out the window and said, 'Because what have I ever done?'

Clara laughed. 'You're fifteen. What has *anyone* done at fifteen?' She for one had passed her matriculation and failed at sewing.

'I'm not *likely* to do anything though, am I?'

'You'll have to wait and see,' Clara said. She couldn't think what else to say. '*I* think you're terrific.'

Now Clara gave him some new plimsolls and a book on adventure sports and he looked startled. 'For me?' he mumbled, close to tears again.

'I can't see anyone else who'd like plimsolls,' Clara replied, and she won a faint smile. She couldn't understand it. He was, as Miss Webb had described him, a lovely boy. His behaviour was good at home and school. His teacher said he was exceptional – 'not that that is unexpected, given that he is a Pell.'

Clara had got marbles for Patricia, which Ivor said was fine now. She had struggled with what to get him and ended up with a spotted teapot with a note about how much she loved coming over for tea, and she also gave him a hand-knitted sweater and a moleskin notebook. She spent more on him than she should have, more than they'd agreed, but she still felt slightly on the back foot with him. It was important to let him know that she appreciated him and if that was through material things, well, it was better than nothing.

For Stella she got an expensive tin of pilchards, which the ungrateful cat left in her bowl for ages, making the entire house smell.

After dinner, they sat around cracking walnuts in the parlour. The older guests were groaning about overeating, the younger children were playing with their new toys. It came up that Ivor didn't have a middle name and the children were incredulous. Ivor didn't mind not having a middle name but the children felt it was a grave injustice.

'We will give him a name!'

'For Christmas!'

'We could vote, but then we might end up with something we all dislike.' Clara laughed.

'Like the Conservatives!' shrieked Gladys.

Clara shushed her because Miss Fisher was looking po-faced.

'Humphrey because he looks like Humphrey Bogart,' Florrie said and then, when everyone laughed, insisted, 'He does though!'

'Humphrey Dumphrey sat on the wall,' said Gladys.

'I like it,' decided Trevor.

'Me too,' declared Frank.

So poor Ivor became Ivor Humphrey Delaney.

Later, although she'd only had one whisky – perhaps it was the brandy from the pudding? – Clara was feeling squiffy. She pulled Ivor over to the mistletoe that Trevor had expertly hung only that morning.

'I've got one more thing for you.'

She saw a flicker of something in his eyes.

Oh God, she realised, *he thinks I'm going to accept his proposal.*

'A big kiss,' she said, leaning in fast so she didn't have to see his hopeful expression any more.

The children whooped and clapped, and Clara and Ivor laughed. Florrie looked around and said, 'Isn't anyone going to stand under the mistletoe with me?' The children screeched in mock-terror but Clara couldn't help noticing that right at that moment, Jonathon sloped out of the room.

25

Anita couldn't decide whether to have a New Year's Eve party or not. It would be a great opportunity to celebrate – Anita did like to mark an occasion – but on the other hand, the living room looked shabby and neither Dr Cardew nor Evelyn were the most sociable of people. And Evelyn had extremely important exams when she went back to school. (All Evelyn's exams were extremely important. Poor Evelyn.)

'What about baby Howard?' Clara joked. 'Has he got extremely important exams too?'

They were sitting in the kitchen at the home, the day after Boxing Day. Dr Cardew and Trevor were playing chess in the parlour, and Jonathon was out running. Peg and Gladys were playing Newmarket. Evelyn and Florrie kept coming in silently to listen to the grown-ups, but Clara and Anita were wise to this and shooed them away.

'Howard loves nothing more than being the life and soul of the party.'

Anita's fears that Howard was 'behind' had long gone. Now two years old, he was picking up things at a pace. Anita had examined his fingers for musical promise but had found none –

nevertheless, and 'far more importantly', he recognised Beethoven and one of his first words was Bach. (Ivor said it was more likely bath, but never mind.)

'You'll have to decide if you're having a party quickly,' Clara pointed out.

'Tsk, there are still three days...'

Eventually, Anita won the great party decision – was there ever any doubt? – and Dr Cardew and Evelyn were railroaded into helping. Evelyn said she'd help with the catering, which Anita greeted with fury – 'she must learn that she is the host, not the servant,' while Dr Cardew said he'd be on hand for accidents.

'What accidents are you expecting?'

Clara faced similar opposition in the home.

'Do I *have* to go?' Jonathon asked immediately. He would opt out of everything if he could. Clara said he didn't have to, but she wanted him to, and he gave her another small smile.

As for Gladys, Trevor and Frank, excitement about life with the Mounts was – as Clara liked to joke – mounting. All through the Christmas holidays, the three had kept saying, 'It's our last...': 'It's our last trip to the playground', 'It's the last haircut', 'It's the last hand-me-down pair of socks...'

The Mounts wrote that they had organised chess lessons for Trevor – 'I'll be better than the teacher,' boasted Trevor ungratefully. They had arranged for some friends to come round for Gladys – 'girls from the village, the same age, good families...' 'They will be wonderful,' decided Gladys, ever the optimist. And for Frank? Mrs Mount whispered, 'We think he might like flying lessons!'

This Clara did not tell Frank for fear he might spontaneously combust. With joy.

The Mounts were playing the 'it's our last' game too. Mr

and Mrs Mount had spent their 'last Christmas without children' with family friends in the Cotswolds. 'We are going to make the most of it,' Mrs Mount had said, dabbing away her tears (she did cry easily) 'but believe me, Miss Newton, I can't wait.'

February third had been ringed in the calendar for a long time.

Anita certainly knew how to throw a party. The house/surgery looked wonderful. She had decorated with fresh bowers of flowers and vases of plants. There were candles on the high shelves, providing a beautifully flattering light, and those were probably how they had managed to get rid of the house's usual antiseptic smell. Much of Lavenham was there and she had friends up from London too. Milling around were Sir Alfred, Mr Dowsett, the postmistress and plenty of people who Clara had never met before. Julian and his girlfriend, Margot, were there too, and Margot kissed the air beside Clara's cheek.

'When are you marrying that handsome neighbour of yours?'

Margot had a way of talking like they were intimate, old friends, even though they weren't.

Clara mumbled something, hoping Ivor, who did look handsome, hadn't heard. He was admiring the fish with Frank, and Frank was telling his usual story: 'And then I spotted that it was dead, and Miss Newton said it was just a silly fish...'

Margot placed a cool hand on Clara's arm. 'Miss Newton, I'd snap Mr Delaney up quick if I were you. There's a dearth of eligible bachelors in the country, especially ones so *desirable*.'

Desirable? Was that a warning? Clara wondered. But Margot's wide eyes were as blank as ever.

The Norwood Nanny whisked the under-threes upstairs, but Anita insisted she come down and circulate once the babies fell asleep. The nanny changed into a frock, and it was strange to see her talking among the guests when usually she was changing nappies. She still expressed herself in the same way though.

'Better the devil you know,' she said sagely when asked to choose between the whisky and the vodka, and 'easier said than done,' about Julian's new year's resolution to make more money.

Jonathon stayed hiding in the kitchen with the aproned staff and with Evelyn, who had appointed herself chief dishwasher, but Florrie, Maureen and the rest of the children hung around the buffet and danced. Ivor said he didn't want to dance, which was disappointing, but Clara knew better than to press him: he knew his own mind.

Anita had chosen the music skilfully and there was a lovely mixture of Christmas favourites, big band numbers and even a few reels. And then of course, later in the evening, Anita herself sat down at the piano to play. Everyone watched her slight frame sway as her fingers worked delicately over the keys.

When Anita was complaining about Howard's behaviour or Evelyn's social awkwardness, it was possible to forget her traumatic history. Anita had survived the concentration camps but lost most of her family there. When she played the piano though it was somehow a reminder of how she had suffered during the war, and all she had endured. Clara was touched to see Dr Cardew too gazing admiringly at his talented and resilient wife.

Clara thought about the years that had gone by. The time that was passing so quickly now. She remembered a kindness from her father – a rare thing – he let her stay up for New Year's Eve once after she had promised to be no trouble. It occurred to her now that maybe it was because he knew it was their last together.

After Anita had finished, Ivor whispered, 'Come outside with me, Clara.'

Patricia was staying in the nursery here for the night, so for once Ivor was a free man. It was cold in the garden, and Clara could see her breath in white wispy clouds – in between Ivor kissing her. He was getting amorous. (It was the whisky; he always was a terrible drinker.)

'Are you still worried about those pranks?' he asked presently.

Ivor still used the word 'pranks' for the incidents. She imagined it was because he didn't want to worry her.

'Not really,' she told him, pretending she was more confident than she was. If it was Ruby doing it, then goodness knows how that would pan out. 'There haven't been any for... I think they're just attention-seekers. Nothing serious.' What was it she sometimes told the children about the naughty ones at school? 'They're just looking for a reaction.'

'Sure?'

'Uh huh. Honestly, Ivor, I'm more concerned about us. We're all right, aren't we?' She couldn't say the word *love*, but that was what she meant.

He looked at her tenderly. Maybe he was drunk, but he was more effusive than usual.

'I'm all yours.'

'Did I hurt you? At the beach in Hunstanton?'

He drew his breath sharply. 'Yes and no.'

Ask me again, she thought. *I'm ready.*

But he didn't. He kissed her and said, 'When do I get you all to myself again?'

'Soon...'

She and Ivor looked at the stars, but whereas usually he liked to point out Sirius and the Milky Way, tonight he was more interested in nibbling her collarbone.

Nineteen fifty-one was becoming nineteen fifty-two and that sounded like something in the future. The nineteen-fifties. What would the decade bring? There were new inventions all the time. One day, everyone was talking about televisions and electronic bicycles, the next there was talk of white fish wrapped up in breadcrumbs shaped like fingers. She remembered as a child working out that in 1952, she would be thirty. She remembered thinking her life would be over, she would be past it. In many ways she did feel like that, but in other ways, in the more important ways, she had only just begun.

Just sometimes, it felt like the world was theirs for the taking.

Tonight was one of those times.

26

New Year's Day, and Clara woke to find red paint splashed all over their back lawn. Ruby-red streaks set against the green grass. It looked like blood. There was even a trail where someone must have lugged tins of paint from the garden back into the street.

Ruby-red. But surely not Ruby?

Clara was horrified. It must have taken some effort and – this is what frightened her the most about it – someone had worked hard to do it. No, that wasn't what frightened her the most. What frightened her the most was what they – whoever it was – might be planning to do next.

She went and spoke to Ivor – he might have heard something in the early hours – but she didn't want anyone else to know and she desperately wanted to clear it up before the children woke up and saw. Ivor came over with a bucket of soapy water and a half-asleep Patricia. And questions: 'Any ideas who...?'

She couldn't tell him her latest suspicions. 'No...'

'You said there hadn't been anything for ages.'

'There hadn't,' said Clara heart-sinking – then nervously

she told him about the tripwire, adding the caveat that she was sure it could have been, well it absolutely might have been, put down *ages* ago.

'Or it could have just been put there recently?'

'Well, yes,' admitted Clara. Her cheeks burned. 'I suppose.'

'You should have told me,' Ivor said, his expression tight. 'You have to call the police.'

INCIDENTS AT THE HOME (in chronological order)

Roses flattened in the garden

Tomatoes thrown at windows

Newspapers possibly stolen/undelivered

Bikes removed and dumped in field x 3

Stone smashed kitchen window

Tripwire in the garden

Red paint splashed on the lawn

27

Clara wanted the children to be asleep before she telephoned the police, so she waited all day and all evening until there was silence from the bedrooms. After she explained it, in a low voice, the police said they would send someone round the next morning. She felt a mixture of pride – that it was worth bothering them – and fear.

These are traumatised children, she thought. Who would do this, and why?

Clara knew who the policeman was because the florist Mrs Garrard had pointed him out to her in the street once. PC Walter Banks rode a bicycle and Mrs Garrard, who saw herself as a matchmaker rather than a busybody, said he was a bachelor and highly eligible at that.

'Any mistletoe still up?' he said, as he walked into the home.

When Clara handed him the paper listing the incidents (in chronological order), PC Banks grinned at her and said, 'You didn't?' as though the fact that she'd compiled a list was the unbelievable thing.

'I thought you would want to see them,' she said lamely. 'And they tend to take place at the weekends...'

He read through the paper and made some marks in his flip notepad, but did nothing to inspire confidence.

'Tomatoes?'

'Yes, and bicycles.'

'It sounds like April Fool's.'

'But it's all the time...'

PC Banks sat back in his chair with his arms folded like he was enjoying a trip to the seaside. 'I'd love another cuppa... Yeah, just kids having a laugh.'

'We feel it's more than that.'

The 'we' sounded more powerful than a mere 'I'. She should have got Ivor here. He would have made PC Banks take it seriously. It was awkward, just the two of them. She wondered on what scale he could be classed as eligible. Not any scale that she would use, that was for sure.

She wondered if she might suggest Ruby as a suspect. She resolved that she would not. Can you imagine if she was wrong? Ivor would come down on her like a tonne of bricks.

'You used to have Clifford Harvey here? Bit of a trouble-maker. Could it be him?'

'He lives in a reform home in Hunstanton now, and he's not allowed out to visit here.'

'Or perhaps someone who didn't like him? It would be fair to say young Clifford didn't make many friends here.'

That was true – but why would someone who didn't like Clifford attack the home when Clifford was clearly no longer here?

Looking out the window, PC Banks complimented her on the garden, then said abruptly, '*Has Anybody Seen My Gal?* is at the cinema.'

'Is it?'

'It's the new Rock Hudson. It's meant to be funny.'

'Good,' Clara said, growing more nervous even than before.

'Good as in you'll come with me?'

'Uh no. Good as in I'm glad it's funny.'

'Come on,' he said. 'Give a guy a chance. You give all the children a chance. Why not me?'

An entirely different notion, thought Clara. Spurious. For one, children were a vulnerable group – you, PC Banks, are far from vulnerable. And the fact he was trying to lump them all together... Clara did not like that one bit.

'I am in a relationship, thank you.'

She thought PC Banks would leave it there, but he was nothing if not persistent, if not in crime-solving, then in the clumsy art of seduction.

'Who with?'

'Who with? – Oh um, Mr Delaney.'

PC Banks made a chopping motion at his arm. 'Not the fella who does the sewing?'

'Yes. Ivor Delaney.' Clara ignored the pathetic hand gesture. PC Banks was getting on her nerves now. Everything was. 'The upholsterer.'

'But he's only got one arm,' PC Banks said incredulously, as though this quirk would disqualify Ivor from the pool of dating possibilities. It was 1953! If you eliminated all the men with one arm...

'I am aware.'

'He lost it in the war?'

You couldn't get anything over this detective. 'That's right.'

'You're engaged?'

So it all hinged on this. Unless Clara was the property of someone else then she was still fair game. It was as clear as day: PC Banks was happy to override her wishes but he didn't want to tread on another man's territory.

Clara felt weary. 'I am,' she lied. To her consternation, it worked like a charm. PC Banks fixed his helmet back on his head and became the detached professional again, sailing self-righteously to the front door.

'Good luck with that.'

It didn't make sense that it would be Clifford but then it didn't make sense that it would be Ruby either – Ruby with her fur throws, high heels and lipstick was not the kind to carry around tins of paint. Or bicycles for that matter. Still, PC Banks had been pretty certain that Clifford was the most likely suspect and it would be helpful to rule him out – what was it Maureen called it? 'A process of elimination'. And after all, hadn't he been awful while he lived with them? It wouldn't be beyond him.

So Clara called Clifford at his school in Hunstanton. It took several attempts to get through to him: one time he was swimming, another time in detention; the third time, someone fetched him. She remembered that wild building with the bars on its windows and the impervious grey sea. She thought about Clifford telling everyone he'd sung on television once. She thought about no one caring.

His voice seemed deeper each time they spoke.

'Miss Newton?'

'Hello, Clifford. I was just wondering how everything is?'

Clifford wasn't a great talker. Only on the subject of Anita Cardew did he become animated. His respect for her had never wavered.

'Do you ever come this way – to Lavenham, I mean?'

'Not allowed.'

She felt he was telling the truth and she was relieved. 'Do you want us to come and see you again?'

He paused and the pause was painful. She felt like a zip had stuck suddenly, unexpectedly.

'I don't mind.'

CHILDREN'S REPORT 16
Florrie Macdonald

Date of Birth: Unknown. Florrie thinks she is fourteen years old and her birthday might be in March.

Family Background:

Left at a children's home in Suffolk when she was approximately six. No documents from that time exist. She had been to eight different institutions including notorious [REDACTED] home.

Health/Appearance:

She doesn't like her glasses and refuses to wear them. Tall, slender girl. She needs feeding up. No nits, capable of haircare. Teeth okay.

Food:

Extremely fussy. Does not like most biscuits or cakes. Does not like sandwiches or meat, pies or stew. Likes beetroot and cucumber.

Hobbies/Interests:

She doesn't like animals. Not interested in other children. Dislikes baking and cooking. Hates cards and board games. Likes cycling short distances. Find out what motivates her?

Other:

Make friends with Maureen or Evelyn? Try sports or music with Anita?

28

The children went back to the school after the Christmas holidays, but Peg, Gladys and Frank soon had rotten colds, went down like dominoes and had to have days off. Mysteriously, Clara's children were always healthy enough to attend Sunday School. There were appointments at the dentist's and the optician's. The dentist was enamoured with Jonathon's teeth; they were a 'textbook example'. Unfortunately, Frank and Trevor's were a disaster zone and they were booked in for several treatments.

Clara looked after the house and kept her notes up to date. There was a small incident on Trevor's birthday – Clara put some candles on a cake, and they were singing 'Happy Birthday'. Trevor had been so overwhelmed that he'd curled up on the floor, and Clara had been so worried she'd nearly called Dr Cardew, but eventually Frank was able to speak for him.

'He's crying A. because he's happy and B. because he's never had a happy birthday before.'

. . .

When Mrs Horton got in touch saying she had information Clara immediately thought it would be about the attacks, so, when Mrs Horton had said she knew a specialist in London who might help get Florrie to eat, Clara was taken by surprise. She protested that it wasn't necessary, but Mrs Horton said she had been watching Florrie over Christmas and again at Anita's party and 'Florrie didn't eat a thing.'

Clara *knew* Florrie didn't eat much but she had convinced herself it wasn't a problem. And then she thought of all the meals that Florrie said she ate but might be skipping. And of all the things she pushed away or stirred or hid.

Immediately, Clara experienced a familiar wave of self-loathing. Was this another thing she had screwed up? Diet and food weren't an area she was comfortable with and while her magazines helped with recipes, not-eating hadn't been featured. She wanted to say it was no big deal, Florrie was fine as she was, but the offer of outside help was tempting.

'He is a food expert, is he?'

'He's an expert in everything,' Mrs Horton replied airily.

PC Banks had been so disappointing that Clara wondered if she trusted experts anymore. Nevertheless, she spoke to this expert's secretary over the telephone. At first the secretary sounded dismissive but she called back the next day and her tone was warmer.

'A friend of Mrs Horton?' she said. 'He said he is happy to see you,' and she arranged an appointment for Clara – no charge.

Clara navigated to Harley Street with Ivor's instructions, and it was easy to find. It wasn't until she was at the top of the steps, right outside the impressive black door, that she saw the shiny plaque: 'Dr Lawrence Q. Morgan'. There were several letters after his name and then the word that sent a chill down her spine: 'psychologist'.

A psychologist was not what she was expecting. She remembered her father talking about the 'funny farm', joking about strait-jackets and bars on the windows. A distant relative was 'carted off' to one (it was always *carted off*) and when she was naughty, her father would say, 'You'll end up carted off if you're not careful.' And then she remembered how Mrs Horton had said it was an expert she was going to see. It was Clara who had assumed Dr Morgan was a food expert. Dammit. She might as well have got advice from Beryl – '*what star sign is she then? Well, Aquarians like to eat fish.*'

Dr Morgan's secretary greeted her as if all was normal. Fortunately, there was no one else in the waiting room as Clara waited, wondering if she should creep away. This was a waste of everyone's – mostly her – time. At home there were accounts to look at, boot polish to buy, vegetables to chop.

And then one of the many doors opened and a friendly wiry-haired face appeared. Dr Morgan had thick feminine glasses, and a firm handshake.

'You didn't bring the young woman in question?'

'Oh...' It hadn't occurred to Clara to bring along Florrie. It struck her that the fact it hadn't occurred to her was revealing in itself.

The office had a long leather sofa, a framed picture of a man who might have been Dr Freud and a statue of a cross-legged Buddha with impressively long earlobes. Dr Morgan started out by telling her the field of enquiry was new. *Field of enquiry,* she thought. She'd never heard that before. It sounded like a place for intellectual ponies.

She wished he *was* a dietician.

Dr Morgan was intense, as though he was used to talking to important people. She wondered what stories people came to him with and tried to imagine herself coming here with her own issues: Marriage to Ivor. Her childhood. Michael. Judy. She couldn't imagine rummaging around in her memories for him. Good gracious – how long had the man got?

Clara explained that she was the housemother of a children's home, and he said he knew all that. She told him she was here about a girl with – she used the phrase Mrs Horton had told her – *disordered eating*.

It was odd being here, but before long she found that she liked that he listened. He was a good listener. It made her wonder – what was it that made a person a good listener? She thought it might be because they paid such attention to what someone was saying. She looked up – she had missed half of what Dr Morgan was saying, which was ironic.

'We're increasingly thinking disordered eating is a manifestation of something else. For example, distress, lack of power, feeling unloved or unworthy.'

'Right,' said Clara, thinking of the diet plans she had cut from the pages of *Woman's Own* with their calorie-control regimes. He didn't mean those, then? This had nothing to do with Clara's abysmal cooking?

'I'd just like her to eat a square meal, at least once or twice a week,' she said. She felt defeated suddenly. It seemed she was barking up the wrong tree a lot recently. Not just Florrie, but with Ivor, with Davey – maybe even with her father. How could she have such certainty and yet be so mistaken? And she thought about the attacks on the home and how sometimes it felt she was being rightfully punished – it was just a shame the children suffered for it too.

Dr Morgan was continuing, his hair bobbing about as he talked, seeming to have a life of its own: 'It's most likely a reaction to underlying issues.'

Clara thought of her aborted attempts to get Florrie to consume not only cabbage soup and burnt porridge, but

Christmas pudding and the roof of the gingerbread house. 'Underlying issues or not, Florrie still needs to eat.'

She thought of the malnourished children in the war. The great struggles to get food for them. Worse, the people in the concentration camps they'd seen in the films that came from Belsen. Those poor people didn't look human any more – that's where refusing food got you.

'The source goes deeper than food. If it weren't food, it would be something else.'

She knew it, she just hadn't joined the dots. Didn't the children's struggles often manifest in extraordinary ways: in arson, in silence, in promiscuity? Each of them was not so much a cry for help as a call to be acknowledged or recognised.

For a moment, Clara saw things so clearly it was like lamps being put on in a dark room: Florrie was a girl in pain – by not eating, she was medicating herself.

'Not all eating disorders come from trauma or psychological problems,' Dr Morgan was saying. 'But many do. We have to ask ourselves – what is the root cause? – what lies beneath the distress? The tendency is to offer a quick fix, to give a solution – "she doesn't want to eat – I will make her eat!" This won't work. We need to think – why does she feel like that? – not "here, take this, you'll feel better".

Clara paused, a little dumbstruck.

'Why are you so interested in young women's health?' she asked eventually. It seemed not many people were.

'I have five daughters,' he said. 'We neglect girls at our peril. The world is often unfair to the female sex. It is hard to change the world though, so in the meantime, we just have to prepare them for it the best we can.'

'So, what should I do about Florrie *practically*?' Clara didn't mean to sound impatient. She focused on the button on the armrest.

'Treat her as you would any person in crisis. With security, trust and acceptance. The food is not the issue – something else is.'

'And how do I find out what is?'

'By listening.'

It was probably a beginner's question, but she had to ask: 'How?'

'By spending time together. I recommend sharing experiences. Or books.'

The two hands of the carriage clock were up as if in surrender. Her time was over. There had been no quick fix.

'How about you, Miss Newton?' he asked. 'You are carrying a lot.'

She liked that term – 'carrying'. She said her usual, 'I'm fine,' as she stood up and straightened (Anita's) jacket.

Afterwards, she would wonder what came over her, but at the time it seemed a natural thing to do. There was something about Dr Morgan that invited confidences. She might tell him anything and he wouldn't be shocked, he wouldn't be appalled. She felt here at last was someone who might be able to lead her away from the confusion in her head.

'There is a man.'

He chortled. 'There often is.'

'He seems to love me...'

'That's a good start.' He smiled at her and for a moment she thought how different her life might have been with a gentle father, a father like this.

'The thing is, he wants to marry me.'

'And you don't want to marry him?'

'I do, but I don't know *how*...'

'What is it you don't know?'

'I love him, but I love my work. It feels like it's my...' She felt embarrassed saying the word with its faintly religious connotations, but it was the one that fitted best: 'Vocation. I love the children...'

'The children?'

'At the home. I don't want to give them up. I can't. They need me – and I suppose I need them.'

There is also Patricia, she thought. Perhaps if Patricia were a different kind of child – a child who was malleable or easy-going – things would be easier. Or perhaps if Patricia were not Ruby's child, Ruby with her fashionable figure and selfish nature, she would warm to her quicker. Or perhaps if Patricia were six or seven years older, Clara would enjoy being with her. People think if you like children, you like all children, or that if you like children, you like babies. Not true. Clara loved the children in the home precisely because they knew the difference between pavement and road, a hot kettle and a cold kettle.

She stared at Dr Morgan beseechingly.

'The best thing to do would be to tell him, be honest, tell him how you feel.'

The thought of telling Ivor all that *muddle* made Clara's stomach ache. He was still peevish that she hadn't told him sooner about the line that tripped up Frank. 'What if I'm too late?'

'Then you'll have learned something for next time,' he said. It was the truth, but Clara couldn't help thinking it was bleak.

'How do you know Dr Morgan?' Clara asked Mrs Horton on the telephone that evening.

'I don't know him well,' Mrs Horton responded.

'That's not what I asked.' From that evasion, Clara *knew* she was on to something here, she smelled it. Mrs Horton must have known she was rumbled too, for she chuckled.

'He asked me to marry him – over thirty years ago.'

'And you said…?'

'No, obviously. I had my work, and I would have had to…

you know how it was in the old days. I have to go, Clara. Anyway, I am happy you went.'

As Clara placed down the receiver, she thought of the alternate lives Mrs Horton had had before she'd met her and probably still had. Each of us has a thousand possibilities in front of us. A thousand different ways. Marrying someone – or not marrying someone – was a huge fork in the road, but there were a zillion tiny forks in every road too.

That evening, the children were in the kitchen, and Florrie was making patterns in her carefully made stew with her fork.

'It's better than it looks,' Clara pointed out, and, 'It's important to have meat and potato,' but after that, she left it.

What was the point of starting an unwinnable row? The food was a symptom, she reminded herself, she had to find the underlying cause. And after the moment of crisis had passed, dinner went by peacefully.

29

Ivor had to take some work to London and Anita's Norwood Nanny was having a week off to see her family in Chester. Anita would have looked after Patricia but she had enough on her hands with Evelyn's exams, baby Howard's education and the choir and 'Clara, do you not realise how hard the Bach Mass in B Minor is?'

Evelyn, of course, would also have done it – she begged both Clara and Ivor for babysitting opportunities – but her private school did long hours and Anita was strict about Evelyn's limited free time.

'Why don't I take Patricia?' offered Clara. She knew it was high time she and Patricia spent some time together. The conversation with Dr Morgan had reinforced that. Clara had the usual chores: cleaning, cooking, peeling vegetables, getting rid of the mysterious something on the floor of the shed; but perhaps Patricia wouldn't get in the way too much?

'I feel bad,' Ivor said. 'Especially while the attacks are still happening. You've got a lot on.'

Clara noted he no longer called them 'pranks'.

'Ivor, it's under control,' she told him. She hated for him to think she was weak or incapable. 'And Patricia and I will have a lovely time together.' (This was doubtful, but...)

'All right, I'll feel worse if I can't afford to heat the workshop. Thank you, Clara. I'll make it up to you.'

He proposed a date in a couple of weeks' time. Just the two of them. She'd get Sister Grace, he'd get the Norwood Nanny, and he would take her to a surprise location.

He laughed: 'It's a surprise because I don't know where it is yet.'

Patricia had four toothy-pegs and a swagger in her walk. She had a disconcerting way of looking at you, like you had just made a bad smell, but she laughed much more than she used to.

'She likes "The Wheels on the Bus",' Ivor said as he handed her over.

'Isn't that dangerous?' said Clara.

He stared at her. 'The song. The wheels on the bus go round and round....'

'All day long,' said Clara quickly. 'Yes, of course. I was just... my singing is terrible.'

As soon as Patricia was released, she started screaming: 'Park. PARK. Wah, Wah, Wah.'

I can't go all the way to the big playground today, thought Clara. It was an hour's round trip.

'If you're a good girl this morning, I'll take you to the little playground later,' she promised.

Patricia wasn't a good girl particularly. While Clara was rolling out the pastry for a pie, she came in chewing the white bishop chess piece Trevor had lost last week. When Clara was bringing in the sheets, Patricia rearranged Peg's shells. What she had done was interesting –a sort of hexagonal pattern – but Peg did not like anyone touching her treasured collection.

Then Patricia found an old recorder stuffed down the side of the sofa, and with that, she made a terrible racket.

'I'd forgotten we had that,' said Clara, wobbling on a chair to put it on top of the wardrobe. She then launched into song: 'The drivers on the bus go honk, honk, honk,' which, gratifyingly, made Patricia roar with laughter.

Patricia ate Clara's lunch, a spam sandwich, with more gusto than the other children put together, which was heartening, and she enjoyed chasing Stella. In the afternoon, Clara took her to the rusty swing on the wasteland where the children spent hours. Taking Patricia was a different experience to taking the children, she reflected, because this was Ivor she was standing in for. With the children at the home, the people she was standing in for were unknown.

Patricia sat one end of the old seesaw and Clara on the other, making it go down while Patricia went up, up, up. But when it was at its highest point, Patricia – for reasons known only to herself – decided to get off. She dangled from the seat, leaving Clara stuck. She could try to leap and save her, but if she did, the seesaw would descend super-quickly and throw her.

Fortunately, Patricia got herself out of the problem, but for a few moments Clara had frozen. The idea of taking an injured Patricia back to Ivor was too horrifying to contemplate.

Patricia was anti-sleep, Clara knew that. Yet Patricia seemed to find Clara as tiring as Clara found her, and she snuggled down into the pram and under the blanket, her fingers wrapped round her mallet. Clara didn't even have to sing. Clara parked her out in the garden under the oak tree that lined the back fence. Stella was washing her paws out there, and Clara was able to get on with her chores, relieved at the respite. She knew young children were tiring but this was ridiculous!

At ten to three Clara walked up to the children's school and collected Gladys, Peg and Frank. Frank's teacher wanted to discuss Frank's reluctance to remove his hat, his active imagination and his verbal tics.

On the way home, it started to rain. Thick round drops came down, darkening the pavement, and Frank's tongue came out to catch them. Jonathon and Trevor returned drenched and serious, followed by Florrie, who was drenched and gloomy. Clara made them hot drinks to warm them up.

At four o'clock, Clara looked out the back window – and to her shock saw the Silver Cross pram out in the garden. She had completely forgotten it. Patricia...

Clara ran for dear life. It was the worst thing ever.

What had she done?

She expected to find a drenched, screaming child, but mercifully Patricia was still fast asleep. Clara couldn't believe it. *Thank you, God*, she began. It took her a few seconds to realise that when she had left Patricia out there, she had not put up the hood, she had not tucked her into the blanket, and she absolutely had not put her under the canopy of the trees.

Someone else had done all that. Someone had been by and made sure Patricia was safely out of the rain. Clara didn't know what to think. Okay, so it could have been a concerned bystander, someone who had seen the pram was getting wet – but wouldn't a concerned passer-by come and tell her too? Wouldn't they knock and say, 'Afternoon, Miss Newton, remember the baby you left outside?' No, it looked to her as though it must have been the person/people behind the attacks. It had to be – who else would do this anonymously? They might be prepared to terrify the children but were they saying they had nothing against the baby? This baby in particular, or babies in general? It certainly meant she couldn't rule out Ruby just yet...

Nothing added up, but for the moment, this was good news.

Clara shunted the pram inside and hoped none of the children asked where Patricia had been.

'The mummies on the bus go shush, shush, shush.'

DEAR MR SOMMERSBY

RELATIVE? I AM MORE THAN A RELATIVE OF THE CHILD – I AM HER FATHER. AM I TO UNDERSTAND THAT PHYLLIS MIGHT NOW BE ON THE OTHER SIDE OF THE WORLD? YOU HAVE LOST TRACK OF MY GIRL AND WE ARE LEFT TO SUFFER THE LOSS?

YOU MAY THINK I AM A PERSON OF NO CONSE-QUENCE BUT I CAN ASSURE YOU I WILL LEAVE NO STONE UNTURNED IN MY QUEST TO FIND PHYLLIS.

MR BURNHAM

30

Clara hadn't forgotten Dr Morgan's advice about listening more to Florrie. At first, Florrie resisted; she certainly didn't want to be read to, that was for babies, but Clara insisted they shared ten minutes reading a day, just the two of them.

At the library, Mr Dowsett could hardly contain his excitement. 'A new reader!' he said. 'Haven't had one of those for a while.'

He helped advise Florrie on which books she might enjoy and eventually, Florrie settled on *Wuthering Heights*.

'Good luck,' Mr Dowsett said, winking at Clara, after he'd made her promise that she would come to the next Jane Taylor Society meeting. (She had missed one but hoped he hadn't noticed.)

After some complaining, Florrie did take to it and soon they were both enjoying their reading time. Sometimes Florrie couldn't wait to find out what was going to happen and read ahead by herself in the day. Clara didn't mind.

'What's wrong with Cathy?' Florrie asked one evening when they were nearing the end. 'She doesn't eat, does she?'

Clara knew she had to tread carefully here. She was out of her depth, but she had to keep paddling.

'I think her heart is broken, she is feeling trapped, she can't see a way out, and she seeks to take control of her world in the only way she can.'

Clara thought of Evelyn, who used to have the opposite issue – she would stuff down every piece of food she could to stop her thinking, to stop her feeling. And how had Anita dealt with it? By keeping her occupied, keeping her loved, keeping her safe.

A few evenings later, they had read together for fifteen minutes and then Florrie put down the book and started to tell Clara about her family.

'Did you know, my dad was married to someone else?'

'Uh, I didn't.'

'That's why he couldn't look after me. But when Mama put me in care, he promised he'd find me. He said, give me a month and I'll be back. But then they moved me and I didn't see him again.'

Clara swallowed. Florrie's own mother put her in care? Clara was used to mothers torn apart from their children through death or desperation – had Florrie's simply given her up? She didn't ask.

But a few days later, Florrie brought it up again: 'The other children here, their mamas are dead, aren't they?'

'Not all, Peg's had to give her up—'

'Mine couldn't wait to get rid of me.'

Once Florrie started talking, she didn't want to stop.

Another time she said, 'One of the men in the foster home hurt me.'

'Do you want to tell me what happened?'

'No.'

'No one is going to hurt you any more.'

'I know that,' Florrie said, folding her arms. 'Now.'

'I'll make us some tea.' Clara was going to add 'and a slice of Anita's meringue', but she told herself, *Not yet.*

Florrie disclosed more horror stories. About older brothers and uncles. There were kind men too, but the kind men went away. She had uncorked the bottle; and now some blood-red cold truths were coming out.

Clara listened carefully and then went back to her own room and wept. It felt like she was carrying many burdens and they were getting heavier and heavier. One day, mightn't she just snap?

Clara had arranged to see Ivor on Friday evening, but at bedtime Florrie wanted to talk again and Clara didn't feel she could cut her off, not while she was in mid-flow. Plus, she wouldn't be much fun, she knew that.

She listened to the litany of ways Florrie had been let down. Sometimes violent, sometimes emotional. Often, Florrie ended her stories wistfully: 'My papa promised he would come and get me one day.'

Clara knew – from her experiences with Rita and Gladys – that these things could happen, but she also knew it was unlikely. Hope might be a wonderful balm, but it could make a wound even worse if it was based on a falsehood. And some-times even when family members came back it didn't work out – Clara remembered Evelyn's poor mother and Terry's awful grandmother, and worse, Peter's uncle, and shivered.

'What was your papa like?' she asked.

Smiling, Florrie remembered a handsome man in a Lombard hat, a cigar. 'He is younger than the other dads,' she said. 'Smarter too.'

Clara wondered if she was confusing him with someone from a film, an actor maybe, but Florrie's description never wavered: 'He couldn't take me in because he was married, see,' she repeated, 'but as soon as he divorced his wife, he would come and get me. He said that, he told me that.'

The first time, Clara had asked Miss Webb if this was in any of the files at the council and Miss Webb swore there was no such thing. But perhaps she had changed her position slightly because, the next time Clara asked, Miss Webb didn't suggest Florrie was lying or that it was imaginary. Instead, she said she'd see what she could find out and for the first time, Clara believed she actually would.

31

Once again, Clara was beginning to hope that whoever was orchestrating the attacks on the orphanage had given up. Maybe the sight of defenceless Patricia out in the rain had caused a change of heart?

That seemed to be the case, until one cold afternoon towards the end of January. Clara was walking the girls to Anita's house when Mrs Garrard rushed out of the flower shop, closely followed by Bertie the dog. Bertie had got so fat, Ivor had taken to calling him a puff pastry on legs.

'I got a telephone order for ten lilies...'

Clara told the girls to walk ahead, she'd catch up in a moment.

Mrs Garrard was agitated. 'They insisted you ordered them, but I knew straight away there was something fishy going on.'

Clara swallowed. Peg and Gladys were skipping up the road. They looked so innocent.

'They said they were for a funeral at the home.'

This was so shocking that at first Clara didn't know what to say. It went beyond even the previous incidents; it was evil. All her relief that the pram had been moved to shelter now vanished.

'What did they sound like?'

Mrs Garrard said the voice was muffled, but she thought it was young and male.

Who could it be? wondered Clara. *And what were they planning to do next?*

Funeral flowers? She wasn't mistaken; that was sinister, wasn't it? Worse even than red paint on the lawn.

It felt like they were under siege.

After she dropped off the girls, Clara was still in a fretful mood when she saw Joe – Maureen's ex-love – walking the other way on the high road, a determined look on his face. Lavenham was a small town, and Clara would have imagined she'd see him often, but she hardly ever did.

They exchanged greetings. Joe looked older– he'd had to grow up fast, she thought. He used to be an honorary resident of the home, and Clara had been very fond of the lad – until he got another young woman pregnant.

'How's the baby?'

'His name is Vincent.'

'Aw, Vinnie,' said Clara automatically.

'Janet doesn't like Vinnie,' Joe corrected as though he explained that a lot.

Clara asked the appropriate questions: Vincent apparently was a good sleeper and smiley.

'You're lucky then,' she said, thinking of Patricia, who was neither of those things.

Joe bit his lip. It was clear he didn't feel lucky. Then he asked in a low, conspiratorial voice, 'How is Maureen doing?'

'She's well.' It wasn't Clara's place to say more. Maureen was busy with college, she was rebuilding her life. Clara crossed her fingers and hoped Joe wouldn't get into Maureen's heart again. The last thing Maureen needed was more complications.

Joe nodded like he understood and as though he regretted giving in to the temptation to ask.

'I was going to send her some flowers for her birthday,' he said.

Flowers? Clara's mind whirled. *White lilies?*

But what would Joe's motive be? she pondered. She couldn't think of any, but she was feeling that suspicious, had she bumped into the Prime Minister she probably would have interrogated him.

'Do you ever come to the home, Joe, I mean in our garden? Have you ever seen anything strange?'

He looked at her like she was a madwoman. Which was how she felt.

'No...'

'You never saw our bikes, or tomatoes or anything?'

'Uh no, I didn't,' he said. 'Why?'

'Just wondering.' Clara had become a housemother with limited experience, and she always encouraged her children to try things out. It was at this moment that she realised not *all* jobs were for everyone. Detective, for example, was not for her.

That evening, Clara slipped off to tell Ivor to cancel their 'surprise' day out. She couldn't go away now, not with the attacks on the home. Although the children weren't aware of the extent of them, they mightn't feel comfortable without her. She certainly wouldn't be able to enjoy herself without them. Without her there to protect them, anything could happen.

'No surprise!' she said to him, 'But I'm sorry, I don't think I can go on our day out this weekend.'

Ivor was sympathetic at first: 'Who's ill now?'

'No one's ill this time.'

Was that annoyance that flickered across his face? She had noticed he was rubbing his arm quite a lot recently – perhaps he was in pain again. She should have at least brought something over, beer or cakes maybe, to soften the blow. Why did she never think of things like that? She was just thoughtless some-times. Other women did kind things so naturally.

'Is this just an excuse?' he asked.

He didn't trust her any more, he wouldn't have said that before.

'Of course not, I'm desperate to spend time with you,' she said.

And then she told him about the lilies – she didn't want to worry him – and he was furious. 'We have to find out who is doing this,' he said urgently, and of course he understood why she was cancelling, of course.

32

It was early February and Trevor, Frank and Gladys were getting ready (or rather, Clara was getting them ready) to go to live with the Mounts. Clara felt tearful as she packed each of their bags. It was emotional every time a child left, but this time felt worse because it was three – three at once! It was foolish though, because the Mounts were so lovely – she'd joked to Ivor that she'd like them to adopt her.

She packed Frank's collection of aeroplanes. There were an incredible nine now. Mr Mount was going to build him a model airport complete with runway. Then she packed Trevor's chess set. Although the missing bishop had been returned by Patricia, there was still a missing knight. Peg had lent him a shell to make up for it. She packed their Bibles and Trevor's had a bookmark in it, which made her feel melancholic: Trevor *had* tried, with an open mind – which was more than she had.

In the girls' room, she packed Gladys' flute, her encyclopaedia and her other bits and pieces. The three children hadn't been with Clara all that long, but they had made a massive indentation on her heart.

She told herself she should be glad they were going, especially now, especially when 'no one is trying to hurt you' seemed like a distant memory. Someone here in Lavenham did want to hurt them, or at least frighten them. Life would be safer elsewhere.

Even before the Mounts suggested they'd fill the pond in, she'd known they'd be perfect for the children. Mr Mount wanted to be a father, Mrs Mount wanted to be a mother. Everything else was just the icing on the cake.

At eight o'clock that night, Clara heard a rustling in the garden. A definite rustling, a disturbance. Her nerves on fire, she got the torch and looked for something to use as a weapon. She remembered suddenly those first few days of the war when they had expected Nazis to parachute into the city and everyone was going over the elaborate ways they would kill them – Judy would frying-pan them to death; no, not fry, batter them over the head, while Clara proposed an iron—

'As if you know what to do with an iron,' Judy had laughed.

Now, Clara picked up a kitchen knife, put it down and grabbed a wooden spoon instead. She swapped it for a chopping board, and decided on second thoughts to take both. And then she was off. This was where the attacks would end. No more funeral flowers or rocks through the window. This was it. She'd got them now.

The someone was trying to get in the shed. The cheek of it. The someone was a shadow, taller and broader than Clara. They didn't need to force the door; it was never locked. They were soon inside. Clara crept after them, regretting not having a knife. Her feet sank into the long grass. Finally, she slung open the shed door. She was ready for the confrontation. This was long overdue.

'Halt! Who goes there?'

That's what they said in the films.

She shone the torch around, her rage overcoming her fears. A figure backed against the wall, light in their face and the whites of their eyes – they were petrified.

'Evelyn! What on *earth* are you doing?'

'Hiding,' Evelyn whispered. 'Sorry, I didn't mean to bother you.'

Had Evelyn been the one attacking the home?

Nooo, it couldn't be her. It wasn't possible.

'Darling,' said Clara. She could feel the relief all over her body. She expelled long breaths. This was sweet Evelyn. Clara put the wooden spoon down on the top of the piano and it fell, making a plinky-plonk noise as it hit the keys. Steadying herself, she asked, 'Who are you hiding from?'

Evelyn didn't say anything.

'Let's go back in the house.'

As they crossed the lawn, Clara was trying to think what to do first – she had to communicate to the Cardews that Evelyn was safe, but at the same time she decided that Anita would have to wait while Clara tried to get to the bottom of what this was about.

Evelyn said she didn't want anything, but Clara made her some hot cocoa and set out the biscuit tin. She was quiet – as you'd expect – and on the verge of tears. Clara tried to think of her recent encounters with the girl, but could only recall her being enthusiastic: about knitting, about her musical instruments, about her new school, about Howard, about everything. Evelyn worked her way through her drink and the digestives and, as she chewed, one tear slid down her cheek, which she quickly, ashamedly wiped away.

'Are you going to tell me what's going on?' Clara coaxed.

'It's Mama Anita,' she said.

Clara knew Evelyn called Anita that, but it still sounded unusual. She said it like it was one word: *Ant-eater*.

'She wants me to become a doctor.'

Clara knew this. Anita had never disguised her naked ambition for Evelyn – she had sown the seeds of Evelyn's towering career long ago and had always hoped to nurture it.

'And?'

'And I don't think I do.'

Clara paused. She didn't want to get in trouble with Anita – after all, the other woman was her friend and she knew that while Anita could be thick-skinned and would laugh at herself over many things, the issue of parenting was a different matter. On bringing up her children, her skin was wafer-thin: you gave your opinion on this at your peril.

'It's not about her,' Evelyn said as though reading Clara's mind. 'It's me. I want to be a midwife.'

It seemed impossible that Anita wouldn't understand. But Evelyn went on: 'She wants me to be the first woman doctor in Suffolk – or the first dark-skinned female surgeon in London, or this or that...'

Clara sneezed. Stella had come in and Evelyn clutched her up, continuing into her furry head: 'Mama Anita wants me to change the world – but I just want to have a little quiet life.'

A little quiet life, considered Clara. On the one hand, if the children, the lovely children like Evelyn, didn't fight for their rights then mightn't it be the bad people who made all the decisions? But on the other hand, what was the point of fighting for your rights if you were denying yourself the right to be happy? And also, whoever said little quiet lives couldn't change the world too?

It felt like when she did her beloved personality tests in *Good Housekeeping* and the score came back between As and Bs. Clara was a fence-sitter – but then she knew she shouldn't see that as a negative, she could try to conciliate between the two.

And didn't Clara want a little quiet life helping young ones reach their potential? She of all people should be able to understand that Evelyn wanted a little quiet life delivering babies. Anita would have to accept this too.

And just as she was thinking this, it occurred to her that Evelyn's dreams were perhaps similar to Maureen's – and maybe she herself had to be more respectful of that too. (Only Maureen's training was blooming expensive!)

Evelyn agreed to go back home if Clara would talk to Anita. As it was so late, Clara whispered to Florrie that she was going out for a moment and to be alert. Florrie scowled and said, 'You smell of biscuits,' like that was a terrible thing.

Evelyn washed her face, pulled up her socks and rearranged the ribbons in her hair. She was so mature, it was like she was born wise. The Buddhists thought you were born and born again until you reached enlightenment, and Clara liked that. If she had to choose a religion, she might choose Buddhism. Or Judaism maybe. For the cakes.

The street was quiet except for their footsteps. A fox ran away. Evelyn was wearing a good-quality coat and beautiful leather boots. Clara took Evelyn's lovely warm hand like she used to – it was an automatic thing – and Evelyn said, 'Sometimes I like to pretend I'm not the odd one out.'

'Do you feel the odd one out with the Cardews?'

'Not always...'

Clara thought how brave Evelyn was around wasps, how gentle she was around babies. It hurt to think that she was struggling. Their footsteps echoed down the road, and she thought of how many times she had trodden this path with troubled children.

'Although to be fair, they're all pretty odd...' Evelyn laughed. 'That's why I like them.'

Clara laughed too.

'Sometimes,' Evelyn said and her small voice faltered, 'I dream that my dad comes from America to find me...'

Clara hesitated. 'Your dad died, darling. You know that.'

'Sometimes people come back though, don't they? Rita's mum – and your father did.'

'I never thought my father was dead,' Clara said quietly, although she supposed it may have appeared like she did. 'Your father died in the war, Evelyn, I'm sorry.'

They carried on walking. Click, clicking on the cobble-stones. The echo seemed to reverberate for miles.

'I love Dr Cardew though,' Evelyn said quietly. 'He is kind.'

Poor Anita – she was mortified when Clara turned up with Evelyn. She answered the door in a long dressing gown with a tassel belt. Clara had never seen her look so un-Anita-ish, and she didn't want to look directly into her cold-creamed face. Evelyn was sent up to her room to change into her nightclothes. Anita was acting composed but her fingers with all her rings on were shaking as she made tea.

'I thought she was in her room,' Anita told Clara. 'I honestly thought she had gone to bed.'

Dr Cardew was at a conference in London delivering a paper on contagious diseases. That was one good thing: Anita's humiliation need not be exposed – unless she wanted to share it.

'I think she felt she was letting you down.'

Anita looked at Clara and Clara could see the conflict etched on her face – her ambitions were strong, but her desire to support her adopted daughter won out.

Evelyn came back downstairs quietly. She was in a white cotton nightdress that went all the way to her toes, the collar lacy, her face serious. She looked like someone out of a Victorian melodrama.

'Evelyn,' Anita said. 'You could never let me down, you must know that.'

They hugged but there was a tension in Evelyn's straight-backed response.

'I don't want to be a doctor, Mama.'

'But...' To Anita's credit the 'but' did not flower into anything. 'I only want the best for you – I thought it was for the best,' she said softly.

'It isn't what I want.'

'Then I understand that.'

Clara knew that Anita wasn't pleased, though. She had had dreams for her Evelyn and it would take a while for her to read-just. Hopes weren't recalibrated overnight. Her heart was set on one thing, and to be told it was impossible meant she would feel its loss. She would grieve its failure to come to fruition – even if she didn't intend to. It would be hard. Anita was a woman who lived by force of will, and she expected others to live that way as well. It made her impatient, it made her less empathetic, but her love for Evelyn would override that.

Anita came over a few days later clutching a tin, and Clara understood it was her way of saying thank you.

It was a brown and white cake, and she sliced it as Clara made the tea: 'Evelyn's been trying to make this for a while, and finally ...success!'

Clara agreed it looked marvellous, although she was more interested in what Anita had concluded than the cake.

'Everything is against girls like her. I just wanted her to show the world, for her to be a triumph against adversity, to be an example or a story.'

'She doesn't want to be an example or a story.'

Anita picked at her cake slice. 'I know that now,' she said primly. 'This is marmorkuchen,' she went on. 'My mother used to make it at home before the war. I haven't wanted to eat it for a long time and then suddenly I did. Evelyn found the recipe.'

Clara picked it up. There was something familiar about it. 'Marmor? Is it what we call marble cake?'

'Maybe.'

The chocolate and the vanilla were mingled, together but each clearly itself, each swirling around each other, like brown land with white rivers running through it or white land with brown rivers running through it – hard to tell which. Or perhaps like her and Evelyn's fingers interlocking as they had been on the walk home. 'Beautiful,' she said.

'She is,' said Anita, misunderstanding. 'She really is.'

33

Sometimes Clara would pick up the telephone and no one would speak. She had tried to see if there was a pattern, and had worked out that these calls occurred mostly in the late evening and early on Sunday mornings. They made her disinclined to answer the telephone at those times.

So, the next Sunday morning when the telephone wouldn't stop ringing, she ignored it. Gladys, getting ready for 'last ever' Sunday School, came downstairs to pick up and Clara told her not to. Then Florrie asked what was going on.

'I'm ignoring it,' said Clara.

'I can see that,' Florrie said in a schoolmarm voice. 'Why?'

Clara decided it would be easier to face the caller than to explain it all to Florrie. She picked up the telephone.

A voice took a breath. 'It's me,' it whispered. Clara was no wiser, but she was running out of patience.

'Who IS this?' she snarled. 'Why don't you clear off—'

'Isabelle Mount.'

'Oh, Mrs Mount!' Clara trilled with relief. 'It's a terrible line.' She put her hand over the mouthpiece. 'Everything's fine, girls. Shoo-shoo.'

Despite Mrs Mount's insistence that Clara call her Isabelle, she couldn't. Mrs Mount was too gracious, too posh to be on first name terms. She was more upper-class than Julian's Margot.

Despite the extensive paperwork, Mrs Mount had taken to calling Clara for reassurance every few days. She was, she admitted, an anxious person. What would be their preferred first supper? She wanted to get books for their bedside tables, which ones should she choose? Curtains – what are their favourite colours?

'We'll see you at two o'clock. They'll be ready.'

There was a long pause, and then Mrs Mount squeaked. 'He's left.'

'Pardon?'

'Monty. He said he can't do it any more, he's gone.'

Mustn't panic, Clara told herself, once she'd put down the receiver. Last-minute nerves were a thing. She remembered the night she had stolen away from the home. Recently, she remembered it as the night she and Ivor got to know each other better, but it was more than that. It was the night she thought she couldn't cope. It was the night she was aware of the enormity of the task ahead of her – and didn't think she was up to it.

She tried to think of other adoptive parents who'd had wobbles. Victor – who took on Alex – had been reticent at first. Billy and Barry's aunt and uncle had held back for some months. And the woman who adopted Joyce had said, 'I drove into a lay-by and cried. I feared I was doing the wrong thing.' The woman didn't tell Clara that at the time – in fact, she was smiley – it was only afterwards she admitted it. 'Doesn't everyone?' Clara had said. 'It IS daunting. It's appropriate to feel daunted.'

All entirely reasonable.

It was a shame the Mounts weren't having these wobbles together, as a team; it was disappointing the wobbles weren't bringing them closer, but driving them apart – but Clara could forgive Monty this. Had he disclosed his doubts earlier, who knew how Isabelle Mount would have reacted? No, it would all come out in the wash.

So she told the children that it was a normal hold-up. Typical council, she said; they were easy to blame because usually it was their fault.

'This is what they are like,' she harumphed, and told Gladys that yes, she might unpack and practise her flute, as long as she put it back; Trevor could ask Dr Cardew for a game of chess 'but he will probably be too— okay, bye...'; and Frank could continue his plane's long and arduous journey through South America.

Funnily enough, it was Florrie who was the most aggrieved. She'd had her eye on Gladys' pillow, for some reason – they were all the same – and she complained that she'd already said her goodbyes.

'You can say them again, can't you?' Clara said impatiently, because Florrie could be trying. 'It's not like you can run out of words.'

'I suppose.'

Sometimes, Clara thought she should be commended for all the things she didn't say to the children. They got annoyed with her when she said the wrong thing, but they didn't know that she was like an iceberg, and up to 80 per cent of the possible wrong things she *wanted* to say were hidden or submerged.

'I can't wait until tomorrow,' Frank said later as she tucked him in.

'Oh yes hopefully,' said Clara, stomach dropping. 'Or maybe next week?' Kids are like elephants – they never forget.

'A. They've got everything a chap could want. And B. The planes will reach Antarctica.'

.   .   .

Mrs Mount was outside the house at quarter past eight the next morning.

'I hid behind some bushes until I saw the children had all left for school,' she wept, which was odd yet characteristically thoughtful of her. When Clara last saw her, her slim figure had looked modern; now she just looked starved. It didn't help that her face was washed out from crying, her eyebrows and eyelashes barely visible.

Reassurance, that's what Mrs Mount required. Clara had all her wobble-stories lined up; in fact, she'd written some down so she wouldn't forget them. She might even mention her own disastrous first night.

'He's stolen everything from me.'

Clara gasped as Mrs Mount clarified: 'Figuratively, not literally.'

Realising she might be in for a long morning, Clara got the best teapot out. Mrs Mount took a seat at the kitchen table, then buried her face in her hands and wailed, prompting Stella to bolt faster than she had for ages.

'Mrs Mount?'

'Oh, it's all such a cliché,' she moaned. 'It sounds like something from *Woman's Own*.'

Clara nudged the pile of her favourite magazine on the dresser out of Mrs Mount's eyeline, but the other woman was too overwrought to notice Clara's reading habits.

She continued in this vein for some time, suggesting great offences but not explaining what had actually happened. Finally, Clara put down her cup and interrupted.

'Mrs Mount, what on earth is going on?'

Mrs Mount looked up at her in bewilderment and then wept again. 'Isn't it obvious? He has been having a... thing.'

This didn't sound like a wobble.

'Are you certain?'

Mr Mount was attractive, there was something stylish about

the way he wore his mackintosh like a diplomat, but he had
seemed a family man, a devoted husband. And Mrs Mount was
adorable. No man could do better than her.

'Oh, I'm sure,' Mrs Mount snapped, suddenly alert, 'I
discovered them.'

She... discovered them? Like Stanley discovered Dr Living-
stone, I presume.

Part of Clara wanted to fall into a flaming pit of gory details;
a larger part of her most definitely did not. Discovered in
flagrante? She remembered the time she had made a discovery
of her own: Mrs Horton grappling with Mr Horton in her car
before they were married. Five minutes later and things could
have been – well, bleach in her eyes wouldn't have been
enough.

'That must have been awful.'

'I don't know what to do.'

Once again, Clara was spellbound by the disconnect
between the public image and the private life. The gap was
enormous.

The tea was too strong – she hadn't had her mind on it – but
Mrs Mount said it was the way she liked it. Even in the face of
such pain, she kept her manners.

'I always vowed I wouldn't put up with it anymore.'

Anymore? Oh God, so he wasn't a first-time offender
then?

That Clara might have a conflict of interest here seemed to
have escaped poor Mrs Mount. But for Clara, it was staring her
in the face. She was the housemother of the children Mrs
Mount was about to adopt. They'd passed all the checks. (The
nature of those checks seemed to vary from one officer to
another, but still...)

'It must have been a shock,' Clara said, and 'here's my handkerchief,' but she was determined to stay neutral.

Mrs Mount drank tea, ate biscuits like she hadn't eaten in

days – she probably hadn't – and gradually the heart-breaking sobs became less frequent.

'You won't tell anyone.'

'Who would I tell?' Actually, Clara reflected, she should inform the council – but no, there was no need to tell anyone yet.

'Perhaps I should forgive him?'

'I can understand...'

'It's the third time, Miss Newton. Three times, and this was so public. Everyone is laughing at me.'

Stay neutral like Switzerland, Clara reminded herself. *You are supposed to be good at staying on the fence. You did that with Evelyn. Do not steer her.* Steering would be wrong. And it could easily backfire. An old memory – she had tried to get her dearest friend Judy to leave the husband who beat her, but Judy sided with Arthur in the end.

'For the children's sake. What do you think? The house is ready. We're so ready – that's why I can't understand.'

'It's up to you,' said Clara.

Switzerland wasn't *that* neutral. It accepted loads of Nazi money and stolen artworks. And people were saying the Vatican wasn't neutral either.

Mrs Mount had a bogey on the end of her nose. Clara had to ignore that too, poor Mrs Mount.

'Maybe he's just doing it because he is afraid. It probably doesn't mean anything.'

How many ways are there to say 'it's up to you'? Clara pondered.

'I know you'll make the right decision,' she said, and then she decided to take the plunge, 'there, you have a...'

Nose wiped and blown, Mrs Mount collected herself. She apologised for taking up Clara's time – 'I shouldn't have come. It's private between a man and a woman. What happens in a marriage...'

'You have to do what you think is for the best. Not just for the children,' Clara said – wary that this was leading – 'but for you.'

At the same time, Clara now knew that the Mounts' house wasn't the paradise she had pictured. Forget the chess, the flying and the promised friendships, it might be a domestic war zone, and she knew better than many what that could be like. Did she want to send children there now?

But Mrs Mount was also thinking, and she had come to a different conclusion. She stood up and proudly announced, 'I will try to make it work.' It was as though she were talking to a hundred people instead of just Clara. Maybe in her head, she was. 'I forgive him.'

34

On the morning of the sixth, Clara woke early and started thinking about the chores of the day ahead. It was a Wednesday. Gladys, Frank and Trevor were supposed to have gone to the Mounts three days ago, but that was still up in the air as they all waited for Mr and Mrs Mount to come to their decision.

Maureen was going to meet Clara for a cup of tea on Liverpool Street and Clara was looking forward to it. Maureen hadn't visited the last few Sundays – Sunday School and church had put a temporary halt to their meetings.

Once Clara had washed the bedsheets, she walked through the kitchen. The wireless was on, but it was so quiet that Clara didn't believe her ears at first.

The King, who retired to rest last night in his usual health, passed peacefully away in his sleep early this morning.

Clara was so tense about possible threats that for a fleeting moment, the thought entered her head that this was another strange incident directed at her – but very quickly, she realised it wasn't.

She put her hand to her mouth. The King represented all that was great. He had stayed in London during the war –

during the Blitz. He wasn't one of those who wriggled out of it. He was one of the people. Clara had liked the King more than she liked his scoundrel brother, that was for sure. And she liked the way he had overcome his stutter.

Although her inclination was to have a good sob, Clara was already running late. At the station, she saw from Maureen's expression that she already knew, and Maureen threw her arms round her, which was unlike her. It was a good feeling to be hugged by Maureen and Clara savoured the moment.

'Big Joan heard it on the wireless, but we're not meant to have the wireless on when we're typing so we couldn't say anything. Isn't it awful?!'

The tea shop was abuzz with it. You could tell something was up as soon as they walked in. Some girls were sobbing into their aprons. The girl who came over to welcome them was red-eyed: 'You've heard the news?'

'Terrible,' muttered Clara and Maureen echoed her, 'So terrible!'

'Even our manager is in tears and she never cries,' the girl said, her face a mixture of excitement and fear.

They put the news on loud.

'Poor Princess Elizabeth,' said Maureen, echoing Clara's thoughts. Then she grabbed Clara's hands. 'I wonder how she feels.'

They ordered their tea and Clara looked at Maureen's pale face. 'Are you okay?'

'I sometimes dream about my dad dying. And when I wake up, I'm sad he's still alive.'

'Oh,' Clara said. 'Sometimes people grieve more if their relationship is tricky, they grieve what they didn't have.'

Maureen chomped on her teacake. 'I grieved all that a long time ago. My father is dead to me.'

The people on the table behind turned around and looked disapprovingly. Fortunately, Maureen was oblivious.

Clara thought about her own father. Had she been too hasty when she'd sent him away? How would she feel if he died now? she wondered. She would not feel indifferent, she was sure of it. She would feel distressed. She didn't feel like Maureen – her father wasn't dead to her. Maybe it was time to get in touch?

Everyone talked to everyone on the train home. It was like getting the tube during the Blitz. 'What a shock.' 'Poor Elizabeth.' As she walked down the road, Mrs Garrard, all in black including her pillbox hat, waved her over.

'Bumper week for flowers,' she said, then hastily rearranged her features. 'I mean, shocking news.'

'The poor princess...'

'Queen now.'

'Yes. Where is she?'

'Africa somewhere.'

'Kenya.'

'Gosh. So far from home.'

It had nothing to do with Clara, and yet it was monumental, and you could feel it was. Here was history knocking at their door again – it would take a heart of ice not to let it in.

Clara had to tear herself away from the wireless when she heard the children coming back from school. They already knew, and the noisy ones were full of questions, the quieter ones more subdued.

'It is sad,' Gladys said, trying to cuddle everyone.

'Gerroff!' yelped Trevor and Frank in unison.

'It's very sad,' Clara said. Now the shock was wearing off, she was feeling more and more upset. Poor King... Poor Prin— No, poor *Queen*.

It was a terrible time for change too. There had been so many changes recently – not just for the nation, but in her own life. Jobs, deaths, boyfriends, parents – and all the while the

King had been so steadfast and steady (unlike his scoundrel brother) and that's what they all wanted right now. A constant, something you didn't have to think about – like an old armchair or a faithful dog. The last thing they needed was the upheaval of a new reign, a new person on the throne. It wasn't that so many things would change – she could only think of coins and stamps when the children asked – but it was the change itself. She didn't feel strong enough or ready. It made her heart sink.

Queen, they would have a queen! And she was so young. Younger than Clara was! Clara thought taking on eight children was a shocker. The Queen was taking on the country!

'He was old, weren't he?' said Florrie.

'He wasn't *that* old,' corrected Clara. 'He was fifty-six.'

Florrie pulled a face as though anyone over twenty-five was expendable.

Frank's teacher had talked about it at afternoon registration. Frank explained to the others. 'It means A. There will be a queen. B. She will have to be coronated.'

Clara turned up the wireless loud so she could hear it while she washed the sheets.

Peg and Gladys had been told – or concluded – there'd be a party at the school when they put the crown on the Queen's head and were arguing over what they would go dressed up as. Gladys wanted to go as Mary – not Nativity Mary this time, but 'Mary who sat on a tuffet'.

Peg wanted to go as Bo-Peep but she didn't want to have lost her sheep and could she take shells instead?

Frank said he would go as a plane.

'A pilot, you mean?' said Clara.

'No. A Spitfire.' He ran around the room with his arms outstretched, making puttering noises.

'What will you go as, Trevor?' asked Gladys.

'We'll be living with the Mounts by then.' Trevor peered

suspiciously at Clara, who managed to make a non-committal sound.

Jonathon said his father and his grandfather would have been devastated by the King's death, and Clara patted his hand as his eyes filled with tears. She realised it was one of the first times he had volunteered any information about them, and she thought it might be progress.

That evening, she let the children stay up late to listen to the wireless too. They'd remember this: better than remembering they missed out. And also, it might help distract them from thinking about the Mounts and the adoption that might or might not be happening.

In the end, the decision about the children did not fall to Mrs Mount. Mr Mount decided he was not for turning. He was going to throw in his lot with the other woman. The moral of the story he had decided to take from the King's untimely death was 'Life's too short.'

That morning, Monty had marched through the newly decorated show home, voided the cupboards and emptied drawers. He had grabbed documentation to show that everything was in his name.

'He even,' sobbed Mrs Mount on the telephone (Clara was spending a lot of time on the telephone recently) 'took the leg of lamb I got for dinner with the Ballards on Sunday.'

He was 'deeply' in love with the other woman. Mrs Mount related, still in tears, 'oh and he apologised to you and Miss Webb for being such a bother.'

Bless her, Mrs Mount had done exactly what Clara would have told her not to do (had she the foresight!); she had squeezed the address out of him like toothpaste, then gone tearing to the other woman's house and begged her to let her Monty go.

'We have three children,' she told her on the doorstep. Satisfyingly, she told Clara, the doorstep looked like it hadn't been swept in ages. Which raised the question – *what must it look like inside?* Fastidious Mr Mount wouldn't like that!

The other woman had looked startled apparently, then said it was the first she'd heard of it, 'and anyway,' she had added, 'Monty is a free man.'

'Monty is a free man' was a sentence that provoked and enraged Mrs Mount even more than 'Life's too short'.

'He is *not* a free man,' she ranted to Clara numerous times. 'We were adopting children. Orphans! We were changing their lives. Look what he's done.'

Clara would never have suspected the large number of swear words Mrs Mount had in her vocabulary. If the children had heard any of those, they would probably have loved her even more.

Mrs Horton offered to tell the children that the adoption was off if Clara couldn't face it, but Clara decided that wasn't appropriate. It was her job. She had to do it.

She brought the three into the parlour.

'There's been a change in circumstances...'

'I've had six changes in circumstances. I'm used to them,' Trevor said philosophically. 'And I'm glad I'm staying on at school. I like my school.'

'And I love it here,' Gladys said fervently. 'As long as we're together.'

Clara gulped.

'It's all right. A. As long as you don't take my hat. Or B. Try and drown us,' Frank said, which gave Clara goosebumps.

'I'll do my best.'

Frank stretched his arm up in the air, flying his Spitfire as high as he could reach: 'Nyaaaaaaaaaaaaaaaaa, chocks away.'

Mrs Horton did however break the news to Miss Webb, who was so shaken by it that she had refused to come into the home at first. Said she'd been to church; she'd studied the Bible and she would forgive Mr Mount in time – but meanwhile, she was devastated.

It transpired that Miss Webb had had a few failures since she'd been at Suffolk Council. One adoption had fallen through – no one's fault, a family bereavement. Another was wavering because of a job loss. It was her unlucky year. She had pinned her hopes on the Mounts – and look where that had got them! The process was like pinning the tail on the donkey and sticking it in its eye.

'You never know,' Clara said, impressed with this analogy.

Clara would also never understand Mr Mount. Mrs Mount struck Clara as someone who didn't even need a guide on 'Keeping Your Husband Happy'. She would be following all the tips without any effort at all. She was probably an excellent cook, a dependable seamstress, kept a tidy home, and Clara didn't imagine her undergarments were all pink, but they were sure to be lovely. It was Mr Mount's loss. Fancy giving all that up for a roll in the hay with some girl from the office.

It was so good to have Ivor to confide in again though. They mulled it over in his workshop.

'People do odd things. Self-sabotage,' he said when she told him. She couldn't work out who he sounded like at first. And then she did. It was Dr Morgan the psychologist.

'It's like they feel they don't deserve happiness,' he added. 'I can understand it, can't you?'

A couple of nights later, Clara woke in the dead of night. She had had strange dreams about Patricia and her gavel pronouncing her guilty. GUILTY! And then her father throwing tomatoes and rocks at her, only it wasn't her father, it was someone else she couldn't make out. It was as though the person was on the tip of her tongue.

She remembered that Miss Cooper had left the council – breaking Mr Sommersby's heart in the process – and now worked in Parliament. Politics. Central government. Messy Miss Cooper. She remembered Mrs Mount mentioning a doorstep that hadn't been swept. She remembered Miss Cooper had met someone at work, but nothing had yet happened...

As soon as the children left for school, she called Mrs Mount. 'I know you told me before – but what does Mr Mount do exactly?'

'He can rot in hell for all I care,' came the reply. Clara made a non-committal sound and then Mrs Mount sighed. 'He works in Parliament.'

'And what's the name of the other woman?'

'Why do you want to know?'

'I just had an inkling...'

'It's not my secret to keep. Cressida. The woman's gone running to Mummy and Daddy apparently. Home-wrecker. Because of her—'

Clara gulped. 'I meant her surname?'

'Cooper, I think. Why?'

'No reason...'

Dammit. What a mess Mr Mount had made.

It seemed to Clara that people like he and Miss Cooper blithely made decisions based on lust that had huge wide-ranging repercussions for many other people for many years. It was a reminder that whatever she and Ivor decided, they had to proceed with the utmost caution.

35

It was spring and Lavenham looked particularly beautiful. There was a hanging basket contest in town and the shopfronts were charming and colourful. It felt almost like nothing bad could ever happen here. Clara remained wary though. She got new locks fitted on the front and the back doors and she had Anita's window man fit locks on some of the windows too. The offenders had never touched the inside of the house, but you never knew. She made certain that her emergency box and her first aid tin were replenished.

She did keep wondering who it was: her father, Ruby, Clifford, the potato-faced boy, Davey... All could have been the culprit but none of them seemed to fit exactly. Then she decided it could have been a combination of them, but that didn't ring true either.

Clara and Ivor never did get their surprise day trip. Under the circumstances, Clara was still reluctant to leave the children. However, she felt she was, slowly, regaining Ivor's trust. She looked after Patricia twice, and both times Patricia seemed to enjoy her time with her (and neither time did Clara forget her in the garden).

Jonathon was her unhappiest child at the home, but even with him there were occasional glimmers of light. He liked hanging out the washing; he said he enjoyed seeing everything drying on the line. When Clara saw the washing, she just saw another burden – it was one of the worst aspects of her job – so to have Jonathon volunteer was quite something.

Despite their setback, Gladys, Frank and Trevor continued to prosper, and Clara took pride in that. Trevor was playing chess for his school, Frank made friends faster than anyone and sweet Gladys lit up a room. They had got over the Mounts quicker than Clara would have suspected. She supposed they were used to being let down.

Clara continued to strengthen her bond with Florrie and to be a sounding board or a shoulder for her to cry on. Books provided a useful way into Florrie's head. One evening, they were reading *North and South* by Elizabeth Gaskell and talking about Margaret's attraction to mill-owner John Thornton.

'There is someone I like,' Florrie began enigmatically.

Would a romantic interest help? Clara wondered, or make things worse? Perhaps it depended if it was reciprocated or not.

'Can you guess who it is?' Florrie asked playfully.

The milkman's boy who went to Sunday School – he was a chirpy chap who loved his horse. This was too easy.

Florrie looked horrified. 'Not him!'

'Oh!' Clara mumbled, wrong-footed.

'Guess again.'

'I don't... How can I guess? Anyone I know?'

Florrie lifted her shoulders, her teeth over her lip. 'It's Jonathon.'

Jonathon?

'What?'

Florrie bristled and Clara regretted being transparent. 'He's like your brother,' Clara said quickly. 'You're both... you know.'

Florrie scowled. 'He is not. We're not related.'

'Yes, but...' Clara floundered. How could she put this? 'It's not the done thing.'

'Ivor and Ruby were together here, weren't they? They were married and Ruby is Patricia's mum.'

It was a stab in the heart. *Don't say anything*, Clara warned herself, although she wanted to know how Florrie knew about it.

Florrie seemed to remember herself. 'I know you and Ivor are together now but you're not even married, are you? They had a baby...'

'Patricia isn't Ivor's child.'

'He says that,' Florrie said darkly.

'If he says that, it's true,' snapped Clara. She could have lost her temper with Florrie then. She took a deep breath. She mustn't overreact. She thought how it must appear to the young girl. It must seem as though Ivor and Ruby were the real pair, and Clara was just some Johnny-come-lately. Not even married. Not even engaged.

'Is there anyone else who's caught your eye?'

'There is a man who works in the petrol station... I think his name is Joe.'

It felt like Clara was frantically steering a ship from an enormous iceberg. 'What's wrong with the milkman's boy again?'

Ivor promised to attend the Easter meeting of the Jane Taylor Society, but at the last minute he had to do some work. Clara didn't mind too much because Anita came, and it was always fun to listen to Anita's slightly off-kilter analysis of the world. Today, she was talking about the poor attendance of her choir members and Howard's genius: 'He takes after me of course, Dr Cardew can't hold a note.'

Mr Dowsett the librarian was behind a tower of books when

they arrived. 'Florrie might like this,' he said, handing her a slim paperback. 'There is a teenage protagonist who feels alienated from the world.'

'Terrific,' said Clara doubtfully, taking a chair.

Mr Dowsett took to the lectern at the front and began, as he usually did, with a poem. '"Contented John",' he said, with his usual enthusiasm.

> *If any one wronged him or treated him ill,*
> *Why, John was good-natured and sociable still;*
> *For he said that revenging the injury done*
> *Would be making two rogues when there need*
>   *be but one*

Anita had leant over Clara, smirking: 'Who does "Contented John" remind you of?'

'Who?'

'Ivor, of course...'

'Ha, ha,' said Clara scowling. 'Hardly.'

'She probably was in love with him too.'

'Jane Taylor never married,' explained Clara primly.

'Like someone else I know,' retorted Anita.

Some late arrivals were making a big noise in the back of the library when Mr Dowsett collapsed. For a moment – it could only have been three or four seconds, no more – there was a kind of collective stilling, a waiting, like the needle had been taken off the gramophone but still the record spun, a moment before the furore began. Then Anita was crouching on the floor next to him. 'Clara, get Dr Cardew,' she shouted. 'Go now. Tell him it's his heart.'

'And then the ambulance came,' Clara said, her eyes filling with tears again as she retold the tale to Ivor later that evening. 'Everything happened so quickly.'

Mr Dowsett was so grey and tired and looked so small on the stretcher.

'I'll come with you,' she had said; he looked lost and mumbled, 'What? Where to?'

And she had explained, 'They're taking you to the hospital.'

'No, think of your children.'

That was what he had said: think of your children.

'It must have been horrible.' Ivor rubbed her shoulders. 'He's recovering, Clara.'

She choked back a sob. She had missed the last Jane Taylor Society meeting in summer. Too busy, always too busy. And now her old friend was fighting for his life.

She had gone to the hospital though. Anita drove her, but waited in the car. Clara took violets because when she saw them in Mrs Garrard's shop she remembered how they both loved the Jane Taylor poem of that title.

She had the copy of *The Catcher in the Rye* in her bag that he'd lent her for Florrie. He was sat up in bed, his white beard merging into the white sheets and the white room, and he admired the purple petals of the violets and said they would brighten up the place.

'Clara, will this convince you to take over the Society? I'm not going to be around for ever.'

'You're not going anywhere,' she said, more confidently now she'd seen him, now that he was still making jokes and had some colour back in his parchment cheeks.

He laughed. 'I am getting older.'

'We're all getting older.'

'And Mrs Dowsett wants to do a little bit of sightseeing before I go. I've always promised her Ireland.'

He held her hand. She was surprised by how wrinkled his hand was, and its size – no bigger than a child's.

'There's not many who appreciate Jane Taylor as much as you and I do. You'd be a good ambassador for her.'

Now, with Ivor, she thought about her father, who was also – let's face it – getting older. He was older than the King and older than Mr Dowsett. She folded some paper into a grubby swan for Patricia, who stared at her doubtfully. Ivor was finishing a big order and concentrating hard, but he listened and then he said, 'Maybe your father has changed, people do. I have.'

'How?'

'In many ways.' He nudged his chin onto his shortened arm, then nodded over to Patricia. 'My life is full of things I would never have expected.'

He turned his dark eyes on her. 'Wonderful things.' It made her catch her breath.

'Do people ever have a fundamental turnaround though? He used to be so intolerant. Inflexible.'

She remembered her father lined up next to her in the church, the smell of boot polish, talking out of one side of his mouth as the organ played and while the vicar preached love and understanding. *Why can't you be like the other children, Clara? Why can't you just obey?*

'What about you?' Ivor said. 'You used to be a pen-pusher, you hated kids.'

'I still am a pen-pusher.' Clara was laughing though; she knew Ivor wasn't being totally serious. 'And I never hated kids – maybe that's just how you saw me.'

'And maybe intolerant and flexible is just how you see *him*?'

'Maybe.' She wondered if Ivor was hoping she'd change her mind about other things. 'I don't have time for him,' she said finally. Ivor didn't say anything. 'Although maybe I should give him a chance.'

'I don't know if it's giving him a chance – just listen to what he has to say.'

Clara kissed him. 'Why do you have to be so sensible?' She saw his expression change, just imperceptibly. He didn't like that. 'I mean so clever... I'll call him.'

'You will?'

'I owe him that – and myself too maybe.'

'So you're taking over the Jane Taylor Society?'

'I can't turn down Mr Dowsett, can I?' Clara said thoughtfully. 'He's been good to me. And I love Jane, of course.'

She was flattered to be asked, and she supposed she could make time if she wanted to. It was for the community, after all. It was important.

Ivor looked like he was going to say something, but then changed his mind.

36

On the telephone, Clara's father sounded cautious rather than grateful, but then he agreed he would come to visit.

'Oh, but you can't stay at the home,' Clara said. This of all things was important to clarify. She couldn't *possibly* live with the man. There was kind and there was being a doormat.

She heard him take a sharp intake of breath. She expected him to say, 'What will people say?' but what he said was: 'If you know anywhere I could stay, I would be indebted.'

He would come at the end of May; and by the middle of May, Clara was a bundle of nerves. Inviting him felt like a huge mistake, and she still hadn't found him somewhere to stay. He mustn't stay in the home. The hotels would be too expensive for more than a few days. And she didn't want him staying at Ivor's either.

It was Beryl who came to Clara's rescue. Her midnight-wandering tenant had died. She had lodgings that were basic but had everything he would need. Clara wasn't sure what to say at first. Beryl was such a character and her father was not, but basic lodgings with everything needed would do (especially since she had no alternative).

'I'm not sure if you'll get on,' Clara warned her. What would this chain-smoking hairdresser have in common with her near-teetotal, evangelical father?

Beryl said, 'As long as he doesn't wander around in his underpants, he'll be an improvement on the last one.'

'I can't promise that,' Clara said po-faced and Beryl roared.

When Clara said her father was a Capricorn or maybe Aquarius, she wasn't sure, Beryl said, 'The stars are aligned.'

This time Clara laughed too.

The day her father came, Clara told herself not to make a fuss, she didn't want him to expect something every time, but she made a sausage and onion casserole, which wasn't bad, although the dumplings were so salty she had to throw them away. Before he ate with the children, she introduced each individually to him – it was good for them to get practice in manners.

'Pell's an unusual name,' he said to Jonathon, who stared at his feet. Jonathon had been running again. When she asked him where he went, he always said nowhere. It was as though he were running from himself.

Her father was studying Jonathon's face. 'There was a Maurice Pell who won the Victoria Cross. One of the few to do so twice.'

'That was Jonathon's father,' Clara said uncertainly, as Jonathon had clammed up.

Clara's father seemed incredulous to have found this diamond in the rough. He shook Jonathon's hand again and again. It was almost as if he was hoping some magic would wear off on him.

'Good lineage, eh? What a legacy!'

'Father, what about the other children?' Clara prompted.

Gladys played the flute for him – she was quite the entertainer – and Peg offered to play the drums. (Frank had given up drums because – A. they're boring. and B. they're very boring.) Her father started playing chess with Trevor, then quickly had to admit Trevor was out of his league. He seemed surprised by this. Trevor asked him which piece he thought was the most powerful (he asked everyone), and Clara's father said definitely the bishop. Clara groaned but Trevor and her father proceeded to have an in-depth discussion about the Church. With Frank, her father talked planes and trains and later, when Peg drew him one of her new religious scenes, he said how joyful it was that they were a Christian household.

After a couple of hours (and that was long enough), her father said he would head off back to Beryl's.

'What will people say?' he asked, hovering at the door.

'About what?'

'About my staying with the local hairdresser?'

'I imagine they'll say you'll get a good haircut there.'

Clara's father looked astonished but then he laughed loudly and for too long. 'I expect they will.'

By day three (even before day three) Clara's father was irritating her in all the ways he used to. He was critical, snobby, rigid; and yet at other times he tried to have a joke with her or the children.

One day, when Jonathon came in wearing a cap, her father put on a funny high voice and said, 'Hello, sailor!'

Jonathon was smiling but not as he put on his running shoes and ran away.

'What's eating him?' persisted her father.

Another time, he asked Clara out of the blue if she had 'the' nits. Then he laughed. 'Beryl told me you're partial to them.'

He told Florrie that if she smiled more, she'd be pretty. Florrie fluttered and didn't seem to mind, but Clara did.

And then Clara noticed that there had been no attacks on the home since he'd come. Coincidence? Yes, probably. Still, it was *something* she wrote it in her files.

On Sunday, the children trotted off to Sunday School and her father went to the church while Clara stayed home. She told him she was sick. There was no way she was going to sit in church with her father, absolutely no way. Church had been the source and the place of their most vicious battles. Didn't he remember?

'Vicar is soft,' he decided when he returned. 'Soft' was a favourite insult. 'Wouldn't have gone down with my lot.'

'He's popular,' Clara said defiantly (even though this was something she cared about not one iota), but whereas when she was young her father would have argued or dismissed her, instead he responded mildly, 'I will take your word for it.'

I will take your word for it? Did anything encapsulate his turnaround better than this one phrase?

One afternoon, when her father had been in Lavenham for about two weeks, Mrs Horton came bearing fruit cake and she acted formally and so did Clara's father. It was funny to see them together, these two who, in their individual ways, were such influences on her life.

Mrs Horton told stories about her mother-in-law: she was one of twelve children and was a nurse in France in World War One. Clara's father said that he was brought up by his grandparents after his mother died of cholera and his father was killed in the Boer War.

'I never knew that,' Clara said.

'I never spoke about it,' he said. 'I wasn't allowed to as a boy so old habits...'

'What were they like?' she asked although she had a sinking feeling she already knew.

He shook his head as though he didn't want to remember. 'It was a different time.'

Mrs Horton and her father also talked about cheese. Clara

learned that her father hated a blue cheese but was partial to a Red Leicester.

In contrast to his critiquing of Clara's offerings, Clara's father's praise for the fruit cake was fulsome. Clara left the room to clear up and when she came back, Mrs Horton touched her arm.

'Your father wondered if he could take the boys to the play-ground some day?'

It was like they spoke a different language and needed an interpreter. Clara would never have expected Mrs Horton to be the interpreter, and she wasn't sure she liked it. 'The one with the rusty swing or the proper park?'

Her father looked helplessly at Mrs Horton.

Mrs Horton spoke for him: 'I think your father will go wher-ever you recommend.'

Clara was feeling exasperated. 'Whatever he prefers... I doubt he's ever even been to a park before.'

Clara offered to do his washing, she may as well, she did so much anyway, but he said he'd do his own; there was a laun-derette near Beryl's.

'God knows, I should have learned sooner,' he said, a colour creeping over his cheeks. Clara looked away, determined not to feel sorry for him.

37

Walking down Shilling Street one afternoon in mid-June, Clara felt a thud on her back: first one, then two. Shots. Bullets.

Clara ducked down low. She was breathing loudly. She could hardly believe it. Back to then, 1940. She squatted. *What was happening?* The past was pressing in on her, so much past she could hardly fit it all in her mind.

She felt sick. Reaching around her back to feel for the damage, she felt a sticky revolting feeling in her fingers: blood – it had to be. Fearfully, she brought her hand round to take a look.

It was something clear, something translucent.

It was egg, Clara realised; she had been egged. Fury turned to indignation to humiliation. Who had done this? She could see no one, but wait, did she hear laughter there over by the cedar trees? And then a scuttle of movement. She heard a rustle from the hedgerow but still couldn't make out anyone. It could be animals. It could be unconnected. What would she say if she found them, anyway?

So, whoever it was, was back. Once again, it hadn't gone away; she'd been lulled into a false sense of security – like the

Phoney War – and it was back worse than ever. She was complacent and a fool.

There was something mortifying about this in particular though. She had been hit with eggs. It was not funny. She felt ashamed. Perhaps she would have told Ivor, but he was up and down to London and even when he wasn't busy, Patricia was there, swinging her mallet with her cool appraising Ruby-like eyes, and Clara still felt mortified that she'd left the child outside in the rain all by herself.

Her father was reading the newspaper at the kitchen table, which ruled him out. When she walked in, though, she knew instantly that she wouldn't tell him what had happened. The attacks were starting again, and her father was back, and she couldn't separate the two.

He looked up and said, 'Two of Beryl's customers said they know you – one is a teacher at the school, and another works in the greengrocer's. And they both said you are an asset to the town and a great role model for the children.'

'Why sound surprised?' Clara snapped.

He looked uncertain. 'I wasn't – I was just repeating it.' Then he stuck his face back into the world news.

Later, she said to him, 'What on earth were you doing sitting in Beryl's shop, talking to her customers?'

He shrugged. 'Beryl doesn't seem to mind.'

Clara wasn't a great role model for the children that evening. Or an asset to the town. Wash your hands. Brush your teeth. Some soup, Florrie? No, Trevor, I don't have time for chess; put the plane down, Frank, not in my face, I don't. Stop biting, Jonathon – you know what will happen. Yes, Gladys, I love you. STOP!

· · ·

About a week after the egging, there were no milk bottles on the doorstep. The milkman and his boy were usually as reliable as the Earth going round the sun. Even when his horse had laminitis. Even when his poor wife had a stillbirth, the milk had been there. So Clara knew it was odd.

When later she saw the milkman, she asked him if there'd been a problem on the round. He said he'd delivered her milk, absolutely, and his horse, a big chestnut mare, flared her nostrils at Clara as if to ask her what *her* problem was.

The next person she saw was Miss Fisher and she told her about the missing milk. Miss Fisher was slightly dismissive. On its own it sounded like nothing. 'There's been other things too,' Clara said, hoping to convey that there was indeed a pattern. 'In fact, I was egged in the street recently.'

'Egged?' Miss Fisher repeated as though she had heard incorrectly. 'Are you sure?'

Now Clara began to wonder if the attacks were perhaps a concerted effort for her to lose her mind. Someone wanted her carted off. Certainly, Miss Fisher was looking at her strangely.

That evening, Clara decided to ask the children. They could often think outside the box and come up with theories that would never occur to her.

'Do you have any idea who could be doing these strange things?' she asked them. And they didn't ask what – they knew exactly what strange things she was talking about. (She clearly hadn't hidden them as well as she'd hoped.)

Peg wrote 'chrimnals'. Which was true but did nothing to progress the investigation.

Trevor thought it was Nazis. 'Maybe they've buried treasure in our garden and they've come back for it.'

'Would Nazis steal our milk?'

'If they were thirsty, why not?'

Clara moved on to Frank – the most outside-the-box thinker she knew – 'What do you think, Frank?'

Frank thought it could be:

'A. Teachers.'

'Why teachers, Frank?'

'B. Because you haven't done your homework.'

On the other hand, it was sometimes hard to get a straight word out of Frank.

Florrie yawned and said she didn't give a toffee about any of it, she was more exercised by the bee that had the temerity to buzz around the light fittings, and she went off to read *The Strange Case of Dr Jekyll and Mr Hyde*.

'Any thoughts, Jonathon?'

Jonathon looked guilty, but then he always did; it was the set of his features, the way the shadows fell. He put his fingers to his lips, then, remembering, put his hand back in his pocket.

'It might be...'

'Who?'

His shoulders were up. 'Someone who doesn't like us?'

Clara nodded encouragingly. 'Do you know anyone who doesn't like us?'

He shrugged. 'Most people, I guess. No one likes children in homes.'

At that, Clara thought her heart would break. 'How do you mean?' she asked softly.

'We're ne'er-do-wells, aren't we? We're good-for-nothings.'

'No,' Clara began, 'that's a terrible thing to say and says more about them than you,' but Jonathon wasn't listening. He was slipping on his Christmas plimsolls. The soles were already thin from wear. He was such a raggedy fella and looked younger than his age. She watched him leave, shut the front gate carefully behind him – because he was a good boy, a thoughtful boy – then he thundered away towards the pink sky.

· · ·

Mrs Horton was hardly any more informative. Over the telephone, she preferred to talk about Clara's father – 'he was nothing like I imagined' – and she was now firmly of the 'boys will be boys – this is just pranks' school of thought.

'Aren't pranks supposed to be funny?' Clara retorted.

But then a few days later, Mrs Horton dropped by the home with six warm scones – 'save some for your father' – and a new theory – actually, she explained sheepishly, it was Mr Horton's theory.

'Could it be a prospective parent that didn't work out?'

'How do you mean?'

'An adoptive parent who was scorned. Some of them get agitated when they are turned down, don't they? Could they be behind the attacks?'

Who had they scorned? wondered Clara. There were a few, not many. By the time the hopeful parents got to her they had usually gone through the council checks. (Clara would have liked to have said *fairly rigorous* checks, but she didn't think they were particularly.)

She remembered suddenly ex-resident Terry's grand-mother; she'd been turned down, but she was surely too infirm to do anything on this scale. Then there were the clowns who had wanted to take Peg – but they had eventually and happily adopted someone else. There was Peter's uncle...

'You don't think it could be James Clarke, do you?'

'He's still in jail,' said Mrs Horton. 'Not out for another six years.' She considered Judy's violent husband. He also was in prison; she was sure of it.

Now Clara thought about it, there were more enemies: Sister Eunice, the former housemother; Mrs Harrington, the former childcare officer; Star of Stage, screen and wireless– Donald Button; the officials involved in the Australia child migration project – but none of them disliked her that much, surely?

Goodness. Clara suddenly blushed. She hadn't realised she was so unpopular. She was the baddie! She was the dislikeable character in the B-movies who everyone wanted to get rid of. In fact, she had probably made more enemies in the three years she'd been at the home than she had made in her entire life up to then. (It was almost as though people don't like you when you advocate for the interests of children!)

If not an outsider, could it be an *insider*?

Certainly, the tricks had started *after* Florrie had come. But after Trevor and Frank came too. And then there was Jonathon.

'What about a birth parent then?' Mrs Horton was also floundering for ideas.

'A birth parent who didn't want to give a child up?'

'You'll have to go through the files again, Clara,' Mrs Horton said as she sliced the scones in half. 'You know what these would go with? Cheese.'

CHILDREN'S REPORT 17
Jonathon Ainsley Pell

Date of Birth: 1 September 1938

Family Background:

His father was one of Britain's most decorated war heroes, Maurice Pell. His grandfather was a commander in World War One. His grandfather took care of him – or he took care of his grandfather until his death.

Health/Appearance:

A slightly scruffy, pleasant-looking young man who looks younger than his years. A nail- (and finger-) biter, he must learn to stop.

Food:

Jonathon should probably eat more, particularly leafy vegetables.

Hobbies/Interests:

He goes running five or six times a week. No other interests.

Other:

Jonathon seems permanently sad.

38

The children broke up for the summer holidays and the shape of Clara's days changed once again. They became elongated and fat around the middle – lunchtime – and there was never enough food in the larder.

Jonathon ran every day and Clara worried about feeding him enough; he was all bones. And Florrie was eating slightly more now, which was a relief – more than a relief – but crikey, it was expensive too. Mrs Dorne organised a church summer school, which was helpful for keeping them occupied.

'Goodie, more lepers and pillars of salt,' Florrie said, but she went without fuss. Clara thought Florrie was developing a nice deadpan humour recently. And she sometimes went over to help Ivor with sewing as well.

Today, Clara's father was going to the department store in Bury. Beryl needed a lipstick; her father needed a tip for his cane. Clara felt the imperative for both had been exaggerated but he was out of her hair, which was good.

Clara sat in the garden with a bowl of cherries on her knees, enjoying a rare moment of peace. She picked up a cherry and ate around the stone. She could never manage to do it delicately. *Was there a way to do it delicately?* Some people could push the stone out with their tongue. She had to put her fingers in her mouth to fish it free. Which wasn't dainty or civilised at all. And then her fingers got cherry juice on them, which might run down her blouse or her skirt.

Clara was glad her father rented from Beryl since it meant he was near enough but not too near. There *was* something between them. Blood ties. Love-memory. Duty. Loyalty. Training. The way he washed up his plate in line with the children after tea was endearing. He didn't used to do that. The way the children, especially Peg, adored him.

One day, Clara saw him wandering down the high road by himself when he didn't know she was there, and she said to herself, 'That's my father,' and there was a treacle feeling in her stomach. He didn't kiss her, hug her or even say her name when he saw her, but she knew his expressions, and it was a smile – it was a tiny one, but it was a smile, and it was for her.

As always when she had a moment to herself, Clara's thoughts turned to Ivor. She had seen him today, with Patricia, and they had talked about a possible day out in the future.

It was over a year since Ivor had proposed to her and nothing much had changed. Thank goodness for that! He had accepted and adjusted. She shouldn't be surprised; he was a master at alterations after all. But yes, she had hurt him. He probably regretted asking her, but he had – and her response, her 'I don't know' hadn't gone away.

The thing was: she still didn't know.

How would she know?

What she knew was that she loved being at the home. Yes, the washing and the cooking were low points, but the emotional care, the responsibility and the actual looking after the children were her life. There was nothing like it in the world.

It seemed silly, but, just as Anita had this alive look about her around the Festival of Britain, Clara felt at the core of her that she was in the right place at the right time. Being house-mother was exactly where she ought to be.

How many people seek that feeling and never find it? It wasn't exactly happiness; no, it wasn't happiness – Clara got downright bad-tempered and miserable at times! – but it was that much underestimated state, contentment. She had a quiet certainty that she was doing something – doing something right for the world AND right for her.

How rarely did those two align?

And now Ivor was tempting her with something that was also right for her, it was also what she wanted – but it would take her away from what she had now.

He said marriage didn't have to change anything at the home and they'd find a way through, but she still couldn't see how, and she was terrified that her happiness with Ivor would be to the detriment of the children – children who'd suffered so much already. Children who deserved better. (Look at Mr Mount, she reminded herself, or indeed her own father – who would want to be like them?)

And yet, she adored Ivor and wanted to be with him. He was her friend, her partner and her love. It was a quandary that was unresolvable.

Miss Webb dropped by to give Clara her paperwork for prospective adopters – this time for Jonathon. Clara was relieved, for Miss Webb had been tempting her with them for some time. (It was like Clara was a donkey and she had all the carrots.) Miss Webb didn't stay long, she just asked Clara to read the papers as soon as possible and said that she enjoyed seeing Mr Newton at church: 'You must be so proud: all that missionary work!'

The prospective adopters were a military family who knew Jonathon's father and his grandfather. They had already brought up five young army officers! They could give Jonathon the support he needed to take over where his extraordinary father had left off. They talked about Sandhurst, discipline, marching and weapon training. They said they were excited to be involved in 'lighting the torch of one Pell to the next'.

Clara gulped. She felt exhausted just reading about them. She remembered Miss Webb once saying, *housemothers can't be the judge and jury, Miss Newton*, but Clara also knew that she mustn't let that stop her making her opinion heard.

These people could not have been less suitable for shy, nail-chewing Jonathon if they'd tried.

Her father was back and at the door, ranting about a hat: 'I left it on the garden gate, and it's gone!'

Clara called in the children but none of them had seen anything. Nothing strange had happened for a while – not since the egging – and as always when it went quiet, she hoped the incidents were over for good.

No such luck.

Unsurprisingly, her father was agitated.

'I liked that hat,' he said, sitting at the kitchen table looking dejected.

'This sort of thing has been happening for a while, I'm afraid,' Clara explained tentatively.

'How do you mean?'

It occurred to her then that nobody knew about all the incidents. She had shared with Ivor, Anita, Miss Fisher and Mrs Horton, but each of them had heard only half-stories, bits and pieces. She was the only one who knew the whole extent of it.

'Uh, we've had problems like this for a while... I've even spoken to the police about it, but they didn't do anything.'

She gave him an outline of some of the attacks but again she found herself holding others back. For example, she did not tell her father about the egging (there was something about it that was just too humiliating) but she told him about the paint on the lawn. She also told him about the stolen milk – in fact she had run out, because yesterday's one was missing.

'I don't like the sound of this,' her father said as he drank his tea black. 'It's not on.'

And Clara was suddenly struck again that, for all her father's faults, she liked having him around.

There was no way she'd tell him that, though.

A few days later, Miss Webb called to ask Clara's thoughts on the prospective adopters for Jonathon. Clara screwed her courage to the sticking place and said: 'I don't think they're the right people.'

Miss Webb went quiet down the line as Clara braced herself to fight her case. But it wasn't necessary. For once, Miss Webb agreed.

39

There was a charity dance in the Cloth Hall. The Cardews were going. Anita said she hadn't had a chance to dress up for ages, although Clara thought that Anita dressed up every single day! Health permitting, Mr Dowsett was hoping to go – 'Don't forget you're taking over the Jane Taylor Society, Miss Newton, I'm counting on you...' Mr and Mrs Garrard were going; and no social occasion was complete without a Julian White: 'Save a dance for me, Clara.'

The Hortons were not going since it clashed with bowls, and Miss Fisher was not going because she had something with the church. She also said, wasn't Clara's father wonderful? 'He knows the Bible inside out,' which was reminiscent of Sister Grace's equally glowing verdict: 'He's such a God-fearing man, Clara, why didn't you tell me?'

All the praise for her father made Clara feel isolated somehow.

The children were excited about the dance too, even though they weren't going – Clara wasn't sure why.

Once again, Clara was wearing that dress Ivor had made – her favourite dress – with pearl earrings, and Beryl had styled –

or sculpted – her hair. While spraying in enough hairspray to repel local wildlife, Beryl surprised her by saying that she too was coming to the dance, and that Clara's father had *personally* invited her.

'Oh!' coughed Clara, unsure how to react to this news. Beryl and her father, at a dance together? 'I'll see you there.'

On the evening of the dance, Sister Grace came to mind the children and although Clara joked that it must have been in her contract to say, 'Oh, Miss Newton! You look divine!' every single time she saw her – a notion Sister Grace denied – it was always encouraging to hear.

Then Ivor knocked for her, looking impeccable in his suit for smart occasions, and it was a joy to walk down the street arm in arm with him like a regular courting couple (Patricia was with the Norwood Nanny, so Clara didn't have to think about her or Ruby at all).

She was keen to dance with Ivor. Davey's insinuation about dancing had hurt her but she wouldn't let him spoil it for her. She *did* used to like dancing. She *wasn't* showing off her pins.

'We've never danced together before,' she said to Ivor when they arrived.

'I'm not in the mood,' he said.

Clara laughed. She knew she'd be able to persuade him.

The band were The Beats, which made Clara apprehensive – she remembered sharing a flirty cigarette with the trumpeter at Mrs Horton's wedding – but then she realised with relief that the trumpeter wasn't the same man as last time. Musicians moved on as often as childcare officers.

Her father asked her to dance. Clara shrugged but then Ivor nudged her, 'go on,' so she had to acquiesce, and they waltzed around the room together. She didn't want to speak to him, not this close, and he didn't want to speak to her. It wasn't terrible but Clara was relieved to be returned to Ivor. 'I want to dance with *you*,' she said, fluttering her eyelashes a little. What else did he imagine the evening was for?

He looked her over, and she couldn't tell which he was: annoyed or impatient. 'I don't dance, Clara,' he said through gritted teeth.

'I've seen you dance with the children hundreds of times!' Peg on his toes, Alex hanging off his arms.

'Not in public,' he said shortly. 'Never.'

'But you can do anything,' she said girlishly. 'You're my hero, I know you can!' He never let his arm get in the way of – what? – holding a baby, keeping a business, riding a bicycle.

'I can't,' he snapped and she realised she had gone too far. She blinked back tears; why had she upset him? And she tried to pretend she was happy.

Then Julian had to ask her to dance, and she refused, but again Ivor said, 'Go,' in a weary voice, which put her in a difficult position. She got up and the first thing Julian said as he held her was, 'Trouble in paradise?' and she snapped back, 'None of your beeswax,' before he twirled her around, reminding her what a good dancer he was, but it didn't matter any more. She wanted to be back with Ivor, dancing or not.

When Julian deposited her at their table (sour-faced Margot was waiting her turn), Beryl and Ivor had gone to the bar, leaving just her and her father, and he was sozzled. He wasn't used to champagne, certainly not free champagne. Mind you, neither was she. She was tightly wound – petrified that she might have hurt Ivor again and that dancing with Julian had made everything worse.

'You look like your mother,' her father said suddenly and, Clara thought, inappropriately. 'Specially when you're...' He gestured at her clothes. 'Dressed up.'

Now her fury was directed towards him. 'Didn't Mother want to come back from Africa?'

He raised his champagne glass to his mouth, then set it down. 'She did.'

'Then why...?'

'I didn't think she was dying.' Her father was next to her but from his expression he was far away, in Africa in a small airless hut, her mother on a straw bed, turning from side to side.

To see an old man weep is a disturbing thing but Clara was unmoved. How could he not have known? Everyone knew. She wondered if her heart was made of ice. '*She* knew she was,' Clara said. Maybe it was spiteful. It was true though.

Her father's chin sank to his chest. 'I know and I'll never forgive myself.'

Beryl and Ivor had returned and were standing over them. You could smell Beryl's hairspray from Ipswich.

'What have you done, Clara?' Beryl snapped. 'Oh, Mr Newton! I knew disaster was in the stars.'

Clara's father blew his nose on a large handkerchief. 'I'll live,' he said bravely. 'Just winded by a memory.'

Beryl scowled at Clara. 'This is supposed to be a dance. A jolly night out. Stop going on about the past. We all make mistakes. Can't you see he's changed?'

Ivor put his hand on Clara's shoulder. 'You all right?'

Clara got up, grabbed her bag. Her father and Beryl could see their own way home.

Sister Grace was ready to go when Clara got back. Usually, Sister Grace would praise the children, but tonight she was grave: 'I don't want to worry you, Miss Newton, but the children are concerned.'

'Why? What's happened?'

'The strikes on the home. Gladys told me what's been going on, then the boys mentioned it, and even wee Peg wrote me a note saying how scared she was.'

Clara swallowed. She hadn't expected this. 'I see.'

'And then I found this.' Sister Grace led Clara outside by torchlight to the quieter side of the house. Someone had chalked 'Leave this town' on the pavement there.

Clara gazed at it in surprise. This was a new and nasty one. While the writing was somewhat childlike, the message was clear. Disaster in the stars. Whoever it was wanted them – or perhaps her – gone. It was an attempt to be menacing, she supposed, but she was still hurt by her father and upset about Ivor, so instead of feeling menaced, Clara felt even more furious.

She picked up a nub of chalk and wrote, 'YOU leave us alone'. It was satisfying.

Sister Grace watched, then wrapped Clara in a hug. As she made off, she said, 'Find out what this is about, Miss Newton. It's not fair on the children. And you don't know what they're planning next...'

INCIDENTS CONTINUED (chronological order)

Patricia's pram moved to shelter (a good thing!)??

Lilies ordered 'for a funeral'

Egged in street

Stolen milk

Father's hat stolen from the gate

Chalk message outside

40

The rain washed the chalk markings away before anyone saw them, and Clara's father didn't mention their argument at the dance again. It was as though that had been washed away too.

One afternoon a couple of days later, her father came to the home bursting with something to tell them. Clara was sweeping the floor and the children were laying the table for tea. Clara sniffed. Her father smelt of something or someone vaguely familiar, but she didn't know what.

'September the sixth...' he said.

'What about it?'

He raised his feet so Clara could sweep under them. There was something about this that stuck in her craw.

'A treat – for you and the boys. Frank will like it most. And you maybe, Jonathon.'

Jonathon was passing around the plates. When Clara's father looked at him, he shrank further into his shell, if that were possible. Gladys collected the cutlery and dished it out.

Her father was full of glee. 'Isn't anyone going to ask what it is?'

Jonathon always did his best. 'What is it, sir?'

'Farnborough Air Show.'

'Farnborough Air Show?' repeated Clara. 'That's over a hundred miles away.'

Her father looked annoyed. 'It's the closest and the best. We'll get there and back in a day – the children will love it. I've got five tickets. Who is with me?'

Jonathon shivered. 'I don't think—'

Her father poked his finger at him. 'Your father especially would have loved it.'

Jonathon left the room. His face was scarlet. Clara heard him pull on his plimsolls and then the slam of the front door.

'What's the matter with the boy?' Clara's father snapped.

Frank and Trevor were excited and this mollified him somewhat, until Frank suggested Gladys come. Gladys squealed and then asked quietly, 'What are you talking about?' When Clara explained, she wrinkled up her nose. 'I might if it were puppies.'

'No, it has to be Jonathon,' her father argued, and then softened his tone at Frank's scared look. 'Jonathon will get the most out of it. He's a Pell, isn't he?'

Worrying about a fly, Florrie pushed away her plate and stomped off. Clara was always concerned that she was back to her old not-eating ways again, but when she went up to see her, Florrie said that she was fine, she was just going to read.

'Do you want to come to the air show?' Clara asked. She didn't like the way her father had left the girls out.

'Nope,' Florrie said, her finger following the words on the page. It was *The Catcher in the Rye* – she said it was brilliant. And she had been chosen to do a reading at her school. 'Teacher said I'm one of the best readers now.'

At least Florrie was happier.

Back downstairs, her father said the tea was 'not bad at all, Clara,' while Peg got out the playing cards. They were happy too. It came to her – her father smelled of Beryl's cigarettes.

. . .

He left to go to his lodgings just after eight, but within a minute he came crashing back into the kitchen, looking as though he'd seen a ghost.

'My wheels are flat as pancakes.'

'Pancakes? Mmm,' said Trevor, who'd just eaten two bowls of soup *and* Mrs Horton's Battenberg cake.

Clara's father held out three shiny iron nails in the palm of his hand. The evidence. Gathering around him, the children stared in awe.

'Someone must have dropped them,' Gladys deduced. Clara watched as her father knelt down and gravely said, 'How careless.'

Then he looked at Clara over Gladys' head and in a low voice said, 'This is going to cost a fortune. This is criminal damage. You need to go to the police.'

'I already did,' Clara said faintly. 'It wasn't helpful.'

Although it was dark, Frank and Trevor went outside to look at the car tyres and to pick up nails; they seemed to think they were a gift. Her father said he would take a taxi back to his lodgings and get the tyres fixed the following morning.

'Who do you think it was?'

Whoever it was, Clara was fed up with it. It was a systematic campaign or a vendetta or something and it was exhausting. Could she rule her father out? Surely she could – it wasn't like he'd be doing these things against himself. Unless he wanted her to be grateful to him or something? Unless he wanted her to need him?

As they waited for the taxi, her father said gruffly, 'I can stay tonight if you like. If you're worried.'

Clara looked across at Ivor's workshop, shut up and uninviting. She wished he were there, but he was away again. He'd gone the day after the dance.

'No need.'

. . .

After she'd washed up, tidied and got everything ready for the next day, she went up to the girls' room. They were quietly reading. Whatever Sister Grace said, it wasn't clear if they were concerned about the things that had been happening or not.

In the boys' room, Johnathon was asleep, and Trevor and Frank didn't seem anxious either. They were playing aeroplanes and shooting all the people on the ground. And then suddenly Frank's plane was blown out of the sky. The plane whirred in his hands, made a circle in the air, once, twice, and then swooped, smashed into the ground, reared up again, until finally it met its resting place on a pair of pants.

41

On the evening before the air show, Jonathon was out running and Florrie was reading in her room. Her father was in the parlour with Peg, Gladys, Trevor and Frank and he was telling them a story. He was a good storyteller, making sure to combine elements that the children enjoyed: for Trevor a competition, for Frank a vehicle, often without a pilot or driver, for Peg a religious element and for Gladys a happy ever after.

Although it was almost three months now since he'd come back into her life, Clara was never not surprised to see him there, tucked up in her home like a part of the furniture. Something that also surprised her was the way he talked about her mother.

'She was tolerant of me,' he said. 'Even though I dragged her around the world. She was a good wife – I can't say I was a good husband.'

Clara was surprised at his softening or dissolving. She knew people changed – wasn't one of her basic philosophies that people *can* change? – but she hadn't expected this. His stiff upper lip had loosened – but would hers?

'We're all right here.' He waved her away. 'Why not go and see your young man?'

Clara liked that phrase, 'your young man', and she hadn't seen Ivor for a few days. It was kind of her father to notice. It was probably Beryl's influence, Clara thought, although she quickly dismissed the idea: Beryl and influence didn't sit well with her.

At the workshop, Ivor was pleased to see her. Patricia was fast asleep, apparently tired out after collecting acorns with the Norwood Nanny and baby Howard (Anita had asked them to stop calling him *baby* Howard but it was a hard habit to break).

Clara and Ivor kissed leaning next to the sewing machine.

'Have we got time?' Clara pulled his wrist round to see the face of his watch. 'It's been ages.'

'If you're sure you want to?'

'I always want to.'

He jumped up, then went to the back of the workshop, where he unclipped the end of the telescope. 'Right then.'

Clara walked over to him, smiling broadly. Enveloping her, he guided her to the eyepiece.

'Tell me what's what,' she said, although sometimes the sensation of him being close meant that, magnificent as they were, her mind would not stay on the stars.

'Concentrate,' he said softly – he knew her heart was wandering – and she laughed. 'I *am* trying.'

And he pointed out all those tiny white lights, those billions-of-years-old stars that Jane Taylor once peered at too.

'Do you think there's life on other planets?' he asked when they had done.

'Like little green men?'

'They don't have to be little green men.' He laughed. 'They could be big blue women...'

'I don't know.'

She lacked scientific curiosity about this, she knew. But

there was a reason for that – all the life she needed was here, in this room.

'I don't want to go tomorrow,' she admitted. Pulling away from her, Ivor looked at her worriedly.

'I thought you and your father were getting on better lately?'

'I suppose we are... It's not just that.'

It was the thought of aeroplanes. She had managed to get used to them in daily life – you had to – but to go to watch them roar overhead? To go and *admire* them? It seemed a bizarre thing to do for a day out. She could not get what Michael used to say out of her head: 'I'm not afraid of flying, I'm afraid of crashing.' It would be raking it all up again.

The sky could be so beautiful – Ivor showed her that. If only they could leave it be; there was no need to sully it.

Clara licked her lips. Ivor was still waiting for her to speak.

'It reminds me of...'

'What, Clara?'

'Oh, you know... the war.'

Dear God, it was nearly twelve years since the Blitz now, she should have recovered, everyone else had. She couldn't know for sure, but she would put good money on it that no one else was replaying it in their mind as often as she was. Sometimes, she felt she lived more in the past than in the present.

'I know it was a long time ago, I should have put it all behind me.'

'It's not that long,' he said. 'I've got things older that in my cool box.'

'That says more about your cool box than anything.' She smiled.

But then she was back there, in the Blitz, panic rising like steam, racing down to the shelters. Sometimes you went so fast, so automatically, that you'd get to the bottom, to the tube station, and you'd wonder just how you got there. You wouldn't remember your route. You couldn't recall another way of living. You became like a rat lurking on the tracks – obsessed with food or mating. Holding Judy's soft hands when they were both frightened out their minds. The memory of near-misses. The trauma of direct hits. The here today, gone tomorrow. The greengrocer who was too slow. The hysterical air raid warden, the tiny boy lost.

'You've never told me much about it,' he said.

There were too many things to cover. It had become a blurry, jostling mess in her mind. What about the night they found the hand? Was it the same night that the neighbour who popped back into her house for the boiled eggs from the stove – a pregnancy craving – had been crushed when her ceiling collapsed around her?

Sometimes, the day after, in the cold light of day – *wasn't that phrase appropriate?* – she would scour the newspapers. She wanted places and names. She wanted validation, or vindication, she wanted it known. But she didn't want to talk about it then. No one did. And she didn't know how to do it now.

'I know you don't want to hear about it,' she said.

'I think a lot about the war too,' he said. 'And I know many other people do – Dr Cardew. Anita. Mr Horton. You're not alone, Clara. I'm always happy to listen.'

She nodded.

'You don't have to go tomorrow, not if you feel it will be too hard.'

She was tired of herself suddenly. Why did she always have to bring the war up? It was like she took a peculiar pleasure in rummaging through the darker recesses of her past. She had to get over that. She sighed. 'I just sometimes feel like I've had all my new experiences already – like I've dealt out all my cards without... without meaning to and I've got nothing left in my hand.' She remembered when Gladys, Frank and Trevor had thought they were being adopted and were talking about everything being 'their last'. Their last bath, the last sleep, the last day at school. 'It feels as though everything is behind me.'

His dark eyes were so sad as he looked at her that she regretted being honest.

'But I'll go. I want to show the kids it's all right.'

'You've got plenty of cards left,' he said quietly. And she knew he was right about that. She had to learn to enjoy the present and look forward, but still. It was hard.

42

When she got back to the home the children were in bed, even Jonathon, and her father was washing his cup in the kitchen, his back hunched over. He turned round, startled to see her, and then he smiled. He always looked older than she imagined – she couldn't avoid the fact that he *was* getting older.

'Thank you.'

'What for?'

'The time with Ivor, it's tricky with the children.'

'I can imagine,' he said gruffly. 'It's nice you've found a special someone.' But he couldn't leave it there. He never could. 'I hear you're refusing to marry him. May I ask why?'

This was definitely from Beryl.

'I'm not refusing. There's no need to marry Ivor yet,' she said.

'He's a nice man.'

'You didn't think much of him at first.'

His exact words had been: 'There's something fishy about a man who sews.'

He paused as though there were lots of ways he could

respond to that, he just had to pick the best one. 'I've been wrong about many things.'

She nodded. If he thought that sufficed as an apology for all the years of horror and absence, then he was mistaken.

'So why aren't you getting married?'

Why did her father always have to spoil a nice moment? 'I just don't see why all relationships have to end up in the same place. It's just convention...' She paused. She remembered Florrie once saying, 'I just don't see why you have three meals a day. It's just convention,' and how that had annoyed her. Did she sound like Florrie? She hoped not. 'I'm not trying to be contrary. It's like – there are other directions to go. You don't have to go from A to B, you could go on a more circuitous route, say G to H.'

Cheerfully, her father said, 'Anyway, it's obvious he's a good man – you have my blessing.'

I don't want your blessing, she thought, insulted that he thought she might. 'I'm not interested in marrying – it doesn't suit some women.' She paused. 'My mother, for instance, would probably have been far happier if she hadn't been married to you. Certainly, she'd probably still be alive.'

Sore point. And yes, she had touched a nerve. His face turned bitter. That, that was the face she knew well.

'You need to grow up, Clara.'

There, the way he said her name, the way he always said her name, all lips and viciousness.

'Grow up? *I'm* not the one who went gallivanting around the world oblivious to everyone else.'

He stayed silent as she continued, 'I'm the one running a household of six here – some of these children are traumatised, let down by every adult they've ever known.'

'And I sympathise with that.'

She squared up to him. 'Why would I add to their suffering? I'm not going to be the one to put other things first – like you did. Whether it's church or my love life, I'm not. They deserve better. Let yourself out.'

She stormed self-righteously upstairs. Her father had had to go and ruin everything again. But she was mostly angry at herself – she was the ridiculous one for expecting anything different, hoping that he'd changed

Clara needed to calm down after the interaction with her father. He brought out the worst in her. And every time, every single time she thought they could get on, be civil, she found either that she couldn't or it involved such a superhuman effort that it was not worth it. Was she meant to forget the way he beat her and then kept her mother in Africa? Was she supposed to swallow all of that just for the sake of keeping the peace?

If there was a machine that could reconfigure your memory to block out all the bad bits, that would be really something. (No doubt they'd invent one, one day.) Would she want one? Yes, probably. Her bile was getting in the way of lots of things. She didn't want it to. How much better life would be if you could only hold on to the good stuff?

There was a sausage-shaped lump in her bed. Clara was in such a stew she didn't feel like dealing with little Peg; nevertheless, she put her arm round the girl and smoothed her hair. 'What's up, sweetheart?'

Peg shoved her notebook at Clara. Her thumb pointed to her writing: 'I am scard bout the nails.'

Clara looked at Peg's trimmed fingernails. And then her own – all the better for typing with. 'Why are you frightened about nails?'

'Who dun it?'

Ah, she meant the nails under the tyres.

On the next page, there was a drawing like Munch's *Scream*

but in stick fashion. Perhaps it was Peg, perhaps it was Clara. Whoever it was, was clearly petrified.

Peg stuck out her lower lip.

'I don't know who it is – but it's nothing for you to worry about, Peg. I'm going to sort it.'

Peg shook her head, then scribbled furiously: 'You must now.' She underlined it, twice for emphasis.

Clara told Peg to look away, and put on her nightgown. Then she sat and rubbed night cream into her face, giving her time to think of a response. 'It's probably just unhappy people. People who didn't have a good mum or dad and are trying to get attention.'

'Can I stay?' Peg wrote sleepily. 'Snug as a bug in a rug?'

'You know I have to be up early,' Clara whispered.

But Peg was still scribbling. 'What makes a good mum or dad?'

The first thought that occurred to Clara was how hard it must be for the girl to see other children go off to their permanent families, while she was always left behind. Miss Webb was trying to find her a match, but her non-speaking put off most prospective parents.

The second thing she was going to say was – the mum or dad who stays is good. But the longer she thought about it, the more Clara was glad she didn't say it.

Peg's mother hadn't stayed. Her own mother hadn't been able to stay. Maureen's hadn't been able to stay. Hadn't, couldn't, wasn't able to. The result was the same. Who was to say they weren't good?

Peg's hair was spread out on the pillow like a Spanish fan. Her breath smelled of milk. She had changed – from tiny skipping girl without teeth to confident and assertive, solid and smart; but she still didn't speak. Now, her eyelids flickered a few times and then closed. She still had a pencil in her fist.

'I don't know if that's the right question,' Clara mused.

'What makes a mother good? – Love, I suppose. But more than that...'

Peg had fallen asleep. Untucking the notepad and pencil from her clenched fingers, Clara was going to carry her back to her own bed, but then decided to let her sleep there – snug as a bug in a rug – instead.

Dear Mr Burnham,

This is my final word on the matter. I have no knowledge of any child by that name.

On a personal level, I sympathise. I hoped to have children, but it wasn't to be. Nowadays, I devote my days to improving the lives of other people's children and it's a choice I never regret.

I recommend that you also move on with your life. I can assure you that it is most likely that Phyllis is thriving and has no need for the upheaval that your reappearance would inevitably bring to her life.

Many thanks,

Mr P.P. Sommersby – Head of Children's Services.

43

They set off at half past five, when it was still dark. The boys slept leaning on each other in the back of the car and Clara dozed off in the passenger seat. She hadn't expected to feel this way, but it was nice to get away from the home and her worries sometimes.

Jonathon hadn't come though. He'd woken up with a sharp pain in his stomach.

'Have you been sick?'

'Yes,' he mumbled. He wouldn't meet her eye.

She couldn't have him feeling like that on a long and possibly bumpy car ride. 'You'll have to stay home,' she told him, and he staggered back to bed without complaint. If he were one of the younger ones, she might have stayed home to watch him, but Sister Grace was coming for a couple of hours in the morning and then Miss Fisher. She had a weird feeling he was lying about being poorly *and* that he had planned it in advance, but there wasn't time for a debate. Increasingly, she felt he had a secret. She had wondered briefly if it could be *that* secret – the incidents – but she had quickly dismissed that as unlikely.

They arrived in Farnborough just after nine. There were

signs for the air show everywhere. The organisers appeared to be in high spirits, some of them smoking cigars at the gates, another singing 'Danny Boy'. The skies were blue and cloud-free, which was just what you wanted, as Clara's father had explained several times. Clear visibility was the key to turning a good day into a great day. Neither of them mentioned the row. And when Clara had told him that Jonathon was poorly and wasn't coming, he didn't, as she had feared, get uppity or call him peculiar again. He just said, 'What a shame,' and then, 'Hope the lad feels better soon.'

It took her father ages to wind down his window and then to make small talk with the man taking the money and checking tickets. Her father did love his small talk nowadays, which was funny because Clara remembered him as an impatient man who wouldn't give anyone the time of day.

'You've come all the way from Suffolk?'

'Indeed. We have some excited children in the back,' her father said.

And the man looked in and waved. He had a moustache and tiny cat-teeth. 'Beautiful sky for it.'

'They're from an orphanage.'

For her father, to do good wasn't enough; he had to be *seen* to be doing good.

All the goodwill Clara had been starting to feel towards him was draining away again. He didn't realise, though; he was grinning as he drove.

'Why did you have to tell him that?'

Her father's mouth fell open, yet it felt staged somehow. 'Was it wrong?'

She stared straight ahead at the man gesturing them forward. There were cars either side of them all trying to line up straight, all careful not to get too close. 'Forget it.'

.   .   .

There were people lined up all along a barbed-wire fence and they found a small space and stood between them. The fence gave you a kind of honeycombed view. The children squeezed their noses through the gaps and Clara tutted, although she knew it was normal that they would – it was what they were there for.

She was still concerned about Jonathon but then decided she had done the right thing, although she expected that her father, for all his kind words, disagreed. She was wearing her respectable hat – the one she'd bought for the weekend in Hunstanton – and her father complimented her on it. That made her dislike it but it also made her laugh – she needed to stop being contrary. It was just a hat.

Frank and Trevor were bursting with excitement and also ravenous. She was glad they didn't need to go to the loo all the time – if ex-resident Denny were with them, she'd have seen more porcelain than planes. The brothers had better bladder control. When she said that, more to herself, her father said, 'And you say I speak too much!'

Clara had packed Scotch eggs and cucumber for lunch. The cucumber had gone mushy, and she wished she'd packed it differently, but she hadn't known how. Somehow mushy cucumber never seemed to feature in Anita or Mrs Horton's picnic lunches.

'Did they not eat breakfast?' asked her father, amazed at the boys' appetites. It was another thing that proved he didn't understand children. Had he forgotten how hungry a car journey can make a child?

She told the children to find somewhere to sit, but there wasn't any room. More people were flocking to the honey-combed fence. And then the planes were moving into position. There was a roar of noise. Frank was wearing his hat as usual, but she covered Trevor's ears until he brushed her hands away.

She thought Gladys would have enjoyed this. It still irritated her that her father hadn't invited the girls.

A pilot walked right in front of them, deep in conversation with two other men. He stood out: he was taller, he held himself with more confidence than the others. He was wearing a brown leather coat that came to his knees, with a furry collar and those aviator goggles over his cap, that always reminded her of a frog. The crowd started clapping and he grinned and saluted them. He was a peacock. He suddenly reminded Clara so much of Michael that it felt like someone was walking over her grave. It was inevitable, she supposed, that she would make the comparison. She remembered a conversation she had with Michael in a Lyons tea room in Leicester Square – they hadn't been together long.

'What's it like up there?' she had asked him.

'It's cold, it's noisy and your teeth shake.'

'Even yours?'

Had he nibbled her finger? Yes. They were sitting opposite each other, and he'd grabbed her hand and put it in his mouth as though it were a macaroon.

'Even mine. My head, my teeth, my legs, right down to the bones. It's marvellous.'

'What's the matter?' Clara's father interrupted her thoughts. She pulled herself together, head high.

'Nothing, why?'

'You look glum,' he said.

Her father didn't know anything about Michael. The huge gaping hole he had left in her heart on Christmas Eve 1944 wasn't visible to the outside world. Not unless she told them, anyway. And although it made her sad, it also meant Michael was just hers somehow, all hers. Michael was a private thing, a safe thing, like a photo in a locket or a lock of hair in a wallet. Their love affair was a story she didn't have to share.

'I'm worried about the attacks – you know, the nails, your hat.' If it was him, she'd get the definitive answer now, she told herself; he'd give it away.

He father looked her right in the eye. 'Hopefully it's just silly kids,' he said, and she was none the wiser.

While they waited, Clara's thoughts drifted to Ivor again. She knew that he was waiting for a decision soon. He never said it aloud, but his eyes did. He wanted that commitment from her and until then he wouldn't be satisfied, not truly. 'I don't know' wouldn't hold him in place for ever.

'We're all right as we are,' she had said. But 'all right'? All right wasn't special, was it? Didn't they deserve more than all right? 'Clara, I'm asking you to marry me – not abdicate,' he had said, but perhaps that was something they hadn't properly established. What exactly *was* he asking? Did he *want* her to be mother to Patricia? Clara liked the little girl now, but she still didn't feel herself around her. Sometimes when Stella stared at her with a hard expression of disapproval, it reminded her of Patricia. Although to be fair, Patricia did not make her sneeze. She couldn't tell Ivor this. If she did marry him, she would have to love Patricia, no doubt about it: she wasn't going to be like those nuns or those housemothers who didn't. She would not be the evil stepmother. She would not think about Ruby all day long.

Her father thought they should get married. Mrs Horton thought they should. Marilyn, Maureen and Anita thought they should, even Farmer Buckle probably did although she'd never asked. Ivor thought they should... And she thought they should too. What was stopping her?

She felt for her respectable hat – it was still there.

. . .

Nothing was happening yet. A few people clapped but it soon petered out. The planes were moved around. Clara queued for a telephone, debating whether or not to bother, but the people ahead of her were finishing quickly and she thought she may as well.

When he eventually picked up, Jonathon sounded chirpier.

'I'm feeling better,' he said.

It was a relief. 'You didn't want to come, did you?'

'Not... no,' he admitted. She could imagine his worried face, blood on his fingers.

What could she say to that? 'Okay, well, be a good boy.' As soon as she said it, she regretted it. Of all the children in the home, Jonathon didn't need to be reminded to behave. 'I mean, you don't have to be good. You're worthy, Jonathon. You are loved. Just as you are.'

There was a pause and then he said, 'Thank you,' in a quiet voice.

In that moment, she felt that it was imperative to connect him to the future. She wanted to join up today and tomorrow; that is, she wanted him to think about all his tomorrows. He had to see that the world was his oyster.

'Tomorrow, let's...' She floundered, looking at the queue that had formed behind her, 'do something nice.'

He had already hung up.

Holding his tin plane, Frank pointed to the sky. He had two favourite planes, a Spitfire and a Hurricane: the one Clara had given him and the one he'd been given in hospital by the Mounts.

The Mounts had disappeared from their lives. 'Easy come, easy go,' Miss Webb had sniffed disapprovingly. Despite Mrs

Mount's promise to stay in touch, Clara had guessed it would be too difficult. Poor Mrs Mount. It would be a constant reminder of what she'd lost.

There was a speaker on a table nearby giving a commentary, but it was fuzzy and unclear. Her father kept putting his finger in his ear and twisting it as though trying to tune himself in. Trevor was leaning on the honeycombed fence. Munching on mints, he was concentrating less on the planes and more on the crowd. Or perhaps he was going over chess moves.

The sky was beautiful. 'Day Six is a winner,' a man next to them said to his girlfriend. She fluttered then looked over at Clara, weighing her up.

An old woman sat on a deckchair and called Clara over: 'Any of the children fancy a Murray Mint?'

'Mince?' said Trevor, wrinkling up his nose. 'I've had enough mince to last a lifetime.'

Clara declined but Frank rushed beside her, panting like a puppy.

'I was here yesterday,' the old woman said, her breath spicy, 'My, you're in for a treat. Wings like monsters.'

Alex would have loved this, Clara thought. Terry and Denny would have too.

The first planes took off and soared overhead. The noise was loud and the old woman was laughing. 'See how they go!' she shouted over the roar. 'Bet you want to fly one, boys.'

Clara's father shouted back, 'I know I do!' and everyone laughed.

Frank did too, but he also wanted ice cream from the van. Clara huffed. Murray Mints, Scotch eggs... She had promised them ice cream, yes, but later in the day.

'Can't you wait until this afternoon?' She knew her father would disapprove but something made her push against that, so she said, 'Go on then, boys.' They were delighted. She wasn't usually a pushover. 'Be quick!' she urged them.

'Oh, I'll have a 99 then,' her father shouted, grinning at her. The planes had put him in a good mood. 'If you can't beat them...'

She watched Frank take the lead, then Trevor, pushing through the sea of people, and charging up to the van. She watched them hold out their coins, the copper glistening in the sunshine. She watched a woman with a net over her dyed brown hair like a spider's web lean out the van, her hand cupped around her ear.

So Clara was not watching the beautiful sky when it happened. She just heard the terrible, terrible noise. It was the same sound they used to hear during the war.

A cry of destruction.

It was the same, same, same, and time was frozen, yet time went so fast, and she was mouth-open in horror and then something slammed against her, crashing into her from the side, sending her flying. And the blue sky went black.

44

Clara dreamed that she was under the belly of a plane on fire and Michael was on fire, screaming to 'Get out!' Only it wasn't Michael, it was Ivor.

She was lying on the ground, and someone was leaning right over her, and she was under a coat that she sensed wasn't hers. She couldn't open her eyes, but she knew it didn't feel or smell like hers. For a silly moment, she thought of the attacks on the home: had this something to do with that?

And then she thought: *Where are the boys?*

When she managed to open her eyes, just a fraction, all she could see was smoke, like fog, a world of confusion but slowly she could make out someone's – her father's? – relieved face looming over her. She took in petrified eyes and she wanted to cry. The acrid air was making her eyes and throat sting. Where had their lovely day gone? She coughed repeatedly, trying to clear her throat. It was on fire. Everything was hotter than it had been.

'You're going to be okay,' the someone who was maybe her father said. 'Don't move.'

'Frank and Trevor?' she whispered. 'Find them.'

And then the man was gone and above her was only sky – the same sky as before but now not blue but swirling smoke. He'd told her to stay there but she was too hurt or too shocked – she wasn't sure which – to move anyway. She closed her eyes again. Where were the children? *Was* that her father?

Touching the side of her head, she realised her respectable hat had gone. It never worked out with that hat. Her fingers travelled across her scalp before reaching a point that was compellingly sticky. She thought of the eggs that landed on her coat once. She thought of the punch she had withstood at the potato boy's house in Ipswich. The meat she had put on her cheek. *I will ask someone for steak*, she told herself, and they will cart me off. Her eyes and throat were sandpaper-dry. Parched, that was the word. Slowly, she pulled her fingers around in front of her eyes to see them. Red, blood-red, but light red. She remembered from the Blitz – bright red not too bad. Superficial wound, that was it. As if it was a wound concerned about silk nightgowns and lipsticks rather than serious things.

Swallow your spit, she reminded herself, *that's what you do when your mouth is dry.*

She tried to keep her eyes open now. She would sit up in a minute, she promised herself. Jonathon was okay. Her Jonathon was safe at home. Clever Jonathon. What about Frank and Trevor? And her father?

She tried to get up but her head was too heavy, like it was a separate thing to her. Someone said, 'Stay there, lady,' and she realised there was a man lying next to her – so close to her, they were almost snug as a bug in a rug – and it was he who was talking to her. She was puzzled that she hadn't realised he was there. Was he the one who talked to her before or was that her father? She inclined her head to look at him. She didn't recognise him. He was about her father's age but not so dignified. He had blood over his eyebrow and forehead. Did she look as bad as he did? She recognised his scarf.

'They want us out the way.'

'I'm...' She pulled herself into a sitting position and felt dizzier. She was a slow-motion thing, like a puppet on a string.

'My children. One boy is wearing a hat. And the other one likes chess.'

She couldn't have lost them. She couldn't have taken them from that house of terror only to lose them. She couldn't have. She would never forgive herself. Gladys would never recover.

Darling Frank, A. the dead fish, B. loved being tickled.

Dear Trevor declaring, 'I'll always look after my family,' telling her about his chess victories: 'It makes me feel I have a purpose.'

Clara noticed she had a big gash on her leg too. Funny it wasn't until she saw it that the pain made itself apparent.

God, she would do anything to make sure they were all okay.

'Best to stay still,' the man said. 'She'll be back in a minute.'

'Who will?'

'Nurse.' He chuckled. 'She *says* she's a nurse.'

She could hear sirens. Air raid sirens. Thoughts of Judy.

'Ambulances,' he said.

'What happened?' she asked but he was no longer listening, he was trying to gesture to some people standing in a huddle nearby to come over. *Was it a bomb?* she asked herself.

Now she was upright, she could survey the area. Where there had been children and families and revellers and plane-spotters, there was now a canvas of emptiness, steel wreckage and a few people lying still and others treading around them. There was even a bloody deckchair. Where was the kind Murray Mint woman? And most importantly, where were her boys?

· · ·

Oh God, could it be – was that them? Yes! They were alive! They were safe! She saw Trevor leading Frank, his arm protectively over his shoulder, and she called out, and Trevor spotted her. They both looked shell-shocked. Unbelievably, Frank still had ice cream around his mouth and in his hair. Trevor was blinking and stuttering.

'Can we go home?' he whispered.

'Yes... You'll need to help me up though.'

Frank's eyes were glazed. He said, 'A. A plane fell out the sky and B. We couldn't find you anywhere.'

The nurse came back as they were tugging at Clara to stand. She introduced herself as Sister Marshall.

'Husband here?' she asked briskly.

'No, but my father is... somewhere.'

'You'll be all right.'

The nurse made Clara sit down again, then bandaged her head. She worked deftly on her, the product of years of training, then she lit a cigarette and passed it to her.

'Take that, calm your nerves.'

'A life-saver,' agreed Clara after a glorious puff, and Sister Marshall gave her two to save for later.

The boys were sat cross-legged, staring at her. She had to find her father. She got up again.

'I shouldn't let you go,' said Sister Marshall.

'My legs are fine, just wobbly,' Clara said. 'It's my ribs that hurt most.'

'They'll hurt for a while,' Sister Marshall said, 'but they'll mend.'

'My father is tall.' She showed with her hands. 'About this much taller than me.' She felt useless suddenly. She was like a giant slug after someone had poured salt on her. 'He's wearing a grey overcoat.' Or was he? 'And a shirt and trousers.' *Obviously he was wearing trousers.* Would he turn up at the air show in just his underpants?

'If he's not here, best go to the hospitals,' Sister Marshall said. She was sharing her cigarette with the lying-down man now. 'They took the worst-injured there.'

45

Clara would have to take a taxi. The thought of dragging herself and two bewildered children cross-country filled her with dismay. Plus, the expense. She didn't have that kind of money with her. There must be an alternative.

She saw a young blond man picking his way through the detritus. He was holding a notebook and had a camera round his neck. He appeared uninjured. She went over to him, and he winced at her, 'You want to get your head checked over, you do. Looks nasty.'

'I'm looking for my father.'

'Have you looked in that tent?' He pointed.

'What is it?' she asked.

'The dead.'

'No, he's not dead, I think I already saw him.'

He stared at her.

Suddenly the most tremendous noise filled the air. She winced. 'They're not flying again?'

Half of her wanted to scream – the other half wanted to applaud. They'd fallen but they'd got back on their bikes. Hadn't she always told the children that?

I'm not afraid of flying, I'm afraid of crashing.

She thought of the pilot. Perhaps he had a girlfriend or a wife who would be getting a telegram soon. A woman for whom life would never be the same. A woman for whom this would be her story – would be her *only* story, if she let it. (And it was hard, wasn't it, to not let it define you?)

Perhaps there was a mother about to be devastated. A mother, like Marilyn, who could never let herself be still anymore but whirred and whirred all over the place like a spinning top.

It took her breath away. Michael. It wasn't fair.

'Can I have your name and number?' She was shocked the man was still there. She came back to earth.

'What for?'

'Once you're all cleaned up, I'd like to take you out some time. Cheer you up.' The look he gave her made her squirm.

She shook her head. Jesus Christ, even here, even now. What was wrong with people?

Clara joined the queue for the telephone. When it was her turn, she tried the home, but no one answered. Then she tried the Cardews and it was such a relief to hear Anita's voice, and when Anita said, 'They're on their way, dear girl,' Clara almost cried. She inhaled on her cigarette for dear life, then blew smoke clouds, then coughed. Anita said that when Ivor heard about the plane crash on the wireless he had made his way straight to theirs. They had also been listening to the wireless – and they *had* heard about the plane crash, but they hadn't realised Clara and the children were there until Ivor told them.

Dr Cardew and Ivor had raced off in Dr Cardew's car, and Anita had thrown a couple of blankets into the boot 'for the poor souls'.

'I can't find my father.'

'It's going to be fine.'

'And Anita...?'

Thank goodness for Anita, she truly was the most brilliant friend.

'Yes?'

'Please make sure the children are...' Clara couldn't finish the sentence though, her voice was cracking.

'Of course,' Anita's voice came back clearly. 'Hang on, Clara.'

So Clara waited with the boys. But it was a different kind of waiting, knowing help was on its way. Her help, her people. Frank and Trevor were shivering, blue-lipped, and Frank said his teeth hurt – they always did under stress – but she managed to get them to drink hot sugary tea from the emergency tea station. Yes, it was just like in the war.

'It's going to be all right,' she told them over and over, and, when she explained it was an accident, no one was trying to hurt them, both made noises of relief. And still they waited. Time was rolling on and most of the spectators who could had gone home.

The sky turned pink and orange, still determined to be beautiful even today of all days. Clara and the boys watched the cars streaming out. There were only a small number of cars coming the other way. And then, at last, there was Dr Cardew's car with Ivor hanging out of the window.

Oh, the blessed sight of them.

'We're here, we've got you,' Ivor said.

Were there ever better words?

'I can't find my father,' she said. 'He's missing.'

But they had not come directly. They had taken a guess and he was in Farnborough Hospital, not too far away.

Oh God, she wanted to collapse again but this time with joy.

'I'll take the boys back and you can spend time with your father. Although you need to get looked at properly,' said Dr Cardew.

She and the boys got in the car. She leaned across Ivor's shoulder. She would say yes to him if he asked her again, of course she would. What kind of man raced cross-country to help her? A good man, that's what kind. The kind of man you married without a backward glance.

She couldn't wait to see her father. She would forgive him for everything – he had paid penance. She would tell him that she loved him. She had never said that to him before. And he would tell her the same. She had been wrong about love. She thought it had to be 100 per cent butterflies. In fact, it came with a side serving of irritation, obligation, and a large dollop of history.

She pictured him, bewildered in his hospital bed. How relieved he would be to see her. She might even let him come and stay at the home while he recuperated. No, of course she would! Miss Webb could see to it that it was all fine with the council. He couldn't go back to Beryl's, that was for sure. She would feed him stews, casseroles and the Red Leicester cheese he liked, until he was built up. This was their chance to start again.

They stopped at the hospital car park. There was a row of pigeons on a fence, eyeing them up. There were two ambulances there unloading people and some families walking out of the hospital in ragged, half-burnt clothes.

'You can go now. I'll be back soon,' she said, kissing Frank and Trevor on their foreheads. 'You've been brave.' But Ivor was getting out of the car too.

'I'll just see you in,' he said.

'No need.' She no longer felt light-headed, she felt cool and in command again.

'I want to. We need to get some idea of the situation.'

She wanted the boys safe at the home. Fed and watered. Up-skip into bed. It was getting darker. The stars were coming out. She remembered her mother used to say, 'Like my old man's teeth.' She would look after her father for her mother's sake. It seemed impossible that she wouldn't.

'What if they've moved him?' The thought had just occurred to her.

Ivor looked at her with that tender expression that she loved about him and said, 'Then we'll work something out.'

She had never loved him as much as she did then. 'Then we'll work something out.' Of course they would, they always would, because that's what they did. Clara would have thrown her arms round him and slathered him in kisses, but they had already reached the reception desk. A woman looked up, with a stern face, or was it a tired face? What a day she must have had. Clara smiled, hoping to disarm her, then remembered – she must look a fright herself.

Ivor spoke. 'We're here to see a Mr Newton. They told us he was here about thirty minutes ago – brought in from the air crash.'

The receptionist hesitated for just a moment, and then went clomping off. Clara watched her deep in conversation with another exhausted-looking woman. She heard this woman say, 'Newton, was it? We have his wallet,' and they both looked over at her. She sensed something but she didn't know what.

People are vague, Clara thought. She wondered if she might offer her paperwork support. Never underestimate the impact of good filing systems.

The receptionist pushed back her shoulders and then returned to the desk. She said she was looking in her notes. Her fingers were trembling. 'Augustus Newton. Is that him?'

Finally!

'That's him!'

'We had four in from the air show – I just want to check it's the right one,' the receptionist explained apologetically.

'Of course.'

'I have date of birth: twenty-eighth of December 1892.'

'Correct,' Clara said, more cheerful now things were being properly documented. She turned to Ivor. 'He was brought up by his grandparents. Quite sad, I think.'

The receptionist continued. 'His address is Beryl's Brushes.'

How incongruous that that was her father's current address. Clara could have laughed.

'Are you his next of kin?'

'I'm his daughter.'

'I'm sorry to have to tell you this, but he's gone.'

Sigh. Another mad goose chase. *Which hospital was he at now, then?*

'I've come all this way.' Clara thrummed her fingers on the desk. 'You could have kept him here. I don't want to go charging about the countryside tonight.'

The woman was looking at Ivor as though to say, *help me.*

'I'm sorry, there was nothing they could do.'

'Clara.'

She heard Ivor's voice, her favourite voice; it was in the distance. It was like she was spiralling off, ascending into the velvet sky to the twinkling age-old stars, and he was calling her back, tethering her to earth.

'CLA-RA.'

BBC NEWS

For five days, Britain and indeed the world turned to Farnborough, and we marvelled at what we saw and heard. As we looked at the latest aircraft that had swept Britain to the forefront of aviation we remembered the men behind the scenes, whose initiative and inspiration had created them on their drawing boards.

And we thought of the men who flew them first, like John Derry, test pilot of the de Havilland 110, but those who watched during the five days could never know the feelings of the men whose job it was to take an aircraft through the sound barrier again and again... and perhaps as we thrilled to their daring we almost forgot that on each and every flight death flew with them.

But those who were there on the sixth day would never forget. For it was on that day that a fault developed on Derry's black aircraft and he and his observer flew in another. The aircraft broke through the sound barrier and then flew low over the airfield. Now the split-second disaster in slow motion.

Far better not to show the harrowing scenes that followed. The heavy death toll is testimony to the tragedy. Almost at once Derry's friend Neville Duke flew a Hunter through the sound barrier again, flying like progress must not stop.

John Derry was an explorer in an unknown world whose barriers can only be penetrated by one such as he. Their courage and skills have won us great victories in the skies and they will go on.

46

Dark, regretful nights and days followed. Clara was in a lot of pain. She needed stitches in her chin and on her ear. She had broken ribs, which made breathing difficult – it felt like she was being knelt on by a giant. Ivor was in the background; her father was in the foreground. The children drifted in and out.

She looked terrible but somehow that felt appropriate because it reflected her inner turmoil. Her poor father. *Her poor father.* Thank goodness no one asked what his last words to her were, but she knew them, she couldn't stop replaying them.

Oh, I'll have a 99 then. If you can't beat them...

She had had to break it to the children. Not Frank and Trevor, who were already aware, but the others. Ivor suggested that he could do it, but she knew his sentiments on death: 'Remember before you were born? No? Exactly – it's just like that,' and she thought this required a more diplomatic touch. Peg and Gladys had grown especially fond of her father and they were vulnerable to feelings of abandonment. And then Miss Webb offered to do it, and Clara surprised herself by letting her. There was no point in soldiering on in distress, she should take help where it was offered. Hadn't Judy once admired her for that quality?

Miss Webb took the girls into the garden and they sat in the shade of the old oak tree. When they came back in some time later, they were both satisfied that Clara's father was in a much better place, heaven in fact, and he would be having a marvellous time – reunited with his loved ones – and looking down on them occasionally. 'But only when we're naughty,' Glady said.

Both looked slightly tear-stained and when Peg handed her a note, Clara took it nervously for what it might bring up – she didn't think she could cope with any penetrating questions – but it only read, 'Miss Webb promised us liqrish.'

Clara spoke to Florrie and Jonathon together. Florrie said she was sorry for Clara and talked about her own father and how she missed him. She still thought he was alive, clearly. Then she took off upstairs with *Brideshead Revisited*. Jonathon lingered, playing with his fingers, and then he said he was sorry he didn't go to the air show, perhaps if only he had been there... and Clara's heart ached. She told him, not at all. She insisted he was not to worry about that, *never* to worry about that, did he understand? It wasn't his fault. Finally, he nodded, slipped on his plimsolls and went out for a run. Clara slumped by the fireplace. She was too exhausted even to get up to light the fire.

Anita invited her into her pristine garden the next day and handed her a crocheted blanket to put over her knees. It was a pretty autumn afternoon and the sun was low in the sky.

Baby Howard was counting ladybirds on a rug.

'Now say it in French, Howard,' ordered Anita. '*Un, deux...*'

Howard set off in French.

'I'm not an invalid,' Clara protested, handing back the blanket, but Anita said shock was a horrible thing.

'I'm not in—' Clara began but Anita insisted.

If she was in shock, it hadn't affected her appetite, unfortunately. Clara couldn't resist two slices of Anita's hot-from-the-oven apple strudel with two cups of extra-sugary tea as Anita hovered around her.

'How do you always look so smart?' Clara asked her. Clara was avoiding mirrors but it was obvious she was a mess. Dr Cardew had said her ear might never look the same again. Ivor joked if it was good enough for van Gogh, then it was good enough for him.

Ivor. Her heart beat faster when she thought of him. Patient, stoical, evergreen Ivor.

'You don't look terrible, that's ridiculous, Clara,' said Anita firmly before adding, 'Although, why not see if Beryl has an appointment this week? And you know, you can always borrow anything of mine. I have clothes coming out of my—' She stopped abruptly, 'closet.'

Clara had seen a lot of Beryl recently. On the night of the air crash, she had been going to break the news to her on the telephone as one of many calls she had to make, but Ivor had asked Dr Cardew to take them there first, even before they went to the home.

When they told her, Beryl had screamed, said she always knew it, and that it must have been because of his rising sign.

Suddenly, Anita shot out of her chair. 'They're not for eating!' she shrieked. Howard was putting ladybird number *trois* to his mouth.

Clara couldn't stop laughing, especially at Howard's aggrieved expression.

'Wait till your father hears about this,' Anita said as she carried him wailing back into the house.

Clara went to Beryl's Brushes the next day. Although her ribs hurt, she was keen for normality. Beryl, still weeping, used a whole bottle of hairspray, so determined was she that Clara's hair would not let her down for the funeral. It was difficult to be told repeatedly that her father was a wonderful man; Clara chewed her lip.

Sometimes over these past few weeks he had been wonderful. Many times over the past few years he had not been wonderful. Not nearly. And yet her ability to process that confusion, to speak of all that, was over. She felt like a felled tree in a forest. She should have yelled about it when she had the chance. Made peace somehow.

'You did make peace with him,' Ivor insisted. He was good at propping her up.

Kind of, but not with myself, she thought. *Not with my past.* She hadn't reconciled herself to that.

Anita popped over later that afternoon with a vat of soup, because she knew Clara had been feeding the children a shambolic diet of crackers and ham and because she wanted to admire Clara's hair.

'It's highly flammable,' Clara warned her and pretended to preen.

'Good thing it's not a cremation then.'

They looked at each other and laughed.

'Ow,' Clara said, clutching her ribs. 'I wish it wasn't a church service.'

'You don't have to believe—' Anita started.

'I *don't* believe,' Clara interrupted her firmly.

Anita looked at her sympathetically. 'It's not my religion either. But you can still feel that people, that we, your family, your community, are holding you up.'

I don't, Clara thought. Church was her father's place, not hers. But she didn't say that.

. . .

The jowly-faced vicar strode up to the home, his robe flapping in time with his strides. There was something majestic about him from a distance, which dissolved when he was close up.

'Ah, Miss Newton, the irregular churchgoer. One minute she's there, the next she's gone.'

'That's me,' she admitted, flushing with embarrassment. She hadn't realised the vicar had noticed her skulking around.

His jowls reminded her of a boxer dog, although his sympathetic smile was like a Labrador. He must have been over sixty but there was something boyish about him. The glint in his eye maybe. Clara had heard he was a big sports fan. No one was allowed to disturb him when Northamptonshire were playing. He said cricket was how he knew there was a God.

'You don't seem keen on my services.'

She could lie but lying to a vicar – even a 'soft' one - was a step too far. 'It's not you. It's just not my thing, sorry.'

He shook his head pensively and the jowls jiggled. 'Fair enough. Why do you come then?'

Clara looked around her. *Did he not know?* 'The children go to the Sunday School, and they love it.'

'I'm not sure I follow?'

'So, I have to attend.'

She thought of Mrs Dorne's softly spoken words. *No attendee...*

He made a face. 'I don't know if that's right,' he said eventually.

'Oh.' Clara was startled. 'That's what I was led to understand.'

'We don't all have to believe the same thing, do we?'

'No.'

'For me, the Lord is apparent in every step, every breath every ball thrown and every hit of the bat, but I have enough empathy to understand that is not the same for everyone.'

'Ri-ight.' She shifted her weight from one side to another. *What was he saying here?*

'Forcing people is the worst thing. How can we be compassionate if we are more concerned about bums on seats than hearts and minds?'

She laughed. She couldn't help it. *The vicar said bums!*

'That you do go shows remarkable stoicism.'

'Thank you.'

'But how about if I release you from that burden and say the children and you are both welcome to attend, but without obligation or expectation?'

'Thank you...'

'Now, Miss Newton, could we perhaps retire to the garden to talk about the funeral?'

'It's chilly,' she said before remembering herself and adding, 'Of course.' She started to lead the way. 'Why the garden?'

Were trees another way he knew there was a God?

He mimed smoking a cigarette and she laughed in surprise. They sat side by side on the bench and he listened to her pain. As she spoke, she had a vision of baskets overflowing with water and he was holding them for her, he kept fetching infinite baskets when they overflowed.

She told him she had no idea what he should say. He asked gently if he had free rein and she thought of wild horses. She was relieved, she said yes. She didn't see how she could pretend things were perfect. She thought of the mother and the house she had lost; she didn't know where to put her feelings about that.

They went through three cigarettes each and when he got up to go, he said apologetically, 'I like cigarettes far too much.'

The Garrards had helped Clara decide which flowers to have, and they arranged them beautifully. Bertie Garrard was less professional. When Mr and Mrs Garrard were in the kitchen, the little dog had yapped at Stella until she sloped off, and then he'd left a deposit under the kitchen table. Clara thought there was a smell but she didn't realise what it was until Frank – it had to be Frank – stepped in it and squealed loud enough... To wake the dead.

The church was crowded. The first six pews on both sides were full. Clara shook her head, although her hair never moved. Her father couldn't have known all these people – it was impossible.

Ivor took the seat next to her on the front row, as she'd asked him to. He looked handsome in his smart suit and trilby. No Patricia – she was with baby Howard and the Norwood Nanny. Clara hadn't asked Ivor to arrange that but she was glad he had. And she was sat on the side that she could hold his hand.

'How are there so many people?'

'They came for you, Clara,' Ivor said and she felt this warm butterfly feeling in her stomach. *They came for her*.

The children took up two rows of pews. They were wearing school uniforms, which Florrie had complained about, but they didn't have enough smart clothes and it seemed the easiest option. She'd had to have another talk with Frank. He'd somehow got the wrong end of the stick and thought her father was going to be flushed down the lav. Clara couldn't work out why until she remembered the silly dead fish.

Maureen came, with dark roots showing through the bleach, her face serious. Big Joan and Little Joan sent their condolences. Clifford was there too, pulling at his collar. Ivor had somehow managed to get him time off from his reform school, got him on the train and helped kit him out. Clifford had been remarkably empathetic. He could be sensitive like that. He said, 'I'm sorry your father died,' and he didn't say 'passed on' or 'passed', which was a euphemism that Clara was increasingly hating.

She'd had telegrams from Billy and Barry. And one each

from Rita, Joyce and Terry and their families. Secretly, she had hoped for one from Peter – always her favourite boy – but none came. Instead, and it almost made her cry, her dear child turned up that morning with a sombre-looking Mabel, hugged her and said, 'I'll see you at church, Mum.'

'How did everyone find out?' Clara asked Mrs Horton, who was there with Mr Horton – and Mrs Horton senior, who kept loudly asking, 'Who died?'

'I keep in touch with most of them.' Mrs Horton blushed.

'I didn't know.'

Trevor wasn't there. He was representing Suffolk Schools in the Under-18 chess championships. There had been some question about whether he should go or not, but Clara had insisted. Of course he should go. She had asked Dr Cardew – if he wouldn't mind awfully – if he could go along to support him. After all, it was his fault Trevor played chess so competitively. Dr Cardew said it would be his pleasure.

There was the coffin. There were the Garrards' flowers. Clara could feel Ivor gripping her hand as though he was trying to stop her from floating away.

Her father's body was in that box.

The vicar spoke. 'I only knew Mr Newton for three months. Before he was in Lavenham, Mr Newton was travelling the world. Bringing Christianity to the natives. Hoping to civilise the uncivilised. A man who dreamed big. A man who – like Jesus – hoped to be a powerful vehicle for change. He even sold his property and most of his worldly possessions to give to children.'

Peg looked up, surprised. She scribbled in her notepad and nudged Clara's shoulder from behind. 'To us?'

Clara shook her head. She wouldn't be hurt – she wouldn't, not any more. 'No, Peg, not to us.'

'To other children?'

'Yes, Peg.'

'Why?'

Clara shut her eyes, whispered, 'Because he didn't know us then, Peg.'

The vicar was continuing: 'A religious man. A God-fearing man. A remarkable man. A man who made mistakes. He came to me and said he had made mistakes.'

At this point it felt to Clara like he was addressing her directly.

'He said he had taken his family for granted. He had taken his wife for granted. He had taken his daughter for granted. He wanted to mend those mistakes. Unfortunately, he didn't get the time. But the spirit was there. The compassion was there. He came to make amends, Lord. He came to make amends.'

Everyone said it was a lovely service, and, back at the home, everyone said it was a lovely spread. It was a hotchpotch, Clara told people, her face red, but it turned out fine. Anita had baked apple strudel, Evelyn had provided her now-famous marble cake, Mrs Horton had gone for two Victoria sponges and Julian and Margot had brought chocolates from Paris that looked not unlike Bertie's deposits but never mind.

Julian said Clara looked fantastic. When she demurred, he stepped closer to her: 'Sadness suits you.' Then he stepped back. 'Although what have you done to your ear?'

Julian hadn't brought Bandit, her favourite dog, who would have been by far the most welcome guest of the three, but he said Clara could come round for a cuddle next week. 'And—' he began hopefully, a glint in his eyes. She put a finger to her lips. 'No, Julian.'

He was incorrigible. *Rather Margot than me*, she thought. *That was one lucky escape.*

Mrs Garrard had brought flowers back to the house too, and now she went on a hunt to find jugs. She came in, shaking her head. She had found one in the boys' room with marbles and a sock in it, and one in the girls' room filled with shells and Peg's notes.

Everyone was having a good time, and why shouldn't they? Clara went around saying, 'We must celebrate his life, let's not be miserable.' She was telling it to herself though. Everyone else – except Beryl maybe, who was sitting in a corner rocking and taking Peter's cigarettes – appeared fine.

Her father was dead. Like King George VI – and that was where the similarities between the two ended.

Clara went out for some alone time in the garden. Her father loved this garden, she said to herself, which wasn't strictly true but he had said some nice things about it. She was just thinking of some of those things when she heard a noise from the shed. Evelyn was making sandwiches in the kitchen – it wasn't her this time. Heart in her boots – not attacks again, not today! She wouldn't be able to— Yanking open the door, she found Florrie and... Clifford! passionately entwined on the muddy shed floor. The boy had always been a ladies' man but this was ridiculous.

'What is going on here?' Clara bellowed.

'We were just talking,' said Clifford. It was shocking how easily the lies tripped off his tongue.

One teensy part of Clara admired how brazen they were. She and Ivor had been tiptoeing around for months trying to find some privacy – these two had known each other for five minutes and... boom! Nine-tenths of her was appalled and outraged. It was indecent: the timing, the location, everything about it – Clifford was the last thing Florrie needed.

Clara pulled Florrie up off the floor – she was lucky not to get clonked on the head with the rake – and pulled her into the house. 'Straight to your room. And stay there.' She did well not to roar.

Ivor was in a happy huddle with Mr Horton, Mr Garrard

and Mr Sommersby. They were drinking whisky, and had already quaffed plenty by the looks of things. Clara marched over to them and glared. Her sanguine mood had disappeared, all was bleak again. Her father was dead. *And they were knocking back the whisky?* 'You need to take Clifford back.'

As Ivor got up, he made a face as though she was being bossy. Clara wasn't having that!

'Now, please,' she insisted. 'Or I will not be responsible for what happens...'

Once she was sure Clifford and Ivor had gone, Clara went to make sure Florrie was still in the girls' room. She wouldn't put it past her to be running away to join the circus with Clifford. But Florrie was still there, combing her hair, a dreamy look on her face in the mirror.

'Sorry, Miss Newton,' she said. 'But love waits for no man.'

Good grief.

'He's more myself than I am,' added the reflection of Florrie.

'No,' snapped Clara. She was not entertaining delusions of Catherine and Heathcliff in her home, not today.

And then Trevor arrived home, euphoric because he'd won, he was Suffolk Schools champion, and he couldn't believe it.

'What do you want, a medal?' said his brother enviously, and Trevor was delighted to show him that yes, indeed, he had a medal, nurh-nurh. Frank tried to pull it off his neck and they started grappling and then it was Jonathon, surprisingly, who pulled them apart.

'Don't you realise this is Miss Newton's bad day?'

Clara snorted. 'Miss Newton's Bad Day' sounded like one of the (sadder) stories she read in *Good Housekeeping*.

'She's an orphan now like us,' he continued. And Clara smiled wanly at him. She wanted to say it was different, she was an adult, but she had a lump in her throat at his kindness.

The boys apologised and settled down at the cake table.

The other children weren't tired and after the guests had gone, waving best wishes into the night, they wanted to play Newmarket because – Gladys said it in a low voice – it was the game Mr Newton had liked best.

'I didn't know that.'

Clara would be hanging out the washing or roasting pota-toes and she would see that he and the children had been playing something, but he always got up when she came in.

'He was good at it,' Gladys said, in a voice much wiser than her years. 'He said it was all down to luck, but I think he had a secret way about him.'

'A secret way about him' was a good way of describing him.

Her father's lodgings at Beryl's had consisted of a simple, unremarkable room – smaller than she'd imagined. She remem-bered Beryl telling her that the basics were all there. Now she thought, *basics must be different for everyone* – there wasn't much here. The wallpaper was a mustard-yellow pattern and the curtains orange-checked. Beryl hovered by her, smoking as though her life depended on it. Clara had gone to 'clear it out' but there was hardly any clearing to be done either. His collec-tion of clothes, the Bible, and a bowl of bruised-looking apples. It looked forlorn and made her sad.

He was alive when he bought those apples, she thought to herself. It was obvious, but it was painful too.

'He travelled light,' Beryl said. 'That's courage,' she added firmly, exhaling.

'Is it?'

He was orphaned too, she thought. The image of her father, as a small boy, having to live with his grandparents and never speaking of his parents again, made her well up.

'I could do your hair again – it's only been a few days and

you look like you've been dragged through a fence backwards,'
Beryl said. 'That's not a compliment, Clara.'

'I didn't think...'

'And it doesn't reflect well on me,' Beryl added to hammer
the point home.

Clara swept through her father's wardrobe, his case, his
bedside table. Beryl asked her what she was looking for.

'I'll know it when I find it,' she said as Beryl lit up another
cigarette.

'I was fond of your father,' Beryl said gruffly.

Oh God, thought Clara. She had been determined not to
pry into the nature of their relationship. Landlady and lodger
did the job, thank you. This was worse than the idea of Clifford
and Florrie.

'And he was fond of me.'

Here it comes.

'We were a great comfort to each other.'

Clara's voice was high-pitched when she said, 'Thank you,
Beryl.' What she meant was: *Please, Beryl, I have enough on my
plate without this image.*

Beryl left her, shaking her head about jealous Leos—

'I'm not a Leo, Beryl!'

'Mean-spirited Scorpios then.'

She was looking for a photograph or a letter or something, a
memory of his life. A drawing by Peg, a picture of her. That's all
she hoped for – a sign that he loved her... But there was only the
book he had tried to give her that first time he visited: *Baby and
Child Care*. The book she had refused. One of the many snubs
she had subjected him to over the last few months.

For Clara, it was scribbled on the first page, *I'm sorry*.

47

One week later, and Clara still wasn't sleeping well. She was so tired that she didn't pay much attention when milk went missing again, and she was sure there were some more malicious calls. Another time she answered the front door steeling herself for something unpleasant, but it was the postman, and another time it was Trevor and Frank playing Knock Down Ginger.

'On your own home?' she asked incredulously. 'I don't think that's how it's done.'

She was no closer to finding out who was doing it. When she remembered that she had suspected her own father, she was suffused with a terrible shame. She hadn't been as good as she should have been.

But Ivor was just the right amount of sensitive, and Anita made cauliflower soup and Mrs Horton made seedy cake. Miss Webb was embroiled in a complicated situation with a foster parent who was excellent but for a gambling addiction, and Clara was pleased that it had nothing to do with her or the children and that it kept Miss Webb out of the way.

Mostly, all Clara could think about was how much she

missed her father. She had only just got him back and now he was gone. This seemed unbearably cruel.

She liked the book her father left her. The writer, Dr Spock, was one of the new types who believed in kissing and hugging. Until then Clara had been making things up with the children as she went along – largely by thinking nothing much more than how she would like to be treated – but now it felt like there was an actual science behind her theories. She understood why her father had left it to her, and she felt she understood him better too. He hadn't had it easy, she could see that now.

One morning, feeling slightly less shattered, she decided to go shopping. Anita and Beryl were right, she *was* letting herself go. She needed to pep herself up. Ivor had been accepting about her bloody ear, but there was a limit to these things. There were some handbags she'd seen recommended in *Good Housekeeping,* so she decided to treat herself to one, or some gloves maybe.

The department store had dark revolving doors that never failed to remind her of Ivor and their date last year. She wished he'd have come with her today – he might have if she'd asked. She squared her shoulders and made her way past the make-up girls, thinking maybe if Maureen did drop out from secretarial college, she might work somewhere like this. It was good to see the city coming back to life – rationing ending. Stockings and lipstick were back. It was funny how in the war years she was desperate to have them again, but now she'd grown so used to going without that she didn't have the same appetite for them as she once had.

She was browsing one cosmetics counter when she heard someone's voice from the perfume section: 'Clara, is that you? Michael's Clara?'

It was Nellie, Davey's Nellie.

Clara froze. There was no getting out of it. She didn't know whether or not to pretend she didn't know about the situation with Davey.

Nellie was pretty as a picture – looking no older than Clara remembered her – and was perched on a stool filing her nails. She usually had a hard expression like she expected you to cross her, but she was smiling, properly smiling, at Clara.

'Well, look who it isn't!'

'I didn't expect to see you here!' Clara said, which was true.

She couldn't not go over to the counter, so she did, and Nellie told her she'd been back home nearly six months now and 'America didn't work out for me, but it was all a terrific adventure' and 'My goodness, isn't this something? – meeting up after all these years.' And then in a low voice, she added, 'Help me, my supervisor is a dragon.'

Clara looked up and saw a hawk-eyed supervisor glaring in their direction.

While she wasn't looking, Nellie sprayed something on the inside of her wrist. 'There, that's French, that is.'

Clara felt overwhelmed as she picked up another and sprayed again.

'This one smells even more French, if you know what I mean.'

Each spray made Clara's wrist tingle.

'Sniff,' Nellie instructed. 'All the girls are wearing this one. It's youthful.'

Clara understood that Nellie's supervisor wouldn't allow her to have a normal conversation.

'Very youthful,' she agreed. Then whispered, 'And have you seen Davey since?'

'Nope, and I never want to see him again.'

The dragon supervisor had crept up behind her. 'Less gossiping, Nellie. You've been warned!'

Nellie smiled somewhat desperately at Clara and, once her supervisor had moved away, mouthed, 'Keep talking.'

'I'll take that one,' Clara said loudly, 'the large, yes, please. And...' she whispered, 'are you okay? It must be difficult starting again?'

Now Nellie looked grateful. She inserted the bottle into a box, explaining something about the stopper, and then she asked if Clara wanted it wrapped. Then in a lower voice, 'I was just happy to get away from there.'

It was that bad? And then Nellie told her the price of the perfume and that was shocking too but in a different way. It seemed outrageous to buy such a thing for herself.

'How about you?' Nellie said in a low voice. 'You never met anyone after Michael?'

'I *have* met someone,' Clara said, watching as Nellie expertly wrapped up the box.

'But no ring,' said Nellie, blunt as anything. She grinned at Clara's expression. 'Excuse me, I'm dreadful at noticing things like that. It's the first thing I look at.'

Clara looked at her fingers, which were bare – the way she liked them. For some reason, perhaps it was that she'd known Nellie a long time ago, or perhaps it was because she was unlikely to see her again, or perhaps she was dizzy with the perfume, but Clara felt she could confide in her, here among the Givenchy and the Chanel boxes.

'I'm nervous,' she said quietly.

'That's not a surprise, is it?' Now Nellie had her sale she was chirpier. 'Michael died when you were what – six months engaged?'

'Three...'

'I didn't know a couple more in love than you two. You were happy, weren't you? No wonder you're nervous.'

'I hadn't thought of it like that.'

'Not that you were engaged and he died? That hasn't crossed your mind at all?'

Clara shrugged.

Nellie fiddled with the wrapper. Then as her supervisor came back, she shoved her wrist under Clara's nose, insisting, 'It's good to have a spare. What do you think of this?'

'Mm, that's strong,' inhaled Clara hopelessly.

'It would be complimentary...'

The supervisor nodded sternly and passed.

'Thing is, Clara, it's not going to happen again. This fella you're keen on – is he in the RAF?'

'Ah, no...'

'What is he?'

'An upholsterer.'

Nellie burst out laughing. 'What? He covers settees...?'

Clara couldn't help feeling offended. 'He does lots of other things too, he's talented...'

'It's not exactly a high-risk occupation though, Clara. Not like being a fighter pilot in the war.'

Clara winced in embarrassment. 'I know that...' Was she afraid of losing Ivor? It had occurred to her, and presumably to him, that she had been happy enough to get engaged to Julian before, and of course to Michael. She told herself that her reticence with Ivor was because she was cautious about the children – all of them – the ones at the home and Patricia, and she didn't want to lose her vocation. And that was certainly true. But actually, wasn't it also because neither of the men before had threatened her emotional equilibrium as much as Ivor? It was Ivor who she rotated around: he was her world, the rest were just satellite moons of... which planet did Ivor say? Jupiter.

Meanwhile, Nellie had collected herself. 'And the other thing is Michael was a gentleman.' It was as though she was saying 'unlike Davey'. 'Which means – you've got taste in men.' She winked. 'Which means I bet this one is a good sort too.'

Clara felt exhausted again. How had she managed to over-complicate everything? It was like perfume. She did not like the spicy smells or the weird fragrances. She should know that something simple, something natural, would be more her.

'You're good at advice.'

'Any time,' Nellie said earnestly. 'I'm not just a pleasant smell.'

Clara laughed, before realising Nellie was being serious. She knew she had to ask something else: 'There's been a few nasty incidents at my home lately – you don't think Davey would do something like... like throw stones or trample on flowers or...'

She had imagined Nellie wouldn't waste an opportunity to bad-mouth Davey but in fact, as Clara hurriedly explained, she looked surprised. 'Oh no, that doesn't sound like Davey. I mean, if he did anything horrid, he would be the first to own up to it.'

Clara thought that was probably true.

'They were crazy times, weren't they?' Nellie's eyes were wistful as she handed over the package. 'I sometimes wonder how we all go round looking normal, knowing what we do.'

Clara went home having spent a large portion of her budget on a large bottle of a spicy perfume that she disliked and no handbag or gloves, which she had wanted. She decided to give the bottle to Florrie – never mind that she was so profligate it would probably last her no more than a week. Florrie was another one who could probably teach Clara something about living in the moment.

Later that afternoon, Clara sat out in the garden reading *Good Housekeeping* fiction. She wouldn't usually 'time-waste' but she was being gentle on herself. Her body still ached. It wouldn't do to get ill – or iller – and this was a sweet story about second chances.

There was a rustling in the tall trees at the back. Evelyn again? Was it Stella – no, she was inside – or a brave fox?

There was definitely someone there.

Suddenly, the someone fell from one of the higher branches in the tree. He yelped as he banged from one branch to the next, and then hit the ground on his side. And then another person appeared and yanked him up, shrieking, 'Come on!'

Aha. Caught red-handed! There was a fleeting glimpse of boys, a flash of legs in shorts, black boots.

She ran through the house and managed to intercept them as they made it to the front. There they were – two of them – grey pullovers and red caps chasing away down the street. They did not go as fast as they might, though: one of them – she supposed it was the one who'd fallen – was limping.

'Come back here!' she screeched after them. They attempted to go faster but the wounded one was making heavy work of it.

Vaguely aware she was making a spectacle of herself (but goodness, the time for worrying about that was long over), she bellowed, 'Stop right there!' She would catch the toerags, she would.

There was her bicycle. The bicycle that never got ridden. The bicycle with the decorative plant in the basket.

She gulped. She placed the plant on the ground and wheeled the bicycle to the road. The injured one was crying that he couldn't go faster and saying to the other, 'Go, leave me!' It reminded Clara of a war film she had seen recently. She hopped on to the saddle – the easy part. She could do one foot off the ground, then the other, but not at the same time. It was time to take a leap of faith. She remembered Dr Cardew saying just last week, 'The ribs are healing nicely but don't do anything stupid.'

Was this stupid?

Very.

Why had she never properly learned to cycle? Ivor had wanted her to! She held her breath and got on with one foot still on the ground. Pedal, for goodness' sake, pedal! And then she was off, pedalling down the high road, and she could hardly believe that by her feet alone – oh, and everything else – she was moving. The boys remained in view. If one of them wasn't wounded, she wouldn't have stood a chance, but he was, and she did. These were the people who'd turned her life upside down. She could have forgiven stealing the odd bottle of milk, but she wasn't going to let go the fear they'd caused in her already fearful children. That had to stop, limp or no limp.

Faster she pedalled, she had almost caught up with them now, and the hobbling boy was struggling; he urged the other boy to go and she was yelling at them both to stop, but they lumbered on. The stronger one had put his arm round the other and was encouraging him forward. She was equal to them now.

Stopping would be a problem but, heck, her face was a mess anyway. She came alongside the stronger boy; he was now wriggling out of reach but, somehow, she reached out, grabbed his shoulder with one hand, he bellowed, she bellowed and they all collapsed into a heap on the pavement.

The one she had trapped was a carrot-topped, red-faced boy. He looked nothing like the monster she had conjured up in her head. The other boy, the injured one, was blubbing into his (filthy) knuckles. She didn't recognise either of them, in fact she had never seen either of them before in her life.

The injured one helped her up and then they both stood in front of her, and even their body language seemed to admit 'game up' as clearly as a king laid down in chess.

'Who on earth are you?' She was grazed all over but she was worried about both of them too. And then another boy joined them, *where did he come from?*, with round spectacles and a flat cap. Very downcast he looked too.

'You got caught then?' he said to the others.

'Yes, they got caught,' Clara told him peevishly. 'And I suppose you're part of it too?'

'He's my brother,' said the injured one.

They were children! 'Who *are* you?'

'Nobodies,' said the limping one, which made the spectacle-wearer snort.

'What were you doing in my garden?'

'Nothing!' said the strong one with the red face.

'I know this isn't the first time. Why have you been doing this?' Clara could not contain herself. She picked up her bicycle, saw wearily that the chain had come off. She proceeded with a diatribe of what they had done, from the tomatoes to the chalk message. She felt suddenly ridiculous. Up close, the criminals were all small and frightened. The limping one was snivelling. Still, she could not just forgive them now: she needed information.

'And then there were the eggs,' she continued, fury rising at the memory.

'You tell her...' said snivelling one.

'No, you...' said the other one. 'I'll fix it for you, missus.'

He bent down to put the chain back on her bicycle, and his hands grew oily and black. 'I'm good at mending things.'

'You're good at breaking things too,' she said severely, and he glowered at her over the wheel.

'We get money if we do stuff. One shilling for a little job – two for a big 'un.'

'What? – who? Who sends you money?'

They shrugged. Clara's heart – or was it her ribs? – ached now. Dr Cardew would not be pleased with his patient.

'I will go to the police if you don't say.'

'He said you are a witch.' The brother pushed his spectacles back against his freckly nose.

'I can assure you I'm not.'

'That's what he said.'

'He said you are like the one in "Hansel and Gretel",' bicycle-fixer added, wiping his oily hands on his shorts. (His mother would kill him, surely?)

'And you believed that?'

They looked at each other cautiously.

'It seemed true.'

'You think I put children in a pie and eat them up?'

'Worse even than that,' said the spectacle boy ominously as Clara struggled to imagine what could be worse.

They stared at the cracks in the pavement. Snivelling one finally said feebly, 'My leg hurts.'

Clara stopped herself from saying, 'good,' and instead gave them all her beady glare.

'And this "he" who said it... Who is he? I want a name, please.'

She knew they'd tell her. They seemed as weary about it as she was. They looked at each other some more and then finally the spectacled one muttered 'Johnson' and although Clara hadn't heard the name in a while, she knew exactly who it was.

Potato boy and his father.

Of course it was. How could she have been so blind?

'You smell,' said the stronger one abruptly.

'That's rude.'

'No, I mean, nice.' He sniffed thoughtfully. 'Kind of French.' He coughed. 'I don't think you are a witch.'

'He said he wants us to kidnap one of the children in the orphanage. He'd give us big money – and you'd give us bigger money too.'

'Kidnap?!' Clara yelped, and a woman who was walking by turned round. Clara waved her away. 'What *on earth*?' she hissed.

'Not for long and not properly,' he added swiftly, as though suddenly aware he'd gone too far. 'Just to give you a fright.

That's what he said. He said, you'd go nuts and pay up if any of them went missing.'

'I would.'

The thought of it! Peg or Gladys pinned up against some wall, unable to escape, their eyes filled with tears. Or Frank or Trevor calling out for her, or Florrie desperately trying to use her guiles, or Jonathon hoping to be polite enough to go undetected. It was unbearable. Unconscionable.

The boy poked his toe into the ground. 'We wouldn't have done it anyways.'

'I know you wouldn't,' Clara said, although she knew nothing of the sort. 'And which one of you kindly straightened up the pram for me when it was raining?'

Snivelling one grinned. 'That was me!' he volunteered, his expression gentle. 'She is a sweet baby!'

'She is, thank you. That was thoughtful,' Clara said, and she wasn't completely acting.

The bicycle-fixer straightened up. 'So, what will you do? You can't tell him we told you. He'll kidnap us then! Or worse.'

'Don't worry about him. I'm going to take care of him,' Clara said boldly.

The relief that she knew who and what it was now rapidly overtaken by a new problem:

How was she going to take care of this?

'What you going to do with us then, missus?' snivelling one asked. Clara felt the sorriest for him and she handed him a handkerchief. She racked her brains. *What was she going to do with them?* For so long she had been wondering who it was – but now that she knew, she still had to deal with it.

'I would like you boys to come to tea.'

They all looked at each other uncertainly. It was almost worse than if she'd said she would go to the police.

'I am not going to eat you,' she said wearily. 'Or worse. Jam or cheese sandwiches?'

They looked petrified. She felt like the big bad wolf.

'I said, jam or cheese?'

'Bloody hell, jam,' stuttered the bicycle-fixer.

'Jam,' added the sniveller.

'Who on earth would choose cheese?' muttered the brother under his breath.

'Maybe not me but I know someone who would,' Clara told him tartly, 'thank you. I take it that's another jam then?'

Mrs Horton knew where the Johnsons had moved to, but she wanted Clara to involve the police or the council now. Clara said she was going to have words first and then if it ever happened again, she wouldn't hesitate to call them both. She was fired up and furious but neither PC Banks nor Mr Sommersby (especially in his current lovelorn incarnation) had inspired confidence. She trusted them on some issues, but this was certainly not one of them.

The boys in town weren't the real problem and if she didn't sort it out at the base, pull it out by the root – who knew? They might simply employ other children to make trouble.

'He hit you last time...' said Mrs Horton as she drove, her face drawn.

'Then he won't hit me again,' Clara responded illogically. She wished she had done something sooner. Wishing it would go away by itself had not paid off. It hadn't with Judy's husband, it hadn't with Peter's uncle, it hadn't with the Australia scheme. She should have learned by now: bad people aren't going anywhere, you can't ignore them. You have to fight back.

And now that she knew where it was coming from, it seemed obvious. It had been staring her in the face for months. Of course it wasn't Davey, or Ruby, her father or Ivor – what madness was that? The one thing she wasn't certain of was who exactly the instigator was – was it potato-faced father, potato-faced son or both?

It was a windy day and even the leaves and branches were trembling. Mrs Horton drove like a maniac and by the time they arrived, Clara's shoulders were clenched and her throat dry. Nothing could be as scary as Mrs Horton's driving, she thought.

This street was marginally nicer than the one in Ipswich but the house had the same flaky paintwork and doomed air of neglect as the other one. The front garden was overgrown and there were prickly plants everywhere. Spilling into the street was a pyramid of glass bottles.

The potato-faced boy pulled open the door. He had a swollen, black eye and she wondered if it was from his father. She'd bet it was. She remembered the way they treated the children, her boys, and she hated him then.

'Oh, it's you,' he mumbled. So he *did* recognise her. He went crimson slowly from the neck upwards. It was like watching a red tide come in.

'It is,' said Clara. All the things she was going to say disappeared. He was just a boy too. An enormous, badly parented boy, but a child all the same.

'You've been attacking my home,' she said, surprised how matter-of-fact she sounded. She thought, *Ivor would kill me if he knew I was here.*

'I haven't,' he said.

'You've been paying other people to do it for you.'

'No, I didn't.'

She knew he was lying, and he knew he'd been caught. 'You have,' she said. 'And I won't have it. It's over now.'

And then the potato-faced father joined his son on the doorstep, and Clara swallowed. Maybe she should have let Mrs Horton get out of the car and come with her. Two against one was pretty scary. Or maybe she should have got Ivor to come after all.

'You can't prove anything,' the father said confidently.

'Oh yes, I can. I have documented everything and I know these boys have been receiving money from you. They are prepared to testify in court,' she said. Actually, they hadn't got round to that, and she hoped they wouldn't have to. But it was something to threaten them with.

The man continued to stare at her intimidatingly, fists clenched, while Clara continued to hold her ground. She couldn't back down now. She could do this. She'd lived through the Blitz – she wasn't going to let evil win. He was a tyrant; just because he was home-grown didn't mean he was any less dangerous.

'Sod off,' he said and then to his son, he said, 'Don't worry, she hasn't got anything on us.'

He stalked back into the house but the boy hesitated, just for a moment, and Clara took her chance. Addressing him directly, she said, 'Sometimes, our fathers can ask us to do bad things. Or we might even do bad things to get our fathers' approval...'

The boy didn't move away. He swallowed and she focused on the way his Adam's apple travelled down his pasty throat.

'Come in,' called the father. It sounded like he'd gone upstairs. 'Leave the silly cow.'

But the boy couldn't leave. He seemed stuck. 'We don't get any money any more,' he said sullenly, 'because of you.'

'You didn't *deserve* that money,' she told him, and she was surprised how courageous she sounded. The advantage of being unequivocally in the right, she supposed. 'You weren't looking after those children, they were having a terrible time.'

She thought of the dreadful state Trevor and Frank had been in and how they had flourished since they first arrived.

'We lost *everything* because of you,' he added weakly. He was trying to hold on to the wreckage of his beliefs when he knew everything was up in flames. 'It was good before you came.'

'I'm sorry for what's happened to you, but it wasn't my fault. And hurting me or hounding the children won't help you, not in the long run.'

'The council are bad,' he whispered, and Clara thought for a moment there were probably a few opinions they had in common after all.

'You know what you have been doing is wrong,' she told him firmly. 'Think about if you want to make something positive of your life or not. And if you ever do, come and find me; I'll be there to help you. If it's not too late.'

Then she turned on her heel and marched off. Luckily, she didn't get caught in the stinging nettles in the garden or trip over any of the rubbish. If this were a war movie, she would be like an American general, coming in late but sorting it out to cheers and cigars all round.

She could feel the boy's eyes on her as she got in the passenger seat, as she smiled nervously at her friend.

'All good,' she told Mrs Horton. 'Let's go.'

48

The parlour looked cosy, and there were still cards on the mantlepiece from Gladys' birthday. Clara went around with a feather duster, but the room was still tidy from the big clear-up before the funeral. They were expecting between three and five guests today. She spread out the red and white checked table-cloth that Ivor had made for her and smoothed it down, smiling at the 'C.A.N', Clara Agnes Newton, in the corners.

Gladys and Trevor were going to act as tour guides. Peg gave them a Union Jack on a stick, like she'd seen tour guides use at the Festival of Britain. Clara was surprised she remembered. They'd wanted to put up an umbrella too, but Clara said, 'Not in the house.'

'Because it's bad luck?'

'And because you'll knock everything down with it!'

Gladys said should they charge an admission fee, and Clara said no, not this time. It was an idea for the future, she thought. Gladys might be a businesswoman one day.

Frank, Trevor, Gladys and Peg waited. (Jonathon was out running and had said he would be back later.) Florrie was waiting too but she was also reading *The Catcher in the Rye* for the hundredth time and feigning indifference.

'Are the children coming to liv here?' scribbled Peg urgently and Clara tried to explain again. They'd never had visitors their own age to the home before and they didn't know how to behave.

At four o'clock, a cluster of children appeared outside the door. The one with spectacles announced that his friend Stanley had wanted to come along too. Stanley looked older than the others; he was tall and wiry with an easy smile. He shook hands with everyone and said he recognised Trevor from chess club. Trevor looked pleased and embarrassed. The snivelling one had perked up and said his leg had healed. Frank ushered them in solemnly. Clara thought for a moment he had once again lost the power of speech but he soon livened up: 'Shall we do a tour first?' he asked, and their guests, suddenly wordless, nodded.

'This was once the home of Jane Taylor,' said Trevor.

'Who's she?'

'I knew that!' said the brother who couldn't believe in cheese. 'Mum told us. She was the one what did "Twinkle Twinkle, Little Star".'

'And other poems, forgotten in the mists of time.'

'I've never been to an author's house before,' he said. He made *author* sound like *awful*.

'Or an orphan's... Are we allowed to say that?'

'What?'

'Orphans?'

Frank shrugged. 'A. It's true, isn't it? B. We don't care.'

'Why do you speak like that?' the former snivelling one asked. 'You know – A and B...'

'A. It's how clever doctors speak,' explained Frank, 'and B. I like it.'

'Nice,' said former snivelling one. 'I mean, A. Nice. B. Super.'

They were chatting as they were led around in a procession. Trevor had decided the route: up to the boys' room, across to the girls'—

'Can we show them your bedroom, Miss Newton?'

'Absolutely not!'

A peek at the bathroom, down to the bathroom in the basement, up to the parlour, then into the kitchen, where the white-bread sandwiches were piled up on the side. Gladys said they were like fluffy pillows for tiny heads.

'My mum says you're from London,' bicycle-fixer said.

'I am,' said Clara. That seemed innocuous enough.

'And she said you're having it off with the man who lost his arm in the war.'

All the children chortled and Gladys made the 'oooh' sound she always did when the subject of romance came up.

'Does she now?' responded Clara mildly. She had to admire the grapevine in Lavenham. Nothing was sacred. And there was nothing she could do about that so it was not even worth trying.

Clara made tea. Jonathon came in, breathing heavily from his run, and then Florrie appeared and grabbed a plate. Clara smiled encouragingly at her.

The boys ate everything up and then former sniveller, who was the most cheerful of the four, asked if there was going to be cake too. Who did he think he was, Little Lord Fauntleroy, asking for cake on a weekday? Trevor scoffed, but Clara interrupted: actually, she did happen to have a nice Victoria sponge.

The boys wanted to play marbles. Trevor was furious with himself though; he'd forgotten to show them the garden and the shed.

'Let's go out now.'

They opened the back door and were ready to launch.

'Wow,' one said.

'This is more like it!'

'You're lucky,' Stanley said to Florrie.

'Thank you,' said Florrie, looking closely at him. 'It could be worse, I suppose. At least there are no phoneys here.'

'I know what you mean,' he said.

Maybe Clara didn't have to worry too much about a Clifford and Florrie love story after all.

That night, Clara's strange dreams were back, yet they were not distressing. There was a judge in a wig that was more like Marie Antoinette's than anyone in the judiciary but this time it was not Patricia, nor was it Mrs Harrington – it was her father who brought the hammer down: *You are allowed a life*, he said, and he was smiling.

49

Clara couldn't find Stella. Peg had noticed she was missing first, but Clara hadn't noticed nor even wondered why she was sneezing less. Then she wondered if the potato-faces had something to do with it, but she didn't think they would dare. And Stella did like to go on walkabout.

But Ivor hadn't seen Stella either, and neither had her biggest fan, Miss Webb. It occurred to Clara that if Stella died, so soon after her father, it would be horrendous for the children, but then she told herself to have faith. Stella was surprisingly good at crossing roads, she was fit as a fiddle, there was no reason to think she was no longer with them.

But it was two days now...

It was also raining and a man at the front gate was ineffectually trying to lift the hinge with one hand and protect his Lombard hat with the other.

Clara was just about to go shopping. She didn't mind the rain today, there was something renewing about it. She saw the man struggling and called out to him: 'Can I help?'

'Is this the Shilling Grange?'

Clara had given up correcting people. She had to face it:

The Michael Adams Children's Home had never caught on. Some names just don't, however much you might want them to. 'It is.'

'I'm looking for a girl, my daughter. Her name is Phyllis Burnham.'

'I'm afraid there are no Phyllises here.' She paused, since he looked so wretched. 'Do you want to come in out of the rain anyway?'

She could go shopping later.

In the kitchen, she saw that he looked younger than she had initially thought. Maybe in his early thirties? He had handsome features and was cleanly shaven. He smelled clean; the scent reminded Clara of Nellie's counter. He could have been a movie star, but he said he worked in parts for airlines. He said he was searching for his daughter. He had been to every children's home and every foster family in Norfolk and Suffolk. Clara's was one of the last and then he would just have to consider giving up.

Clara apologised that she could not be of more help. She had just poured the tea and laid out the fly biscuits prettily on a plate when he said, 'I used to call her Florrie sometimes, it was a pet name.'

Her heart thumping wildly, Clara excused herself and called the council. Florrie's papa had come? Fortunately, Miss Webb answered the telephone and said she'd take a look in Mr Sommersby's office and call back. It was difficult having tea and biscuits with the visitor and trying to quell her increasing excitement. They talked about the rain, 'quite welcome,' his family – he had remarried last spring and his new wife was a doll and as eager to meet Phyllis as anything. Clara studied his face: she thought in the eyebrows there was something of Florrie, or perhaps in his narrow shoulders and the way he held himself.

The telephone rang.

'I have found letters,' Miss Webb said in a subdued voice. 'Many of them from a Mr Burnham.'

She knew it!

'How can we prove it's him – and her?'

'I have an idea – ask him to write something.'

'I can't... What?'

'Just do it!'

Clara asked him and, looking bemused, he wrote on one of Peg's scraps: MY NAME IS MR BURNHAM AND I AM LOOKING FOR MY DAUGHTER PHYLLIS

Miss Webb whispered down the telephone, 'Is it all in capitals?'

'It is, yes.'

'Excellent. What does he know about her?'

Clara asked him. He said he couldn't think what to say. Not a thing.

'What about the last time you were together?'

He said, 'It was a long time ago and the thing was I didn't know it was the last time, otherwise I might have... I don't know what I might have done...' And Clara nodded. This was a feeling she understood.

She wasn't going to cry today, she had shed enough tears lately, but it was hard. Florrie was the girl, the Phyllis, he had been looking for. How happy would Florrie be – after all these years.

He added, 'She was just a dot, the tiniest thing when I last saw her.'

The tiniest thing.

The girl who wanted to stay tiny.

Clara would have told him then, but the children were due home in less than thirty minutes. She asked him if he'd like to meet them and he said, 'I suppose I might as well, since I'm here.'

It stopped raining and the sun came out. Clara opened the kitchen window and straight away, a fly flew in. He said that was something else he remembered: she used to particularly hate wasps.

Clara's emotions were mixed. Yes, she was elated, yes, YES, but what the hell had happened? It looked like – just as they had with Frank and Trevor – children had been lost, children had been forced apart, children had been abandoned – and not by the parents but by the council themselves! It was almost too much to take in.

And another thing that occurred to her was that while she had been forced to focus on potato boy and his father's threats to the home, she had taken her eye off the other real although less tangible threats to the children's well-being, which were the council's policies, deliberate or otherwise. It just was unconscionable. Having to deal with these immediate issues wasted her time and energy, time and energy that could have – should have – been spent here. She didn't know what to do with this information. It made her angry at the potato boy and his father all over again.

But she had to set it aside for now, she had to. This was Florrie – Phyllis – and her father's moment.

Ten minutes past three, and there in the high road, leading the procession, were Gladys and Peg. Gladys was rabbiting as she walked. Peg was laughing and holding something, a shell maybe? Next was Frank, limping – *oh God – what had he done to himself now?*

'Is this...?' Mr Burnham said.

'The junior school children,' explained Clara. 'The high school children will be along soon.'

Next, Jonathon and Florrie. They weren't talking but they strolled along companionably. Clara waited.

'Whose cat is that?' asked the man suddenly.

Clara realised that it was Stella, out in the street. Stella was back! And Clara's heart soared. 'Oh, it's ours!'

The children were all crowded around Stella, now talking nineteen to the dozen.

Clara could hardly wait any more. Mr Burnham was gazing out of the window, transfixed. If he was Florrie's father he would recognise her and she would recognise him.

'Is that...?' he asked, wringing his hat. 'It can't be.'

'We call her Florrie... I didn't know she was ever a Phyllis.'

She had never seen anyone react like that. It was like he melted in relief and happiness. His voice came out croaky: 'Is it really her?'

She nodded. 'It is.'

She wanted to call over the wall to Florrie, 'Look who's here!' but at the same time she wanted to freeze-frame this moment. It was such a beautiful sight, all six of the children gathered around the cat, who was letting them adore her as though it was her due.

Even Jonathon was laughing as he crouched down to pet her, even Florrie.

And then Stella – the least loyal cat of all – tired of the attention and walked off, over to Ivor's, and the children straightened up and reached the gate.

Clara registered how pale Florrie's father looked now. He'd gone all white and shiny. His hands were shaking so much that he crossed them under his armpits, but that made him look even more nervous.

They were opening the gate; they were in the garden now.

'Stella's back!' shouted Trevor and Jonathon at the same time.

'Hello!' shouted Gladys. 'Have we got visitors?'

'Welcome,' shouted Frank. 'Are you a new boy?'

Trevor shoved him in the back. 'It wasn't funny the first time you said it. It's not funny now.'

Peg was in next, tugging at Clara's hand. She wanted Clara to look at her paper: 10/10 spellings, it said, and there was a big tick next to them. *Well done, Peg.*

Jonathon shielded his eyes, saying, 'Good afternoon, sir.' Well-mannered as ever.

Only Florrie did nothing for a few seconds but stood frozen. Then, she called out, 'Daddy?' Then she flew, she flew into his arms.

50

A few days later, Clara visited the council. She marched up to the second floor, where, she had been advised in confidence (if she hadn't had Mr and Mrs Horton on side who knew what she'd do) that there was going to be a meeting of several bigwigs – a good opportunity to set out her case.

She didn't hesitate but knocked firmly on Mr Sommersby's door.

'Come in, come in,' Mr Sommersby called out, clearly in expansive mood today. There he was, behind his desk, and also Mr Horton – the mole – and two other men she didn't know. There was no sign of Miss Webb. Mrs McCarthy – the Head of the Council – wasn't there either – it would have been nice to have her present, but this would have to do. The men all held cigars and the smoke felt oppressive and made her eyes sting.

'I only need five minutes,' Clara said.

'I'm happy to give you five minutes,' Mr Sommersby returned, looking around him, 'if everyone is in agreement?'

'I'd give her more!' said one of the men she didn't know, a podgy man with a moustache.

Clara was glad her hair was frozen in position. She had seen

Beryl again that morning for an appointment and had even given her hairdresser a kiss on her damp cheek. Thanks to Beryl, her hair felt like a helmet as she went to war. She would hate to be here feeling bedraggled – she was a match for any of these men.

'What can we do you for?'

Clara was just about to launch when Miss Webb came in, carrying a wobbly tray of drinks. She blushed when she saw Clara.

'Did you remember the sugar this time, Miss Tebb?' one of the men asked and Miss Webb, avoiding Clara's eyes, said that she had. She made it to the desk and dealt each person a cup. The tray was swimming with tea. Then one of the men poured whisky from a bottle into his mug and then everyone else's: 'Well, we are celebrating, aren't we?'

They clinked their cups together and cheersed each other. Miss Webb looked around for a seat, then, giving up, she backed against the window.

'Go ahead, Miss Newton,' Mr Sommersby said, still in a jolly tone.

Clara explained what had happened with Florrie's father as the men stared at her. She hid her fury behind a tone that she hoped was methodical, rational and honest. Being emotional would get her nowhere – they would dismiss her if she was.

'I don't understand how the council lost track of the poor man and his daughter. This father was repeatedly misinformed that his daughter was not with us! It's incompetence – at all levels – and it has huge ramifications for people's lives.'

She drew a breath. 'And it's not the first time children have gone missing in Suffolk. I've seen siblings separated too. Gladys lost her two brothers for years. Children torn from their parents, sisters taken from brothers... it's not what the Curtis Report recommended. It shouldn't happen.'

She mentioned the 1946 Curtis Report, the Government

instigated enquiry into the care of children without homes because she knew that was the thing most likely to pique their interest. The distress of children wouldn't, but any legal ramifications might.

'Something has to be done,' she said finally. The officials looked at one another. The one who would 'give her more than five minutes' looked green around the gills. He scribbled in a notepad. For a few moments, his spidery writing was the only sound in the room.

Then Mr Sommersby cleared his throat. First, he thanked Clara for her heartfelt story.

Clara blushed. Heartfelt was not a compliment in the council, she knew that. Hearts were considered a negative.

Mr Sommersby said, 'You certainly paint a picture. I'm taking all this on board, Miss Newton. What we are doing here – what we are achieving here – is clearly worth its weight in gold.'

Clara blinked at him. *This was what he had taken from her impassioned speech?* He seemed utterly oblivious of the terrible role he had played in all this. Did he not realise what he had done? Or did he realise and just not care?

Mr Sommersby took another sip from his cup. 'Excellent tea, Miss Tebb.'

There was a chorus of thanks and approval. For the fine refreshments.

Or did he realise and was engaged in covering it up? Clara glared at him.

Miss Webb was scarlet.

'Is it time for a toast?'

Clara blinked again. She couldn't believe this. *What were they celebrating?*

'To the new queen!'

'Feels funny to say queen!' said notepad man.

'And a national holiday.'

'Excellent work, Phil. I can't think of a better way to celebrate the Coronation than a week off work.'

'What?' said Clara, all pretence of good manners forgotten. At that moment, she loathed Mr Sommersby, all of them. She loathed them far more than potato boy and his father. Potato boy and his father were stupid and cruel, but Mr Sommersby and the council were calculating and careless. And they were the ones who had the power.

Mr Sommersby's expression turned sheepish, but only for a moment. 'Senior management holiday only, I'm afraid, although I daresay there'll be some hours in lieu for you housemothers too. Not until next year, mind, don't get too excited!'

The notepad man slapped Mr Sommersby on the back. 'Well done,' he said, while Mr Horton buried his face in his papers and Miss Webb examined her fingernails.

It was so bad it was ridiculous, thought Clara on her way home. It was a distraction and they were papering over the cracks – cracks that her children, and other children, were falling through.

But she would not go tilting at windmills, she would not waste her energy here. Mr Sommersby and his incompetent cigar-smoking, whisky-swilling cronies wouldn't always be the ones in charge. She would write to their senior, Mrs McCarthy, and she would get an apology for Mr Burnham and for Florrie; and, even more importantly, she would try to work out ways and systems to stop it from ever happening again.

They mightn't be prepared to do anything – but she would. She wasn't going to let this go. The world was unfair but there were also good people. And yes, she would change what she could. She would never give up. Yet at the same time, she told herself firmly, as she walked the long way back from the station, she would be sure to get on with her own life too.

51

Ivor and Patricia came back from London the next morning. He and Clara had arranged to go for a walk together in the afternoon. Around midday when she went over, Patricia was still in the workshop, but Ivor said the Norwood Nanny was coming to pick her up pronto. Patricia surprised Clara by welcoming her with a big kiss and a rousing rendition of 'A Sailor Went to Sea, Sea, Sea'. It was a song that usually never failed to depress Clara: 'All that he could see, see, see was the bottom of the deep blue sea, sea, sea' – but the way Patricia sang it was cheerful and made her laugh.

Ivor grinned at her as he rummaged in his bag. 'It's nothing much, but we got you these.'

'What...?'

A pack of playing cards.

'New memories,' he said. 'I know you deal out a lot – this is so you feel you've got plenty more memories to make.'

She sat down, feeling tearful. Ivor had remembered what she said; he always did. She had taken him for granted, she knew that. She always liked to think she was the opposite of her father, and yet, in some ways, she had done the same thing to the people she loved as her father had.

She had expected Ivor to be there for ever and that was exactly what her father had done to her mother and her.

While they waited for the Norwood Nanny, Clara told Ivor about the latest goings-on at the home. How thrilled Florrie was that she would be going to live with her father and his new family soon. How Clara would love to find parents for Gladys, Trevor and Frank, but did such sainted people who wanted to take on three children exist? She told him that she was still worried about dear Jonathon – why was his confidence so low? What could she do to help him? And her concerns about Peg – would she ever learn to speak? (It looked less likely every day.) And would Peg ever find the loving family she deserved? She talked about the children who had left the home but still had no families of their own – Peter, Clifford and Maureen – and how she would always try to support them, complicated as it was. Then she said there were new children on their way, and Ivor suggested that when they arrived, they all go on a bicycle ride together, Clara included.

'That is not going to happen.'

Then Clara told Ivor about her tentative plans for the Jane Taylor Society meetings and he laughed: 'For someone who was reluctant, you've certainly thrown yourself in,' and she laughed too: 'That's the story of my life!'

Then she felt terribly awkward and added, 'sometimes,' in a small voice that, thankfully, he didn't seem to notice.

When the Norwood Nanny finally arrived, 'better late than never,' Patricia waved goodbye to Ivor and then cried out, 'Want Ca-ra!' as she was efficiently spirited away.

'Wow,' Clara said, confused. 'Do you think she meant me?'

It still seemed more likely that Patricia was demanding to be transported in Anita's latest automobile than that she would be calling for Clara.

'I'm sure she means you. It was the marbles that did it – and then the new Polly bear. She's been keen on you ever since.'

Clara had searched high and low for a replica of the bear that Patricia had lost on a double-decker bus last summer. She had eventually found a similar one in a toyshop near Maureen's college, but she had been apprehensive about giving it to her. What if the little girl thought it was a poor imitation, a fraud or worse – perhaps Patricia might see through Clara's shameless attempt to win her affection?

'Patricia's not *that* easily won over, is she?'

Ivor had slung his arm round her. 'I regret she might be.' They both laughed, and then he coughed. 'Your hair is very—' he started.

'Beryl,' she finished.

'I like it though,' he said. She thought he was lying but it made her smile anyway. 'Are you ready to go out?'

Clara stammered. Wasn't it awfully breezy? (it wasn't), and he laughed and said, 'Don't worry – that hair will withstand anything!' When, excruciatingly, he *still* didn't get that hint, she said, 'Maybe we should just go and see if everything is all right upstairs, IN YOUR BEDROOM?'

Once he realised what she was suggesting, he was enthusiastic and also, he said, embarrassed that he hadn't thought of it himself.

A couple of hours later, they were downstairs again and Clara was sitting by the telescope at her favourite table under her favourite window, watching the clouds drifting by. As Ivor made the tea, she was growing more nervous.

'It's now or never,' she told herself, which was ridiculous because it wasn't: it was now or tomorrow, or the day after tomorrow, or next week.

But it *could* be now. And if it were now, she had only thirty minutes before the children started arriving home from school. Deep breath. Let's go. *He'd give you the moon if he could,* she remembered Farmer Buckle saying.

'You know you said you wouldn't ask me again... what you asked at the beach?'

He poured the tea and brought it over to her. Was she imagining it or did the cup struggle in its saucer? He was usually steady-handed.

'I do remember.'

She imagined her elephant in the room, walking over to the door – and, with its trunk round the door handle, twisting it wide open and letting itself out.

Ivor went to fetch his own cup. He sat down, then got up and straightened the curtains. Then he looked at her expectantly. 'You were saying?'

So he wasn't going to make it easy for her.

'How about if I asked you?' she asked softly.

She thought fleetingly of Michael again. Her last love. Nellie was right – she *was* afraid. But she would get over the fear. She would get over it now. She had been the tortoise – in a world made for hares. She'd never be a hare, but maybe there was a middle way.

Ivor stroked his chin, breathed in slowly and then out. He took up his cup, put it down again. His hand was definitely wobbling. It looked like he was trying not to smile.

'There is that, I suppose.'

Now Clara's hands were trembling too. She set down her cup.

'Well, go on then,' he said.

Clara took a deep breath. This was it. Everyone knew they should be together – Mrs Horton, Maureen, Anita, Beryl, Marilyn, her father – everyone but her. And now her father was gone, and Clara felt she couldn't take anyone for granted any more. You never knew what was round the next corner, you had to do what was best for now. What had the psychologist said? 'It is hard to change the world, so in the meantime, we just have to prepare children for it the best we can.'

Well, she knew how hard it was to change the world, but she should remember that she was part of the world too and she could change the little things. She could help make the children happy and Ivor happy and – and this was the important bit – make herself happy as well. They would work something out. She didn't know what yet, she didn't know how, but the finer details could wait.

'Ivor Humphrey Delaney—'

'Actually, I can do without the Humphrey,' he interrupted, but she continued.

'Will you marry me?'

'I never want to be without you,' he said, gazing into her eyes. 'You must know that.'

As she held his hand across the table, tears came to her eyes. His too.

'I'm sorry I took so long.'

He nodded. They squeezed each other's hands so tight it was hard to know where his began and hers ended.

'I knew you'd come round one day. I know you're a thinker,' – he winked at her – 'it takes you a while to put your whole self in.'

'You still haven't answered though, not properly.'

She knew what the answer was – she just wanted to hear him say it out loud.

'Clara Agnes Newton,' he said as she let out a hoot of laughter, 'I would like nothing more than to be your husband.'

A LETTER FROM LIZZIE

Dear reader,

Thank you so much for choosing to read *The Children Left Behind*. If you enjoyed it and want to be kept up to date with all my latest releases, just sign up at the following link. Your email address will never be shared and you can unsubscribe at any time.

www.bookouture.com/lizzie-page

It feels like just days ago that I was writing a 'Letter from Lizzie' for my last book, *An Orphan's Song*, but I realise, incredibly, that it was over ten months ago – time certainly has flown while I've been staring into my computer screen.

I hope you enjoyed *The Children Left Behind*, the fourth book in the Shilling Grange Series. I have so enjoyed writing this one – well, all of the books actually – why? I guess I like the larger canvas, I like that we – you and I – know the characters inside out. (I hope that you still like Clara; I know some people find her irritating, but I do pour my heart and soul into her.) Writing a series has been a huge joy for me – I hope it has been for you readers.

Some of the children are amalgamates of children I know and love. I have three children and one stepchild, and two grand-stepchildren – quite a few for someone who, like Clara, was always ambivalent about motherhood. Some of the children are entirely imagined but with issues I know well. I like being able to shine a spotlight on some of the things children – and their carers – go through.

The Farnborough Airshow was a terrible tragedy of 1952. I hope I have represented the incident fairly and have honoured the thirty-one people who died, including pilot John Derry and flight-test observer Anthony Richards. I have also sprinkled other current events throughout *The Children Left Behind* including the re-election of Churchill and the death of King George. I believe 'external' or political events such as these have a huge influence on our lives, and I wanted to show how Clara and the children are affected by such things. As I was writing, it was the funeral of Queen Elizabeth, and it was interesting to get a feel for the similarities and differences between then and now.

Finally, to Clara and Ivor. They are my perennial problem. Some of the feedback I received after Book Three was that I simply couldn't keep Ivor and Clara apart anymore. One reader wrote: 'They are grown-ups – why don't they just talk to each other?'

Of course, there is a reason why they can't 'just talk to each other' – as J.K. Rowling says, 'happy relationships make bad fiction...' If Clara and Ivor's relationship were smooth, then where would be the story? Plots need obstacles. Nevertheless, I got the message. Holding these two back artificially won't work – I can't hold them back any longer. But they also need to have some tough testing times, painful though it is.

I am writing Book Five now – and it's the finale of the series, so I had better get on making those times very testing and very tough.

Ivor and Clara are together, but will they get their happy ever after? You'll have to read it to find out.

Thank you again for your time. It is so appreciated.

Much love,

Lizzie

facebook.com/LizziePage
twitter.com/LizziePagewrite
instagram.com/lizziepagewriter

ACKNOWLEDGEMENTS

Thank you for reading Book Four of the Shilling Grange Series – I'm so pleased that readers have stuck with me and Clara and the children. Without you, I couldn't do this – thank you.

Thank you to my fabulous publishers, Bookouture – a huge and growing company that never makes their writers feel small. I have as usual been so well looked after with this book (any aspiring authors out there, do get in touch with them – they are the business).

My editor on this book has been the wonderful Rhianna Louise, who is now on maternity leave. Best of luck, Rhianna, your help has been invaluable.

Thank you to the proofreaders, designers, marketeers, the whole team (who to my horror, I sometimes forget to thank). I'm hugely grateful to Jacqui Lewis, my marvellous copyeditor, who has saved me from humiliating myself a gazillion times. Thank goodness for your eagle eye. Remaining mistakes are my own fault. And also to Jane Donovan, fabulous proof-reader and missing word spotter.

And thank you too to the audio reader Emily Barber, who has gone over and above with this series. Your reading is always a delight.

Huge thanks as always to my first editor Kathryn Taussig – without her, there would be no orphans. (Uh, that sounds wrong, doesn't it?!) She planted the seed of this story into my head and I'll always be grateful for that.

Much gratitude to friends who stick by me and my weird

schedule – sometimes I'm in my writing cave and other times I'm coming up for air. You are very kind and supportive.

I miss my friend, the lovely and supportive Julia Marriot.

Thank you to my sister and all my lovely nieces. I do declare I have the best nieces and grandnieces in the world. Always thanks to my family, who let me get on with it, let me go on about it, and thank you for your excellent and bizarre ideas too. I love you all very much.

Made in United States
North Haven, CT
19 July 2023

39265335R00236